The
Black Friar

S. G. MacLean is an historian specialising in the sixteenth and seventeenth centuries. She has written four highly acclaimed historical thrillers set in Scotland, as well as a series set in Oliver Cromwell's London. *The Seeker* won the 2015 CWA Endeavour Historical Dagger. S. G. MacLean lives near Inverness.

The Black Friar

S. G. MACLEAN

Quercus

First published in Great Britain in 2016 by Quercus
This paperback edition published in 2017 by

Quercus Editions Ltd
Carmelite House
50 Victoria Embankment
London EC4Y 0DZ

An Hachette UK company

A CIP catalogue record for this book is available
from the British Library

PB ISBN 978 1 78206 847 1
EBOOK ISBN 978 1 78429 338 3

Any omission should be notified to the publishers,
who will be happy to make amendments to future editions.

10 9 8 7 6 5 4 3 2 1

Typeset by Jouve (UK), Milton Keynes

Printed and bound in Great Britain by Clays Ltd, St Ives plc

To Andrew

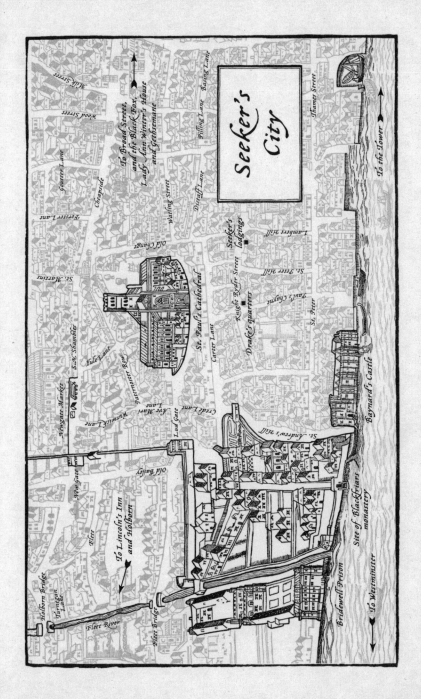

ONE

The Black Friar

January, 1655: seventh year of the English Commonwealth and second of the reign of Oliver Cromwell, Lord Protector
Gethsemane almshouse, Aldgate

Goodwill Crowe straightened himself, brushed grit and stray rushes from the front of his jerkin and his hose. Nathaniel was too frightened, Patience too astonished to say anything. Only Goodwill's wife, Elizabeth, had something ready on her lips.

'An abomination.'

Goodwill nodded. 'Yes.'

'Idolatry. An offence to the Lord. In this house.'

Patience glanced quickly at her brother then lowered her eyes again, before taking her lead from her mother. 'Idolatry.'

Nathaniel ignored his sister's look. He was still watching his father, waiting. At last it came.

'And you, boy, what did you know of this?'

Nathaniel stammered. He could feel his mother's eyes on him, and he knew the stammer would anger her all the more. 'N-nothing. I knew nothing of it, F-father.'

Elizabeth Crowe's voice was cold. 'You slept but three feet from him, how could it be that you did not know of this?'

Nathaniel lowered his head and said nothing. It was better, always, when he said nothing.

'He must have stolen it,' said Patience, emboldened. 'He had the look of a Papist, or a thief.'

This Nathaniel could not tolerate. 'Gideon is no thief.'

'So what has happened to Mother's bloodstone ring?'

Nathaniel screwed up his face in sudden frustration and annoyance. 'What?'

'Mother's bloodstone ring. It's been missing since the day before he disappeared. Is that not so, Mother?'

'You didn't tell me of this . . .' said Crowe to his wife.

Elizabeth's mouth scarcely moved when she talked. Not like those other times, when she preached, thought Nathaniel. Not like when her voice filled a room or churchyard, inflamed her hearers, stopped passers-by in their tracks. Here, in their home, about the streets of Aldgate, Elizabeth seldom spoke, and her voice, when she did, was low, her words slow and something terrifying. 'It was a trifle,' she said, 'a vanity. Why should I concern you with such a thing when you are so engaged on Godly works, with the major and others?'

'All worldly possessions are trifles, vanities,' Goodwill

replied. 'But theft is a sin, regardless of the value of the thing stolen.'

Elizabeth said nothing. Nathaniel knew though, that the ring, the cheap, old ring, had belonged to his grandmother, Goodwill's mother. Nathaniel could just remember his grandmother. She had been the last person, before Gideon Fell had walked into their lives, to brave Elizabeth Crowe's bile to the extent of being kind to him.

Nathaniel tried to glance at the picture his father had brought out from beneath Gideon's straw mattress. He hadn't lied – Nathaniel never lied – he'd never seen the picture before, hadn't known about it. He'd seen Gideon put things there sometimes – not the picture, other things – but Gideon had told him it was better for him not to know about these things, not to ask, and so he hadn't.

Nathaniel didn't like the picture; it was dark, and something in it frightened him. A dark tangle of trees, rocks and bushes. Goodwill held it facing out a moment and Nathaniel could see it better. Men sleeping at the base of a rock. Three men sleeping, but another awake. He knew then what it was. It was idolatry, a false image, a graven image, the depiction of Christ. Nathaniel knew that, he had been taught it all his life. But still he wanted to reach out to the wakeful man and say, 'I'll stay with you, I'll watch with you.' He knew what was going to happen to the man. It was the Garden of Gethsemane.

'What will you do with it?' Elizabeth Crowe said to her husband.

'What do you think?' he said. 'I'll keep it for now. There is a sign in this, somewhere, I am sure, or I would not have found it. I will keep it until I better understand it, and why Gideon Fell came here.'

Elizabeth nodded, and Goodwill, rolling the canvas into a scroll, left the small almshouse chamber that his son had for a time shared with Gideon Fell and returned to his work across the yard.

The room was still disordered from Goodwill's search, the cot upturned and the bedding on the floor. Elizabeth surveyed the place a moment then looked to Nathaniel. 'Clear it up,' she said, and turned to leave, Patience in her wake.

As she passed him, his sister paused and murmured, 'So much for your friend, now.'

Nathaniel had had a bellyful of her. 'G-go to Hell, Patience,' he said.

In Samuel Kent's Coffee House on Birchin Lane in the heart of the city, all the talk was of Parliament. Parliament holding out against Cromwell, refusing to recognise his right as Lord Protector, threatening to cut the army, wrest it from his control.

'But they can't expect Oliver to give up the army,' said Samuel, the old soldier who ran the coffee house. 'He can't govern without it.'

'Oliver has no intention of governing without the army,' responded Elias Ellingworth, who'd been holding court.

'Parliament, though, he would happily do without. It cannot be long before he claims Divine Right.'

There was an uneasy shifting on the coffee benches at this, and a lull in the conversation that was shattered only by the arrival of Gabriel, the coffee house boy. He had been at Custom House Key, noting the day's prices for the merchants who called into Kent's in the course of the day, too busy to see to such matters themselves. Samuel's niece Grace had been teaching Gabriel his letters, and he carried the worth of all the stocks of the day in his head, ready to list them on the board Samuel had hung up on the wall. Today, though, Gabriel was out of breath, having run faster than ever all the way back up to Birchin Lane from the river to be first with the news, and there wasn't a figure still in his head when he got there.

'Glory be! What on earth is it, boy?' said Samuel when Gabriel had skidded to a halt at the top of the coffee house steps. 'Is it an armada?'

Gabriel took a moment to get his breath, shaking his head vigorously to emphasise the import of his news. 'No.' Then he hesitated, a new and terrible thought come to him. 'But maybe . . .'

A merchant, George Tavener, was on his feet. 'Good Heavens, lad, take a seat and tell us what the matter is.'

A stool was thrust beneath the panting boy, and at last he had gathered himself enough to speak. 'A monk. Dead a hundred years. All bricked up in Blackfriars.'

Elias Ellingworth, the lawyer, looked at the child

quizzically. 'That's hardly news, Gabriel. There'll be lots of old Dominicans buried there. There are places still in London where you've a good chance of digging up a monk's skeleton every time you put a spade in the ground. A few are bound to be turned up now and again at Blackfriars.'

But Gabriel shook his head all the more emphatically. 'Not a skeleton. Fresh as you or Mr Tavener there. But dead, and all bricked up there since old King Henry put his Spanish queen to trial in Blackfriars to get rid of her, before he could get rid of the monks too.' His voice became quiet with terror. 'Now they're coming back, to get their revenge, Dan Botteler says.'

'Dan Botteler!' said a haberdasher, tutting as he put on his gloves ready to go back to his shop. 'Dan Botteler's mother dropped him on his head long ago, and he hasn't spoken a word of sense since.'

The others, having similarly lost interest in the boy's story, went back to their coffee and their pipes.

'But what if it's true?' Gabriel looked around him, beseeching.

'*You'll* not need to worry about it, true or not, if you don't get back down to the quayside double quick, to get the prices of Mr Tavener's stocks.' Samuel Kent brandished his stick threateningly. 'Better take your chances with Queen Catherine's ghost!'

The boy was up and out in the streets again before the laughter from the coffee drinkers had died down.

'Strange, all the same though,' said Elias. 'A body to lie

uncorrupted so long. There are ways, I have heard, of preserving them, but behind a wall? I cannot fathom that.'

'Don't trouble yourself over it,' said Tavener, 'it'll be all over the *Intelligencer* by Monday, with every lurid theory you could want.'

'Yes,' said Elias, gathering up his papers for his business in the courts, 'and never a word more said about Protector or Parliament.'

In the depths of Blackfriars, Damian Seeker looked upon it. Walled in alive. Dead now. Very thoroughly dead.

The stonemason was prattling, never taking his eyes from the recess he'd unwittingly revealed in the far wall. 'Heard of it before, mind, in bogs and suchlike, on the moors, bodies kept perfect, hundreds of years. Never seen it. Not till now.' The man was rooted in the doorway, reluctant to move any closer to the corpse, as if fearful the black-robed figure was not quite dead.

Seeker stepped impatiently past him into the small, roofless chamber that, many incarnations ago, might have served as private chapel to the priory, but was now scarcely fit for the stalling of pigs. The stonemason continued to babble, addressing himself now to Seeker's sergeant, Daniel Proctor.

'Lack of air, I suppose, that preserved it that long. I mean, the Blackfriars haven't been hereabouts for a hundred years or more, have they? Lack of air.' He nodded confidently, rubbing his arms in an attempt to stop the shivering. 'Or a miracle?'

Proctor shot him a warning glance. Talk of miracles was not to be encouraged, and would certainly not improve Seeker's mood. The man shut up.

Seeker called Proctor over to him. 'Take a look, Sergeant,' he said, before glancing over his shoulder at the stonemason. 'And you, wait outside.'

Once the fellow had gone, Seeker took his knife from its sheath and carefully used the flat side of the blade to draw the cowl back from the face of the dead man. There was a slight tug as the black worsted reluctantly came away from the dried blood stuck to the man's hair. The light in the chamber was poor, but sufficient for their purpose. Daniel Proctor was no stranger to the sight of corpses in varying states of decay, but he took a step back from what Seeker's knife revealed. 'It isn't possible.'

Seeker nodded slowly. 'It shouldn't be possible, yet it is.'

'But how can it be?'

'That I don't know. But here isn't the place to find out. Guards!' he shouted, and four of his men came quickly into the dilapidated chapel. 'You two, get a cart and covering to take this body up to the coroner's court at Old Bailey. You, fetch the alderman of Farringdon Ward, and tell him to get himself up there.'

'What will you tell him?' said Proctor.

'That the body was preserved through lack of air. That it is being moved under guard for fear of some pestilence. That will keep the curious well back.'

'And if the people start to talk of miracles?'

8

Seeker looked again at the face of the man revealed by the cowl. 'Let them. Better talk of miracles than the truth.'

'Whatever that might be,' said Proctor quietly.

'Aye,' agreed Seeker, 'whatever that might be.' He moved closer, the better to examine the man's face. 'I could do with Drake's view on this. Bring him to me at the coroner's.'

'What should I tell him it's about?'

It hadn't occurred to Seeker that Proctor didn't know Drake's discretion as he did. 'He won't ask. Just bring him.'

Once his sergeant had gone, Seeker went to stand in the doorway of the old chapel, blocking off the sight inside from curious eyes. The stonemason and his apprentice had been taken for questioning, but Seeker knew enough of masonry to know that the brickwork masking the body had not been left undisturbed near a hundred and twenty years, since the Dominicans, the black-robed friars, had roamed freely from this place that still bore their name.

Seeker turned his back to the corpse in the wall and surveyed what Blackfriars was now. Derelict, damp, its walls gradually falling into the stinking Fleet. How was it this had ever been a place of God, a parliament, a court for Henry Tudor's queen? No pleasant gardens left around the crumbling cloister, no richly robed ambassadors of foreign kings to be flattered and painted here, no angelic voices rising from the choristers of the Chapel Royal. It was as if the depravity of Bridewell facing it across the Fleet had crept along King Henry's gallery, dragging with it the spores of an irresistible decay.

'Pull it all down, best thing for it,' Daniel Proctor had said when they'd arrived, summoned by a sharp-eyed constable who'd guessed there might be more to the stonemason's macabre find than met the eye. Stamping his feet to fend off the chill of the freezing January morning, Seeker had grunted his agreement. Whatever had drawn the Dominicans to this site on the Thames four centuries ago was long disappeared, violated, built upon and built upon again. At the last it had been a theatre, shut up for years now, a place of nuisance and debauch, until the Commonwealth had put an end to it. London needed cleansing, and sometimes the only way to do that was to pull down and begin again.

TWO

Carter Blyth

Before the cart bearing the covered corpse had even cleared Ludgate, rumour as to what lay beneath the heavy sacking had begun to run. It was the last friar, bricked up for that he had refused to leave; it was the princes, starved to death in the Tower by their uncle of Gloucester, their poor young bones found at last; the thing had no head – a lover of Anne Bullen; it was Plague. That last they liked the least; that last kept them further from the cart than the others had done; there was no good story to be told if the thing beneath the sacking was that last.

Up at Old Bailey, there was a great deal of low murmuring amongst the officials of the coroner's court. They should be given their place: this was not a matter for the army. But any protestations the alderman of Farringdon Ward or the coroner of Middlesex had considered airing died on their lips when they saw Seeker follow his soldiers, bearing their burden, into the building. Lawyers and ward officers stepped further into the shadows, grateful not to be noticed, wary already about what might lie beneath the covering of the stretcher. 'Dear God,' murmured one, 'is it not enough that he pursues the living?'

The arrival a few minutes later of the apothecary John Drake did little to quell the air of apprehension growing in the corridors and doorways.

'Drake. Why have they called him? What need has a dead man of an apothecary?'

The coroner regarded the alderman with a mild contempt. 'You believe Drake is an apothecary? Have you ever been into his place on Knight Ryder Street? Do you know anyone who has? Whatever alchemy he practises there, there is nothing honest in it.'

The men stepped back as Drake moved quietly past them. He was tall, and his sweeping black robe did not quite mask an unnatural thinness. A slight stoop further shaded his already shaded eyes from the curiosity of observers. His sallow skin and long black curls caused many to declare him a Greek, and Drake was happy enough to let the assumption pass: there were too many still in Cromwell's England who did not share the Lord Protector's desire to readmit the Jewish people from their five-hundred-year banishment. Even without the distinctive cap and robe of his craft, Drake carried about him an air of mystery, and there were those who suspected his alchemical practices owed more to old magic than to the new science.

'You mark me,' whispered the alderman, turning from the coroner to his constable, 'a monk dead a hundred years and more, his body scarce corrupted, and now that fellow called upon. There has been something unnatural here.'

Seeker, too, was of the view that he was in the presence of something unnatural, but his thoughts had little to do with alchemy, or miracles, or talk of magic. He nodded briskly as Drake was brought into the room, and had everyone else but Proctor leave it.

The apothecary was no more disposed to unnecessary preliminaries than was Seeker, and went straight over to the body, trailing welcome scents of bergamot and jasmine to contend with the pungent smells emanating from the cadaver that had indeed begun to decompose. Seeker followed him, while Proctor waited by the door.

'Tell me what you know, and what you wish to know,' said Drake.

'This corpse was uncovered less than three hours ago, behind the wall of a building in Blackfriars long out of use, by the mason inspecting it for demolition. It was clothed as you see it now.' There was no need to ask if Drake recognised the type of clothing; Seeker knew it was the Dominicans, the friars of the Inquisition, who had driven Drake's family to London in the first place.

Drake nodded. 'The robes of a Dominican friar.' The apothecary walked around the table on which the body had been laid, sometimes bending to inspect it a little more closely, sometimes using a thin wooden baton to gently ease clothing back from flesh.

'And what is it you would know, Captain?' he said, apparently concentrating on the bare feet that extended beyond the hem of the robe.

'How old is this body? How long has this man been dead?'

Drake turned his head towards Seeker, raising an amused eyebrow. 'The body, I would say, Captain, is around as old as yours. Forty, forty-five years old, perhaps. Many decades younger than his clothing, which as you see,' he said, indicating points on the sleeves and around the neck area, 'has begun to rot in parts, and been troubled by moths and, I suspect, mice. As to how long he has been dead,' he straightened himself, 'a matter of a very few weeks.'

Seeker nodded. 'And the manner of death?'

Drake peered closely at the man's mouth, the tips of his fingers and toes, then lightly separated some of the hairs at the back of the man's head. 'Unpleasant. You see there has been bleeding, though not any great amount, from a blow to the back of the head, but the skull is not cracked and I don't believe that is what killed him. The passage of time muddies the picture, but I believe this man died through suffocation. Deprivation of air.'

'Strangulation?' But Seeker thought he already knew the answer to that.

Drake shook his head, and indicated the man's neck, and the lack of chafing or bruising around it, before carefully raising one of the corpse's hands, and indicating the fingertips. 'You see that his neck shows no marking of strangulation, yet his fingertips are worn more than ragged – the skin has almost all been scoured away. There are traces of soot in the creases of his hands, and,' here stooping to examine the man's nose, 'his nostrils. More than in the common run of things. And his nails,' he straightened himself and brought his own index finger to the nails on the fingers of the left hand, 'you see they are badly broken and worn down, what's left of them filled, I suspect, with the same manner of crumbled brick and powder you will find on the wall behind which he was enclosed.'

So it was as Seeker had suspected. 'He was bricked up in there alive.'

Drake let the dead hand fall. 'That at least would be my assessment. Also, I doubt very much that this man was a wandering friar.'

Seeker knew he hadn't been, but was curious all the same. 'What makes you say that?'

'His feet. They are not the feet of a man who has walked the world in sandals.'

'No,' said Seeker. 'They are not. Thank you, John.'

Drake inclined his head slightly and left without further farewell, other interests already calling him.

Daniel Proctor approached the figure laid out on the table once more. 'It's him, then?'

'Looks like it.'

'What will Thurloe say?'

Seeker considered. Whatever Thurloe had to say, he suspected, would go halfway to explaining why the man in front of them had been bricked up alive in the old priory of Blackfriars. 'That is what I intend to find out.'

★

Thurloe would not be found in his usual offices at White-hall, that Seeker already knew. The Chief Secretary, on whom the government of England, the survival of the Pro-tectorate, the security of the Lord Protector himself, so much depended, was ill. He had been ill for weeks, and refusing to countenance any retreat from the rigours of his office, until Cromwell himself had ordered him to betake himself to his bed, 'And not in Whitehall, Thurloe, or I will set my dogs on you!' Too ill to argue any further, Thurloe had left many instructions with his most trusted Under-Secretary, Philip Meadowe, and consented to remove himself as far as his old chambers in the attics of Lincoln's Inn. Cromwell had decreed that all business meant for Mr Thurloe should be brought for the time being before Mead-owe instead, but Thurloe had summoned Seeker to him before finally agreeing to leave in the litter that had been called for him.

'You, Damian,' he had said, applying all of his meagre strength to his grip on Seeker's wrist. 'You will come to me, if you come upon any business that is not for others to know of. You know the type of business of which I speak. You will not fail me!'

Seeker had known. Any business so dark, so far in the murk that its outlines could hardly be seen. What had been found at Blackfriars was of this business.

Seeker did not often have cause to be at Lincoln's Inn, and he was glad of it. It was a pleasant place, he could see that, if you belonged in such places, but Seeker knew he did not.

The gardens, with their high brick walls, their walks and arbours, their well-clipped lawns and pinned back roses were too precise, too ordered, there was no freedom in them. A place where nature was not loved but tamed, and Seeker, be he never so controlled, was too rough-hewn for such a place. Within the portals of Lincoln's, its panelled walls, polished floors, corridors echoing with assured laughter, voices trained to expectation and ambition, the easy companionship of those who expected to get on in the world, the set of his face, the tread of his boot on a step, the very sound of his voice seemed to stop all of that in its tracks. The porter who met him didn't even ask what he had come for. 'I will take you to Mr Thurloe,' he said.

After several turnings and stairways, they came to an attic corridor, and halfway down it the porter tapped lightly on a panelled door, giving his name. The door was opened, and Seeker had to stoop slightly as he stepped into a small, over-heated sitting room. The porter nodded to him and left. Seeker recognised the manservant who could occasionally be glimpsed flitting through the corridors and doorways of Whitehall, always just in the background of the Chief Secretary's daily life.

'How is he?' asked Seeker.

'A little stronger, though far from fit for business, but I have instructions that you are to be let to see him, should you come. I pray you do not keep him long.' The man disappeared through an inner doorway and a few moments later came through it again, more slowly, behind him a man younger than Seeker, not yet forty, and younger-looking still, like a curate or nervous junior lawyer. The man would have passed unnoticed in the street, like any other clerk or city-dweller of middling stature. Short and slight of frame, only the great dome of his forehead under long, lank fair curls, matted now to that forehead, marked him out as different, somehow. 'Such a brain, Seeker, such a brain as holds the secrets of the world in its chambers,' Cromwell had once said to him of his Chief Secretary. ''Tis a mercy God gave him to our side and not the other.'

Thurloe came closer into the light, and Seeker saw that the man on whom the Protector so depended was still gravely ill. Overwork, he thought. Thurloe was killing himself with overwork. The eyes were red-rimmed and the always-pale skin as rough and dry-looking as cheap paper. The small, thin hands that held within them the invisible strings of a network of agents and informers extending to the edges of Europe and the New World were clammy, and trembling. Seeker had seldom seen Thurloe outside Whitehall, or Hampton Court, for the Secretary was rarely prepared to remove himself far from the centre, the person of the Protector, and Cromwell still more rarely disposed to spare him. It was bandied in the taverns and the coffee shops that even the Lady Protectress was constrained to go through Thurloe first, should she wish to see her husband.

Thurloe made no comment as his servant helped lower him into the more comfortable-looking of the two chairs by the fire, and set a heavy woollen rug over his knees. The man then told Seeker to call him if the Secretary required anything and disappeared once more through to what Seeker supposed must be Thurloe's sickroom.

'Well, Damian,' said the Secretary as the departing servant pulled to the door, 'I'll wager this is nothing good.'

'No,' said Seeker, 'I don't think it is.'

'Tell me then,' said Thurloe, reaching for the cordial his man had set on the small table beside him.

Seeker handed him the glass and waited for him to swallow it down, before telling him of the morning's find at Blackfriars, and the apothecary Drake's assessment of the corpse.

Thurloe listened without interrupting, saying only at the end, 'A puzzle indeed, but I think there is something you have yet to tell me.'

Seeker took a breath, tried to keep the challenge out of his voice. 'It's Carter Blyth.'

Thurloe's face registered something, a mild flicker, before he pursed his lips in thought a moment. 'You are certain?'

'Completely certain. As is Daniel Proctor, who also saw him.'

'Hmm.' Thurloe leaned forward suddenly. 'You swore Proctor to secrecy?'

'Of course,' said Seeker.

'Good.'

Thurloe sank back, his bout of animation having exhausted him.

'I've left the body covered and locked under Proctor's guard in the coroner's court.'

The Secretary nodded, considered a moment before speaking again. 'It is a bad business we have on hand here.' He looked up at the still-standing Seeker, indicated the chair opposite him. 'Sit, Damian. This may take some time.'

Seeker took a plain oak chair and sat down awkwardly, his helmet in his hands, the feet of his black leather boots closer to the fire than he would have liked. He waited.

'You know that Carter Blyth was one of our agents in the Netherlands?'

Seeker nodded.

'He kept a close eye on enemies of the Protectorate – Royalists colluding with foreign interests, especially the Spanish. Any Papists passing through. Presbyterians too. Radicals involved in the printing of incendiary works. Businessmen trading with the wrong people, showing an interest in the wrong sorts of goods.'

Seeker knew what agents of the Protectorate did in foreign cities – they joined the churches, patronised inns and coffee houses, traded at the bourse, insinuated themselves into the society and trust of those who might wish ill to Oliver's regime, and gleaned information on those persons' contacts in England. By such means, only a few weeks since, a plot involving London's gunsmiths and other city merchants had been uncovered, and those involved pulled from their beds and slung into the Tower before they had had time to find their slippers or bid their wives farewell. The security of the regime depended upon its foreign agents as much as it depended upon the army at home. It would not have been the first time that an agent had been found dead, having clandestinely returned to his own shores. Seeker might well have believed this to have been the case with Carter Blyth, and would not have troubled Thurloe with it, had it not been for one detail.

'Carter Blyth died in the gunpowder explosion in Delft three months ago.' He looked bluntly at Thurloe. 'You had me attend his burial in Horton churchyard.'

Thurloe was matter-of-fact. 'It was necessary. For the sake of authenticity.'

'Authenticity of what?'

'That he was dead.'

Seeker said nothing.

Thurloe took a careful sip of his cordial. 'Believe me, Seeker, it was not done to make you a fool, but because if you were there, no one would question our certainty. It suited me that Carter Blyth should be believed dead.' He looked at Seeker directly. 'I had other work for him to do.'

'That was not an empty grave I stood by at Horton,' Seeker said.

The Secretary was dismissive. 'Some nameless fellow who'd died in Newgate. More use to the Commonwealth in death than he ever was in life, and none to miss him.'

Seeker thought of the worn-out woman who'd stood across the grave from him in Horton those months ago. 'And Blyth's widow?'

A shrug. 'She doesn't know. Grateful for the pension we gave her and didn't ask too many questions.'

'And,' Seeker spoke slowly, 'should we have any idea how Carter Blyth came to be walled up alive in Blackfriars, in the guise of a Dominican friar?'

Through his weakness, Thurloe smiled. 'As well I have never needed to use you in diplomacy, Damian. I fear we have some work to do yet on your subtlety, but yes, you have come to the point. I can tell you what Blyth was doing back in London, but as to the rest? That I will require you to discover.'

It was over half an hour later that Thurloe finished. 'You may have Proctor to assist you, but no one else is to know what you are about.'

'So who else does know, apart from the generals?'

Thurloe shook his head. 'Not the generals, not Oliver himself. Only me, and Blyth, who is evidently dead, and now you. This could touch to the very highest ranks of the army, and to the Council of State. I am not certain yet of who is to be trusted. It would play right into the hands of Parliament to see the army so divided against itself, and the Protector so under threat. They think that Cromwell cannot rule without the army, but they have yet to comprehend that should Cromwell not control the army, God himself would be hard put to do so.'

Seeker knew that Thurloe believed as vehemently in Oliver's providential right to rule England as did the Protector himself. But there was a line, a gulf now, between what such as Cromwell and his circle believed, and what many who had fought alongside him in the army had understood to be the end point of their struggle, their revolution. The Levellers, who had fought for equality amongst men, and been told clearly by the generals eight years ago at Putney that there could be none, had begun to make their voices heard again, and now they had been joined by those of the Fifth Monarchists, who were not satisfied that any should rule England but Christ himself, on whose return they waited avidly, and for which they actively prepared. Those men that thought they had been fighting for equality and the rule of Christ were not content that a captain of horse from the Cambridgeshire fens should sit upon the throne of England.

'The army is under control now, surely?' said Seeker. 'Overton, Ludlow, Alured, Saunders, Okey – they have all been cashiered, court-martialled, imprisoned.' Five senior army officers, amongst them the Protectorate's seconds-in-command of Scotland and Ireland, caught in three separate conspiracies against Cromwell in the course of the autumn and winter, all of them known to have plotted with the notorious Leveller pamphleteer John Wildman. Wildman was still at large.

'They were but the head,' said Thurloe, 'and when we cut off the head we set the rest of the beast to writhing.'

Seeker chose his words with care. 'That has a flavour of the Fifth Monarchy men to it.'

'More than a flavour,' said Thurloe, in a manner that told Seeker they had come to the heart of the matter. 'It was about the time the conspiracies had come to light and the trials of the colonels begun, that Oliver held a dinner at Whitehall Palace for the members of his Council and other key figures he can rely on, to discuss how the army was properly to be brought back under control, how the threats to his power from the Levellers and Fifth Monarchists within it were to be addressed. The usual number of guards had been posted within and outside the banqueting hall, and by the end of the dinner it seemed that nothing was amiss. But when the guards within opened the doors for the Protector and the rest of his party to leave the hall, they found their fellows gone from the other side, and words daubed onto the walls in blood. Animal, possibly,' Thurloe added as an afterthought.

'What words?' asked Seeker.

'Mene, Mene, Tekel, Upharsin.'

' "God hath numbered thy kingdom and finished it: Thou art weighed in the balances and found wanting," ' said Seeker.

Thurloe nodded. 'Belshazzar's Feast.' From the Book of Daniel, the favourite text of the Fifth Monarchists who had believed their struggle against England's king to have been but a step on the way preparing for the imminent bodily return of Christ to rule on Earth. They it was who had urged with the greatest determination the trial of Charles Stuart, attended with the greatest relish his execution. The next step was to have been the march on Rome and the Papacy, that Whore of Babylon. Cromwell's settling of himself instead onto the throne of Charles I had rendered those who had been his most fervent supports the most implacable of enemies.

For a moment, the crackling of the logs on the fire and the occasional gust of laughter from elsewhere in Lincoln's was all the sound between them. Seeker spoke hesitantly. 'But following the feast, Belshazzar was slain in the night.'

Thurloe nodded, coughed, took another sip of the cordial. 'An attempt was made on the Protector that night. It came to nothing – I'd had him removed from Whitehall by boat as soon as the scrawling on the wall was seen.'

'The perpetrators were caught?'

The Chief Secretary shook his head. 'And neither were the guards who had been on duty at the outer door of the Banqueting Hall found. It seems they had contrived to slip away unremarked, their uniform and arms forestalling any questions, or notice even. A warrant has been put out for them, but the army is so riddled yet with Fifth Monarchy men I doubt they will be found.'

'Round them all up then,' said Seeker. The thing was clear to him and he could not comprehend that it had not immediately been done. 'They hardly hide that they have insurrection in mind anyway – there isn't a street corner on which one of their deranged preachers isn't calling for the Saints to rise and prevail against the Beast.'

Thurloe regarded him for a minute and then raised his hands feebly. 'The Lord Protector won't allow it. He is still in hopes of bringing the Fifth Monarchists of the army back into the fold. Harrison, Overton – they fought at his side, they were among his closest friends and he prays daily for their restoration to him; he misses their comradeship.'

'He trusts too far,' said Seeker, more blunt than he was wont to be on the subject of the Protector, but he knew Thurloe would not need reminding that Overton had denigrated Cromwell as 'A tragical Caesar acted by a Clown,' or that Harrison, who still freely walked the streets and had become the figurehead of the Fifth Monarchy men, proclaimed the Protector 'The dissemblingest most perjured villain alive'.

Thurloe attempted a smile but the effort defeated him. 'I do not, though. I do not trust at all. We are alert to the danger of a rising by the Fifth Monarchists, and you know we have the means to defeat it, but I fear they will make another essay on the Protector's person, that they will try to mask it while our attention is taken by watching for the beginning of their rising. *That* is why I brought Carter Blyth back from the Netherlands when I did, and told no one, absolutely no one.' Thurloe took a moment to summon what strength he had and Seeker waited until the Secretary was ready to continue.

'I recalled Blyth to London and had him embed himself with a group of Fifth Monarchists known to meet at St Pancras. Others in the city and throughout the army have been charged specifically with tracking any plans for a rising, but Blyth's instructions were to seek out and report on any deeper, more specific threat to Oliver himself.' He looked directly at Seeker. 'I don't know how high any such conspiracy might go, how close to Oliver's person those involved might be. That was why I could not risk telling *anyone*.'

'Seven weeks ago? What have you heard from Blyth since then?'

'Each week, for four weeks, I received intelligence reports from him. For the last two, I have had nothing.' Thurloe looked to the fire and then to Seeker. 'What lies under a shroud behind the locked door Daniel Proctor guards confirms my fears: Carter Blyth was compromised, and has paid the price for it.'

Seeker was of the same opinion. 'But not even Meadowe knew Blyth was back in London?' It was widely known that, increasingly, the young linguist who'd been brought in to assist and gradually replace the blind Milton as Secretary of Foreign Tongues had become Thurloe's overworked right-hand man in the handling of agents.

Thurloe shook his head. 'Philip has been fully occupied, God knows, in keeping an eye on what's coming in from the continent – on the Royalists. One deluded scheme after another, each more crackpot than the last, despite Hyde's efforts to bring them into line.'

It was commonly believed in Whitehall and Westminster that Edward Hyde, the exiled Charles Stuart's chief minister, was responsible for the only sense spoken or good counsel ever given in the refugee court. It was said that Henrietta Maria, the queen mother, ensconced in her Parisian exile, loathed Hyde with a passion, something that only served to increase the esteem in which the Republicans held the man.

Thurloe continued. 'The Sealed Knot still reports to Hyde, whose advice tends to the biding of time, but there are those, less patient, who have been throwing wild ideas at Charles himself.'

When Seeker had first heard the name 'The Sealed Knot', under which English Royalists at home colluding with their counterparts abroad had lately chosen to organise themselves, he had laughed. A sealed knot had no loose end, nothing that could be tugged, manipulated, worked upon until the whole came apart. A sealed knot was strong, limitless, the purpose of each part of it working in harmony with the rest. Those Royalists who had plotted the overthrow of Cromwell and the return of the Stuarts had lurched from one desperate, ill-conceived scheme to another, their indiscipline, loose tongues, carelessness and self-interest condemning each attempt to failure almost before it started. And now they thought if they would but organise themselves, and give themselves a name, all would be well.

Hyde, traipsing round Europe after his king, had been relieved at first, it seemed, to have one set of fools to deal with and hold at bay instead of twenty, and stop them doing his royal master's cause more harm than good. But the word from Charles's court of late was that the plotters were becoming restless, tiring of Hyde's caution, and hell-bent on action.

'They're not completely without guile, though,' Thurloe

continued. 'We've learned of late that they've been circumventing our surveillance by communicating with one another at race meetings. Clever that. Of course, we'll have to put an end to race meetings now, but it's for the greater good. And this frayed end of the Sealed Knot was behind the arms smuggling we uncovered amongst the gunsmiths only a fortnight ago.' The Secretary took another sip of his cordial and looked over to Seeker. 'Our old friend Lady Anne Winter will be mixed up in it somewhere, I am convinced. I have just yet to work out how, but she is closely watched and we are working on it.'

'Huh.' Seeker did not quite smile. The woman was as brazen in her royalism as she was formidable. Her mind and her morality travelled pathways that could hardly be comprehended, still less foreseen. He was not sorry that she was, on this occasion at least, someone else's problem. 'You think Royalists are behind Blyth's death?'

Thurloe breathed deep. 'That would be convenient, but I doubt it. Nevertheless, while they play out their petty shows, their *panem et circenses* for the masses, it will divert attention from our problems with the army, and from what I require you to do.'

Bread and circuses. Seeker had little knowledge of the Latin tongue, but that at least he understood. Better keep the populace diverted with cheap entertainments and leave the ruling of the country to those who knew better how to do it. 'You wish me to find his killer.'

The Secretary nodded, draining his glass. 'And I want to

know why they did it and how much they knew — what they were trying to stop Carter Blyth reporting to me.' Gripping the arms of his chair, the secretary began to attempt to raise himself from the seat. Seeker moved to help him, turned to call for Thurloe's man.

'No!' insisted Thurloe. 'Let him be.' He collapsed down into the chair. 'That cupboard.' He raised a trembling hand towards the upper row of panelling in the wall behind where Seeker had been seated. 'I have the key.' He fumbled in the pocket of the heavy woollen shag-lined gown tied with a silk cord over his smock, and handed a small brass key to Seeker. 'The leather case on top. Bring it to me.'

Seeker went across to the wall and, without recourse to the footstool set beneath it, succeeded in reaching the lock in a small door he hadn't previously noticed, and pulling out the leather case he found on top of some ledgers there. He relocked the door and handed the case to Thurloe, who shakily undid the ties. Taking a sheaf of papers from inside it, he handed them to Seeker. 'These are my transcriptions of the reports I received from Blyth, although I doubt they will do much to help.'

Thurloe waited while Seeker read the reports, and then spoke, summing up what Seeker was thinking. 'There's very little in them that we didn't already know. A few names of Levellers suspected of supporting the late unrest in the army, some coming and going with associates of the lawyer John Wildman who are already being watched, a lot about Major-General Harrison.'

Harrison. Seeker remembered seeing Thomas Harrison in the field, fighting in the parliamentary armies like one possessed. Harrison, who had truly believed that by defeating Charles Stuart's army and then severing that man's head from his neck, Parliament had been preparing the way for the thousand-year reign, in person, of Jesus Christ. He and the others who now called themselves 'Fifth Monarchists' had been mesmerised by Cromwell once, as he led them in the field to astonishing victories that could only be God-given, but they would not have it that he should rule over them in peacetime. Where once there had been love and loyalty, now there was virulent hatred and vitriol. The New Model Army had spawned offspring its leaders struggled to control.

'And Wildman has not yet been found?' enquired Seeker, still giving his full attention to the paper in front of him.

'No, but once he has been, he'll be looking at the inside of the prison cell for a good few years – he goes too far this time. The word is that this "Declaration" of his is worse than Lilburne's "England's new chains". But these chains will bind him tight and shut his mouth so long he'll wonder that he ever thought to open it.'

It was indeed rumoured that this new "Declaration" against Cromwell that Wildman was thought to have in hand was so provocative and incendiary it would be banned as soon as it landed in the Censor Office. Seeker had come across a rough draft of it only three days since in the garret at Dove Court, and had burned it before Maria's eyes. He had known, from the night over two months before, when he and Elias Ellingworth's sister had finally given in to their feelings for one another, that such conflicts would come between them. His assertion that it was either burn the pamphlet or arrest her had done nothing to assuage her fury.

Seeker could feel Thurloe's eyes on him. 'There are reports though that Wildman has been seen in the company of the lawyer Elias Ellingworth, and to frequent his home at Dove Court.' Thurloe's voice was careful, and it told Seeker everything he needed to know. 'I think, perhaps, you should look into the matter, Damian.'

'I will,' said Seeker quietly, the words just edging out from his clenched jaw. He turned the papers over. 'There is no indication where Blyth lodged.'

Thurloe let a coughing fit pass. 'It was necessary that he should be very deeply embedded. For his own safety and the security of his mission. All I know is that he went among the Fifth Monarchists, at St Pancras on Soper Lane, posing as one of their number to gain their trust. It had always been his practice to send the fullest details by a more secure cypher only when he was certain.'

'How were the reports transmitted?'

'In the usual way. I arranged a covert location, then informed Dorislaus at the postal office that anything directed to that place should be brought directly to me on intercept, without being opened.'

Seeker nodded, and glanced again at the bland reports. 'And you have had nothing by the second cypher?'

Thurloe shook his head.

'So he had found nothing yet,' mused Seeker, 'and yet . . .'

Thurloe leaned forward, as if they had at last come to the part he'd been waiting for.

Seeker took a moment, as if to clarify in his own mind what it was that left him so ill at ease. 'Blyth hints now and again at another matter, more so as the reports proceed, and not much connected to the mission on which he was sent.' He looked up at Thurloe, who nodded. Carter Blyth had committed a cardinal error – he had veered from the path on which his master had set him, and now he was dead. Now they had come to the point.

Thurloe's voice was low. 'I need to know what it was that Blyth was doing, what trail he was following, that took him to his death. I need to know whether the dangers he encountered were for the Protectorate, or for him alone.' Another pervasive shiver assaulted Thurloe and he clung more closely to the woollen blanket his man had set around him, gathered what strength he had left. 'I want the whole truth of it, Damian, whatever that might be.'

Seeker nodded. 'I'll need the name Blyth went by.'

There were rumours that Thurloe kept the book here, rather than at Whitehall, the book in which he noted the identities of all the Protectorate's agents, alongside the code names that they went by. No one but the Chief Secretary knew those identities. As well, perhaps, that they did not.

Regardless of where he might keep it, Thurloe didn't

need to look in the book. 'Gideon Fell. He called himself Gideon Fell.'

Their business finished, the reports in their leather case returned to their cupboard in the wall, Seeker stood to leave. Before calling on Thurloe's servant he asked, 'And Blyth's body?'

Thurloe was fussing at the fire, shifting a log with the poker. He hardly looked up. 'Say it is diseased, have it thrown in a pit. Bury it deep.'

THREE

Soper Lane

Having left the Secretary to nurse his misery in peace, Seeker walked down the stairways and half-lit wood-panelled corridors of Lincoln's Inn. He could feel nervous eyes on him. Well might there be. There had been few troubles he had looked into that a lawyer was not mixed up in somewhere, and the Inns of Court had long been the haunt of those who would see themselves as 'the coming men'. Even in the war, even in the matter of the death of the King and since then, too many on Parliament's side had written of their affection and regrets to old friends from the Inns who had chosen to follow the Stuart standard.

Seeker paused a moment to look out through the diamond-leaded panes of a window onto the dormant, hard-frozen garden below. A waft of pipe smoke and a burst of laughter came to him from a room he could not see down some corridor to the side. Was that what Thurloe sometimes came here for? Companionship, a brief respite from the duties of office, the friendship of other men? Seeker breathed in the smoke a moment, then stepped out and readied himself to face London's other odours.

The oldest church in England, they said. A fit place indeed for the second coming of Christ. Green and pleasant enough around, if you didn't mind the leatherworkers, old soap-boilers and lounging labourers looking for a day's employment. Seeker wondered how Carter Blyth had clothed himself, comported himself, when first he had come here to St Pancras church to insinuate himself into the ranks of the militant godly. He left his mount, Acheron, by the gate in from Needler's Lane. There were few other souls lingering here on this cold January afternoon. A child with a bucket was making his way from the gate of a house backing onto the churchyard.

Seeker stopped him. 'Where are you headed, boy?'

The child was speechless a moment, and then managed to say, 'To fetch water from West Cheap. My mother hasn't the money to pay the water-bearers.'

'Hmm. And where will I find the preacher?'

'John Spittlehouse? He's usually in the vestry, this time of day. Schooling.'

'You do not attend his school?'

'My father won't have it. Says I'm not to go near them.'

'Go near who?'

'Those Fifth Monarchy men. You should hear them. The terrors they'd put on you, when they talk of the Beast.'

Seeker was taken by a little devilment. 'And how do you know I'm not one of them?'

The boy's eyes went wide and his mouth shaped itself into an incredulous smile that he could not hide. 'You? You're no Fifth Monarchy man, you're the Seeker. Everyone knows that!'

Seeker grunted. 'Your mother's water will keep five minutes, I daresay?'

The boy nodded.

'Good, keep an eye on my horse there.'

As the boy dropped his bucket and ran to take the horse's rein, Seeker approached the vestry door, his boots crunching on the frozen, fallen leaves beneath them. He could hear the sound of the preacher's voice, promising dreadful fates for those who did not believe in the true God, the God of Daniel, the all-conquering God of the Book of Revelation: '"Woe to the inhabitants of the earth and of the sea! For the Devil is come down unto you, having great wrath, because he knoweth that he hath but a short time."' The words were spoken with a terrible relish, and the children who pushed each other through the door past Seeker looked as if they would rather have been anywhere but the place they'd just left.

The preacher was just closing his Bible as Seeker stepped into the vestry past the last escaping child.

'And what do you hope to teach them by such lessons?' he asked the small, thin man whom he knew to be a soap-boiler by trade.

'Enough that they can read their Bible, know their rights, and speak for themselves,' the man replied. He assessed Seeker carefully. 'You haven't come here to learn your letters though.'

'No, nor my rights.'

'A captain of Nol Cromwell's guard? A servant of Jehu! You have no rights.'

Seeker had no interest in trading scripture. 'I want to know about one of your congregation. He might have come amongst you about six weeks or so ago. Went by the name of Gideon Fell.'

The preacher was instantly suspicious. 'Went? What was his real name then?'

Seeker ignored the question. 'You know the man I'm talking about?'

A curt nod.

'When did he first appear here?'

The preacher gave the matter some thought. 'It would have been about six, seven weeks. About the end of November, beginning of December, I'd say.'

'Was he alone?'

Again, a nod. 'At first.'

Seeker would keep that one for later. 'And what story did he tell?'

The man shrugged. 'Same story as most of them. He'd been a soldier – no story there, we'd all been soldiers. Left the army when Cromwell turned his back on the cause of the righteous for his own carnal ends. Went to New

England for a while, Massachusetts, but the Lord put it in his heart to return and join the fight for His kingdom, that's what took him to this door.'

'No doubt. And what happened to him after he came through your door?'

The preacher had begun to occupy himself with tidying the vestry, pushing benches against walls, pulling to the window shutters. He had his back to Seeker. 'He fell in with one of our congregation. Got work, a roof over his head.'

'Who?'

'Goodwill Crowe. Clothworker up by Aldgate.'

A clothworker. Carter Blyth had put his time in the Low Countries to good use, for Seeker knew him to have been a market gardener before the war.

'Where in Aldgate?'

The preacher straightened himself and turned to Seeker, a sour, triumphant look in his eyes. 'That I couldn't tell you, Captain.'

'Won't, more like,' said Seeker. He hadn't more time to waste on the man – he would keep, for now. Any more details he'd have got from him would like as not have been false, anyhow. There were other means of tracking down Goodwill Crowe.

When he got back out into the churchyard, a crowd of half a dozen children had surrounded the horse. They melted backwards at his approach, all but the one he had left watching the beast, who was assured in his new status.

Seeker tossed him a coin. 'You did well. Now go on then, fetch your mother's water.'

The boy retrieved his bucket and started to make his way up the path once more, walking very straight, but Seeker stopped him again.

'And pay heed to your father. Stay away from those men.'

Coming back out the end of Soper Lane by the Great Conduit at West Cheap, Seeker inevitably glanced over to his right, towards the Old Jewry and Dove Court. For years, there'd been nothing but his duty in the army, and then the guard. His service in the wars, and now for Thurloe, for the Protector, was all he had needed. Nothing else, no human being, had been able to touch him. Until the girl at Dove Court. Until Maria. As he stood at the edge of the street, all around him, like a river round a rock, the incessant flow of people of the city passed, intent upon its own business. An ordinary man could join them, merge into them, take up a life like theirs and live it. How would it be, to be an ordinary man? But the flow of people that jostled against one another took care not to touch him. That other life wasn't possible. The bells of St Mary-le-Bow striking two recalled him to the business in hand, and finally turning Acheron to the left, he put thoughts of Dove Court aside, and urged the animal westwards, towards Whitehall.

FOUR

The Secretariat

When she had walked from the gates of Whitehall Palace little over two months ago, Anne Winter had thought she would not set foot back in that place until Charles Stuart had reclaimed his father's throne. It was not that she feared for her life – she would hazard that, if the cause so required – but it made her sick to her stomach to traverse once more the courtyards and passageways at the relentlessly grinding heart of Cromwell's rule.

She would never have come at all had it not been for Charity. Charity. A girl who could have hoped for nothing better from Whitehall than to sleep, unnoticed, in some corner of an unused stable or storeroom, a girl who would have thought it a privilege to sweep the floors of that place. A girl who had never dreamed there could be anything beyond the walls and gates of the city. But now she was gone from the city, disappeared, and Anne Winter had exhausted all other possibilities. She should have come here in the first place.

She knew her way, and the soldiers let her pass, too

awkward in the presence of their dead lieutenant's widow to stop her. November it had been, but seemed so much longer ago to Anne Winter, that her husband had been murdered in this very palace. It was early afternoon now, but she had no fears of finding the offices unattended. While half of Westminster and Whitehall would still be at their dinner in the taverns and cook shops of King Street or New Palace Yard, Thurloe's men, the under-secretaries, the clerks, would be busy at their work, receiving, processing, acting on intelligence, doing their master's bidding, watching and circling each other as they did so.

She came at last to the end of Thurloe's corridor, aware by now of more sets of astonished eyes upon her than had she paraded the Strand unclothed. She was surprised to see the entrance to Thurloe's own rooms unguarded, but that might only mean the Secretary was occupied elsewhere. It was an inconvenience, but it could not be helped. She would wait for him, and she would not leave until she had seen him.

Seeker was looking for Dorislaus. There would be little point seeking him out in his small room at the postal office, behind the admiralty chambers, at this time of day, for Isaac Dorislaus didn't keep other men's hours. Dorislaus would have been up half the night, having begun his work just as other men were finishing theirs. Letters delivered through the day, in innocence or unwarranted optimism, to postal drops at coffee houses, inns and taverns throughout the city

and further afield, would have been sifted for suspect handwriting, address or mark of provenance, and those found of
interest been transmitted to be read and translated by Dorislaus. Any new cypher discovered would be sent to the
Cypher Office where Dr Wallis or one of his assistants
would break the code and report it back to Dorislaus for
analysis. The contents would then be simply noted or passed
upwards, closer to Thurloe. Letters thus compromised
would be resealed, or amended and forged, as required, by
Samuel Morland, who found the world of espionage more
to his taste than the arid debate of his Cambridge College.
Such intercepted letters were then sent on their way to the
unsuspecting recipient who, had they but realised it, could
thenceforth look forward to being watched, reported upon,
perhaps arrested, imprisoned by the agents and officers who
enacted Thurloe's will, all for the security of the state. It
amused Seeker to think that few would give the unassum-
ing Isaac Dorislaus a second look, should they pass him in
the street, and yet Isaac Dorislaus was one of the most dangerous men in England.

He was on his way to the junior clerks' room, where he
knew Dorislaus liked to pass a half-hour with the other
young men, when he heard the sound of raised voices coming towards him up the corridor. The voices seemed to be
coming from the Chief Secretary's rooms. Seeker recognised both of them, and neither should have been there. He
quickened his step, and at his approach the clerks who had
been gawping outside Secretary Thurloe's rooms suddenly

remembered they had pressing business elsewhere. When Seeker reached the open door, what he already knew was confirmed by the figure of the woman standing with her back to him: plum velvet gown, marten stole with chestnut curls escaping from below the hood, and long, pale hands, fine hands, decorated only with a mourning ring: Lady Anne Winter. There were times he had been hard put to extract two words from her, but today, she was in full flow.

'A fitting place indeed! A viper in a vipers' nest.'

'Madam, I would—'

'I never thought to find one in here beside whom Thurloe would look the better option!'

George Downing was bristling, fit to burst. His barrel chest was so engorged with indignation Seeker thought it might snap the fastenings of his doublet. Risen through guile and Cromwell's favour from near-indigent army chaplain to high office within the Exchequer in a very few years, it must have been a long time since anyone had dared to speak to Downing with such open contempt.

'Madam, I am aware you lack the sage counsel of a husband—'

'Husband? My husband said you were not a person on whom any honest soldier would turn his back, that you would have sold a comrade as soon as a foe, if the price was right.'

Downing's dignity deserted him, and he leaned across Thurloe's desk towards her, his face a snarl. 'As you so plainly evidence before me, your husband was no judge of character. Now take your complaint to the alderman of your ward, it is none of our concern here.'

The woman's voice again, incredulous. 'None of your concern? My house is watched every day and reports sent back here as fast as they can be written. There is hardly a chimney sweep nor a baker's boy comes in at the door who is not under the surveillance of this department. Spare me your denials. I can scarce chew my food but I am constrained to spit one of your spies out onto the plate in front of me. You will not tell me you do not know where she is!'

Seeker could not help but let loose a smile. The degree of affront to Downing was something to behold, and the man's ego would hardly submit to such a hammering. Still, the commotion could not be permitted to continue. He walked into the room without knocking, and saw that his arrival only served to increase the burly New Englander's irritation.

'Captain Seeker, I am currently engaged.'

Seeker surveyed him a moment, determined that the other man should know he was unimpressed by his rise in the world since the days their paths had crossed in the army. 'Why are you in Secretary Thurloe's chamber?'

Lady Anne Winter had turned on hearing Seeker's name, and the face, which had been a study of fury, softened, if only a little. 'Captain Seeker,' she said. 'At last, a man with whom one might deal.'

Wary of the impotent outrage in Downing's eye, Seeker spoke cautiously. 'Lady Anne. We have not seen you in these corridors a good two months. How does life in Crutched Friars?'

'Well enough,' the woman replied, 'as you might no doubt know if you would consult this person's files.' She treated Downing to a look of contempt that Seeker in all his dealings with her had never seen. Calm, measured, aloof: those were the words he would have used to describe Lady Anne Winter, had anyone cared to ask. None of these epithets could be applied to her now.

Nevertheless, there was little point in dissembling. 'You can hardly be surprised that your house is watched, Lady Anne. You have made no secret of your continued adherence to the cause of Charles Stuart, or of your contempt for the Protector. If it had been left to me, I would have had you out of London, never mind just this palace.'

To Downing's evident astonishment, Anne Winter now actually smiled. 'Still honest then, Seeker. Perhaps there is hope yet, if there is still *one* honest man in this nest of vipers.' She let the emphasis of that 'one' fill the room a moment. 'I know my house is watched, and you are right, I would expect nothing less.'

'And so?'

'He,' – still she would not accord Downing the courtesy of his name – 'will not tell me what he knows.'

Seeker shrugged. 'Why should he?'

'Because one of my housemaids, a good child of great promise, has disappeared. You know as well as I that the movements of everyone who sets foot in my house, or leaves it, by back door or by front, are watched day and night.' She stared at him and, receiving no response, flung a hand towards the rows of shelves behind and to the right of Thurloe's desk. 'It must be somewhere there, in those books, or in the countless others in this place. It will be written down.'

Downing, not quite mastering his anger, sought to regain control of the interview. 'As I have told this woman—'

But Anne Winter ignored him, continuing to address herself solely to Seeker. 'She is not twelve years old, an orphan from the streets. She'd been passed from one foundling hospital to another, until the last, some old religious house, was closed down, for that the title was found by your Commonwealth's lawyers to be insufficient, and the property allocated to others better inclined to the regime. She was put out onto the streets, Seeker. She is not a knowing child, and too trusting.'

Downing sneered in contempt. 'Trusting? A girl of the streets?'

Anne Winter whipped back round towards him in a fury. 'She would not have *been* on the streets had your—' Then she stopped, as a young man, dressed like most of the clerks in Thurloe's service, although his clothing of better quality, passed by the open door. 'You!' She went after him. 'You, you have been there, you have been one of them.'

The young man turned around, trying to make sense of the woman accosting him, and turned startled eyes on Downing, who along with Seeker had followed her into the corridor.

'I, your ladyship, I do not know—'

Seeker put up a hand to stop him. He had noticed this young man around the corridors lately, or in the clerks' rooms, always looking as if he had somewhere more important, more interesting to be. He carried about him an air of indolence which did not sit well in a place of such industry. 'Who are you?'

Looking at Downing as if for confirmation of his own identity, the young man straightened himself, stood on ceremony a little. 'My name is Marcus Bridlington, Captain Seeker. My mother is a cousin to Major-General Goffe. I have been in the Secretary's service for—'

Again Seeker stopped him. The boy, by links of kinship and friendship, was but a few steps from Cromwell. 'Lady Anne, though she might not realise it, has no call to know this. Go about your business.'

As the young man inclined his head and continued down the corridor, Anne Winter opened her mouth to protest, but Seeker gave her a warning look. 'I will look into this matter when I have the leisure, Lady Anne. For the child's sake, not yours, but you will importune Mr Downing no longer. He has greater matters to attend to than the business of absconding servants.'

Anne Winter, he knew, was an intelligent woman, and he saw an understanding flit across her face. Downing was not a person of whom to make an enemy. She nodded slowly.

'All right. Yes. All right.'

She offered Downing a cursory dip of her head, and went past them both, more composed now than when she had arrived. Seeker took her by the elbow and steered her away from Thurloe's door, and towards the end of the corridor. 'You would do well not to make an enemy of George Downing, Lady Anne.'

'Downing? Why should I fear him? I know all about him and where he came from. A penniless preacher arrived not ten years ago from Massachusetts with hardly a coat to his back. John told me of him. Had Colonel Okey not taken him on as chaplain to his regiment, he would like as not have died an infantryman. He came from nothing.'

Seeker took a moment to reply. 'That may well be, my lady, but what you and your like will not understand, and what has been the defeat of you all, is that men who come from nothing need not end as nothing.'

'How we end, Seeker, God will decide.'

'Perhaps. But in this place, it's for the Lord Protector to say how we live.'

'And George Downing has insinuated himself into the right circles, taken a woman of good fortune and high breeding to wife—'

'Whether you like him or not, Lady Anne, Downing's skills and talents have made him very useful to the Protector.'

'Does Oliver not have preachers enough?'

'I think you know that isn't what I mean.'

'Oh, I know. His skills lie less in the salvation of men

than in the observation, the manipulation of them. John told me: Downing taught Oliver the virtues of a spy.'

Seeker didn't argue with her. Downing's facility for the gathering of intelligence in the field, and for showing others its value, had seen him rise quickly from a chaplain in the now-disgraced Okey's regiment to Scoutmaster General of the army in Scotland, charged with gathering and tracking any intelligence that was to be had. But Downing's rise had not stopped there, and by the time Oliver had appointed the New Englander, a rich and well-connected wife on his arm, to a lucrative post in the Exchequer, he was already well on the way to forgetting he had ever been a penniless preacher.

Before he handed her over to a guard at the end of the corridor, to be escorted from the building, Seeker turned Anne Winter to face him. 'A man that has risen from nowhere to almost the heart of government, who finds himself at the Protector's dinner table, who has half of London clamouring for his favour, is not one to be taken lightly, or slighted. You have enemies enough, Lady Anne. I would counsel you to make no more.'

Back in Thurloe's room, Downing, his colour subsiding, was nonetheless shaken. He sought to assert his authority. 'How did that woman get in here, Seeker? I had heard before that she was mad. She should not have got in here. This place should be better guarded.'

Seeker did not respond other than to call for a guard. While the man was running down the corridor, Seeker picked up Downing's hat from the chair on which it had been set and handed it to him. 'Your office is in the Exchequer. You have no business in Secretary Thurloe's rooms when he is not here.'

Downing bristled. 'I think you forget who it is that you talk to, Seeker.'

Seeker looked at him, any hint of deference he had adopted for Anne Winter's benefit gone. 'I forget nothing, Downing. Not the merest detail. And I take my orders only from the Council of State. Get back to your Exchequer.' He turned then and ordered the guard to have Secretary Thurloe's rooms locked and watched. 'And see that no one, no one but Mr Meadowe, Secretary Milton or the Lord Protector himself is given access to these rooms without the written permission of Mr Thurloe.'

Seeker was still thinking about George Downing when he reached the ante-room where the clerks and under-secretaries were prone to gather. Marcus Bridlington, the young man accosted a few minutes earlier by Anne Winter, was not there, but Dorislaus was, and with him Andrew Marvell, who was intermittently to be found trying to secure preferment in one Secretary's service or another. Passed over more than once, by men less able than he but more amenable to making themselves liked, or by others, like Marcus Bridlington, better connected, Marvell nonetheless had established himself in Whitehall like moss on a neglected step. In order to make ends meet, the young poet

found himself constrained every so often to take the position of tutor to the children of wealthy and increasingly
powerful men – recently the daughter of General Lord
Fairfax, and now a ward of Cromwell himself. His duties
would take him away to Yorkshire, Eton, overseas sometimes, but always he found his hopeful way back to
Whitehall, and the moss grew back on the step. Seeker
knew, because he had taken the time to read Marvell's file,
that his younger compatriot had travelled on the continent,
as far as Spain, had dallied in Madrid, attended literary gatherings there in the homes of the affluent and influential, yet
little in the way of social graces seemed to have rubbed off
on him. Only John Milton, blind Milton, saw something in
him that others did not. 'It is because Milton doesn't have to
look at that sullen face,' Seeker had heard one of the clerks
mumble to another once. Yet for all Marvell's sullen face
and quick temper, something in Seeker warmed to his fellow
Yorkshireman. You'll never get on in Whitehall, though,
he thought.

Dorislaus was laughing good-naturedly at an anecdote of
something that had clearly outraged his companion. Neither man was in the army, nor ever had been, but both
jumped to attention when Seeker's shadow crossed the
doorway. He motioned to them to sit back down. 'Where is
Secretary Meadowe?' he asked.

'Transcribing for Mr Milton. Do you wish me to interrupt him?'

Seeker shook his head. 'No. But when he's free, ask him

to find me anything he has relating to a man by the name of Goodwill Crowe.'

Marvell was again rising from his seat. 'The Fifth Monarchist?'

'Yes, you know of him?'

'We've taken some pamphlets in of late. The usual stuff. Printed by Giles Calvert and the like.'

'Have them sent to my chambers, and any information you have on him or his associations.'

Marvell nodded, pleased, and hurried off back to the Censor Office, to do Seeker's bidding.

'I doubt anything will have come your way . . .' Seeker began to Dorislaus, but that young man was also on his feet.

'Goodwill Crowe? Aldgate?'

'That's right. He has received post?'

'Something,' said Dorislaus, his forehead shaping to a frown as he tried to recall. 'A pamphlet. Nothing much – as Andrew said, the usual stuff. I passed it on to Meadowe's office.'

'The address?' said Seeker.

'Something biblical. Golgotha? No.' The frown deepened. 'Gethsemane. They were directed to him at Gethsemane. It's amongst some old drapers' almshouses at the end of Wood-ruffe Lane, towards Tower Hill.'

Seeker knew it: a likely enough place for Fifth Monar-chists to gather – many of them had been clothworkers before the war, and those not still in the army had returned to their old trade. The clothworkers had their hall nearby on Mincing Lane, and Carter Blyth in his guise of Gideon Fell would no doubt have found work there amongst them without too much trouble.

Seeker was about to leave, and then paused. 'Has George Downing been asking questions around the postal office, of you, or Morland?'

Dorislaus looked uncomfortable. 'I think he has been trying to find out who Mr Thurloe is in contact with, in Charles Stuart's court.'

'And what have you told him?'

Dorislaus shrugged. 'The truth. It was not difficult. Only the Secretary knows the code names anyhow. Morland did say that we suspected the people we were in contact with of being avowed Royalists, but I don't think Mr Downing found that amusing.'

Seeker laughed.

Dorislaus, emboldened, continued. 'And I think he has been getting one of his clerks from the Exchequer to insinuate himself amongst us.'

Seeker waited, interested.

'But it will do him no good.'

'You are on your guard against young clerks from the Exchequer?'

'No, not that. Sam Pepys is very personable, though prone to too much drink and some lewdness. But the thing is, he likes Downing less than we do.'

'Be careful what you say in front of him all the same,

though,' said Seeker. He resolved to have the Exchequer clerk looked into.

As he turned to leave, Dorislaus asked, 'Should we concern ourselves more closely with the Fifth Monarchy men, then?'

'Concern yourselves with exactly what Secretary Meadowe tells you to concern yourself with. Besides, I think the Stuarts and their friends will be keeping you busy enough.'

A happy smile illuminated Dorislaus' delicate face. 'If they but knew, Captain, if they but knew!'

FIVE

Gethsemane

Seeker took a wherry from Whitehall Stairs down the river as far as Custom House Key. He considered Blackfriars as he passed. It told him nothing. That had been Carter Blyth's ending – macabre and grotesque, a tableau in some grim, preposterous masque to entertain and divert those who might come upon it. And it would entertain and divert the people a while, as they swallowed down whatever outrage the vermin scribblers of a hundred news-sheets rushed to feed them – but it would not divert Seeker. The rotting Dominican robes would have been stripped away by now, and burned. Seeker had already stripped them from his mind, determined not to see Carter Blyth in death, but to look at him as he was in the last few weeks of life, as he took the steps that led him to that end in Blackfriars.

Alighting at the quay, he told the boatman not to wait for him, and went by Tower Hill to Woodruffe Lane. The day was already darkening and candles were sending glints of golden light from windows in the Tower. A couple of naval officials making way to their offices on Seething Lane paused in their discussion of the new ship, the *Naseby*, to be named in honour of Cromwell's greatest triumph, and nodded a greeting to him. Seeker could not help but wonder what the army might have done with the vast sums this vessel, aimed at conquering England's rivals at sea, was rumoured to be costing. There were threats enough at home to contend with.

The markets by the river were closing down for the day, and the feel of the streets changing. Business was ending, the hawkers finished touting their wares and the taverns becoming fuller. The cleansers were coming out from wherever they passed their daylight hours, to clear the debris of the day. All underfoot would be filthy again by dawn when the night-soil men would resume their thankless task. For now though, no one got in Seeker's way.

The almshouses were near the top of Woodruffe Lane, where Hart Street ran into Crutched Friars. To one side were the walls, in good solid stone, of what had once been the Friars' Church, now a tenement for drapers and other clothworkers. The almshouses themselves were done in brick and timber. Over the arched entranceway to the courtyard, below the window of the master's dwelling, where the chiselled arms of the founder had begun to wear away, hung a simple wooden sign bearing the legend *Gethsemane*.

Seeker was aware of a movement of the shutter above him as he passed beneath the gatehouse into the courtyard. The sights and sounds of industry came from all sides of the square of fourteen identical cottages serving as dwellings and workshops. A pig was tethered in a pen, chickens pecked around its edges, and a cat observed him from the window ledge of one of the cottages. A boy was employed in chopping wood in a corner, a smaller child in stacking it into piles. Seeker walked towards a door from which he could hear the low and regular murmur of female voices. The two faces that turned to him when he pushed open the door were separated by a generation but little else. Mother and daughter were carding wool, a seam of joylessness in flesh and spirit running from one to the other and offering outsiders no welcome. He addressed himself to the older of the two. 'Where will I find Goodwill Crowe?'

Apprehension darted briefly across the younger woman's eyes, and she glanced quickly at her mother before hurriedly turning her attention back to her carding. The older woman stood up and smoothed her apron. 'What do you want with my husband?'

'That'll be for me to tell him. Where is he?'

The woman addressed her daughter without taking her eyes from Seeker. 'Patience, fetch your father.'

The girl went to do as she was bid. She looked to be about sixteen or seventeen, but everything in her was a younger version of her mother. Not just in the sombre clothing, but in the plain, narrow features, pinched nose and chin, small eyes, like a bird's. He could not tell the colour of their hair, covered by caps so tight against their skulls that not a wisp escaped. Thin lips, the mother's colourless; what passed for bloom, which would soon be gone, Seeker thought, giving a little more warmth to the daughter's features. The older woman was taller, and the hardness of her eyes allowed for no misconception: she didn't fear him; she didn't fear anyone.

'This way.' The mother went out into the courtyard and led the way across to another of the almshouse buildings. Smoke rose from the chimney of this one, but on entering, Seeker saw it was no cookhouse or family dwelling, but a meeting room with rushes on the floor, and plain benches set in a horseshoe around the fireplace. On either side of the fireplace was a simple wooden chair. Ten years of his life flooded from him, and he felt something in his stomach shift. Mistress Crowe pointed to the chairs. 'Take one. My husband will be here presently.'

'What manner of gathering is held here?' asked Seeker, pushing back all thoughts but of the present.

She considered him. 'You said your business was with him,' and walked out without saying anything else. Seeker stood before the fire and thought over the bones of the report on Elizabeth Crowe that Carter Blyth had made and sent to Thurloe with those on the other Fifth Monarchists he had encountered at St Pancras church. Woman preacher. Second wife to Crowe. No pamphleteering known, but preaching of the most virulent kind, and its direction against the Protector but thinly veiled. Uncompromising. Considered unturnable. That was always a key thing for Thurloe: could they be turned? So many of the agents in the Protectorate's pay had begun believing in, serving, the other side. But a few days in the Tower, and a visit from Thurloe, who could often achieve with his soft voice and reasonable offers what the turn of the thumbscrew or the threat of the rack could not, had turned many of them. But no, even a moment's acquaintance had told Seeker Blyth had been right about Elizabeth Crowe – she would not be turned. He thought the report might also have said cold, humourless, unpleasant to be in the vicinity of. How any man could marry himself such a wife was beyond Seeker's comprehension.

It was only a few minutes before Goodwill Crowe appeared. Seeker was not conscious of ever having seen him before, but he was the kind of man he always thought he knew: an army man, of average height, strong build, battle-worn face. Crowe looked to be a year or two older than Seeker, and a few younger than his wife. Coarse, greying brown hair roughly chopped to his shoulders. A beaten leather hat and jerkin, sturdy boots. Strong hands. He was the kind of man who had won the war for Parliament, for Cromwell. 'Captain,' he said.

Seeker nodded.

'You're here about Gideon Fell.'

Seeker was not surprised – he'd expected that the preacher from Soper Lane would have forewarned them. 'Aye.'

Crowe turned to his wife, who had followed him into the room. 'Have the girl bring us some bread and ale.'

'It's for the meeting,' she said.

'Just bring it, woman.'

Once she'd gone, Crowe sat and Seeker did likewise.

'Tell me about Gideon Fell,' said Seeker.

Crowe took a moment, careful. 'I haven't seen Gideon Fell for over two weeks. He was here about a month, from about the start of December. He'd turned up one night at a meeting at St Pancras. Said he was a soldier. Discharged. He was of our belief, and we didn't ask too many questions. He could work a shuttle well enough, and I had work to give him.'

Seeker looked towards the window onto the courtyard. 'You get many of his sort here?'

'A few find their way to us,' said Crowe. 'It's not so easy, when you leave the army, to go back to the life you had before.' Seeker said nothing and Crowe continued. 'They turn up looking for a bed and a day's work, stay a few weeks most of them, then move on when they find something else or manage to get themselves into a regiment again.'

'Do you hear from them again after that?'

Crowe pursed his lips in thought. 'Most of them go on to some other congregation of our sort, carry on the work of the Lord, making ready, and we hear of them now and again, see them if they're back in London. One or two, we don't hear of again.'

Seeker didn't need to ask about that 'making ready'. He knew from Carter Blyth's reports. The Fifth Monarchy men gathered regularly at the Artillery Yard by Spittal Fields and kept themselves in training, exercised their bodies and maintained their weapons and their skills, waiting for the word. The word that would tell them the time to rise up had come, the time to fight had come. He knew that at a word from Cromwell they would march on Paris, march on Rome, tear the great anti-Christ, that Whore of Babylon, from St Peter's throne, as the Saints were bound to do. But Cromwell was not disposed as yet to give such a word, and many of the men Carter Blyth had been watching, inflamed as they were by the preaching of the likes of Elizabeth Crowe, were not disposed to wait much longer.

'And what of Gideon Fell? Did you hear anything from him after he left here?'

'Not a word.'

'Had he told you he was going?'

Another 'no', then a pause. 'Though, I'll tell you, I thought it strange he'd said nothing to Nathaniel.'

'Your son?'

'Aye. The boy's simple. A judgement of the Lord on me, on his mother.'

'For what?'

'I have searched His judgements, but what can mortal man tell of the purposes of God? His mother was taken at his birth, and perhaps the sin was hers. Perhaps it was a chastisement to me, for that I had too great an affection for her – who can tell? He's there, before my eyes, every day, and I strive to atone.'

'Your wife is not this boy's mother?'

Crowe weighed his words. 'She has been in the place of a mother to him. She has done her duty, as my wife. He has never hungered, nor gone without shelter and the word of God. And he has honoured her as his mother, as is right.'

The boy might have fared worse, Seeker thought. He might also have fared better. 'Why should Gideon Fell have told this child of his plans?'

Crowe fixed him with a direct look, layers of practised godliness stripped away a moment, to reveal the man beneath. 'Nathaniel isn't a child. He's twenty-two years old.' Then he said in a lower voice, 'Willing enough worker. God-fearing. Does no harm.'

'And Gideon Fell?'

Crowe shrugged. 'Took a liking to the boy, so's that Nathaniel trailed around everywhere after him. Fell even tried to teach him to read.' Crowe shook his head at the uselessness of it.

'And Fell didn't tell him of any plans to leave?'

'Not that I know. Mind you, I'm not certain that he did plan to leave. He hadn't much to his name when he came to us, and most of that he's left.' He considered this and then said, 'What's your interest, Captain?'

At that point, the door opened again and Patience Crowe came in bearing a tray with two mugs of ale and a trencher of bread. As she served Seeker she studiously avoided his eye. Seeker knew that look – one not of modesty, but fear. He waited until she was leaving before he answered Good-will's question.

'Gideon Fell is dead. His body was found today.'

Crowe's face showed little reaction. 'Where?'

'Blackfriars.'

Crowe sat back in his chair, took a sip of his ale, then rested the mug on his lap. 'There was an old monk found today, I hear, at Blackfriars. Bricked into a wall.'

Seeker said nothing, and Crowe nodded. 'So there was more to Gideon than he chose to tell us, then.'

'What did he tell you?' asked Seeker.

Crowe tore a piece of bread and passed it to Seeker. 'That he'd been born in Norfolk, worked in the wool trade until the war. Fought for Parliament. Tried his luck overseas when the war ended. Came back when he saw how things here were shaping, after Cromwell shut down Barebones, came to stake the claim of the godly.'

'You think yourselves more godly than the Lord Protector?'

'There was a time there was none more godly, but he has forgotten, abandoned what was fought for, and he must heed his warning: "I have somewhat against thee, because thou hast left thy first love. Remember therefore from whence thou art fallen and repent, and do the first works; or else I will come unto thee quickly."'

The weaver's face had taken on a completely different look; there was a clarity in his eyes that pierced Seeker.

'Our claim is to this kingdom, that we might make it fit for the reign of Christ. We wait on Christ, we watch and we do not sleep. We looked for the government of the godly to prepare the way, but Cromwell has failed us. We have made this a new Gethsemane, where we will wait on the Lord, watch with the Lord, and we will not fail him, we will not sleep.'

Seeker thought of the drills at Spittal Fields Blyth had written of. He thought also of the attempt made on Oliver's life in the wake of 'Belshazzar's Feast'. 'You must know if you take up arms against the Protector, you will perish, every one.'

Goodwill Crowe fixed Seeker with a look that was utterly uncompromising. 'We have more in our armoury than guns and bullets. We pray. We preach. We educate the people in their rights, in the means by which their rights are denied by lawyers, judges, church priests, tithes. We challenge those who would set themselves up to rule where only God has right, who have overturned the assemblies of the Godly. Nol Cromwell has forgotten who gave him his victories and why they were given. We press for the armies of England to carry the Revolution overseas, to take it to the very steps of St Peter's and there at last to destroy the Anti-Christ.'

Seeker glanced around him: from the gates of Gethsemane to the gates of Rome. He could have reeled it off himself; it had hardly been worth the asking. 'You spread sedition, then.'

'How can it be sedition to assert the claim of God, of his people? What did you fight for? To set up a new tyrant in the place of the old, to bind the people in new chains?'

'England's New Chains' again. The lawyer Wildman's pamphlet had reached even here. The Censor Office wasn't working fast enough. Seeker ignored Crowe's question and returned to the matter in hand. 'And what did Gideon Fell do in your cause when he was here?'

Crowe pushed out his chin, thought. 'Little. And less as time went on. He started as a fervent hearer when Elizabeth preached, attended every meeting, prayed, read the Scriptures with us. Didn't put himself forward often though. Kept to the back at meetings, didn't raise his voice much. As time went on, he started to miss meetings. Elizabeth spoke to him of it.'

'What did he say?'

'He gave different reasons – that he'd met by chance an old comrade, gone to hear another preacher, been asked to do a job for someone in the city.'

'And did you believe him?'

Crowe pursed his lips. 'No. But I've seen it before. They come out of the army and have no place. Fix on us, tell themselves they believe as we do. But some are weak, their faith too weak – like grain that falls upon stony ground springs up and is burnt in the sun. Gideon Fell's faith fell short, Captain; his name wasn't written in the Book of Life and he knew that. That's why he went.'

Seeker didn't disabuse Crowe of this view of the man who had posed as an acolyte for a month. 'And how did he come to find himself bricked up, alive, in a wall at Blackfriars wearing the robes of a hundred years' dead monk?'

'I have no notions what perversions may have led him to that pass. No interest either. But if you have made it your business to know, then this may tell you something.' Crowe reached inside his jerkin and pulled out a canvas scroll, which he handed to Seeker. 'It was all I found when I searched his chamber, other than a few items of clothing. It was hidden below his mattress. Nathaniel tells me he never saw it before.'

'And do you believe him?' asked Seeker, looking up from his scrutiny of the image on the canvas.

'The boy may be simple, but he doesn't lie.'

'This is a painting of Christ in the Garden of Gethsemane.'

'An affront to God.'

Seeker had no view on that, but he did know one thing: this was not the first time he'd seen this picture. He didn't have to go down many pathways in his memory until he located where he had seen it before: in Lincoln's Inn, in a sitting room that Thurloe had once met him in. It had hung opposite the door. When Seeker had passed that open door earlier in the day, there had been a blank space where the picture had once hung.

'Do you think Fell meant this as a gift for you?'

Goodwill Crowe stared at him. 'I have heard it said of you, Seeker, that you scarcely pay lip service to the Word of God, but surely even you know, and Gideon Fell certainly did, that any such gift, such graven image, idolatrous, would have been a profanity to me. "Thou shalt not make unto thee any graven image, or any likeness of *any thing* that is in Heaven above." This was meant as no gift.'

Seeker nodded and put the rolled-up canvas inside his own jerkin. He drank down the last of his ale and stood up.

'Take me to where you found this, and bring your boy to me there.'

Nathaniel was already in his own chamber when his father appeared with Damian Seeker. He'd tidied the room so that no sign of the earlier disturbance remained, put fresh rushes on the floor, and taken blankets from the laundry press for Gideon's bed, in case Gideon should come home tonight. His mother would be angry when she counted the blankets, but then, Nathaniel thought, she would be angry anyway.

He'd heard of the Seeker before. Sometimes, the boys out in the lane would play at soldiers. No one ever wanted to be the Royalists, but the biggest boy would always be the Seeker, and the others always ran the fastest from him. They'd been coming home one night, him and Gideon, and the boys had been pretending to be plotters, running from the Seeker, but Gideon had laughed and said, 'If it had been the real Seeker, he'd have been waiting in their hiding place for them before they ever got there.' Patience had been trying to scare him all day with tales about the Seeker coming for him, but Gideon had told him Patience was a liar, and cruel. No one had ever said that before, the men and women at the meetings were always praising Patience, although he'd sometimes wondered if his father liked Patience very much. Gideon didn't like Patience, and she hated him, Nathaniel knew that for sure.

The man who came through the door behind his father was much bigger than Goodwill or Gideon. He was bigger than Nathaniel himself even. He had his helmet under his arm but he still had to stoop to get through the doorway. He had a long black cloak on too, and his boots were just like Gideon's. Nathaniel was always noticing things like that, but he didn't tell people any more, because his mother always said such things were vanities. Everything made by man was a vanity. So he hadn't said anything about Gideon's boots, but he'd liked them.

The man fixed him with his look, and Nathaniel tried not to look away, answered as clear as he could when the man asked him if he was Nathaniel.

'And this is the chamber you shared with Gideon Fell?'

Again he gave as clear a 'Yes' as he could manage.

'Good,' said the man, then turned to his father. 'Leave us now.'

Goodwill looked surprised, but made no protest, unlike Elizabeth Crowe and her daughter, who had followed them across the yard. Seeker made a point of barring the door shut on them.

Nathaniel didn't like being shut in, and there was so little light in the room. But the man lit a second candle from the first by the window ledge, took off his cloak, and sat down on Gideon's bed, motioning for Nathaniel to do likewise on the one opposite.

When he had done so, the man looked at him as if to search his face. 'My name is Damian Seeker,' he said.

'I kn-know,' replied Nathaniel.

'Whatever you have heard of me, you should know there

is no need to be afraid of me, if you tell me the truth. Your father tells me you don't lie, is that right?'

Nathaniel nodded. 'Lying is a sin.'

'That's right. But if you lie to me, that will be a crime. And that is worse.'

Nathaniel had never heard anyone speak in this way, and was glad his mother hadn't been allowed to come in. She would have given many texts on the matter, and annoyed the Seeker, he was certain.

The Seeker didn't appear to notice the strangeness of what he had said and carried on. 'Gideon Fell was your friend, was he not?'

Nathaniel bristled. Gideon was not like everyone else. 'Gideon *is* my friend. He will be coming back. He would have told me if he wasn't coming back.'

He shouldn't have argued with the Seeker, he shouldn't have spoken back, but sometimes he couldn't help it, and now he'd be in trouble. Already the difficult smile had gone from the man's face, and his expression was changing. But the look that was in the Seeker's eyes now was like when Gideon had to tell him that he couldn't take him with him somewhere he was going, or that he would be back too late to help him learn his letters that night. The Seeker was sorry about something. Nathaniel felt his stomach go cold.

'I'm sorry, Nathaniel. But you need to understand. Gideon cannot come back.'

Nathaniel could feel his cheeks begin to burn, and in his ears it was very noisy. He put his hands over his ears to muffle Seeker's voice, but strong hands lifted them away. The Seeker was leaning towards him, looking right into his face. 'You must listen, Nathaniel, you must understand. Gideon is dead. Someone killed Gideon.'

'No, no . . .' Shaking his head, his hands over his ears, the strong hands lifting them off again. Seeker's face looking right into his.

'You must understand, and you must help me, Nathaniel. There is no one else. You must help me to find who killed him.'

SIX

Shadrach Jones

It was fully dark by the time Seeker left Gethsemane. It had taken some time to explain to the boy what he would need of him – places he had gone with Gideon, what he'd seen, things Gideon had said to him – especially as, when Nathaniel had first begun to understand, Seeker had hardly been able to stop the flow of words, the information tumbling from him, and while it evidently made sense in Nathaniel's mind, it made little, yet, to Seeker. Two things he had made sure the boy grasped before he left that bolted chamber: that he would be back, and that Nathaniel was not to tell his parents, nor his sister, the things he was telling Seeker. The boy took the trust as a solemn vow, and Seeker left knowing he had won him.

For the last few minutes of his interview with Nathaniel, Seeker had been aware of voices and increased footfall in the courtyard outside. Torches had been lit around the perimeter, and after he left the boy he took a moment to watch as people emerged from the other almshouse buildings: an old woman Seeker remembered touting herself as a prophetess – she'd had a spell in the Bridewell for her deranged ravings about the Protector, and would do so again, no doubt. Three men of different ages, clothed as labourers but walking like soldiers. An itinerant preacher whom Carter Blyth's report had already informed him was in London. From out on the street, through the entrance-way, more people came: a printer Seeker knew of from Blackfriars, whose premises he had not long raided; Christopher Feake, a fanatic who had been in gaol more often of late than he had been out of it; the woman Atwood, who so often disturbed the peace with her preaching up by Coleman Street. All of them had been listed in Blyth's reports, and none was a surprise, but they would all need to be questioned about their dealings with Gideon Fell. Seeker would have to take Daniel Proctor with him when he returned.

It was growing cold, frost beginning to form on the cobbles of the ground and on the branches of an apple tree trained against the wall beside him. Seeker thought he had seen all he was going to see, but then the bell of St Olave's church tolled six, and Elizabeth Crowe, followed by her husband and daughter, emerged from the building the others had just gone into – the one in which he had talked with Goodwill Crowe – and positioned themselves opposite the entrance. Less than a minute later, a man came through it who didn't seem to fit, but Seeker knew that he did fit, all too well. The firelight from the torches only served to make his appearance here all the more remarkable. Any who did not already know him, if there were such in

London, might have thought the man a Cavalier of the most exorbitant sort: russet satin breeches and doublet, a green velvet cape held with a jewelled silver clasp, and descending from beneath the wide-brimmed, feathered green hat, locks any courtier of Charles Stuart would be proud of.

But this was no Cavalier, no courtier of Charles Stuart. This was a butcher's boy. Or a butcher, some said. Major-General Thomas Harrison had never been a man to compromise. He it was who had named Charles I 'that man of blood', when others had thought the King might still be treated with, he who had signed the King's death warrant without flinching, and when Cromwell had tired of court-ing the Parliament that had killed that King, had called in his soldiers to shut it down, and himself pulled the Speaker from his chair. But when Cromwell had been made Lord Protector, and made peace with the Dutch, and forgot that his destiny was to march on Rome, Oliver's greatest friend had become his most dangerous enemy. And he was here, tonight, the highest-ranking Fifth Monarchist in the land, at Gethsemane.

Seeker had made no attempt to conceal himself, or that he watched. When Harrison had been greeted by his wife and daughter, Goodwill Crowe leaned towards him, spoke something to him and then pointed towards the doorway in which Seeker stood. Harrison turned and looked right at him. There was a depth of hatred in that look that Seeker had rarely seen. 'That is no godly man,' Harrison said at last, 'and his day will come.'

Back out on Woodruffe Lane, where the rising sound of the psalms seemed to follow him, Seeker felt for the painting inside his jerkin. He would have liked to take it to Thurloe tonight, but he had disturbed the Secretary from his sickbed once already today: it could wait. Seeker considered heading up to the right. Two minutes would take him to Anne Winter's house, near the far end of Crutched Friars. His earlier promise to look into the disappearance of her young servant came back to him, and he was curious to know what kind of household the widow had made for herself after leaving the palace of Whitehall. More, he wanted to know how much the reality of what went on behind that new-painted green door accorded with the reports of those sent to watch her, but he was not in the humour to deal with the woman again tonight – her troubles would keep until the morning.

He turned, instead, westwards, up by Blanch Appleton and then along by Fenchurch Street to Lombard Street. Two drunkards, sent scuffling out of the George, almost collided with him, and on seeing who he was, remembered they were friends after all, and not so drunk as they might have thought. The watch was lax, but a clampdown was coming, Seeker knew. The tavern-keepers would not like it, the people even less. So be it: day by day they showed that they could not be trusted to govern themselves. Past St Edmund's, he paused a moment at the bottom of Birchin Lane, and there, through the other odours of the night-town, he caught the aromas of coffee grounds and pipe smoke floating down from Kent's coffee house, and from the Turk Pasqua Rosee's, nearby. Sometimes at the end of a long day, just as the place was shutting up for the night, he had found himself crossing Kent's threshold, having a word and a draught with the old soldier who ran it. The coffee man knew that Seeker had somehow been behind the recovery of his niece Grace, a few months back, from an illness that had dragged her into the deep sleep of another world, when Elias Ellingworth had falsely been accused of murder, but Samuel had understood enough never to ask Seeker about it. Sometimes, on his late-night visits, Seeker had nothing to say at all, and Samuel would leave him be, and quietly shuffle around the coffee room, making ready for the next day, murmuring instructions to the coffee boy who knew enough not to trouble the captain. Seeker was weary, and would have liked to pass a quarter-hour with Samuel now, but it was too early: the place would still be filled with lawyers and merchants and newsmen, and nothing would empty it for Samuel faster than the Seeker coming through his door. Besides, he didn't like their noise, their endless babble, their mania always to know how the world moved on, when sometimes all he looked for was that it would stand still.

He continued on his way. Light glowed from the windows of the post house at the bottom of Threadneedle Street. They would be sorting over the last arrivals of the day, brought from drops at coffee houses, inns and taverns, looking out for anything that should be sent to Isaac Dorislaus. Seeker wondered if those who filled the taverns and coffee houses had any notion how much of the business of the Protectorate was conducted by others, through the night, as they took their leisure and their sleep.

He turned off Poultry and up into the Old Jewry. The woman at the cook shop opposite the Angel nodded in recognition. She knew, but knew also that it was better it was none of her business. At the entrance to Dove Court he paused. They hadn't arranged this; Maria's brother might well have come home, instead of taking himself as usual from his chambers at Clifford's or the courts to the coffee house. It had happened once: Elias Ellingworth had returned home for a brief he had forgotten and found Seeker ahead of him on the stairs. The lawyer had assumed he was about to be arrested, and hadn't argued, but simply enquired, 'For what this time?' They had never quite resolved between them Seeker's role in saving Maria's brother from wrongful hanging for murder, only two months before. Elias had tried once, but Seeker had cut him off. It might have made a bridge between them, but for Seeker, it made a further barrier.

Still less had they spoken of Maria. She had assured Seeker that her brother did not know. But what then, if Elias didn't know? How were they ever to proceed, any of them, if Elias didn't know? How were they to proceed anyway? End it, he told himself every day. Just end it. But not tonight.

Maria heard the sound of footsteps on the stairs. It wasn't Elias. She knew the footsteps. The listening for them accompanied her every waking hour, so that she didn't know she listened for them any more. He was her constant thought, whenever she was in the garret alone, even when she knew he would not be coming, even when she knew that it was not possible that he should come. But not tonight; it wasn't a good thing that he should come tonight.

She went to the door, opened it before he could reach it.

'Captain Seeker!' she said to forestall him, and saw the question form in his eyes before he reasserted himself.

He looked at her curiously. 'Mistress Ellingworth. Is your brother at home?'

'Elias hasn't returned from Clifford's Inn yet.'

'Then . . .?' She saw the confusion on his face, saw him look past her, through the door, which she had thought too late to pull to behind her.

She watched his expression gradually change, lose its mobility, harden. She became aware that his breathing had quickened, become more shallow, as if he was struggling to stop his wonted composure abandoning him. He moved past her into the room, and spoke to her without taking his eyes off the object of his question. 'Who is this?'

The young man who had his back to them, with whom Maria had spent the last hour talking, as she'd wondered where on earth Elias could have got to, turned slowly round, his clear green eyes bypassing Maria entirely to focus purely on Seeker.

'Captain Seeker!' Maria said again. 'You cannot simply barge into a person's home, be they ever so lowly.' She knew though, that he could, and often did.

'Evidently,' he said, never taking his eyes from the other man.

'Damian,' she muttered through gritted teeth, positioning herself with her back to the other man and hoping he would not hear. She was relieved to see a little of the rage pass from Seeker's eyes. He took a breath and turned to her.

'As you are fully aware, mistress, your brother's activities have brought him to the attention of the authorities on many occasions, to the extent that all his contacts are suspect. Yourself included.'

Maria opened her mouth in protest, but thought better of it. Yet she resolved to remember that last part. He would not have that for free.

'There is a matter I would discuss with your brother. But it will wait. I'll ask again, Mistress Ellingworth, who is this person?' Seeker invested the word with such contempt, he might have been referring to the loathed and long-dead Earl of Strafford.

The man answered for himself. 'My name is Shadrach Jones. I arrived in London two weeks ago, from the town of Boston in Massachusetts. I have come to take up the position of schoolmaster, in Rhys Evans's school at the sign of the Three Nails in Holborn.' It was the voice of a man who expected to be challenged, and who was ready for it. Maria knew the type very well – most of her brother's associates had learned the same attitude.

It was not enough for Seeker, though, who loomed a

little closer to Shadrach Jones. 'So much for why you are in England – for the moment – but why are you *here*?'

Maria looked at the schoolteacher, so pale to Seeker's darkness, rich cream to heavy earth. He was almost as thin as her brother, his red hair, long, slim features and large eyes giving him the appearance of a deer ready to bolt. Nevertheless, he stood his ground.

Shadrach appeared to watch Seeker a moment, as if trying to understand him, before answering. 'I met in with Mistress Ellingworth's brother five days ago, at an evening lecture at Gresham College. There is another tonight that we both wished to hear, and Elias was kind enough to say we should go together, and to invite me here to take a little supper first.'

Seeker continued to speak to Jones, but looked at Maria. 'So you have had supper?'

Jones cleared his throat and Maria flung a hand towards the bare table top, annoyed. 'No, we have not. Elias was to bring it from Wood's cook shop on Cordwainer Street, and as you see, he is not here.'

Just then there was the sound of whistling, and more footsteps on the stair, and a moment later, Elias Ellingworth swung into the room. 'You would hardly credit what—' He stopped short when he saw Seeker. 'Oh. Trouble then.'

'As if you had not trouble enough,' said Maria. 'You are near an hour late, and I see you have brought us no supper.'

Elias looked down at his hands, as if expecting something to materialise there. 'Ah, I had forgotten. But Shadrach and I will get something on the way up to Gresham. We are still in time for the lecture.'

'And what about your sister?'

Elias turned astonished eyes on Seeker. 'Do not tell me the Council of State is concerning itself with the nutrition of London's spinsters now? I cannot think that is why you are here.'

Maria would not have believed Elias could have spoken to Seeker with such levity, that anyone, save herself, could speak to him with any levity at all.

'No, it isn't,' said Seeker. 'I have come to advise you to be careful of the company you keep.'

'What?' said Ellingworth putting down his papers. 'Shadrach's stomach is hardly settled from his voyage from New England. You cannot tell me he has been causing trouble already.'

'Your schoolmaster friend would be well advised to cause no trouble here, whatever may have driven him from Massachusetts, although by the present company, I see he has made a poor start,' Seeker replied. 'But it is John Wildman I have come to speak of.'

Elias sank wearily into one of the room's only two chairs. 'This again? Is every honest man to be hounded for opening his mouth? Can John Wildman not have friends?'

'John Wildman causes more trouble with his pen than even you do. His writings have been behind much of the dissent in the army, and now he has been colluding with Fifth Monarchy men. If they are found to be plotting against the security of the state, they will be brought down, have no doubt of that, and all of their associates with them.'

'I have no truck with the Fifth Monarchy men,' said Elias. 'To replace the Law of England with the Law of Moses? God help us.'

'It's not them but Wildman you should concern yourself about. He is known to have been here recently, on three different occasions. His movements and his contacts are closely watched. If he comes again, report it. Take this as a warning: disassociate yourselves from him.'

Elias narrowed his eyes as he appraised Seeker. 'But why now? And why should you care what becomes of us? Besides, you know threats and imprisonment will not silence me. You have had a wasted journey, Seeker.'

But Maria understood, even if Elias didn't. If Wildman was under close surveillance, and was known to be coming and going freely at Dove Court, their home, too, would be watched, and it would not be long before someone noted that Damian Seeker was there much more often than he had call to be.

There was nothing more to be said, no reason for Seeker not to take his leave now. He took his helmet from under his arm and gave Shadrach Jones one more admonitory look. 'Mind who you involve yourself with. London is not Massachusetts.'

Maria followed him out onto the landing, on the pretext

of seeing him safely gone, and shook her head at him, her mouth a firm line.

'I know, I know,' he said. 'I will study to do better.'

Samuel Kent was pleased with himself. The reactions on the faces of his regulars, as he took the pencil from the young New Englander's hand and made adjustments to the sketch on the table in front of him, was a sight to behold.

'But Samuel,' said Elias astonished, 'where did you learn this? I thought you could not write?'

Samuel smiled and handed the pencil back to Shadrach Jones. 'Write? Who says I can write? Drawing though, that's different. I didn't spend all my years in the army fixing bayonets or digging latrines, you know. Do you know how many sieges I was at in the war? Bristol, Newcastle, Hull – and half the towns in the Germany before that too. Not a siege engine from Nordlingen to Newark that I haven't seen rigged up from one side or the other.'

The young New Englander was paying no attention to the good-natured talk around the serving table of the coffee house, so engaged was he in making refinements to his sketch according to Samuel's suggestions. 'Thank you, Mr Kent. That will be most instructive for my pupils.'

'Dear Lord, help us,' said a hatter not long sat down. 'Don't tell me you're teaching the schoolboys of Holborn to construct siege engines!'

'Ah, no, no,' said Shadrach, smiling awkwardly as if it were something new to him. 'It is to show them the practical applications of mathematics. Elias and I attended a most fascinating lecture at Gresham College this evening—'

'And you studied at Harvard College, Elias tells us?' interjected the merchant George Tavener. 'You must have known George Downing there, before he discovered himself to be a sailor and a soldier and a preacher and a great English gentleman and officer of the Exchequer and I know not what. He taught for a time at Harvard, did he not? Surely you must have some tales to tell of George Downing that London would like to hear. Did he keep as mean a table then as they say he does now?'

The young man had coloured a little. 'What kind of table he keeps I don't know, for he would never have invited one such as me to sup at it. Downing cultivates no one unless he thinks they will be of use to him, and when they have outlived that usefulness, he casts them adrift and never thinks a moment more about it. He would sell his own mother if he thought it politic.'

With much murmuring in agreement, the table had entertained itself a little longer with tales of George Downing's parsimony.

It was just as Samuel was putting on the last pot for the night, and Grace set to work on the night's inventory, that Samuel became aware of a new customer coming in through the door and a murmur of distaste running through the room. The man at the top of the coffee room steps surveyed the company with an unpleasant smile, crooked, almost feral teeth contending for space in a narrow, scab-marked mouth. 'Very jolly,' the man said. 'Very jolly indeed.'

Elias Ellingworth was the first to speak, in his voice a hostility that was palpable. 'Nedham. I hadn't noticed you creep in, or perhaps, nowadays, you prefer to slither.' Samuel felt his old soldier's apprehension of something dangerous approaching. Marchamont Nedham. If Milton was the Protectorate's propagandist to Europe, the Empire, the Papacy, the Royalists in exile, Nedham was its mouthpiece to the masses, and he would write whatever it paid him most to write, regardless of any truth.

Nedham was looking sourly at Elias. 'When I find myself this far down in the world as you are, Ellingworth, perhaps to slither would be the more appropriate attitude. Anyway, I heard the Seeker was sometimes to be found here of a night.'

At this, Ellingworth laughed. 'You aim to tangle with the Seeker? Oh, but that would be something. I would pay any money to see that.'

'You have no money,' replied Nedham, with a satisfied contempt.

'Aye, but I would lend it him,' interjected George Tavener evenly. 'And at no interest – to see you tangle with the Seeker.'

It was seldom that Tavener was put out of humour, and a silence filled the room. It was Elias who broke it. 'Damian Seeker would wipe him like shit from his shoe. He likes to keep his boots very clean, I've noticed.'

Nedham lost patience with being the butt of their

humour. 'It's information I want from him; I'm no more fool than you are, but Whitehall has gone very quiet on his whereabouts since he found a hundred-years-dead Dominican bricked up in Blackfriars. No one there claims to know anything about it.'

The eyes of the coffee boy grew wide at this, until old Samuel flicked a cloth at him. 'You get on with your work, now, Gabriel. I'll not have Grace up half the night, listening to you wailing about dead monks and ghosts and all sorts.'

Grace smiled fondly at the young boy, who was not to be daunted.

'But I told you, Samuel—'

'And I'll tell you,' said the old man with the best semblance of menace he could muster, 'get out to that yard and fetch in more coal, and no more of your nonsense, or I'll put you to Blackfriars!'

'I heard about that,' said the hatter. 'Plague. They say the men that carried it away were in masks. Buried it deep out at Bedlam. I wouldn't go near the Seeker for a while.'

A draper next to him assured him with a shiver that he was not in the habit of going anywhere near Damian Seeker but added, 'The apothecary Drake was called, I hear, to cast spells over the corpse.'

'There you go, then, Nedham,' said Elias. 'Plague and spells. Exactly what you came looking for. Much better the people read about that, than about Cromwell trampling all over their parliament again, just like Charles Stuart used to.'

Nedham drained his dish of coffee. 'Mock if you want,

Ellingworth, but I'll be the one writing your gallows speech when you're dangling from a rope.' And then he was gone, back out into London, to sniff out whatever malodorous tales he thought might divert the masses, please his masters and line his pockets.

'Strange, all the same,' said Tavener after Nedham had left, 'that Seeker should be involved in the disposal of some old corpse like that in the first place. You'd have thought Thurloe would have enough on hand for him, with the Stuarts and their friends so busy polishing their sabres. But they obviously won't let Nedham have the merest scrap of what it's about.' He called over to the counter: 'Has he said anything to you about it, Samuel?'

'The Seeker?' The old soldier paid close attention to the coffee pot he was polishing. 'Hasn't been in. Don't say much when he does come in in any case. Takes his drink, gets a warm, goes out again. Doesn't bother me with his business.' He held the pot up to a candle, to examine his work. 'Makes for a nice change,' he murmured, smiling.

It was many hours later, and far into the dead of night, that Shadrach Jones at last snuffed out his candle. It had been a long enough walk from Birchin Lane, and he had been distracted by almost every shadow.

The last echoes of the lecture had faded, Elias's eager talk and the good-humoured exchanges of the coffee house drifted away, leaving Shadrach with the reality of the thing.

He had heard of the Seeker long before he had ever set

foot in Dove Court, or in England, indeed. Old soldiers who had fought with him spoke well of him, but those who had crossed him, who had fallen foul of the Protectorate, who had found as much to flee in Cromwell's England as they had in Charles Stuart's, would utter some oath when his name was mentioned and pray that God would keep him on the other side of the ocean. The Seeker *found* people, they said. People who did not wish to be found. Shadrach had thought it might be a simple thing to hide himself in this teeming city in a way it was not possible to do in that sparsely peopled world, that vast wilderness of New England. Here, you might hardly notice a man who passed within two feet of you; there, you knew soon enough if another had passed within two miles. He had been here little over two weeks, enjoying the anonymity in his schoolmaster's role, far from the likelihood of ever being spied by George Downing. He had even begun to make acquaintance, friends perhaps, of like mind but little note, and to do what he had come here to do unremarked upon, unnoticed. And as the hour that evening in Dove Court had stretched, he had even begun to wonder if he might find something more in this city of London; but then the heavy step had been on the stair, and into his world had walked Damian Seeker.

SEVEN

At Crutched Friars

The morning was crisp when Seeker woke. He stretched out a hand to ruffle the head of the ever-hopeful hound. 'We should be out in the woods, boy, should we not, catching hares, eh? Hares to send to Maria's pot, while that shiftless brother of hers lets her starve.'

At the mention of the name, the dog had stood up, alert, but Seeker shook his head. 'Not today, boy. She'll have to shift for herself today.' He looked at the animal, and a thought came to him. 'Besides, I have other work for you.'

In a little time, they had left Knight Ryder Street and were on their way to Crutched Friars. The matter of Anne Winter could be got over and done with before he started on the more important business of the day. The dog kept its distance, always ten yards or so behind, when Seeker was on the business of the state. It was only when his master walked through London as a carpenter that the animal knew he might acknowledge him. Only the apothecary Drake, who lived not far from Seeker, beyond the street door of the old

Physicians' Hall, had noticed. 'You fear that people will think you soft, Seeker, to see your attachment to the beast?'

Seeker had shaken his head. 'I fear they would harm him, if they should learn he was mine.'

He should have read the watchers' report on Anne Winter and her household before setting out there. Usually he would have done, however great the inconvenience of going first to Whitehall to call it up before having to turn around and make for the eastern reaches of the city again. But this wasn't Thurloe's business he was on, no matter of import to the state but a petty domestic concern. In truth, Seeker wasn't certain why he'd agreed to look into it at all. For peace. To get Anne Winter away from George Downing. For the missing girl's sake. For the feeling, which he could find no logic in, that he owed the woman something. It suited him better, though, to believe – and he would record the purpose of the visit as such – that it was because despite the best efforts of Thurloe's best men, they had not yet managed to get an agent behind that green door at the top of Crutched Friars to see what this most blatant of Charles Stuart's adherents had on hand there.

He'd gone up Fenchurch Street and down Northumberland Lane to come to the house by way of Poor Jewry, rather than pass by Gethsemane at the other end. He would get this thing over and done with first, before he set his mind fully to the business of Carter Blyth. The hound settled himself at the corner of Northumberland Lane, where a chestnut-seller with his brazier was setting up for the day, and Seeker rapped loudly with the wrought-iron knocker on Anne Winter's door. There was something familiar in the base of the knocker: the Baxton crest. When he stepped back and cast his eye over the fine batten-work panels of the door, he noticed the new-looking hoodmould above the doorhead – the same crest again, carved into the spandrels on either side. Her father's crest, from their seat in Oxfordshire that had been forfeit to the Commonwealth. Cromwell, out of love for John Winter, had gifted the place to his widow on Winter's death, but if the Protector could show tenderness of feeling, Anne Winter had not. She had sold Baxton before her husband was buried, and instead bought this house, here, almost in the shadow of the city walls and Aldgate. She would have done better to return to Oxfordshire and live quietly, as so many of her sort now did – there were plenty that had advised her so; but no, she had instead brazenly set herself up here with her father's crest. No one, not Cromwell, not Thurloe, and not Seeker, yet knew why.

He heard footsteps and then the door swung inwards away from him. It wasn't a housemaid nor a footman who was revealed there in the dim light, but a rat-like man of some indeterminate age between thirty and forty years, enquiring what his business was.

'My business is with Lady Anne.'

'I didn't ask who it was with, but what it was,' intoned the rat, the voice unwavering, a hint of something foreign in it.

Seeker was not accustomed to having to ask twice. 'Fetch

your mistress,' he said. He caught the slightest flinch of the man's hand as it went for the dagger hanging from his tan leather belt. Seeker had him by the throat and against the inner corridor wall before it could get any further. He heard a woman's voice, descending the stairway towards them. 'Dear Lord, Seeker, can you not come through a door like any other man? Would you let my steward go!'

'Steward?' said Seeker in disbelief. 'I had thought him rather a thief or assassin crept in here to do his worst.'

He let go his hold of the man's neck, and was rewarded with the look of an enemy made for life.

'Oh, Richard's worst would be very bad indeed, I grant you, but he is most certainly no thief,' said Anne Winter, emerging into the light from the bottom of the staircase. She was dressed for a morning at home, like the wife of a wealthy merchant, who had no greater concerns than the supervision of the kitchen and the counting of linen. He did not believe the picture for a minute.

She turned to the rat-man. 'Captain Seeker is here at my bidding, Richard.' She paused just long enough. 'On this occasion, at least.'

The man nodded to her and gave Seeker one more glance of unadulterated contempt before retreating slowly down the dimly lit corridor.

'He will not have liked that,' she said, opening the door into a small parlour and waiting while Seeker passed.

'You would truly pass him off as a steward?' Seeker said, removing his helmet as he stooped to pass into the room.

She smiled. 'I do not have him order my wine, or count the coals needed for the winter, but he takes care of the household all the same.'

'He looks more like a cutpurse to me.'

'Cut-throat, perhaps, if the need so arose, but as I said, Richard is no thief.'

'A bodyguard, then?'

She nodded. 'A better one than you might think. No one had bested him before. Not single-handedly. He will not forgive you for that.'

'I will study to tolerate the loss,' said Seeker. 'He'll have crawled out of some foreign Royalist sewer, I take it?'

She shook her head. 'Good Oxfordshire stock – his father served mine, although I believe Richard has spent much of his adult life, ah . . . . travelling.'

'No doubt,' said Seeker, resolving to have the Rat's background looked into. She'd lost none of her shrewdness or her nerve in the two months since she'd removed herself from Whitehall. He looked around the small parlour. There were few of the fripperies he might have expected. It was almost like a man's room, a place of business. The walls were panelled in wood, linenfold. On either side of the stone fireplace were carved leather-backed armchairs – a great chair, for the master of the house to the left, a smaller one for the mistress, to the right. He saw the brief play of merriment upon her lips as she offered him a seat. 'Take your pick, Seeker.'

He had no time for her game-playing and sat in the man's chair. 'I can spare you a quarter-hour,' he said.

'It is more than I thought to have.' She went to the small oak dresser by the door and poured him a tankard of ale from the pewter jug set there.

'The missing girl,' he said.

She sat down opposite him now, folded her hands on her lap, determined not to waste the quarter-hour. 'Her name is Charity Penn. She was a foundling, brought up in some old religious house until the masters of your Commonwealth thought to turn a better profit from it than could be had from the feeding and clothing of orphaned children.'

Seeker could make no defence of what he knew had been done on the discovery of some law unearthed in books covered in mould and dust that had little to do with justice.

'Most of my household staff is from Baxton, but, dear God, I cannot close my eyes to the poverty of this city's children. I found Charity begging in the street, offering to do any work for a hunk of bread and some shelter at night.' She looked to him, angry. 'She was three steps from the stews, Seeker. How is it in this godly England that children are forced to sell themselves for shelter, and men still able to have their way? How is it?'

'Steps are being taken,' he said. 'Those places will be closed down.'

'Not soon enough,' she muttered.

'You took her in when you came here, in November?' he asked, turning the conversation once more to the matter in hand.

'Yes, at Martinmas, and never had a day's cause for

complaint about her. For all that she was so young, she was making fair to be a gifted seamstress. She learned quickly, and when she could not master a task, she tried again and again until she could.'

Anne Winter's hands twisted in her lap, and he noticed that her own fingers were marked with needle-pricks.

'She was a good, Christian child, and if she had picked up any of the ways of the street, I saw none of them when she came here. And she was pretty, Seeker, such a pretty child.'

Anne Winter appeared to think this a good thing: Seeker would have preferred to hear that Charity was knowing in the ways of the streets, and as plain as plain could be.

'Did she have friends? Pay visits?'

Anne Winter almost laughed. 'A child of eleven years? I am not a harsh mistress, Seeker, but servant girls in this house have little time for callers and visits. No, Charity made her friends and her family here.'

'She must have run errands, to markets and the like.'

'Well, of course she did.'

'She could have met anyone there and on the way.' He raised an eyebrow at her. 'Even the lower orders do, you know. Maybe she was not as happy here as you like to tell yourself.'

She opened lips that had become tightly pursed. 'I have questioned the others and they have assured me that she never showed nor spoke of any desire to leave.'

'Church services,' he said.

'What about them?'

He shrugged. It was obvious to him. 'The girl must have come from Puritan stock. How many of your sort are called "Charity", after all?'

'She attended St Katherine Coleman's with the rest of the household.'

Seeker thought of Gethsemane, only one of several gathering places for religious independents of one sort or another within easy walking distance of this house. 'Prayer meetings? Women preachers?'

Anne Winter shook her head. 'She was godly enough, but did not go beyond the bounds of what was required.'

'Like yourself, then?'

Now she did laugh. 'I think your pot is as black as my kettle, Seeker. You scarce go through the formalities, as I recall. Cromwell must concern himself much over your soul.'

'The Protector's concerns are of greater moment than that, I assure you. This girl's family may have come back and found her.'

Again Anne Winter shook her head. 'She had been in hospitals and poorhouses for as long as she could remember. She knew no family.'

Seeker looked round the small parlour again. It struck him that nothing here was for show: it was for utility, or because Anne Winter liked it. The three miniature oval portraits hanging on a length of black velvet ribbon by the chimney breast must, he supposed, have been of her mother, father and brother. None then, of her dead husband, John Winter. The parlour faced onto the street, and her desk, with candle in a pewter stick that matched the jug on the small sideboard, quill pens, ink, a silver gilt pounce pot and paper, was set facing the mullioned and transomed window. Through its diamond panes, she must have seen half of London pass but a foot or two in front of her.

'You can see everyone who comes in or leaves at the door from here,' he said.

'Yes. That is how I come to know Secretary Thurloe's assorted spies so well. They are not really so difficult to spot, once you know what you are looking for. Especially the new, young ones.'

Seeker thought of Marcus Bridlington with his well-made clothes and his startled look: he would have stood out like a sore thumb trying to blend into the streets of Aldgate. Little wonder she had recognised him so easily in Whitehall the previous day. Thurloe liked nepotism no more than did Seeker, particularly when it touched on those employed in his own service, but when it was a question of finding a place for the nephew of Cromwell's cousin, one of the Protector's closest confidants, then there was little that captain of the guard or Chief Secretary could do.

'And do the servants go in and out at this door?'

'If need be.'

'Which others might they use?'

He saw her hesitation. Anne Winter was not about to detail for one of the Protectorate's officers all the exits and entrances to her home. Seeker surmised that there were more, in that case, than there should be. Too near to the river and to the city gates, this Royalist's house. Too easy to arrive unnoticed and slip out unseen.

She had calculated what it suited her to tell him. 'There is a door from the kitchens into the back garden, and another from the basement storeroom.'

'And no one saw her come or go from one of these the day she disappeared?'

'No one.'

He drained his mug of ale and set the empty mug down on her desk, not concealing that he was looking at the papers on top of it as he did so. 'She cannot have been taken from here against her will. She would have been seen or heard by the other servants, or by one of our watchers. I will look into it. But you should know that servants run from their masters and mistresses every day in this city, for any number of causes.' He considered the good quality of everything he had seen so far in this house; a question that would usually have been his first came to mind. 'Did anything else go missing from here at the same time?'

Anne Winter became indignant. 'Charity is not a thief. That was just a coincidence, I am certain of it.'

He had picked up his helmet, been preparing to leave. He put it down again. '*What* was a coincidence?'

She had said something she'd not meant to, but now it was too late, his interest had been pricked. Her shoulders sagged. 'Oh, very well. I'll show you.'

She led him up the wooden stairs in the corner of the hall.

'That newel post is loose,' he said, as he took the second step.

'I'm waiting for a carpenter to turn me a new one, in keeping with the rest.'

At the landing, he could see out of the arched paned window over the back garden. It was somewhat neglected, he thought, and in need of a good clearing. As if she saw into his mind, she said, 'I have been taken up with the inside of the house. The outside has had to wait. I have hired gardeners from Southwark, who will begin upon it this week.'

'Aye, before the spring comes,' he murmured, thinking, by the various newer-looking wall panels, wall hangings in gilded leather or tapestry that they had passed, that she had made herself very busy indeed in this house over the two short months since she had been forced to move from her apartments at Whitehall. He would have liked the chance to look between, behind those hangings. Some other time, he thought to himself.

She stopped on the second floor and, taking a key from the silk-embroidered purse hanging from the cord at her waist, she unlocked the panelled oak door to her left. She stepped in and pulled open the shutters on the deep casements. The room was a different order of place from the small parlour down below, and yet it was of a type with it too. This room was larger, grander, made for comfort as much as utility, and in places perhaps, for show. The one quality, though, in which it was at one with that other, was unmistakable.

'This is an Englishman's room,' he said.

'Or woman's,' she replied, pleased at his reaction. 'But what did you expect? Do you think that English blood runs only in your Republican veins? In Cromwell's? We are as English as any of you, Seeker, however Mr Milton might try to claim our birthright for your side alone.'

What should he have expected? Gilt? Fripperies? Too much lace, too little modesty? Some parody of the lost Stuart cause, of Henrietta-Maria's Parisian exile at St Germains? Somewhere a man would hardly know where to sit? Ostentation beyond the grounds of decency? But no, here was good English oak, a long, well-made dining table and chairs that he would have been proud to have made himself. A dresser displaying fine Staffordshire plate. What was of foreign provenance in the place was there for the quality of it, not the fashion. Italian glassware, Flemish cloth, tapestries that her grandmother must have worked when Elizabeth was on the throne. Again, at either side of the fire were armchairs for master and mistress, English hunting scenes embroidered on the cushions. Who played role of master in this house? wondered Seeker. Not the Rat, that was certain, but then who?

The wide stone fireplace was finely done, but not overly elaborate, a picture frame built into the overmantel. Set in the frame was a family portrait, father, mother, son and daughter, at table.

'Before the war,' she said, 'in the small dining room at Baxton.'

He observed that family who had not known what was

about to happen to them. 'You are very like your mother,' he said.

'She was a better wife,' she said, almost matter-of-factly. 'But it's that I mean to show you.' She indicated the setting of the table in the painting, and the silver salt in the middle of it. 'It was a wedding present to my grandparents, seventy years ago. It was made here in London, on Goldsmith's Row – you cannot see the maker's mark in the painting, of course, but if you look closely, you can see our crest engraved on the side, and a model of my grandfather's favourite hound, serving as handle on the lid.'

Seeker stepped closer to the painting, the better to see. 'Have you an eyeglass?' he said, without turning to her, and in a moment she had fetched one from a drawer in the sideboard. The salt was a beautiful thing, about eight inches in height if the artist had scaled it right, in silver gilt, and the hound on top so delicately worked, so sleek, Seeker could imagine it bounding across ditch and stream in pursuit of its young master's prey over the fields of Oxfordshire.

Anne Winter was caught up in his wonder. 'My husband managed to find the soldier who had looted it when the house was taken. The paintings and much else had already been hidden away, but we were still using the salt.' The simple folly of it seemed to amuse her for the moment. 'I kept it locked away at Whitehall, but I took it here with me. It stood there.' She pointed to the large oak table in the middle of the room.

'And it disappeared at the same time as Charity Penn?' That was it, then. The girl had stolen it and absconded.

Anne Winter shook her head. 'The night before.'

'She might still have taken it, secreted away somewhere before she was ready to go herself. It is not so large a thing, would be a simple thing to hide.' As simple, he thought, as a child, in London.

She sat down wearily in the larger fireside chair, ran her hand over her forehead. 'I cannot believe that, Seeker; that she was a thief, or that she chose to run away. But we have searched everywhere, asked everywhere for more than two weeks. Nothing. I thought your people, who watch the house so closely, might at least be able to cast some light on what has happened to Charity.'

He had never seen her so vulnerable. He knew in his head how the thing would most likely end – a dead child in a ditch or lost to the hands of some beggar chief or brothel-keeper, and yet a few hours of his time might help save this one child, as Anne Winter had tried to save her. 'I want you to write for me a description of the people who have been watching your house.'

'Shall I send it to you at Whitehall?'

He considered. This was not the concern of Whitehall. 'No. Call up your man.'

Little over a minute later, the Rat was standing in front of him. He had guessed right that the man couldn't read. That was good, for a start. He described to him the old woman who lived down a short alleyway at the back of a narrow old house on Knight Ryder Street. 'You will give your mistress's paper, under her seal, to this woman and no one else.' The Rat understood – well-used, Seeker suspected, to such missions.

'Don't put my name on it anywhere,' he said to Anne Winter. 'And you,' he said, addressing the Rat, 'you tell her it is instructions for the carpenter, do you understand?'

The man, whose resentment at having to take orders from Seeker was written on his face, nevertheless nodded, and left.

'And now,' said Seeker, 'I have work of my own to see to.'

Anne Winter accorded him a small curtsy, which she appeared amused to see only aggravated him, and led him back down the stairs. As they descended, a familiar aroma, but one that he had not smelled in any private house before, came to him.

'You brew your own coffee?'

'Gabriel brings me the beans, and has taught my cook how it is done. We don't do such a good job as Samuel, but we do well enough.'

Gabriel, the boy from Kent's on Birchin Lane. Seeker stashed the information away as useful, and walked out into the bright morning, putting Anne Winter's troubles away in their place as he cut through the flow of people from Aldgate down Crutched Friars.

Daniel Proctor was already waiting beneath the stone archway to Gethsemane when Seeker got there. The look on his face told Seeker his feelings on the long morning ahead of him, questioning all the known associates of Gideon Fell.

Proctor was no keener on religious fanatics than was Seeker; each man kept his views on the workings and wants of the Almighty to himself, one reason, Seeker thought, that they functioned together so well.

As they walked into the almshouses' yard, they could see the women of the community through an open door, at work making butter. 'I'll tell you, Captain, if that woman Crowe starts sermonising me . . .'

Seeker laughed. 'First Timothy, chapter two, verse twelve, that should shut her up a good two minutes at least.'

Proctor looked at him quizzically.

' "I suffer not a woman to teach, nor to usurp authority over the man, but to be in silence." '

Proctor was still testing the words on his tongue when they got to the loom shed where Goodwill Crowe and his son were already at work. A smile flickered over Nathaniel's face, quickly followed by an anxious glance towards his father. Seeker waited until they had finished a run of the shuttle.

Crowe didn't look at them. 'You heard everything I have to say about Gideon Fell yesterday. I have work to do.'

Seeker might not have heard him, for all the reaction he had. He took a list from Proctor and handed it to Crowe. 'Have all these people assemble in the yard. Sergeant Proctor will be questioning them, one at the time. Have your wife find him a room.'

Crowe scanned the list. He mentioned one or two who were elsewhere, 'at their godly and lawful calling', and not expected back at Gethsemane until suppertime. Proctor noted the names, and where the individuals would be found.

'I'll want your boy too,' said Seeker, indicating Nathaniel.

'You questioned him yesterday.'

'And will do so again today.'

'I need him here, at his work,' said Crowe.

'You'll do without him a while,' replied Seeker, turning to leave and knowing that Nathaniel would follow him without being told twice. He paused to address Goodwill again. 'The sergeant will be starting with you.'

'M-my father looked very angry,' said Nathaniel, keeping up with Seeker as they crossed the yard.

'Is he not always so?'

The boy considered. 'He is never joyful.'

Seeker looked around Gethsemane. There were apple and plum trees in the yard, that must have given an abundance of fruit in the autumn. The masonry was in good order and most of the old thatch on the roofs replaced by pantiles. An old rose had clambered around the archway, a solitary stubborn yellow bloom, tight as a ball, hanging on in defiance of the January frost. The yard was well kept and cleaner than most in London, poultry pecking amongst the cobbles and the two pigs securely tethered by their sty. The water from the pump in the centre, coming down from the conduit at Aldgate, would be cleaner than that in parts of the city relying on the Walbrook or the Fleet. It should have been a pleasant place, this Gethsemane, a place of industry and quiet companionship, and might have been, had the crew who currently occupied it been swept out, and others, for whom it had been first intended, brought in.

'Come on,' he said to the boy, 'I have something to show you.'

They walked out onto Crutched Friars, past old tennis courts and a bowling green that were now a joinery yard, past Anne Winter's house, which Seeker saw Nathaniel glance quickly at, up as far as the corner of Poor Jewry and Northumberland Lane. Seeker removed his right gauntlet and clicked his fingers. From beside the chestnut-seller's stall, a large shape bestirred itself, a hound getting to its feet. He clicked his fingers one more time, and the dog came bounding towards them. Seeker kept close to Nathaniel, lest he should be frightened of the animal, but a broad smile had spread over the boy's face, and he got down on his knees to greet the large beast as it reached them.

'This is what you wanted to show me?'

Seeker nodded.

'What is his name?'

'Name?' Seeker frowned. 'Dog, I suppose.'

'Is he yours?'

'He is his own; he lives with a carpenter I know, but I can make use of him, from time to time.'

'Like Sergeant Proctor?'

Seeker stifled a smile. 'Not exactly. Will you let him keep you company a few days?'

The look of disbelief which spread over Nathaniel's face was short-lived, displaced by a sudden, leaden certainty.

'My mother will not let me keep a dog. She says they are filthy animals, carriers of disease, untrustworthy.'

Seeker grunted. He wondered if there was any race of beings Elizabeth Crowe did not so denigrate. 'Your mother is wrong. I'll tell her he'll be staying with you for now. And there will be no argument.'

Nathaniel Crowe looked at Seeker in wonder. Even Gideon had never seemed so bent on provoking a fight with Elizabeth. There were many tales told about the Seeker, some bold, some terrifying, but he doubted if any of the boys on the lane would believe this one.

And yet it was so. When they got back to Gethsemane, Seeker called Elizabeth out of the dairy and told her the dog would be lodging with Nathaniel for the time being.

She turned sour eyes on the animal, who responded with a growl. She stepped back and told Seeker under no circumstances would so foul a thing be permitted to remain there. Seeker told the boy to take the dog out beyond Aldgate a while, run him on the old earthworks left after the war, by the Houndsditch, and by the time he returned to Gethsemane, no one would raise a question, still less a boot, to the dog. Sergeant Proctor would be there a good two hours yet, and he himself would return when his business allowed him. Nathaniel did as he was bid without question, losing no time in distancing himself from his mother's wrath.

Once the pair were safely gone, Seeker rounded slowly on Elizabeth Crowe.

'Do you like the look of Bridewell?' he said.

'A house of whores,' she replied, her lips scarcely moving.

'And preachers of sedition. Ask your friend the prophetess there,' he said, indicating the old woman regarding him sourly through the open door of the dairy.

'I preach no sedition,' she said.

'No? How long do you think it would take me to find two people to say otherwise? The boy will keep the dog. Nathaniel is known to have been a close companion of a man who lived here and who is now murdered.' He looked around the half-opened doors and window shutters of Gethsemane. Everyone was watching, listening. 'If he were to find himself in any danger, there is not a soul here, not one single soul, that I would trust to lift a finger to help him.'

The prophetess hobbled out of the dairy to lean on her stick at Elizabeth Crowe's elbow. ' "He that spareth his rod hateth his son; but he that loveth him chasteneth him betimes." '

Seeker turned his eyes on her. 'Raise a hand to him and I'll rip it from your arm.' He called over to Daniel Proctor, who had just finished questioning a discharged soldier who lodged at Gethsemane. 'I have business with Mr Thurloe. See to the hag next. If she says one word out of line, throw her in the Wood Street Compter.'

EIGHT

Rose-Sick

Seeker entered Lincoln's Inn by the main door, and ignoring the curious looks of the lawyers who milled in the corridors, discussing the news of the day, or making their way to some comfortable room to smoke their pipes or take an early dinner in the great hall, he went in search of a Lincoln's servant. He was not long in finding one, or then another, more senior, until the one he most wished to speak to was found and brought to him. The man was stooped, and elderly, and it was joked about the halls of Lincoln's that the place had been thrown up around him. Seeker had seen it often enough; it was everywhere, this assumption of privilege. The students and lawyers, the well-connected young men like the clerk Bridlington whom Anne Winters had accosted during her argument with Downing, who laughed and called the old steward a good fellow, had no idea, no idea at all if truth be known, that such good old fellows knew everything about them, everything they did and said, and thought, and everything that they might be. He told the steward he was here to see Mr Thurloe, but had a matter to discuss with him first. He asked that they might go to the small dining room that the Chief Secretary occasionally used for meetings.

The steward nodded and Seeker followed him. Within a few minutes they had come to the place – a small, comfortable room whose walls were panelled in oak, and lined around with iron sconces. On one side of the large stone fireplace hung a portrait of some ancient judge, on the other, nothing. Seeker cleared a wooden bowl of hazelnuts from the centre of the table, put his hand in his jerkin and pulled out the painted canvas Goodwill Crowe had given to him the previous day and unrolled it, weighing it down with two silver candlesticks from the sideboard. The old man watched what he did and then took in a breath of surprise and Seeker knew he had been right: he recognised it.

'Christ Jesus in the Garden,' he said. 'Never thought to see that again.'

'You know it, then?'

'Oh, I know it all right. Hung here for years, more years than I remember. How it got past the Puritans – begging your pardon, Captain – I don't know. But then, about three weeks ago, it was gone.'

'Where did it hang?'

The steward pointed to the lighter patch of wood across the fireplace from where the picture of the old judge hung. 'There,' he said. 'That's where it was.'

Seeker held the unrolled canvas to the wall. 'The frame?'

The steward shook his head. 'Took that too.'

'Do you know who took it?'

The steward frowned. 'Not much been said, apart from a cock and bull story about a scarred man who came in asking for Mr Thurloe one day. But Mr Thurloe wasn't here and the fellow had gone by the time one of the message boys came down to tell him. Stuff and nonsense.'

Seeker considered a moment. 'What did Mr Thurloe have to say of this?'

The man looked down at his feet and then back up at Seeker. 'I doubt anyone ever told him. He hardly has the leisure to come here – even when he's in full health – and when he has, I'll not let him be bothered by tales of low fellows with scars that won't give their names.'

There was nothing else to be learned from the steward. Seeker dismissed him, telling him he would find his own way to the Secretary's chamber. The man turned away in the direction of the servants' stair, muttering to himself about Thurloe never getting peace. 'Making him ill. Where would Old Nol be without him, eh? Does he ever think of that?'

Arrived on the attic floor, Seeker found the Secretary's manservant to be of the same view, and he was not certain he hadn't heard the man curse under his breath before he opened the door to him. He forestalled the fellow's complaints with a curt, 'Business of state,' and walked into the small sitting room next to Thurloe's sickroom. The heat, which had been uncomfortable on his previous visit, was now overwhelming, the air clammy and the closed shutters only serving to intensify the odour of illness.

'Would a draught of cool air in here not do better for Mr Thurloe's health?' he said, indicating the unnecessary shutters.

The man drew himself up in so far as he could, and made reference to the instructions of the Lord Protector's own physician, who had also counselled that Mr Thurloe should not be disturbed by *anybody*.

Seeker was spared the necessity of making a response by the sound of the connecting door between bed- and sitting room opening, and the appearance of a bent and shivering Thurloe dressed in a long nightshirt, cap and his favoured heavy loose woollen gown. 'Captain Seeker is not *anybody*,' he said, his voice a rasp as he shuffled to his chair. 'You may leave us, Thomas. We have business to discuss.'

Thurloe was shrunken, and looked in worse health even than he had done the day before. Seeker had never seen him look so ill. 'Perhaps your man is right, Mr Secretary, you should be abed. This business will keep.'

'This business will *not* keep!' replied Thurloe with some vehemence. 'You will leave us, Thomas.'

As the man closed the door behind him, Thurloe was taken by a fit of coughing. He motioned to a side table where the servant had placed a goblet of some steaming liquid. Seeker fetched it for him, the aroma of the hot treacle wafting through the stultifying air as he did so. Thurloe gulped some down and sank back, the effort having temporarily exhausted him. The steward's words came back to Seeker and for the first time he wondered who might replace

Thurloe, should he die. Meadowe, perhaps, or even Morland. Not George Downing. However clever Downing might think himself, Seeker was certain Cromwell would not be so far taken in by one so evidently driven by self-interest as the New Englander as to make him his Chief Secretary.

Thurloe wiped his mouth and took a moment to recover himself. 'This business will not keep,' he repeated. 'It is bad enough that I am away from Westminster. Oliver's patience with Parliament is running out.'

Seeker felt a kind of dread begin to creep through him. 'You think he will dismiss it?'

The Secretary nodded. 'Any day now. He doesn't need to wait the full five months laid out in the Instrument. Five lunar months will do. They've had it coming.' He fixed Seeker with an uncompromising look that might almost have had a challenge in it. 'The army must be unwavering in his support: we need to know of any plots long before they see the light of day.'

Seeker told him of Major-General Thomas Harrison's appearance amongst the Fifth Monarchists at Gethsemane, as had been indicated by Carter Blyth's reports. 'They're brazen. Any loyalty they ever had to Oliver is long gone, and they're just biding their time.'

'And as to any direct threat to the Protector?'

Seeker shook his head. 'Their language is full of bile towards him, but I have uncovered nothing so far relating to any planned personal assault.'

Thurloe considered this a moment. 'So it's as Blyth said, but what was he *not* saying? Have you discovered anything of that?'

Seeker unbuttoned his jacket, glad in the stultifying heat to have the excuse to do so, and took out the canvas of Gethsemane. 'All I have so far is this. It was found under Carter Blyth's mattress at Gethsemane. It had been taken from the wall of a room within this building, by a man matching Carter Blyth's description, about a week before he disappeared. He had come asking for you, and both he and the painting were gone by the time a servant came to tell him you could not be found.'

Trembling and flushed with the heat, Thurloe leaned towards the picture. 'Yes, Christ in the Garden of Gethsemane. A dark thing – I never liked it. I met Carter Blyth in the room where it hung when first he returned from Antwerp and I gave him his orders.'

'Over a month before it disappeared,' said Seeker. 'Did you ever meet him there again?'

Thurloe shook his head. 'No, absolutely not. He would have been quite clear that there would be no further meeting between us until his mission had been completed. He was only to communicate with me by the agreed codes and methods.'

'So why did he not do that? Why did he try to find you in person?'

The answer to his own question came to Seeker just as Thurloe gave it.

'Because he did not trust our process, something, someone in our own network. Whatever Carter Blyth found himself caught up in, he believed someone in my service to be involved. And he took that painting as a code, to let me know where he was.'

There was silence between them a moment, save for the persistent crackling of the logs piled high on the fire. The reality of the thing took form and presented itself to their minds: there was someone in the chain of links connecting Thurloe in Whitehall at one end and himself in the field at the other whom Carter Blyth had such cause to distrust that he had left off his vigilance over Harrison's Fifth Monarchists in order to pursue, and in that pursuit he had met his death. Seeker voiced his thoughts and Thurloe murmured his agreement, before being taken by another wracking fit of coughing. The Chief Secretary leaned forward and gripped the sleeve of Seeker's shirt. 'Find this person, Seeker. Find him, and tell no one what it is you do.' Nodding his understanding, Seeker called for the servant to assist Mr Secretary back to his bedchamber, and there being nothing more to be said, and neither man being adept in the matters of illness or companionable conversation, took his leave.

He still felt the cloying miasma of the sickroom hanging around his clothing, his flesh, as he stepped out of Lincoln's. He wanted a moment to disperse it before immersing himself once more in the air of the waiting city. Instead of going directly back out onto Chancery Lane, Seeker walked up between the lawns of Lincoln's gardens, able to admire now the simple geometry, the precision of them. He had of late been taken by the occasional desire to be away and back to the untamed north. To be out with his brothers tracking deer, trapping hares, to hear his mother singing as she worked, to tease and terrify his sister's suitors. But that was all in the past now, so far in the past. His sister was long married, his brothers dispersed and divided by the war, his mother probably dead. He had struggled hard to put away his memories of those times, to obscure them and with them the images of his wife, his child, which still took him from time to time, when he let down his guard. He pushed those thoughts away and made himself think only of the here and now. He focused his mind on the gardens of Lincoln's until he could appreciate the order, the careful structure of the place. He liked the walls that said they were not quite of the city, nor yet of Westminster, either. Outside these two overpowering jurisdictions, the Inns of Court and Old Bailey were of England itself and spoke to Seeker of the incorruptible edifice that was the Law.

There was hardly a soul out in the gardens on this cold January day. A few sparrows and a robin flitted hopefully from bare branch to bleak bush, in search of the few remaining winter berries, having given up hope of the iron ground. But at the south-facing wall, not far from the gate out onto the top of Chancery Lane, a gardener was struggling with the roots of an old and gnarled damask rose that had been trained against the brick. A pick that had evidently been used to break up the ground lay against the wall, and the old man was doing his best with a spade.

Seeker observed him at his work. 'Digging it out?'

'Aye,' said the man, about as gnarled and aged-looking as the wood he was at war with. 'A pity, for she was a beauty once. And the smell of a summer's night! But the ground's rose-sick, won't take no more, grow no more. Needs to be rested.'

The man must have been at least seventy. Seeker took off his cloak and jacket. 'Hand me the spade,' he said, rolling up the billowing white linen sleeves of his shirt. The gardener hesitated, as if he was not sure he could have understood, but did not argue and passed Seeker the spade.

'Have you no one to help you?' said Seeker, as he finally got purchase beneath the root ball and began to heave.

'Did have. A good lad Jed was too. Strong. But he left a few weeks since. Off to sea, I reckon. Always speaking about it. Down to Deptford he was, every chance he got. Down to look at Old Nol's new ship. Reckon he got took on. Pity, he was shaping well to be a good gardener. Ah well, not much adventure here for a young lad, I suppose. I told the masters, but they haven't got me anyone else yet.'

'There must be plenty looking for work,' said Seeker.

'Oh, that there is,' replied the man, 'but I don't have the authority to take them on. Need the masters' say-so for that. Course, maybe Jed'll get fed up of the sea, come back again. You know what boys are.'

'How old is he?' asked Seeker.

The man stuck out a lip and pondered. 'Thirteen? Fourteen maybe? Big strong lad. Bright, learned quick. Did me well.'

Seeker said he'd ask around the next time he was down at Deptford.

The rose was well rooted and the ground hard, but Seeker enjoyed the labour.

'You're a man's done plenty digging, Captain, I'd say.'

Earthworks, trenches, pits, graves: sometimes it felt like he'd dug up half of England in the war. And fertilised the ground with blood.

With a final heave and groan, the rose at last came away. Seeker let out a long breath and pressed his hands to his back, feeling the pleasure of hard work done. He handed the shovel back to the gardener. 'Tell the masters again you need someone. Tell them Mr Thurloe said so.'

NINE

Nathaniel

Seeker wanted to get Nathaniel away from Gethsemane, to talk to him where the sharp shadow of Elizabeth Crowe did not fall, where his father's disappointment and his sister's malice did not permeate the air. He had thought at first to take him walking with the hound out across the fields to Islington, to take their supper perhaps at the King's Head, but he was finished his other business too late, and it was already darkening by the time he walked up Woodruffe Lane towards the almshouses of the Fifth Monarchists. It was growing colder, too, promising a bitter night that he would not enforce on dog or boy.

'He'll be back here before the curfew,' was his response to Elizabeth Crowe's protests that Nathaniel should not be out in the town.

'You have not the authority,' she said, as her husband watched them quietly from the door of his loom shed.

Seeker could feel his patience ebbing away. 'The lad is twenty-two years old. He can make his own judgements.' Then he leaned a little closer to the preacher-woman. 'And besides, I have all the authority I need. Every time I step in through that archway, or you step beyond it. You would do well to remember that.'

Nathaniel didn't ask where they were going, but talked incessantly as he kept pace with Seeker, the dog loping ahead. The boy clearly relished being out in the night, and his eyes darted from side to side, taking in everything, commenting on anything new to him, and anything that had changed. The defect of speech which crippled him under his mother's tirades and admonishments was all but gone.

It didn't take them long, going by Fenchurch Street and onto Lombard Street, to come to Birchin Lane, and at the top, the door to Kent's. Here, as the dog settled himself across Cornhill, Nathaniel froze.

Seeker stopped in the act of pushing open the door of the coffee house. 'What's the matter?'

The stammer was back. 'I – I am not a-allowed to go into those places. They are t-temples of d-depravity.'

'It is not a tavern, Nathaniel, it's a coffee house.'

Nathaniel nodded. 'I kn-know. It's the milk of Hades, b-black and noxious. It makes men mad.'

Seeker smiled. 'I think some of them are mad already, but a good man, an old soldier I know, keeps this house – there is no drunkenness or lewdness here. You are right though, the beverage is black and foul, but there are other things to be had here. Come, it will be warm and we can talk freely.'

There was an unconcealed hiatus in the coffee house talk when Seeker followed the young weaver into the coffee room. Seeker was glad, for Nathaniel's sake, to see that the place was not so busy as usual, not so glad to see the Massachusetts schoolmaster, Shadrach Jones, seated there, taking his pipe with Maria's brother. He slid a look quickly over them and turned away to usher a bewildered-looking Nathaniel towards the private booth. As he beckoned Samuel over to them, a low murmur set up and conversations began to build again.

'What can I do for you, Captain?' said Samuel, nodding briefly to Nathaniel as he did so.

'I will take a jug of your bracket, and my friend here a bowl of your chocolate. After that we would like to be undisturbed.'

Samuel nodded and hobbled away, calling instructions to Grace and Gabriel about the hot spiced and honeyed ale, the chocolate and the captain's pipe. Gabriel appeared with tobacco and flint and Seeker observed Nathaniel closely. When the boy had gone back to the counter, Seeker said to Nathaniel, 'You know him.'

Nathaniel nodded. 'I've seen him go into the house with the green door, on Crutched Friars. He doesn't go in by the front, but by a side passageway down into the garden. He often has a package with him.'

Seeker had not realised before quite how observant Nathaniel was.

'And have you ever been into that house, with the green door?'

Nathaniel shook his head.

'Or Gideon? Did he ever go there?'

'I saw him look at it sometimes, just when we were passing, but I never saw him stop or go in.'

A thought struck Seeker. 'Do you know anyone else in here?'

Nathaniel looked over at the serving table and carefully studied each of the men seated at it. 'That is Elias Ellingworth,' he said. 'He came to a meeting at Gethsemane once, but left before Mother had finished preaching. I don't think he liked it, and Mother was greatly offended.'

Seeker stored the image away for future amusement. 'Anyone else?'

'That merchant, with the loud voice . . .'

'George Tavener?'

'I think that's his name. He came to Gethsemane once, to order some bolts of cloth, but Mother asked too much for them, and so he left.' Nathaniel made a tired face. 'I don't know the names of any of the rest, although I have seen that physician about, and the carpenter too, I think.'

By the carpenter, he seemed to mean Shadrach Jones. 'No,' corrected Seeker, 'he's a schoolteacher, although he claims to take an interest in mechanics and the like, it is true.'

'Oh,' said Nathaniel, colouring.

'All right,' said Seeker, taking a drink of his bracket, and leaving his hands warming around the pewter cup that Samuel always kept for him. 'What I really want you to tell me about are the places you went to with Gideon, tell me about the people you saw him meet and speak to, what you know about where he went when you weren't with him.'

Nathaniel looked uncomfortable, and Seeker thought he knew why. 'You cannot keep Gideon Fell's secrets for him now, Nathaniel. You have to tell me what you know. No harm can come to him in this world worse than has already come.'

And so Nathaniel began to talk, and Seeker had to slow him a little sometimes. Gideon had always made sure to attend Elizabeth Crowe's preachings when Major-General Harrison was expected. Nathaniel thought Gideon must want to get to know the major, because he always seemed as close by him as he could get while Elizabeth preached. He'd never noticed Gideon say much to the major, although he'd attended carefully any time the major spoke, which was strange, because Nathaniel didn't think Gideon had really liked the major.

No, thought Seeker, Carter Blyth would not have liked Thomas Harrison. Carter Blyth, as he recalled him, had been an honest, decent soldier, clear that he fought for the good of the people, taken into Thurloe's service because his courage and loyalty were beyond doubt. Thomas Harrison brandished his Bible and brayed what he called his honesty even in Cromwell's face, vaunted himself on speaking truth to power, but Seeker knew, as did half the army, that Harrison, the son of a Staffordshire butcher, had made several fortunes from the sequestered lands of beaten Royalists. Nothing was said of it, though, by Cromwell's Council of State, for so many of them had done the same.

Seeker returned his attention to what Nathaniel was saying. Goodwill Crowe kept his son busy most days in the weaving shed, but sometimes he'd let Nathaniel away for an hour or so, when he was having meetings with the major and others. There had been a lot of meetings lately, and talking over pamphlets, although Nathaniel could not tell what the pamphlets said. At first, Gideon had taken an interest in those meetings, but after a while less so, until about two weeks before he'd disappeared, he had stopped attending, and then, on those occasions, he would come and find Nathaniel and they would go out walking through the town, and Gideon had shown him places Nathaniel had never seen before. He'd taken him out by Ludgate and to the Inns of Court. 'I thought they would be frightening, those Inns. My father says that those in them keep honest men from justice, and practise to tie our rights up in words we cannot understand.'

In his heart Seeker didn't think so differently from Goodwill Crowe on the matter, but he kept his own views to himself: Parliament had dragged its feet and would not reform the law as the army wanted it to.

'But you didn't find them frightening, the Inns of Court?' asked Seeker, curious.

Daniel shook his head. 'Gideon left me with two gardeners, an old man and a boy; they showed me about the plants and the lawns, and the boy told me of the Lord Protector's new ship.'

Some of the dirt from his struggle with the old rose was still on Seeker's boots. 'This boy was called Jed?'

Nathaniel looked briefly amazed, and then recalled what the children on the lane said, what Patience said: the Seeker knew everything.

'Did he tell you he wanted to join the ship? To go to sea?'

'When he was older, he said. But he wanted to learn about ships first, about the stars, and mathematics and navigation. He was going to go and hear the lectures at Gresham College. When he was older.'

Nathaniel had never seen Jed again, never been back to Lincoln's, after that one time. 'I hoped I might see him again when we went out to practise archery at Conduit Fields. There were lots of other boys there, but I didn't see Jed.'

'Conduit Fields is a long way out from Gethsemane. What took you up there?'

'Gideon had business up at Holborn – we had our dinner at an inn called the Red Lion at Long Acre – I liked the sign, it was very fierce. Gideon said it would do me good to get out into the open spaces, away from the damp of the loom shed and . . .' He stared, realising what he had been about to say, and took a long drink of his chocolate.

Seeker could have said it for him. 'Away from your father and mother.' He wondered whom Carter Blyth might have had business with at Long Acre – the place had been a favourite of Cromwell when he had still lived amongst ordinary men, before the demands of the state had forced him to Whitehall, and his family with him. It was still a favourite of many officers who didn't have to live within the confines of the Palace, and preferred not to be walled in in the city itself.

'Do you know what Gideon's business was, or who it was with?' Seeker asked, but again, Nathaniel did not. He had been left to sport with other young men in Conduit Fields while Carter Blyth had done whatever it was he had gone up to Holborn to do.

Seeker wondered what Blyth's purpose could have been, in taking the boy with him on those occasions – whether it was out of genuine affection, or a means by which to disguise himself better. He had clearly taken care that Nathaniel should not become party to knowledge and identities that might endanger him. As well to leave the hound with him at Gethsemane, all the same.

'When you were out on these trips with Gideon, did you ever think he seemed to be afraid of anyone?'

Nathaniel grinned, as if he thought Seeker to be in jest, but then his expression changed, and he set down his bowl of chocolate.

Seeker watched him. 'Well?'

The boy wrinkled his brow, was troubled. Then he looked up at Seeker, convinced. 'A woman. Gideon was afraid of a woman.'

'Tell me about her,' said Seeker quietly.

Nathaniel was concentrating. 'She had red hair, tied up beneath her cap but with lengths straggling. She is older than me, not as old as you though, or my mother.'

'Go on.'

'She is tall, with broad shoulders and strong hands, and her face seems happy, but I think she is only pretending.' Nathaniel sat back, glad to have said his piece and to have got nothing wrong.

Seeker knew he had to be patient, to play out his questions carefully.

'Do you know this woman's name? Did Gideon tell you?'

Nathaniel shook his head. 'I asked him, when we were leaving, but he said he didn't know.' He glanced at Seeker, worried again. 'I think he might have been lying.'

Seeker sought to reassure him. 'All right. That's all right. He may have had good reason. But tell me, where was it you were leaving, that you had seen her?'

Nathaniel's face brightened. 'It was the Black Fox Tavern, up Broad Street on the way to Gresham College. Gideon had wanted to go up there and see what lectures they were advertising at the college, but he was hungry – Patience had cooked the dinner that day and we could hardly eat it – so he said we should go into the Black Fox and get our supper. And we sat down, and he ordered us two dishes of rabbit stew, which is my favourite. But when the boy went through to the kitchen, and the landlady came out as if to see us, Gideon suddenly got up and said he had brought no money with him, and we could not have our supper there after all.'

'He didn't speak to this woman at all? Nor she him?'

'No. But they looked at each other, and I don't think she was glad to see him at all, nor he her.'

Seeker realised it was getting late, and they would need to

leave soon if he were to get Nathaniel back to Gethsemane before the curfew. No nightwatchman would dare to question him, regardless of what time of night he prowled the streets or who he was with, but he knew, hound or no, Elizabeth Crowe would find it an excuse to chastise the boy once he was gone, and he was determined she should not have it.

They finished their drinks and Seeker bade a quiet goodnight to Samuel Kent. There was silence as they passed the serving table again on their way out. Once they were on the lane, the door to Kent's closed behind them, Nathaniel said, 'Why are they so scared of you?'

Seeker finished putting on his gauntlets, straightened his shoulders. 'Because it suits me that they should be so.'

Nathaniel didn't pursue the matter and they fell into a silent stride back towards Aldgate, the dog at their heels. Seeker was aware that the boy was troubled by something, but left him to ponder it until he was ready. Then, as they were passing the Clothworkers' Hall at the top of Minchin Lane, Nathaniel suddenly stopped.

'What is it?' asked Seeker.

'I am not afraid of you.'

'I don't wish you to be.'

Nathaniel looked down and started to work at the buckle of the bag he always carried with him when he went out of Gethsemane, 'for interesting things,' he had said. From it he pulled a slim volume, in quarto, and handed it to Seeker. 'I think you should have this.'

Seeker turned the volume over in his hands. It was a cheaply bound ledger of some sort, with a symbol embossed on the front that he could not make out in the lamplight of the street. 'What is it?'

Nathaniel shrugged. 'I don't know. I found it amongst Gideon's things after he went away. I knew my father was coming to search his room, and I worried he would destroy it, because they do not like books that aren't about the Bible, and it was Gideon's book.'

Seeker flicked through the leaves of the ledger, but could only see enough to know that it was handwritten and not printed. He could not believe that an agent as experienced as Carter Blyth would have left a record of his activities in the very place in which he had embedded himself. 'You're certain it's his?'

Nathaniel nodded. 'I saw him place it in the recess he'd made by loosening two bricks behind his bed. I think he kept things there that he didn't wish others to find.' He looked away a moment. 'Patience, and my mother, come in searching sometimes.'

'For what?'

Again Nathaniel shrugged. 'Anything they think I shouldn't have.'

That seemed likely enough. 'And what else did you see Gideon put there?'

Even in the darkness, Seeker would have sworn the boy coloured, looked at his feet.

'You cannot get Gideon into any trouble now,' he said.

'No,' said Nathaniel. 'But you will think badly of him, and I'm sure he didn't steal it.'

'Steal what?' asked Seeker carefully.

'It was a jug, or candlestick or something like that. It was made of silver.'

'Did you ask him about it?'

'No,' said Nathaniel. 'Gideon told me what he thought I should know, but there were other things he said he couldn't tell me, so I didn't ask.'

A thought came to Seeker, a possibility that he had not yet found a connection for. 'Could it have been a salt?'

Nathaniel looked bewildered. 'Mother keeps the salt in a small wooden bowl with a lid; it was nothing like that.'

'All right,' said Seeker. The boy was tiring, and it was clear that being asked things he had no answer for upset him. 'Just one more question and then we will get you home.'

Nathaniel waited.

'What happened to this silver thing you saw?'

There was a pause. 'I never saw it after Gideon went.'

An hour later, Seeker was in his chamber at the back of the house on Knight Ryder Street. His landlady had set the fire and put fresh water in a glazed earthenware ewer and set it by the bowl beneath the old mottled-looking glass he would shave by in the morning – it had been three days since he had had the time to visit the barber at his barracks, and he preferred his jaw clean. Fresh candles had been set in the wooden candlesticks on the mantelshelf. He paid the extra for good wax – he had never liked the greasy mutton stench of tallow.

He lit a candle at his table and sat down with the book in front of him. It was a cheap thing, quarto in size and nothing of quality. On the front cover, written in a fine secretary hand, were the words *Register of Scholars*, and beneath the words an inexpertly embossed symbol. It looked something like three nails, crossing each other. A vague, troubling recognition began to seep from Seeker's memory and he pulled open the book. There, on the first page of the volume, written in the same secretary hand, was *Rhys Evans, at the sign of the Three Nails, Holborn*.

Something cold went through Damian Seeker and his fingers pressed harder on the volume under them. He had first come across the name of this place on Holborn only the night before. The man Shadrach Jones, whom he had come upon in the Ellingworths' garret in Dove Court, had claimed to have crossed the ocean, come all the way from Massachusetts, to take up a post at this Rhys Evans's school. He felt anger rising in him that he didn't fully understand, the same anger that had taken hold of him when first he had come across the man, alone with Maria. He breathed deep and waited for it to subside, then turned the first page of the register.

It looked like nothing more than a list of boys' names, little over a dozen, attending the school from Michaelmas until the beginning of December of the year just past, the period just before Shadrach Jones said he had arrived in England. Seeker read through the dates, the names, any marks by them again and again. Cryptography held some interest for him, but if the information on these pages were some code it would be for Dr Wallis and his assistants to unravel.

He closed the book, considering what cause Carter Blyth might have had for having it, how it might relate to Blyth's investigations. Certainly, there must have been a connection between Blyth's visit with Nathaniel to Holborn, and his possession of this book. Carter Blyth had had this book and now Carter Blyth was dead.

Seeker snuffed out the candle and lay down on his bed. He had not pulled to the shutter on his window, and the clear blue light of the moon filled the room. He closed his eyes against it, but knew it would be many hours until he slept. Word was tomorrow would be Parliament's last day, and if that were the case, it might be long enough before he could continue his quest in the fading footprints of Thurloe's dead agent.

TEN

The School at the Sign of the Three Nails

Shadrach Jones opened the shutters of his small room at the back of the Three Nails and looked out over the gardens to Conduit Fields. The sight gladdened his heart. Had he looked out to the front, he would have seen the steady creep of the city of London, which, having burst its bounds, was advancing inexorably north and west. The houses that faced the Three Nails just across High Holborn could scarcely contain the surge behind them, around Lincoln's Inn Fields and up Drury Lane, straggling eventually up to St Giles in the Fields.

Shadrach had only been in England a few weeks, but from his very first sight of it he had loved London; it had drawn him in as belonging. Out in the streets, at the markets and in the taverns and coffee houses, he heard endless complaints about the never-ending growth of the city, the overcrowding, the ceaseless building upon building in the face of all laws to the contrary, the difficulties of travel, the bad water. King, Commons, Parliament, Protector, the filth on the streets was all the same. But those complaints were as music to Shadrach's ears, for in London was the means to answer them: the knowledge in the free lectures, open to all – tradesmen, mechanics, labourers and lawyers – given at Gresham College on mathematics, navigation, the possibilities of architecture and engineering – and Shadrach would be the man to do it. When people asked him why he had come to London, he would mumble something appropriate about England's godly revolution, the rights of the people, freedom of religion. That usually did it, one way or the other, so that they forgot any curiosity they might have had in him.

Freedom *from* religion, he should have said; freedom from the narrow constraints, the suspicion of learning of his own parents; freedom from the suffocating puritanism of Harvard. When the business that had called him to England was finally finished, Shadrach was determined, from his small room at the back of the Three Nails on High Holborn, that he would shape London, and that London would make him. The only pity was that George Downing was here too, but Downing was so risen in the world, and he himself not risen at all, that their paths that had crossed at Harvard were unlikely to do so for a long time, if ever, here.

Damian Seeker, though, that was something different. Damian Seeker he would do his utmost to avoid. The closing down of Parliament by Cromwell, four days since, had been like one of those gifts of Providence such as the Protector himself was so fond of speaking of. For in the coming weeks, if those who knew of such things were to be believed,

Seeker would be too much busied leading raiding parties on printers' workshops and hunting down dissidents to trouble himself over a Holborn schoolmaster.

The work of the previous few days had borne Seeker and his troop on a wave of adrenalin, but the city and its liberties had taken the news of Parliament's closure much more calmly than it had been feared they might. Thurloe, still ensconced in his sickroom at Lincoln's Inn, remained vigilant. 'The most dangerous elements will be the ones we can't see. There might not be apprentices rioting on the streets of Walbrook or Cripplegate, but who's scribbling away at pamphlets to send out across the country, to stir up dissent? Who's whispering mutiny in the ears of likely army men? Don't lose sight of Carter Blyth, Seeker. Don't lose sight of Carter Blyth.'

Their last raid had finished in the early hours of the morning, and Seeker had taken a few hours' sleep in the barracks at Whitehall, but he had woken before daylight, anxious to investigate the school at the Three Nails. Four nights and four days since Nathaniel had given him that book, and not a moment since to pursue it, because Cromwell had finally had enough of Parliament. Today, at last, with all calm, he could allow himself a few hours to see to Thurloe's secret business. The young men of the Secretariat were also less hurried today – he passed Andrew Marvell and Marcus Bridlington in animated conversation as they turned into a cookhouse opposite Axe Yard, evidently intent on an early breakfast. The walk up to Holborn invigorated him. Even at this hour, carts and travellers and traders on foot and horseback were making their way towards the city from villages to the north and west, Hampstead and Uxbridge, and further afield, their concerns for the rights of Parliament a secondary matter at best to their concern for commerce. The country was at peace, stable under the Lord Protector, and those who had to earn their living by the sweat of their own brow understood that.

The trees and bushes of the gardens were stark and bare, and even the snowdrops had not yet broken through the earth, but the birds were busy already and there was a freshness in the air that grew the further from the river he walked. Seeker liked Holborn: there had been good times here, when the King had still been a fugitive and not a martyr, and the army leaders had met at the Red Lion, or in Cromwell's own house on Drury Lane, and all had seemed possible, all that they had fought for had almost been within their grasp. And they had grasped it – Cromwell, Fairfax, Ireton and the rest. Ireton was dead now, Fairfax retreated to Yorkshire and his gardens and his books, and Cromwell was left, with lesser men to guide him. But that hardly mattered; the Protector would hold firm, for England had nothing else.

The Three Nails was not difficult to find – a ramshackle collection of buildings on the north side of High Holborn, next to the neglected and swiftly deteriorating house of a Royalist who had lost almost all in the cause of Charles

Stuart. Another place that needed pulling down. A haber-dasher's fronted the building at the sign of the Three Nails, and Seeker went down the narrow alleyway at its side to the small courtyard, two of whose sides were occupied by Rhys Evans's school.

Off to the side, a dull aroma of porridge infused the air, contending with the more pungent smells coming from the midden at whose edges a roped pig was snuffling. Chickens scattered noisily across the yard at Seeker's approach. Through a doorway he could hear the practised chorus of a grace being offered in young and toneless voices. He waited until they had finished and then pushed open the door. Little light traversed the panes of the room's only two, grimy windows. A dozen boys, aged perhaps between nine and twelve years, were ranged on benches set either side of a long table. They were bent, murmuring to one another, over bowls of a grey and unappetising porridge. At the top of the table sat an elderly, unkempt man with rheumy eyes, whose clothing suggested he might once have known better times. Rhys Evans. Seeker knew, because he had made it his business to know before coming here, that Evans had been a Fellow of long-standing but little distinction in a Cam-bridge college a good while before the war. A Laudian, he had soon been ejected in favour of a Puritan rival. And so now, he kept this school. His file had not taken Seeker long to peruse – Evans had evinced no particular royalist sympa-thies and had made himself amenable enough to the new regime to not fall foul of its several proclamations against teachers trained in the old state-established church. Evans scarcely seemed to notice Seeker's arrival, and only raised his head from his contemplation of the contents of his bowl at the sudden descending silence that enveloped the table. A vague recognition stirred in the eyes before they returned to the contemplation of his bowl.

'Captain Seeker.'

The voice came from the other end of the room. Shadrach Jones was standing some way behind Seeker, by a large pot suspended over the fire.

Seeker swallowed down his reaction to the sight of the American and said, 'I'd have a word, if you please.' He surveyed the awestruck boys. 'In private.'

Jones nodded. He called up one of the boys. 'See it doesn't burn, William. The rest of you, hold your tongues and do not disturb Dr Evans. Consider your reflections on last night's task.' He indicated a door behind where the senile master sat, and Seeker followed him through it, into the schoolroom.

'You do all the teaching then?' said Seeker, jerking his head towards the door of the dining parlour.

'Mr Evans is not fit for it. Has not been some time. God alone knows how long the boys have been covering up for him – months, I think. The older ones have done their best, but some of the younger were scarcely lettered when I came.'

'Hmm. Have you not told their parents?'

Jones sighed. 'It has come on gradually; he has worsened

even in the time that I have been here. To begin with, there was occasional lucidity. I doubt it will be long before he is wholly insensible.'

'And then?'

Jones frowned. 'I will keep the school on, and for Dr Evans? He has no family that we know of, is a member of no craft that will look after him, has lost any college connections he might once have had, has no patron. I would not put him to Bedlam. We will just keep him here, and tend to him as we are able.'

Seeker nodded. Many would fare a lot worse.

'Evans adhered to Laud's church and methods.'

'I know little of that,' said Jones. 'My family fled Laud's England.'

Seeker would have liked to know more of Jones's background, but this was not the occasion. 'In his more sensible times, did Evans ever show any sign to you of royalist leanings?'

Again Jones considered, before giving an emphatic 'No. I have heard him mutter once or twice, "Finished, they're all finished", whenever the name of the Stuarts is raised.'

'And is that often?' said Seeker quietly.

Jones looked startled. 'What? No. Hardly ever.'

'And you?'

'Me?'

'What is your allegiance?'

Jones blinked, stuttered. 'Well, to the Protector, to the Commonwealth, of course.'

Seeker grunted, unconvinced. 'In my experience, there is seldom an "of course". He rubbed a hand over his chin and walked around the room. It was a poor-looking place, as most schoolrooms were, and only a little better lit than the parlour the boys ate in, so much of the light being obscured by the other buildings around the courtyard. Nevertheless, it was well-enough ordered, he would grant Jones that. Three benches were ranged before the schoolmaster's desk, slates and notebooks stacked beneath them. The set fire at one end and brazier at another both waited to be lit. At the teacher's lectern was a book of simple arithmetic, and on a shelf by the door sat a wooden model of some sort of lifting device. 'Yours?' he enquired.

'Yes,' said Jones, coming over to him. 'It's a model for a new water-pump.'

Seeker took a moment to examine the machine, turning it carefully to observe it from different angles. The design was ingenious and the thing well made. Seeker would have liked to see the working model. He resolved to mention it to the Master of Works at Deptford. He returned the machine to its shelf, and as he did so, said, 'Tell me what you know of a man named Gideon Fell.'

Jones looked momentarily startled, before registering his puzzlement at the sudden change in direction of their conversation. He looked at Seeker warily. 'I have never heard that name.'

'What about Carter Blyth?'

Jones shook his head. 'No. I don't know him either.'

'Hmm,' said Seeker. 'And have you ever been to a place called Gethsemane?'

'Gethsemane?' Jones appeared to be genuinely confused. 'Gethsemane? From the Bible? The Holy Land?'

'It's home to a sect of Fifth Monarchists in Aldgate. Are you going to tell me next that you don't know what the Fifth Monarchists are?'

'Of course I know, but why should I . . .?'

'But you have never met a weaver by the name of Gideon Fell?'

Jones sat down, his head in his hands. 'I don't know any of these people or the place you are talking about. I scarcely know anyone in London. I am a schoolmaster.'

Seeker, who had been looming slightly over Shadrach, stood straight. He'd seen people lie brazenly, and people lie out of fear, but he'd also seen people frightened and confused because they didn't know even the beginnings of the answers to the questions he was asking them. He was convinced Shadrach Jones didn't know anything of what he was talking to him about. He changed his tack.

'And what of Dr Evans, does he wander the town? Does he ever speak of the Fifth Monarchy men?' He thought of the woman Nathaniel had told him Blyth was afraid of. 'Does he ever talk of going to the lectures at Gresham, take his supper in the Black Fox?'

Something he'd said had caught Jones's interest, but it passed and the schoolmaster sighed heavily. 'Dr Evans speaks of wonders and horrors that only his mind's eye can see, and his days of attending lectures are long past. Since I came here, he has never, to my knowledge, wandered beyond Holborn Bar or the top of Drury Lane. The shop-keepers keep a lookout for him for us, and the innkeeper of the White Hart, who occasionally returns him to us.'

'I see. Then you will have no idea how this item came to be in the place known as Gethsemane?' From his leather bag Seeker produced the register of the school given to him by Nathaniel Crowe, and held it out towards Shadrach Jones.

Jones looked at the book, examined the lettering, the wording on the front. He opened it, and again a frown spread over his face. 'I don't understand.'

'What do you not understand?' asked Seeker.

'This isn't our register.'

'How so? It bears the name of this school on the front.'

'As does this,' said Jones, opening the lid of his desk and holding up to Seeker's view an identical-looking register. 'From the Martinmas term until now. It was here when I arrived, and I have been making notes and entries in it ever since.'

'And the names? Are the boys named in this pupils here?' Seeker asked, indicating the register found at Gethsemane.

Jones laid the books down side by side and scanned the names. 'Yes,' he began slowly, 'I think . . .' and then he stopped. 'All but this one.'

He turned the book towards Seeker.

'Edward Yuill?'

Jones nodded. 'There is no Edward Yuill in this school.'

Seeker turned through the pages of the book Nathaniel had given him. 'According to this there was: an Edward Yuill is marked among the pupils from the end of September until the twelfth of December, the last day this book was marked up.'

Shadrach Jones's eyes moved, troubled, from one book to the other. Eventually, he gave off looking at the book he had taken from his own desk, and gave all his attention instead to that Seeker had brought with him. At last he looked up, his face pale. 'The hand, in your copy of the register, it is Dr Evans's. I know it from some old accounts and books he keeps – it is an old secretary hand, not so much practised now. It becomes very shaky towards the end, as you see, but that is definitely Dr Evans's hand, and it must have been he who wrote Edward Yuill's name in that register, and marked his charges paid.'

'And whose hand wrote out the names and notes on this?' said Seeker, indicating the copy without Edward Yuill's name in it.

Jones shook his head. 'I don't know. It is certainly not mine, nor Dr Evans's, nor yet any of the boys, for I know all their hands.'

Seeker plucked a pen from its holder on the master's desk, dipped it in the inkwell and held it out to Jones. 'Show me.'

Jones stuttered.

'Your hand,' said Seeker, pushing a piece of paper underneath it. 'Show me.'

Still Jones hesitated. 'What would you have me write?'

Seeker lost patience. 'The first thing that comes into your head, man.'

Jones bent over the paper, and Seeker watched the pen move across it: the movement seemed natural, flowing, and not contrived for disguise, but Seeker would take it to the postal office for examination anyway.

He glanced over the words.

For man (alas) is but the heavens' sport;
And art indeed is long, but life is short.

'Fine sentiments for a New England Puritan,' he said dismissively, setting the paper aside to dry, ready to take back to Whitehall with him. 'And this book was already here and in use when you arrived?'

'What?' said Jones, still looking at the paper on which he had just written.

Seeker began to wonder if the fellow's mind was wandered as much as the old master's. He held up the copy of the register Jones had taken from his desk. 'This. It was here and in use when you arrived?'

Jones nodded.

'Call in the youngest boy.'

'The youngest? Surely the oldest would know more.'

'I don't doubt it,' said Seeker, 'but the youngest will be less practised in lying. Call him in.'

A very little time later, a small and very frightened boy was standing before Seeker, who had taken the trouble to put back on the helmet he had removed on first entering the courtyard of the Three Nails. Shadrach Jones, almost as nervous as his pupil, stood a little to the side.

'What's your name, boy?'

'John Dorward, Captain sir.'

Seeker glanced at the two registers. The boy's name was on both lists.

'How old are you, John Dorward?'

'I am nine, sir.'

'And are you a good boy? A truthful boy?'

'Y-yes, sir.'

The child's face was turning a blotchy scarlet. Seeker knew the thing would hardly take another minute.

'And you have been at this school since Martinmas?'

'Yes, sir.'

'Good. So you can tell me what you know of Edward Yuill.'

The boy, who had seemed to regain a little courage at the previous question, now looked terrified. He looked to Shadrach Jones, stared at Seeker, gulped, and said nothing.

'Did you not hear what I said?' asked Seeker.

The boy gulped again, nodded his head.

'And so you will tell me.'

'I – I can't,' the child whimpered.

'Speak up.'

'I can't.' The tears were coming now, and the child, in utter misery, his face crimson, stared at his feet.

Seeker removed his helmet, stepped forward, and gently

raised the boy's chin. 'Who has told you that you may not speak of Edward Yuill, child?'

Very quiet, and still not looking up, 'William.'

Seeker looked to Shadrach Jones, who went to the door leading to the parlour. He then bent down a little, to look into the young child's eyes. 'You have done well. You must always tell the truth, you understand?'

The boy nodded, still a picture of utter misery.

'Good. Now return to your classmates. You will get into no trouble for this.'

The child ran for the door, almost colliding with Shadrach Jones and the tall, thin boy who was following him through the door.

Seeker regained his full height and his demeanour changed completely. 'What is your full name?'

'William Godmanson.'

'And who is your father?'

'M-my father?'

'It is a simple enough question. If he be not dead.'

'No. My father is not dead. His name is Daniel Godmanson.'

'I see. And has your father ever spoken against the Protector?'

The boy blinked. 'Never.'

'Or for Charles Stuart?'

The blinking became more furious. Seeker resolved to remember the name of Daniel Godmanson and have it looked into.

'No,' said the boy.

'And you?'

'Me?'

'Do you ever speak against Lord Protector Cromwell? For the traitor Charles Stuart?'

'N-no. Never.'

'Hmm. But you tell the younger boys to lie.'

'N-no, I . . .'

'You have told the others they must not mention Edward Yuill, have you not? That they must forget he was ever here?'

The boy stared at him, then his shoulders slumped, and the truth of the accusation was written all over his face.

Jones stepped forward. 'Why did you do this, William? Who is Edward Yuill?'

Seeker was not generally disposed to allow others to intervene in his interrogations, but he decided to let this one play out.

The boy simply shook his head.

'Come, William. This is no game. Who is Edward Yuill?'

The boy bit his lip. 'No.'

'What do you mean "No"?'

Again he shook his head. 'I cannot tell you.'

Now Seeker stepped in. 'Oh, but you will, William Godmanson.'

Again, the boy said, 'I cannot.'

Seeker appraised him. 'Why?'

The boy gulped deeply, looking desperately from side to

side as if for some way of escape that might present itself. His voice was scarcely more than a whisper. 'Because he said he would hurt the other boys too.'

'Edward Yuill did?' asked Shadrach Jones, not understanding.

But Seeker understood. 'Somebody took Edward Yuill, didn't they, William?'

The boy was desolate. 'There was a note, addressed to me. It said none of the boys should ever speak of Edward again, or they would be taken too.'

'Where is this note?' asked Shadrach Jones.

'It said I should burn it.'

'And did you?' asked Seeker with a sinking heart.

All the child could do was nod.

ELEVEN

Dorcas Wells

Dorcas watched the pig turn slowly on the spit. The smell would bring them from all ways: Austin Friars, the Drapers' Hall, Gresham. Up as far as the Artillery Yard sometimes, if the breeze was right. The Black Fox was never empty. Dorcas knew how to run a good house; neither she nor hers would ever go hungry. And they all knew that, knew they would be all right with her. That was why she couldn't understand about the girl. But Dorcas reminded herself that girls were not to be understood – many other things, but understood, no. She'd been a girl once, and foolish. So be it. Her girl would learn, or die. Dorcas, she had learned.

They'd had to be on their mettle, these past few days though, with the closing of Parliament. The town was buzzing, the soldiers were everywhere: Cromwell didn't much like the sound of what Parliament had to say. Stupid, they must be, thought Dorcas: he'd been telling them long enough what he expected them to say. Surely they didn't think he'd had himself set up as Lord Protector so that they might tell *him* what he could do and what he couldn't. They knew now the meaning of the Puritans' freedom. Like Dorcas had found out, long ago. She'd learned, and she'd remembered, and Dorcas had been careful not to make one mistake since. Not until a month ago. She'd thought she'd made a mistake then; nothing had come of it, but still she was vigilant.

She went to the store and reached to an upper shelf for a jar of apple jelly, preserved in the autumn. Apples from the orchard in Fisher's Folly, out past Bishopsgate. She unlocked the spice cabinet and took out a small packet of cloves. They were running low. She'd need to send the boy to Leadenhall for more. Or maybe not. She'd go herself. It might be better to be out in the town, to hear what was going on, things that others might not pay proper heed to, rumours that might die for lack of interest before they ever reached the Black Fox, where they might be better understood. And the boy would be better kept under her sight, for now anyway.

In the kitchen, she gave instructions about the spices. It was nearly dusk, and the tavern was starting to fill already, apprentices, lawyers and gentlemen stopping in on their way up to the evening lectures at Gresham, ward militias coming back from their exercises at the Artillery Yard or at Spittal Fields, ready for any unrest that should begin as darkness fell, needing their bellies filled for watching through the night; people heading out of the city, hurrying home across the fields to Hoxton, Hackney.

Five minutes. She would have five minutes in her private

room, up the stairs. Any in London, almost any, might have come through the doors of the Black Fox and found welcome, but Dorcas allowed no one into this room. She looked around, but something displeased her: a tassel on the cord tying back her bed-curtains had slipped, and the green brocade curtain hung loose. Dorcas put it right. Even in the heat of the summer, where warm breezes rather than cold draughts found their way through the wooden frames and past the shutters on the windows, she kept those curtains closed while she slept, remembering the years under canvas, where a tent provided her only shelter from all that might watch outside, in the night. She sat down on the room's only chair, and pushed aside her walnut dressing-box, the better to contemplate the other object on the table. What to do about it; that was the question. She reached a hand out to trace its delicate lines, turned it, inspected it for the hundredth time for some clue as to where it might have come from. Nothing. She gave over her examination and, as she always did at this time in the evening, opened her casement and leaned out of her window to look out over London, breathe it in. She could take what she liked from this city, but she'd never take too much: only just a little more than enough. She watched the people making their way home up and down Broad Street, along the lanes to Bishopsgate or up to All Hallows for the evening service, some of them who'd scarcely been beyond the walls, others making themselves something new, striving with every step towards some better self, some secret goal. She stepped back, and just as she was about to close the shutters for the night, her eye was taken by one particular figure making its way up past St Peter's and the end of Austin Friars; this one she knew, but couldn't quite fathom. She'd observed him before, couldn't help it – her eyes were drawn to him. Something about him awakened something in her she'd thought dead and gone with her husband on the field of Edgehill. She'd watched him go about his business, his movements sure, his face without doubt, utterly contained in himself and unswayed by what passed around him. But Dorcas knew to look closer at a man, and she wondered if he was truly as certain of his purpose as all the world who moved out of his way seemed to believe. This evening she noticed him first a long way off, a head taller at least than almost everyone he passed, and clothed almost entirely in black. He didn't vary his pace, didn't need to, and his eyes were fixed on his present purpose. For all the sight of him quickened Dorcas's pulse, some things mattered more and she felt dread pass through her. Her mistake would not go unpaid for: Damian Seeker was coming for her.

An hour's further questioning had got little more that was coherent out of William Godmanson. Edward Yuill had been the oldest of the boys at Rhys Evans's school, and the one who'd been there longest. His father was overseer of a plantation in Virginia and his mother was dead. It had been understood that when his schooling was finished he would join his father. He had been a quiet boy, but gifted, too gifted, Dr Evans had said, when he had still been in his senses, to waste his life and talents in the godless swamps of Virginia. An Oxford College at the least should have been his goal. He had been a handsome boy too, William had added shyly. A few weeks before his disappearance he had taken to going out often by himself, saying he was walking in the fields beyond the school or at St Giles's. William God-manson had become curious, and eventually had followed him. He'd lost sight of him for a time, and when he saw him again, it was with a man in a hooded cape, who seemed to be teaching him archery. Edward had begun to go towards them, but the man, catching sight of him, had stood and held the bow in such a way as to leave no doubt that he meant to shoot directly at him. William had run straight back to the Three Nails, and Edward had soon appeared behind him, with a warning that he should never follow him again, nor tell anyone what he had seen. It was not long after that that Edward had disappeared. On the day of his disappearance he had walked out to the fields after dinner, as had become his habit, and he had not returned. In the night, the letter addressed to William had been pushed under the dormitory door of Rhys Evans's school, warning him never to mention Edward Yuill again, and to instruct the younger boys likewise, for fear they might not live to regret it.

And so neither William, nor any of the other boys, had ever mentioned Edward Yuill from that day to this. He'd known nothing of the register, which must have been taken and replaced that same night – it had always been kept in Dr Evans's desk. He didn't recognise the writing on the new register, and his description of the man he'd seen with Edward that day on Conduit Fields was wavering and incon- sistent. Had he appeared to be scarred, burn-marked? William couldn't say – he'd been too far away, and the man had kept his hood up. And this had all happened before Mr Jones ever arrived to teach at the Three Nails? Yes.

Knowing there was nothing else to be had of the boy for now, Seeker had warned Shadrach Jones to bolt the doors and windows of the Three Nails securely, and not to let any of the boys wander abroad alone. Seeker had left Holborn a deal more troubled than he had been when he'd arrived, and the next few hours spent on raids on suspect pamphlet- eers and other such had seemed like honest business against whatever Carter Blyth had involved himself in, which became murkier by the minute.

It was evening before he was able to pursue Blyth's busi- ness again, and this time he was resolved to discover what had taken Carter Blyth, with Nathaniel, to the Black Fox, and what it was about the woman innkeeper that had so much discomfited Thurloe's agent. He pushed open the door, in no mood for the kind of dissembling he'd had to deal with all afternoon. It was the same everywhere: he'd walk into an inn or tavern or coffee house and all fell silent. Good. It saved time.

'Where is your mistress?' said Seeker to the elderly man dispensing ale from behind the short counter.

'Here,' came a voice from behind him.

She'd stopped halfway down the narrow wooden stairway that led directly from the upper floor into the tavern's parlour. It was clear to him that she'd been standing there, watching him since he'd come in. He had a sudden feeling that he'd noticed Dorcas Wells around the town before, without knowing that he had. Nathaniel's description had been accurate, as he was coming to understand it would be. She was a trim, well-built woman only a few years younger than himself – not yet forty, perhaps. Clean and strong-boned, her dark auburn hair showing only a little grey where it was pulled up under a plain linen headdress. Her dress was serviceable wool, dyed a dull rust, the shift beneath it well bleached. She had large, clear green eyes, and strong hands, like a farmer's. She commanded her property with the assurance of any man, and he doubted that many customers troubled to get on the wrong side of Dorcas Wells more than once. Yet there was nothing manly to her, and it occurred, fleetingly, to Seeker that some might call her beautiful.

If his arrival unsettled her, she didn't show it. 'You have the look of a man on business.'

He nodded. 'I'll take a plate of that pork, though, while I'm here.' He put some coins on the counter. Seeker always paid his way. Most tavern-keepers sought to gain favour by trying to refuse his money. Dorcas Wells didn't.

'Bring food for the Seeker, and ale,' she instructed the pot boy. 'Through here,' she said, leading Seeker to a small room above her cellar. There were brooms in the corner, and a half barrel fashioned into a basin, in which a good number of tankards waited to be washed. Against a side wall was a stool, a deal table, and writing materials – where she did her accounts, no doubt. A door in the back wall led out to the tavern's courtyard. The trap door to the cellar was open, the top of the ladder visible.

'Dangerous, that,' he said.

'Useful,' she replied.

'And that?' He pointed to the flintlock pistol hanging on the wall behind her. It looked to be of recent English manufacture, simple, with little embellishment.

'Also useful,' she said. 'What do you want here, Seeker?'

There would be no beating about the bush, then. Good.

'What do you know of a man named Gideon Fell?'

He saw just a flicker of recognition, of surprise, in the eyes of Dorcas Wells, and then saw her glance towards her pistol box.

'I'll ask again, mistress. What do you—'

She cut him short. 'I know no Gideon Fell.'

A knock on the door was followed by the entrance of the pot boy bearing a tray with a wooden trencher piled with slices of fresh-roasted pork, covered in a spiced gravy and hot stewed apple. A large hunk of bread and a jug of ale were also on the tray the boy shakily placed on Dorcas's work table. He had almost tripped over his own feet, in his attempts not to stare at Seeker.

'Next to useless,' muttered Dorcas. She pointed to the

barrel of dirty plates and tankards. 'Get that lot outside and washed. There's hardly a clean dish in the house.'

'I know, Dorcas, but since Isabella run off—'

She fixed him with a look that would have frozen milk. 'Just get it done.'

The boy coloured, but held his tongue as he dragged his burden out into the yard.

Dorcas Wells bolted the door behind him, and stood against it a moment, sighing, weary. She motioned to the stool at the table. 'Sit, eat.' Seeker could feel her eyes on him as he took a knife to the meat, speared it into his mouth. After he had had a few mouthfuls, she said, 'Everyone's jumpy tonight, with Parliament and all.'

'Any trouble here?' he asked.

She shook her head. 'I don't allow any trouble here.'

Wiping up some gravy with a piece of bread, Seeker considered the tavern keeper. There was something she wanted to know of him. Something in particular. Well, it would come if he left it long enough. He hadn't eaten since morning and the smell of the pork had first reached him not far past the Drapers' Hall. He had time. He took a draught of the ale and continued eating.

She began to move around the small room, affecting to examine objects that could have been of no interest to her – a cracked flagon, an inkpot, a coney muffler hanging from the door. 'So,' she said at last, her voice more light than was natural, 'who is Gideon Fell?'

He swallowed down a hunk of bread drenched in gravy.

It was the finest meal he'd eaten in a long time. 'A dead man. Of no concern to you. If you didn't know him.' He looked up from his food to meet her intense look. 'You're sure you didn't know him?'

'I never knew any Gideon Fell.' Another silence, then, 'So what's he to do with my tavern?'

Seeker wiped his mouth and stood up. 'Nothing, it seems.'

He nodded down to the empty trencher. 'More work for your boy.'

Her face finally softened. 'I'm too hard on him sometimes. Not his fault about the girl.'

'What girl?' said Seeker, starting to put on his gauntlets.

'A girl I had helping me, Isabella. She's gone now, and everything falls on Tom.'

Seeker stopped what he was doing and turned to face her. 'How do you mean, "gone"?'

Dorcas Wells shrugged her shoulders. 'I wish I knew. It must be ten days ago or so. I sent her down to the herb market at Leadenhall, to see what was to be had. When she didn't come back I went myself to look for her. No one had seen her. No one's seen hide nor hair of her since.'

Seeker felt some chill begin to creep over him. 'How old was she?'

Dorcas spoke very quietly. 'Fourteen. She'd been with me since she was eight.' Her fingers worried at the edge of her apron. 'She had no call to run away. I'm not a bad mistress, and she was safe here.'

Seeker doubted whether any in the parlour of the tavern, or indeed out around the streets of Bishopsgate and Broad Street had seen the woman before him weep.

'You think some evil has befallen her?'

'What else can it be?' she said, desperate. 'What good can befall a girl – such a lovely girl – alone in the city?'

Very little, thought Seeker. He thought of Nathaniel, coming here with Carter Blyth, of the hidden objects Blyth had stashed away in their chamber – the painting of Gethsemane, the register of the Three Nails. 'Has anything gone missing from here?'

'She was not a thief!'

'I didn't ask that. Has anything gone missing from this tavern since she went?'

'Nothing but the usual – the occasional tankard, dish. But . . .'

He sensed something in their conversation had changed, that now they were talking of something else.

'What?'

'Something appeared here, something strange, but it was a good two weeks before Isabella went.' She assessed him, took a linen handkerchief from the pocket hanging at her side and gave the tears that had started to brim onto her cheeks one harsh wipe. She went to the door. 'Wait here.'

Less than two minutes later, Seeker was looking at the small, ornate silver salt, topped with the model of a hound, that he had previously seen only in Anne Winter's family portrait.

'How did you know?' Dorcas Wells asked.

Seeker didn't take his eyes from the salt that he was examining. 'It doesn't matter. You found this two weeks before your girl disappeared?'

She pursed her lips in thought. 'Two weeks at least. But what could that have to do with it? How can there be any connection between the two?'

'How long after Gideon Fell was here did this—'

She interrupted him. 'There was no Gideon Fell.'

He looked at her in such a way that she should not doubt he thought her a liar. 'Have it your own way.' He put the salt into his leather bag. 'Tell no one of this.'

'I don't understand, Seeker. What's happening?'

'I think it would bring more danger to your house to make any of this known. Keep your boy close by you.'

'What?' On Dorcas Wells's face there was now a look of panic.

'If your girl comes back, or anything else unusual occurs here, or if anyone else should ask you about Gideon Fell, you get a message to me, you understand?'

She nodded, following him out into the parlour. The eyes of all her drinkers turned upon them. Dorcas didn't care.

'Seeker? You will come back?'

'Oh, I'll be back,' he said, surveying those who watched him. 'You may be certain, I will be back.'

TWELVE

The Sketches

Seeker was at his desk in Whitehall early the next morning. In Thurloe's absence, he wasn't sure he trusted many more here than he did in Anne Winter's house. George Downing had almost given up the pretence of interest in his duties at the Exchequer, so often was he to be found haunting the corridors of the intelligence offices. Philip Meadowe was an able deputy to the Secretary, but Seeker was not certain that he was of sufficient mettle to see off that stalking horse alone.

Despite the early hour, there was an air of even greater business, greater hurriedness, than usual on the stairways and corridors around the Cockpit. The closing down of Parliament had everyone on the alert, but Seeker suspected much of the tension was born of an underlying panic at the absence of the usually omnipresent Thurloe. This was confirmed when he ran into a bleary-eyed Meadowe, whose first words were a heartfelt wish for the Secretary's swift recovery and return.

Seeker was sceptical. 'I think his recovery will be slow,

and slowed the more should he return here too soon. But you manage, do you not, Mr Meadowe? Secretary Thurloe has great confidence in you.'

Meadowe breathed deep. 'I *think* we manage, but how can I be certain? The more complacent we are, the more likely we will miss something, and dear Lord, so much is flying this way from the Continent that if we don't miss something, it will be a miracle.'

'The Stuarts are up to something?'

'When are they not? But this time, I think it is something big. The intelligence coming our way, both from agents and by intercept, suggests better organisation than they have ever mustered before. This Sealed Knot of theirs has been wound round several parts of the country, and with the army so unsettled . . .'

'Don't concern yourself over the army. The Protector's name is carved on our hearts. Those who collude against him will be brought down before they even begin to rise themselves up. Their conspiracies have as much force as a twist of damp gunpowder.'

'You believe it?'

Seeker had no doubts. 'Men who believe they are something soon find they are nothing, should they think to stand against Oliver.'

As the two clerks Andrew Marvell and Marcus Bridlington passed, affecting not to be listening to the conversation of their superiors, Meadowe lowered his voice and moved closer to Seeker. 'The Secretary has told you of the attempt made on the Protector a couple of months back by the Fifth Monarchists?'

Seeker nodded. 'Belshazzar's Feast.'

'Well that's where we believe it's most likely the trouble in the army – should there be any – will come from, and Major-General Harrison at the head of it.'

'Only give the word, and Harrison will be crushed,' said Seeker.

Once seated behind his own desk, Seeker opened his leather bag and took out the packet his landlady on Knight Ryder Street had handed to him as he'd left that morning. He hadn't been back there since the shutting down of Parliament.

'Fellow like a rodent brought it, four days since,' she'd said, shivering at the memory.

Seeker looked at Anne Winter's seal, wondered what truths or lies might be contained beneath it, and tore the package open. Four sheets of good-quality paper, carefully folded. Seeker raised his eyebrows in unwilling admiration – Anne Winter had not sent him written descriptions of those who watched her house, but hand-drawn likenesses. Unfolding the first, he found himself looking at the living face of a man he'd last seen dead, one week ago now. Carter Blyth had been a good agent, practised in discretion and, when required, disguise, but Anne Winter had captured him, in blacklead and charcoal, exactly. It was the face, the scarred, burn-marked face that had indeed survived the munitions explosion at Delft. It was also the face of a man trying to look as if he was on his way to something, some place, of greater import to him than that which he was actually looking at. What was in the eyes? What did Carter Blyth see, and what was he looking for in Anne Winter's home?

Seeker set the sheet aside and considered the next sketch. In this he recognised one of the watchers Thurloe sometimes used, a stocky, ordinary fellow with drooping eyes and a careworn face. As far from what many imagined the agents of the Protectorate to be like as could be achieved, and yet Anne Winter had seen and known him for what he was. Seeker wrote down his name and moved on to the next sheet. A young, almost arrogant face, clean-shaven, slightly handsome, but Anne Winter had drawn more than the face, she had sketched in the body, too, capturing the fine lines of the expensive clothing, the sheen of the silver buckles on the shoes, the soft fall of a black velvet cloak over the good coat. Beneath the sketch, she had written, *One of General Goffe's, as I recall?* It was indeed Goffe's nephew, the young Marcus Bridlington, whom she had accosted on her visit here only a week ago, and who had so carelessly told her who he was. 'Hmm.' Seeker doubted that one so naive and so careful of his appearance would have a long career in the intelligence services. It angered Seeker that the lives of other, better men could at times be held in the balance by well-connected, lesser men who were not properly fit for the tasks allotted them, but then one as well connected as

Bridlington would not require a long career in the intelligence services. Some useful alliance, a wealthy widow or promising young heiress of influential family, was probably already being made for him, in some other part of Whitehall, or general's home on the Strand, or Pall Mall, or Wimbledon.

And so to the last piece of paper, the last sketch of those in the state's pay whom Anne Winter had observed watching her house. Seeker smiled and shook his head. 'Oh, Andrew, my lad, she has you to the very scowl.' Anne Winter had not moved below the shoulders in this case, the plain white split-linen collar coming right up under the first suspicion of a double chin. The sullen, pursed mouth, the heavy dark shadow around jaw and above the lip that was almost like a muzzle, the offended eyes, brewing on the injustices of life. Marvell – it could be no other. And beneath the likeness, Anne Winter had written, in her neat, trained hand:

> Much rather thou, I know, expect'st to tell
> How heavy Cromwell gnasht the earth and fell.
> Or how slow Death farre from the sight of day
> The long-deceived Fairfax bore away.

Seeker read the lines through twice, and cursed Anne Winter for her mind games. He could make little sense of what the woman was trying to say. If her words were to be taken literally, she seemed to be accusing Andrew Marvell of treachery against the Protectorate, which hardly made sense. But if they were some kind of coded threat, experience told him to get to the bottom of it sooner rather than later. He copied the lines down on a piece of paper, sealed it, and called for a runner to take it to Dr Wallis in the Cypher Office. Then he sent for the three watchers whom Anne Winter had identified, and called up the file of surveillance on her house. Bridlington and Marvell, neither yet set out on their day's task, were standing before him within five minutes; word had been sent that the third agent was working in the field, presumably already in position, Seeker thought, at Crutched Friars. He would have to have that changed – the man was already discovered, compromised.

A low winter sun had begun to edge its way above the city, and send some shafts of light across the dull greens and browns of the park beyond his windows. He set aside the third agent's report to read by himself, but pulled the other two from the file, where they had been meticulously titled and numbered by one of Thurloe's clerks.

Seeker's eyes were stinging from lack of sleep. He selected first the slim folder containing Bridlington's report, and handed it to the young man. 'Read it aloud, please.'

In a clear voice that had been trained to public speaking, Bridlington read. His observations were languid and, Seeker suspected, cursory. He appeared to recognise few of the callers to the front door of the house, other than the playwright William Davenant, whose arrival greatly animated him, and the known but tolerated Royalist John Evelyn, whose very young wife drew an admiring report. The dress of all three were described in unnecessary detail. Neither the servants of the house nor the tradesmen who called at it had stimulated any great degree of interest in Bridlington, although he did go as far as to categorise the Rat as 'unpleasant'. His attention to detail on Anne Winter's clothing on a day-to-day basis, and the architectural improvements she was undertaking to the outside of her home would have been impressive, had those been the objects of Thurloe's interest, but they were not. Bridlington concluded his report by commenting that the Royalists known to pay call to her were tolerated and indeed approved by the regime, and by offering the assessment that nothing untoward was being undertaken by Lieutenant Winter's widow.

As the young man's report drew to a close, Seeker found himself wishing that it was in his power to dismiss one so useless from Thurloe's service, and indeed in many circumstances it would have been, but not when the vessel of uselessness was one who could call on patronage so close to the Protector.

Bridlington was no doubt aware of this, but what he had clearly not been aware of was that Seeker did not feel himself constrained to pretend to be impressed by a shoddy piece of work, regardless of how well connected its author. When Seeker pushed back his chair, stood up and very volubly began to make his views known, Bridlington's look of self-assurance gradually turned to one of mortified disbelief.

'Pointless. An utterly pointless piece of work. A waste of Secretary Thurloe's time, and mine. You think that Charles Stuart sends his agents by the front door, bearing the Garter and his letters of commendation on a velvet cushion? You think every servant or tradesman to be a harmless halfwit? Every Royalist to be dressed like the Duke of Buckingham, or to blow a trumpet before him announcing himself as Rupert of the Rhine?'

Bridlington, visibly shaken, attempted a reply, but Seeker, risen from his seat and pacing towards a window, waved him away. 'Return your report to the file, and then report to the messengers' room. You can make yourself of use there until Secretary Thurloe returns and considers how better to employ you.'

Bridlington glanced at Marvell, whose eyes were now orbs of astonishment, and who, all unseen by Seeker, gestured vigorously towards the door. Bridlington needed no further telling, and was through it and gone by the time Seeker turned around again.

'So, Andrew,' said Seeker wearily, 'what can you tell me that your so-well-turned-out colleague cannot?'

Casting a defensive eye over his own perfectly serviceable clothing, Marvell licked his lips and began. The voice was halting, the flat Yorkshire tones did not roll as comfortably as Seeker's own; for all that his own gifts and his father's determination had seen Andrew Marvell as well educated as had been Marcus Bridlington, the churchman's son from Hull lacked the polish that wealth could buy, and for all his well-stocked mind and Cambridge training, he was no orator. The words came haltingly and in a monotone, but that was all right: Seeker didn't look to be entertained, he looked to be informed. And informed he was, for Marvell had noticed things, several things, that had escaped his more eloquent younger colleague's interest.

The Rat he too had noticed. He gave no personal opinion on the fellow, but that he suspected he carried a stiletto in his boot, and – Marvell hesitated, cleared his throat – his waistcoat was of Spanish leather, and he was fairly certain, Spanish-made.

Marvell need not have worried – this was a different thing entirely from Marcus Bridlington's admiration of the quality of John Evelyn's lace cuffs. Seeker knew Marvell to have travelled in Europe for many of the war years, and that he had ventured as far as Madrid, where, it was claimed, he had been taught to fence by a Spanish master.

'So, he has plied his trade as a mercenary then?'

'I think it likely,' answered Marvell. 'Lady Anne has taken steps to protect herself and her household.'

And yet they had not been enough to protect a girl not twelve years old.

Reassured that he was not to be subjected to the searing contempt poured on Bridlington, Marvell proceeded. He had noticed that the Rat, mercenary or no, seemed to have an especial oversight of the craftsmen who called at the house. And of craftsmen, he reported, there were several, but while Anne Winter had employed known local men to see to the new pantiles on the roof of her house, the painting of her front door, the weatherproofing and refining of the outer masonry, those who carried out the work inside came from outside London, and were unknown to the local men whom Marvell had asked about it.

What puzzled Marvell most, though, was that he had noticed Anne Winter's house was being watched by another, and not someone he recognised as being in the Protectorate's employ. When Seeker asked him to describe this other, it soon became clear that Marvell, just like Anne Winter, had noticed Carter Blyth watching her house. It made very little sense to Seeker that an agent as experienced as Blyth had neglected his own orders to study the comings and goings at the house of a Royalist widow whose home he must have seen was already being watched. The clear explanation was that he had not been watching it on Thurloe's behalf, but for some other reason. Seeker recalled his feeling, on reading Carter Blyth's reports to Thurloe, that some unmentioned train of enquiry had taken the agent's real interest. He was beginning to think he knew what that might have been. He became even more certain of it when Marvell made his final observation.

'This person, who comported himself as a clothworker out of some old almshouses by the top of Woodruffe Street, seemed less interested in the lady of the house or the visitors to it, than in some young servant girl who had a place there for a time. I have not observed the servant girl of late. The clothworker also appears to have left the area, and at around the same time.'

Relieved, it seemed, to be finished speaking, Marvell looked up, a little flushed. 'That's it.'

Seeker's jaw was tense, he was calculating something, tracking a thought to its source. 'The girl,' he said, 'tell me about the girl.'

'The girl?' repeated Marvell, perplexed.

'The servant girl in whom this scarred clothworker took such an interest.'

'Ah, yes.' Marvell consulted his report once again. 'About eleven or twelve years old. Pale red hair worn loose under her cap. Large eyes. Quiet, wary.'

'Of what?'

Marvell stuck out his lower lip and shrugged. 'Everything.'

'The clothworker?'

'Initially, but afterwards, not so much.'

'Who else did you see her with?'

'No one. She just hurried about her business in the streets and always looked glad to be back at Anne Winter's gate.'

Charity Penn: that was who Blyth had been watching in Anne Winter's house, the house the girl had then gone missing from, just as children had gone missing from the gardener's service at Lincoln's Inn, the Black Fox Tavern, and the school at the Three Nails on Holborn, all places he knew Blyth to have gone with Nathaniel.

Marvell cleared his throat. 'Uhm, will that be all?'

'What? Oh, yes,' said Seeker, but when Marvell made to leave, an idea occurred to Seeker and he stopped him. 'You know the playwright Davenant?'

Marvell's face began to engineer something of a sneer. 'A little. He is a buffoon.'

'And yet well favoured by the Protector and Lady Anne alike. I will procure you an invitation to attend him the next time he goes to visit the lady in her home. You can tell me what they speak of.'

'But if she has already noticed me . . .'

'It will be useful to see which topics they dance around to avoid whilst you are there, and you can get a better look at the people in her house. The servants too.'

Marvell's face was a picture of fleshy sullenness. 'I have seen as much as I wish to of her Rat, of Davenant too. I made sport of him once, and of his work, in a piece he is bound to have seen. I doubt he will take me with him willingly.'

'Hmmph,' replied Seeker. 'If there's one thing Sir William has learned since his release from the Tower, it's to do what he's told. Now get back to whatever you are supposed to be doing.'

Relieved, Marvell passed through the doorway, awkwardly dipping his head to the arriving Philip Meadowe as he did so.

Seeker waited as Meadowe closed the door carefully behind him.

'He resents me,' he said.

Seeker grinned. 'Andrew? He resents everybody. He could never have done the job for Secretary Thurloe that you have done, no matter how earnestly Secretary Milton might have recommended him for it. He has his uses all the same.'

'Aye.' Meadowe settled himself somewhat uncomfortably into the chair across from Seeker's.

'But?'

'It's Andrew I have come to talk to you about. You must believe me that I mean him no ill-will in what I am about to say.'

Seeker nodded.

'The note you sent to Wallis earlier, those four lines . . .'

'Anne Winter had written them beneath a sketch she had done of Marvell. I could make head nor tail of them. I thought Wallis might make something of them. Has he?'

'He didn't need to,' said Meadowe. 'They are no code, but lines from a poem Andrew himself penned seven years ago, a eulogy for a dead Royalist, Francis Villiers.'

'Seven years ago?'

Meadowe nodded. 'He was in circles that he would have done better to avoid, befriended those who were no friends to the cause of Parliament.'

Seeker shrugged. 'Like many others who have been brought into the fold. He never fought in the wars and he is firmly in Cromwell's cause now; albeit that he took his own good time deciding which way to jump.'

'Aye, a good long time, he took,' said Meadowe. 'And there are times I am not certain . . .'

'If he was still in the Royalist camp, Anne Winter would hardly have taken the trouble to point it out to us.'

'Would she not?' said Meadowe. 'I wonder. Sometimes I think the woman laughs at us, for the sake of showing she can. On the other hand, the Protector trusts him, likes his turn of phrase, and Fairfax had him as tutor to his daughter.' He sat back, revived it seemed by the couple of minutes' conversation. 'We should probably keep an eye on him nonetheless.'

'Yes,' replied Seeker, 'we probably should.' But he wasn't thinking about Andrew Marvell penning verses for a dead Royalist boy; he was thinking about what Meadowe had just said – that Marvell had indeed been in the pay of Lord Fairfax, the one man whom the army loved more than Cromwell. More than that, Seeker was thinking about what Meadowe might not know – that Marvell had from their youth in Hull been a friend of two officers – Alured and Overton – lately turned first Fifth Monarchist and then against the Protector altogether. For all he liked his fellow Yorkshireman, Seeker resolved to keep Andrew Marvell close.

As Meadowe rose to leave, Seeker said, 'I'm on my way out; I'll walk with you.'

As they descended the stairway from Seeker's rooms, Meadowe said wistfully, 'Out? What is "out" like these days, Damian? I don't think I've been as far as Scotland Yard since Mr Thurloe was laid low.'

' "Out" is a maze of wickedness and deceptions.'

Meadowe smiled. 'Like here then,' he said almost under his breath.

Seeker stopped at the bottom and turned to face him.

'Remember, sir, my men and I are yours to command in Secretary Thurloe's absence. Regardless of who might assert otherwise.' He nodded towards the far end of the corridor, into which George Downing had just turned, followed by a coterie of under-secretaries and clerks who were struggling to keep pace with him, while hanging on his every word. Seeker stepped aside to let Meadowe pass him, and then stood behind the Under-Secretary, who straightened his shoulders and took up his position in the middle of the corridor, forcing the New Englander to a halt.

'Mr Downing. Is there some business in particular that brings you from the Exchequer today?'

Downing eyed Seeker over Meadowe's shoulder, then addressed himself solely to the Under-Secretary. 'In Mr Thurloe's continued absence, and at this critical time, I thought some greater authority might be required—'

'I have all Mr Thurloe's authority, in his absence, as you may confirm with his Highness the Lord Protector, and I will not have my staff distracted from their duties by those to whom they do not answer.' Meadowe then turned his eyes on the group of young men in Downing's train, all but one of whom, Downing's own clerk, an eager-looking fellow with a lively mouth and intelligent eyes, melted away. Seeker would have sworn that that clerk took pleasure at his master's humbling.

Downing's mouth was a firm line, but his face was crimson. 'Come, Pepys,' he muttered as he turned on his heel. 'We have much business at the Exchequer.'

Seeker and Meadowe watched the pair leave, and Seeker saw the Under-Secretary's shoulders slump as the sound of their footsteps on the stone stairs gradually faded.

As Meadowe groaned and rubbed a hand over screwed-up eyes, Seeker placed a hand on the younger man's shoulder. 'You saw him off, sir.'

The Under-Secretary turned to Seeker, and smiled wearily. 'No. *You* saw him off. I am not so misguided as to think otherwise. But the main thing is that he is gone. For now.'

'Aye,' said Seeker, 'for now.'

THIRTEEN

Suffer the Children

As he went through the Holbein Gate, the watery early morning sun had given up its struggle and ceded the skies to darkening grey clouds. Seeker traced their path: they seemed to be gathering over Westminster Hall. Providence. God angered at what had happened there, or forewarning of worse to come. Not Seeker's concern, until the security of the State made it his concern.

He was soon at Lincoln's Inn: there were questions about Carter Blyth that he could ask no one but Thurloe. Propped up with many cushions, seated by a raging fire in his attic sitting room, the Secretary wrapped his hands around a steaming posset cup, still far from health but determined on business. He listened carefully to what Seeker had to say. At the end, he shook his head.

'No, Damian. Whoever took those children, it wasn't Carter Blyth. He was a truly godly man, not one subject to unnatural perversions – he would not have had to dissemble over much in the prayer meetings and all the rest at Gethsemane.'

Seeker had known many godly men in the wars who had not scrupled to do things no Christian should do, but he kept his views to himself: Thurloe was a sound judge of his fellow men and had known Blyth much better than he. 'The other explanation, then,' he said, 'is that this business of missing children is what Blyth had begun to investigate, the thing that distracted him from his true purpose of investigating the activities of the Fifth Monarchists and their army connections. He was tracking down whoever took those children. He must have come close, and that's why he's dead.'

Thurloe, forcing himself to swallow down some of the hot, thick drink, considered the point. 'I follow you so far, Seeker, but Carter Blyth had never wandered from the orders of his mission before, and I'll speak plain: why should he care about these children, servants and schoolboys whose families are of no account? And why did he not inform me of it as he would of anything else of import?'

To Seeker, there were only two answers to the Secretary's questions, and neither of them would he like. But then Seeker's value to Thurloe was not founded on him giving him only answers he would like. 'Either he did attempt to inform you, and his message never reached you, or the person he suspected was not someone he felt he could name until he was certain.'

He didn't need to spell it out: Thurloe had already grasped the thing. 'Those are not two answers, but two sides of the one: the person Blyth had tracked down is one of our own – someone who has access to our networks, or who is virtually untouchable.' Thurloe ran a hand over his fore-head and screwed his eyes tight shut. 'The news-sheet writers, Nedham and the like, must be kept well clear of this. And God knows, we have not the time for it, just now.' He looked at Seeker. '*You* have not the time for this. Philip Meadowe has need of you at Whitehall, where the vultures are circling; we are on the point of moving against the Fifth Monarchists, and our sources suggest the Stuarts have some-thing brewing. There is more than enough to get on with, without your time should be spent amongst the weavers of Aldgate or the schoolboys of Holborn. Carter Blyth allowed himself to get distracted – killed – over a matter of so little account. The question is, will his killer lie low now, or be emboldened by his crimes?'

Seeker thought of his own daughter, as he had last seen her nearly ten years ago, huge blue eyes blinking at him uncomprehendingly over her mother's shoulder as he had walked away. He thought of Isabella, the girl who had disappeared from the Black Fox Tavern, after Carter Blyth was already dead. 'They are emboldened,' he said. 'It will create a great deal of fear and unsettle the city if these dis-appearances continue.' Seeker was resolved: whatever Thur-loe might counsel, he was not inclined to leave the children of the city to fend for themselves.

Shadrach Jones should not really have left the boys, but after Seeker's visit of the previous day he had spent an anxious day and restless night and decided he had no option: he must go out into the city again, for there was someone he must see. The morning's classes had passed in a blur, and he could not have told afterwards whether he had taught the boys Euclid or Euripides. After a hasty dinner, he had set them translation exercises according to their abilities, and warned William Godmanson to bolt the door behind him after he left, and allow no one in or out until his return.

A careful route, by backstreets and small alleyways, had eventually brought him to his object, and after the encounter had taken place, he had chosen different routes, unlikely routes for the schoolmaster from Holborn to be seen wandering alone. It was just as he'd passed the Fishmongers' Hall, not far from London Bridge, that he realised someone was calling his name from across the street. Shadrach affected not to have heard and carried on, but it came again. He stopped. It was Elias.

The encounter was not to be avoided. Shadrach smiled and waved and stepped into the street, almost coming to grief between a carter heading westwards and some soldiers riding east. He lunged across the gutter as Elias, laughing, pulled him to safety.

'You are not in the woods of New England, now, Shadrach!'

'And thank God for it – there are things in the New England woods that would put even a Billingsgate carter to flight.'

'There speaks a man with a limited experience of Billingsgate carters,' muttered Elias. 'But come, Shadrach, what brings you to this part of town at this time of day?'

Shadrach had his story ready. He patted his bag. 'I was down by the river, at the Three Cranes, making sketches of the lifting apparatus to study with the boys. I plan to make a model with them.'

'More useful than the endless repetitions of Euclid I was subjected to in my schooldays, I am sure. But come, Shadrach, we will go to the coffee house. I missed my morning draught there and am desperate for a dish of Samuel's finest. You can tell me all your news – Maria was asking after you only last night.'

There evidently being nothing for it, Shadrach relented. Half an hour more at this time could hardly do the boys much harm. Besides, he liked Elias's company a great deal better than that of the man he had just been with.

'And will Mistress Maria be joining us?' he asked a little hesitantly as they turned up St Michael's Lane.

'Joining us?' Elias was bemused. 'It isn't proper, Shadrach, for a young woman to sit in a coffee house. She might work there, but to sit and take her dish and talk with the men? It would be a scandal. Would the Puritans of Boston not think it a scandal?'

'We have no coffee houses in Boston, Elias, but yes, I am certain that should there be the opportunity of thinking something a scandal, they would indeed grasp it.'

They walked on, each considering. 'And yet,' ventured Shadrach again, 'your sister is as intelligent a woman, and as well versed in the news as any I have met. Anywhere.'

Elias nodded. 'Of course. If she were a man, well, she

would . . .' Then he laughed. 'She would probably be as poor a lawyer as myself.'

'And she has no suitors?'

Elias looked at Shadrach as if the question had not previously occurred to him. 'She scares them off, and anyway, I don't think, well, no . . .' But he stopped, a thought evidently occurring to him. 'No,' he said quietly, as if to himself, then a more definitive shake of the head and again, 'No. But you, Shadrach. You should talk to her. Talk to her of the Americas. Take her walking even, in the Spring Garden. No, wait, Cromwell has closed it. The Mulberry Garden? Yes. That would be better. Much better.'

Shadrach was not certain whether it was the particular pleasure garden or something else that Elias regarded as better, or indeed, better than what, but Elias seemed curiously distracted and so he left it. By the time they reached Kent's, all Elias's talk was of Oliver's closing of Parliament, and what further repressions of liberty might follow, to the extent that Shadrach was relieved to find there some faces familiar from his previous visit.

Tavener's eyes lit up to see them.

'Move up, move up!' he exhorted, digging an elbow into the somewhat morose figure beside him whose ink-stained fingers suggested a life spent at the printing press. 'Here is our young friend to regale us with tales of life in New England!' It was not long before conversation was of bears, wild cats, alligators and the many fevers to be obtained in the swamps with which the New World teemed. Relieved not to be pressed further this time on any connection with George Downing, Shadrach began to relax a little, and persevering with the coffee, found he began to like it. He was in the middle of telling a tale of one of his many encounters with the natives of Massachusetts to a wide-eyed scrivener when the voices around them suddenly dropped, and the faces around the table became intent upon the dishes of coffee and chocolate in front of them. Shadrach glanced towards the door to see what might have caused this alteration in the humour of the room, and his own heart sank – standing at the top of the steps leading from the street corner door down to the floor of the coffee room, was Damian Seeker.

Seeker scanned the room slowly and his gaze, hardening, soon fell upon Shadrach. He did not mince his words. 'What are you doing here? Who have you left in charge of those boys? The old man?'

Shadrach's face was a sheet. 'No. I left one of the older boys—'

'After what has already happened?' Seeker barked something towards the door and two of his men entered. 'Escort this – *schoolmaster* – back to the Three Nails on Holborn. Be sure to ascertain that all of the boys are accounted for before you leave.'

Shadrach made no protest, and picking up his hat and shabby coat followed the soldiers out onto the street without a word. As he passed him, Seeker hissed into his ear, 'You had better hope to God all is well with those boys you have left.' Then Seeker looked around the room, looked at Samuel, at Gabriel, the bright boy Samuel had found on the streets, given work, food, a cot by the fire. 'Children have been going missing, taken – a boy from the school at the Three Nails in Holborn, a lady's maid from Anne Winter's house in Aldgate, a lad who worked in the gardens at Lincoln's Inn, a serving girl from the Black Fox in Bishopsgate. All children without family by them. All you merchants and tradesmen – have an eye on your apprentices and errand boys, tell your wives to look well to their maids. Know who they speak to.' He looked firmly at Samuel, and at his niece Grace, behind the counter. 'Don't let them out to wander the streets alone.'

A grocer from Cheapside stood up. 'But this is impossible – how is our business to be done?'

Grace had moved unknowingly to where Gabriel was setting a ginger jar back on its shelf, and laid a protecting hand on his shoulder. The boy wriggled. 'I'm near enough thirteen, Mistress Grace, you need have no fears for me.'

Samuel raised his stick and pointed it at him. 'You've no idea how old you are! How old you are is none of your concern – you'll do as you're told and stay by us until the captain says different, isn't that right, Captain?'

Seeker nodded slowly.

Elias Ellingworth shifted his gaze from Grace and Gabriel back to Seeker. 'Is this the truth, Seeker, or is it just another government lie put about to take people's attention from what's going on in Parliament and the army? Your

Protectorate's on the verge of destroying itself and you think the people will be too busy with your peddled fears and rumours to notice? Buried monks bricked up alive? Stolen children?' Ellingworth shook his head, disgusted at the truth he believed he had glimpsed. He picked up the latest edition of Nedham's *Mercurius Politicus*, complete with its lurid account of the macabre finding at Blackfriars. 'Is *this* what you think we are?'

Seeker was weary of the lawyer's diatribes. 'I *know* what you are, Ellingworth. You, and your like. Don't hold your breath waiting for the state destroy itself. You'll be deader than the monk of Blackfriars before that ever happens. Now, Samuel,' he said, making it clear that he had nothing further to say to Elias, 'I'd have a few words with that boy of yours.'

Seeker dropped his helmet onto the table of the private booth at the back of the room, and settled himself on one of its benches. Samuel hastily ushered Gabriel over to join him, hobbling over himself a moment later with the warm tankard of spiced ale Grace had begun to prepare as soon as she'd seen Seeker come in.

Once Samuel had left them, Seeker took a draught of his drink. There was no need for mind games with this boy, such as there had been with the ones he'd spoken to at the Three Nails. He knew Gabriel spoke the truth. 'Lady Anne's house,' he said, and waited.

Gabriel chewed at his lip a moment and took a deep breath. 'She wanted me to show her cook how to prepare the beans – weigh them and roast them and grind them and boil them and all. You see, if you do them too hot for too long—' But Seeker had held up a hand to stop him.

'I'll wager I'll meet my maker before I ever need to know how a pot of that foul stuff comes to be.' Gabriel's colour rose and he looked at the table. Seeker took pity on him. 'But tell me, has the fellow mastered it – Anne Winter's cook – or do you still have to go to the house?'

'Oh,' Gabriel brightened, 'he got it soon enough – not as good as Samuel, mind, but that's to be expected.'

'So you don't go to the house any more.'

The boy wriggled a little, uncomfortable. 'Well, I do you see. Lady Anne – she can't come to the coffee house, can she, for the beans? Especially after all that trouble after her husband died. No one likes to think of that. And Samuel doesn't like the look of that steward fellow she has. Doesn't want him sniffing in here.'

'The man Richard?'

'I think that's what she calls him, but he looks like a rat, and Samuel says he's damned – if you'll pardon me – if the fellow wasn't a freebooter for that Cardinal-Infanty or some such Spanish dirt.'

Seeker suppressed a smile at the unfailing accuracy of Gabriel's rendering of the old soldier's views. 'You do well to listen to Samuel,' he said. 'So you still take the beans there?'

'Yes. And other things Grace sends now and again, receipts and the like for new beverages she's come across. Lady Anne sent her back a book once.'

'What kind of book?'

Gabriel coloured again. 'Couldn't rightly make it out. Poems and stuff, I think. I'll know by next year, Captain.'

Seeker knew Grace was teaching the boy his letters. 'You see that you do. Where do you go when you take things there?'

'At first it was just the scullery, then right into the kitchen one cold day, for a warm and a cake the cook's girl made.' He traced his finger across the grain of the wood on the table. 'Charity was nice. Is she the one you were talking about, Captain, that's been taken?'

'I think so, Gabriel. Do you know of where she might have gone? Who with?'

The boy shook his head. 'She wasn't forward to talk to me, not like the market girls, but she was happy there, liked being with Lady Anne, you could tell that. You'll find her, won't you?'

Seeker wasn't in the business of making promises he couldn't be sure of keeping. 'I don't know. But you keep your eyes open when you're there. And you tell me if there's anything you think I should know of. You know what I mean, don't you?'

A look of understanding flitted across Gabriel's face that Seeker thought presaged the man he would be. 'Yes, Captain, I know what you mean.'

Elias Ellingworth had left, as had most of Samuel's customers, by the time Seeker had finished talking to Gabriel. Seeker took in the empty benches, the table cleared of cups and pipes, the news-sheets Grace was tidying. He might have been carrying the plague. He should have waited until Samuel was ready to close up.

'Nice to get to our beds a bit earlier tonight,' Samuel said. 'Sometimes you'd think they had nowhere to go.'

Seeker placed his empty tankard on the counter and nodded his thanks to Grace before putting his helmet back on and going out into the street. He craved his own bed in the spartan room on Knight Ryder Street more than he did the more comfortable small apartment set aside for his use in Whitehall. For a time, he had spent almost all his time at Whitehall, as if the surroundings of that life might silence the echoes of the other which he strove to forget, but eventually, something in the city, its narrow lanes, secret gardens, unexpected brooks and gutters even, had called to him, and he felt himself more and more often drawn here.

There was little light to be seen as he passed by the end of Dove Court, but he was certain that Elias would be up still, committing his latest outrage to paper, thinking to bring down the state built by Ironsides with the force of his pen. And yet, despite what Seeker had so roundly asserted to the lawyer, they both knew that Elias's words could be as insidious to the fabric of the government as ivy to the bricks of a house. They would creep, and find their way through gaps so tiny they could hardly be seen by those not looking, start to tug at that fabric, fray and unsettle it as ivy would the wall, if no one was watching. But Damian Seeker was watching, and should Maria's brother or his kind begin to trouble the state more than the state could control, then they would have to be crushed, cut down, their very roots removed from the places they had got their foothold, for otherwise, eventually, the state would not stand.

He had almost reached the small alleyway at the end of the house on Knight Ryder Street when he saw her, waiting in a doorway across the street, like a wraith, or worse. When she saw that he had seen her, she came quickly over to him.

He pulled her out of the lamplight to the end of the alleyway at the side of the house. 'What in God's name are you doing here at this time of the night?'

Maria bridled. 'It is not the first time . . .' Her eyes were filling and he cursed his temper.

He softened his voice. 'I *know* it's not the first time, but you shouldn't come here without warning, without it being arranged. If you were seen . . .'

'Seen? Damian, even to you, I think I am invisible.'

He put a hand up to brush back a lock of hair that had fallen over her forehead. 'Invisible? You? Never.' He pressed her against the wall and kissed her, before pulling away. 'But we should not be seen like this.' He took her hand and led her halfway down the passageway to the door that opened into his solitary dwelling.

Little moonlight fell through the room's one small window that in the daytime, when Seeker was hardly ever there to see it, looked into a high-walled backyard and herb garden. Seeker made his way over to the mantel above the fireplace and lit a lamp, then put flame to the fire his land-lady had set in the hearth.

He sat down on the narrow bed, removed his helmet and rubbed a hand over weary eyes. 'Why have you come here, Maria?'

'Why? Can you ask that? Are you truly asking me that?'

'It is not . . . you should not . . .'

'What? I have not seen you for nigh on two weeks, apart from that night you came to our home and practically threatened to arrest Elias's friend simply for being there, for speaking to me.'

'I shouldn't have done that.'

'No, you shouldn't have. But at least – at least it showed you had some feeling for me.'

He paused in the easing off of his jacket. 'Some feeling? Dear God, Maria, all the feeling I have is for you. The only reason I know I have a heart at all is from the ache you have made in it.'

She crossed from beside the door to kneel in front of him, took his hands in hers. 'But why? Why should there be an ache and not joy? I *love* you, Damian. I will offer you, give you, everything I have, everything I am, and I ask nothing of you in return other than that sometimes, for a few hours, you will let yourself be mine.'

He shook his head. 'We can't, Maria, we should never have begun.'

She dropped his hands in anger and disbelief. 'For God's sake, why? Why should we not be happy as others are? I don't ask to be your wife – I will not be *anyone's* wife. I don't ask that we share a roof over our heads even. All I ask is that we, you and I, know what we are to each other, and live that, sometimes.'

He looked up at her. 'You will always be what you are to me now, Maria, what you were that first night. There will not *be* anyone else. But we cannot live as you wish us to live, be as you wish us to be. It isn't possible, and I should never have let it begin.'

She took a step backwards. 'You're not saying this.'

'Maria, there can be no future for us in this world. Even if you were to leave your brother . . .'

She was indignant. 'I will not leave Elias!'

'I know you will not. So how does that work? Your brother will never lay down his pen, never cease to speak against the state until he is made to, and it is on me that that task will fall, one day. You and I both know it. And even if Elias were to be struck down dead this very night, it would make no difference. Your heart is as his, your mind as his: you would take up the pen he had dropped and carry on. You would collude with Wildman and other radicals as he does.'

'And then you would arrest me,' she said quietly.

He shook his head. 'No. No, I could never do that. And then I would not be who I am, and we have returned to the beginning of our circle once more. There is no way for you and I to be together in this world, Maria.'

The sound of some animal rooting in the backyard, of a

door creaking in the slight wind, made the silence between them in the small, whitewashed room unbearable. A teardrop that had formed on her lower lash slowly crept onto her cheek. The fire had taken, but still she was shivering.

Seeker got up and went over to her, pulled her gently to him and brushed the top of her head with his lips. The desolation in her threatened to undo him.

'Can we not have this one, last night?' she said at last.

He said nothing, pulled her closer.

'Please, Damian?'

He continued to hold her. His will was raging with itself inside him. He felt that his ribs might collapse. His head moved slightly, he took in the scent of her hair, brushed her ear with his cheek, then his lips found her neck and they stumbled to the bed.

FOURTEEN

Downing

Downing regarded his clerk and congratulated himself once more on his ability to spot talent. He had known it in himself, seen it in himself, before others had, and that had proved useful. Lesser men of higher birth or greater influence had thought to make use of his abilities, while affording themselves the satisfaction of patronising him. So be it, he had left most of them behind, and now they sought his favour instead.

But this young fellow had not the air of one who intended to be left behind, and that suited Downing well. He had spotted this Pepys's abilities, his sharpness of mind, his power to charm, at an early stage, afforded him his patronage at Cambridge and brought him into his own service. There were rumours the fellow was too fond of the taverns around Westminster – the Dog, the Fox, the Swan – drinking over much and pestering any maid who could not outrun him, but he had never yet failed to perform any office Downing required of him, or to attend his master whenever required, as now.

It was not yet light, and Pepys had been waiting for him,

as summoned, outside his house at Axe Yard, by five. The city along the river was still breathing a dusky sleep, although the streets of Westminster were lit, the cavalrymen in Horse Guard Yard already looking to their mounts, the next duty of guards having their last half-hour sleep before rousing themselves to take over from the night watch.

Across King Street and beyond the gate into Whitehall itself, a light would still be burning in Isaac Dorislaus's office, as he finished his night work on the last of the previous day's postal intercepts, but the corridors around the Cockpit should be quiet now, Meadowe, Morland, Marvell still abed, Milton perhaps just rising in his house across the way in Petty France, looking out onto a park that he could no longer see. Thurloe would still be safely swathed in the blankets of his sickbed in Lincoln's Inn – Cromwell's own physician was not sanguine about the Chief Secretary's state of health, and that suited Downing's purpose very well.

'Is our business at the Exchequer, sir?' asked Pepys, hurrying along to keep pace with his employer, almost slipping on the early morning ice.

'No, it is not. It is in the department of Mr Thurloe.'

'Ah,' said Pepys, opening his mouth to say something else but, evidently finding nothing politic to add, shutting it again. Downing liked that about him too.

Their footsteps on the stairs and corridors leading to the Cockpit, where the Council of State met, echoed in the stone silence. The guards posted in doorways and at stairheads might also have been of stone. Downing did not acknowledge them, and there was no flicker from them as the pair from the Exchequer swiftly passed to the corridors where Thurloe's under-secretaries and clerks oversaw the security of the state.

The captain of the night watch was an officer known to Downing from his days in the army in Scotland, and it was with no great difficulty that he and Pepys gained access to the corridor of the Secretariat. Entry to specific offices and stores was another matter though, for every door was locked, and not even the captain of the night watch had the keys. Had Downing been less righteous, he would have sworn, under his breath at least, but he contented himself with a silent curse on Seeker. 'Who does have the keys?' he demanded of the captain.

'Secretary Meadowe, Secretary Milton and Mr Morland.'

Pepys stepped closer and murmured to him so that the captain might not hear, 'I believe there is also a set kept in the junior clerks' room.'

'Which is also locked,' said Downing, beginning to lose his grip on his patience.

Pepys cleared his throat. 'Yes, sir, but each of the clerks has his own key to that room, and it would take only one of them to obtain the rest . . .'

A brief flicker of hope appeared on Downing's face before fading. 'They are all in thrall to Seeker, terrified of him. They will not countermand his orders.'

Pepys made a grim face. 'And they are quite wise in that, I have no doubt. But there is one who is somewhat resentful towards him – I think he might be prepared to counter-mand the Seeker's orders if someone more influential – like yourself, perhaps – were to make it known he wished him to.'

'Spit it out, man,' said Downing. 'Who is it, and where is he to be found?'

'Bridlington, sir,' said Pepys, chastened.

'Goffe's nephew?'

'His wife's, I believe. The Seeker roared at him more or less in public, reduced him to the status of message boy. He is not well pleased. He is accommodated in his aunt and uncle's private apartments. I can have him here in less than five minutes.'

And indeed, less than five minutes later, Pepys was return-ing with the bleary-eyed and somewhat dishevelled clerk, who was still struggling to tuck the tails of a fine white shirt into his breeches. He looked terrified.

'Mr Pepys has told you why you are here, I assume.'

Bridlington looked uncomprehendingly and somewhat accusingly from Downing to Pepys and back again. 'No, sir, he has not.'

Downing glared briefly at Pepys. 'I need access to the offices of Mr Thurloe's department and to the file library.'

Bridlington bit his lip. 'Captain Seeker said no one was to . . .'

'Captain Seeker is not here,' growled Downing, 'and there are urgent matters of state which will not wait upon an improvement in his humour.'

'Hell might freeze over before such an event,' murmured Pepys.

'And,' continued Downing, ignoring the musings of his clerk, 'I require immediate access to certain papers of great import. I require you to bring me the keys to the offices of the Secretariat.'

A genuine reluctance manifested itself in Marcus Bridlington's frightened eyes and in the deepening pallor of his face.

'Get me the keys,' said Downing, scarcely moving his lips. Behind him, Pepys nodded encouragement and warning: Downing was not to be countermanded on this.

At last Bridlington understood, and led them to the clerks' room, which he unlocked. He then crossed to the small cabinet affixed to the wall opposite the door and unlocked it too. Not looking Pepys in the eye, he handed him the bunch of keys hanging inside. Downing snatched them from his clerk and stalked from the room.

'What does he want them for?' whispered Bridlington to Pepys, as they hurried along behind him.

Pepys looked around him, and finding no one but themselves within earshot replied, 'He means to find the name of Thurloe's agent in Charles's court.'

Bridlington was fully alert now. 'But why?'

'Because the Royalists have something on foot, with their Sealed Knot or some other such thing, and old George there means to make contact with our man in Cologne and get the intelligence of it himself, and so the glory, when the plot is foiled.'

'And will he?' asked Bridlington.

'Hmm, only if Mr Thurloe dies first, and takes half his department with him. But it will do you and I no harm at all to humour Downing while he tries.'

'There will be none of me left to do harm to once the Seeker discovers it is I who let him have the keys,' said Bridlington resentfully.

Pepys clapped an arm around his shoulder. 'Come, Marcus, be of good cheer. You had shot your bolt with the Seeker anyway; Mr Downing there is no more to be trusted than a hungry flea on a cat, but he aims to rise further in this world and it will be no bad thing for you to retain his favour as he does so.'

'No,' responded Bridlington, 'perhaps it will not.'

Downing did not hear any of the exchange between his own clerk and Goffe's nephew: he was intent on his object of Secretary Thurloe's door, the key to which he selected at the third attempt. Again, he cursed silently as he found cabinets and drawers locked.

'I think it possible that he has had the most sensitive documents shifted to his rooms in Lincoln's Inn,' ventured Bridlington.

Pepys took a breath in anticipation of an explosion of anger from his employer, but none came. Downing had seated himself in Thurloe's chair and was thinking. He stretched his fingers and clenched his fists alternately as he did so. No one spoke, the two clerks waiting, watching him. 'Other papers,' he said at last. 'There must be some way in through other papers. But who?' He listed and discounted the names of several known and suspected Royalists, and then he smiled. 'Lady Anne Winter.' He enunciated the words slowly, with a grim pleasure. 'She told me herself, her house is watched night and day. Why would Thurloe watch her so closely if he did not have some specific intelligence regarding her? You' – he snapped a finger in Bridlington's direction – 'fetch me her file.'

'I . . . it may take some time to locate.'

'How difficult can it be? They are arranged by name, are they not?'

'Yes, sir,' said Bridlington quietly. His eyes firmly fixed on the ground before his feet, he trudged off in the direction of the file room. Once he thought the young man likely to be out of earshot, Downing let out a great sigh and said, 'No wonder the Seeker gave him his marching orders – heaven help the Protectorate from such useless milksops. A man should rise by talent, not connection – is that not right, Pepys?'

'Very right, sir. I don't think Mr Bridlington's future lies in Whitehall.'

'Hmmph. It is a wonder the others, that have to prove their worth to get here, tolerate him.'

Pepys drew up the chair at the other side of Thurloe's desk and proceeded to make himself comfortable. Downing was too astonished by the audacity to comment. He was surprised the fellow did not bring out a pipe. 'They tolerate him by more or less ignoring him, and he does nothing to ingratiate himself by making it clear how tedious he finds the work that they value so highly. He prefers to talk of his grand connections, his parents' country house, whom he met at his uncle's hunting lodge in Berkshire. He lacks the style of Meadowe or the wit of Marvell, and for all his puff I don't think he is much practised in social intercourse. Never went to school, apparently – tutored at home. A dull companion.'

While awaiting Bridlington's return, Downing passed the time by letting himself into other rooms in the corridor, and was just about to turn the key in the lock of Philip Meadowe's door when the clerk finally reappeared, bearing a heavy sheaf of papers in a hide cover tied with leather thongs.

'About time,' said Downing, leaving Meadowe's door and striding back towards Thurloe's room, calling for Pepys to take the papers from Bridlington and lay them out for his own examination, setting the most recent reports to the front.

Pepys began to do as he was bid as Bridlington looked on, but a moment after opening the ties on the file he turned raised eyebrows on the clerk. Another minute and he was clearing his throat, evidently casting about for the best way to begin.

'Well?' said Downing.

'It, uhm, appears that Mr Bridlington has brought us the wrong file.'

' "Wrong file"? What do you mean, "wrong file"?'

'What I am looking at is the record of observations on Mr Elias Ellingworth, lawyer, of Clifford's Inn and Dove Court. It may be that Lady Anne features at some point further back in these reports, but at present I cannot see—'

'What?' growled Downing. 'Move aside!' He pushed Pepys out of the way and began to examine the papers for himself, as Bridlington shifted uncomfortably in the corner.

'It – they must have become mixed up, when Ellingworth was thought to be involved in the death of Lady Anne's husband, it was in all the news-sheets.'

'That was over two months ago, Marcus,' said Pepys. 'These reports are of much more recent provenance. You will have to return them and find—'

But Downing had held up a hand, something in a report near the top having caught his eye. 'No,' he said. 'Leave them here. Go and find where the reports on Lady Anne have been put, but leave these here. Pepys, you assist him.'

'But, sir, what if—'

'Now!' said Downing.

The two young men being gone, Downing lit another candle and brought it over to Thurloe's desk. He set aside the top three reports, and opened once more that from almost two weeks ago, recording a new visitor to Ellingworth's home on Dove Court. The visitor had been tracked to his own dwelling and place of employment and his name obtained from the local innkeeper who was an invaluable source of information on the business of those who called to take their ale or have their dinner at the White Hart at the corner of High Holborn and Drury Lane. *Subject's name Shadrach Jones, under-master at the school run by Rhys Evans at the Three Nails. Lately arrived from Massachusetts. No other known associates, questionable or otherwise.*

Downing's breath became a little shallower. This was not good. He turned over the next few reports and began to read more carefully through them. Nothing more on Jones, though. He began to search through past reports, knowing something of Ellingworth's past and reputation, trying to make the connection as to why Jones should have lighted on his company. Again, nothing that offered any explanation.

Downing was replacing the papers in their proper order and preparing to tie them up in their file once more, when he realised something. In his search for more information on Shadrach Jones, his eye had lighted on one name much more often than might have been expected. The name was so unexceptional in the circumstances he had hardly registered it at first – it was like seeing one particular grey stone in a wall of stone – but then he understood that the context, the detail in which it appeared, was wrong. He pulled out some of the papers again and looked at them closely, actually read what was written there. Damian Seeker. Damian Seeker had been observed to go into Dove Court alone, on several occasions, mostly at times when Elias Ellingworth was known to be at Clifford's Inn or in Kent's Coffee House. It was noted that Ellingworth's sister was usually at home at those times. Seeker was rarely there for less than an hour, unless Ellingworth was at home, or observed to return home, and then the duration of the visits was a deal shorter.

No name was given for the watcher: it didn't matter. Seeker and Ellingworth's sister: Downing had Seeker now. Not only would the man not best him again, but he could use him. He separated the relevant papers from the file and rolled them up, tied them with a length of thin ribbon set out for such purposes on Thurloe's desk, and sat back, almost content, waiting for Pepys and Bridlington to return.

After a few minutes of silence, he heard footsteps along the corridor, but they weren't Pepys's easy tread, and had more purpose than he had yet observed in Bridlington. More footsteps followed, and he heard the door to Meadowe's office being unlocked, urgent voices calling to one another. More footsteps.

Downing snuffed out the candles he had set about Thurloe's room, then tied up again the remaining papers from Elias Ellingworth's file and set it carefully under his arm, concealed by his cloak. He went through the near-darkness to the door and, listening a moment, opened it carefully before stepping smartly outside and closing it softly behind him. He had not been observed. Meadowe's door at one end of the corridor was open, and in the flickering yellow light of the candles set there, he could see at least three people in the room, with their backs to him.

When Pepys and Bridlington appeared at the end of the corridor, he motioned Pepys towards him but, handing Bridlington the clerks' room keys, shooed him away, telling him in a low voice to return Anne Winter's file, which he'd only just arrived with, to its proper place and then return himself to his own apartments and forget the events of the last hour.

Then, with Pepys in tow, he casually walked to Meadowe's door as if he had just arrived in the department. 'Is something amiss?' he asked.

'What? Oh.' Meadowe appeared to be too distracted by what he was reading to notice anything unusual in George Downing's presence there at such an early hour. Without looking up, he indicated one of his clerks, who held out to Downing a copy of what Meadowe was engaged in reading. 'It was discovered at a printers off St Paul's late last night. Some have already gone out.'

Downing read the title of the pamphlet he had been given. *'A Declaration of the free and well-affected people of England now in arms against the tyrant Oliver Cromwell,'* by John Wildman.

'So,' said Downing, 'he has finally put his head above the parapet again.'

'And will be lucky not to see it blown off,' added Meadowe. 'The people "now in arms against the tyrant Oliver Cromwell". That can only mean there's an armed uprising planned, and that Wildman expects it to be under way by the time this paper is printed. He will have to be brought in as a matter of urgency, and his co-conspirators found.'

'Do we know where he is, sir?' It was Andrew Marvell, who had somehow appeared behind Downing's shoulder without Downing having noticed.

'He's not in London, that's for certain. I have sent for Seeker.'

'You plan to send him out of the town to find Wildman?' asked Downing casually.

'Who else would I send?' replied Meadowe with a hint of irritation.

'Of course. You're right.' Downing appeared to be weighing his words carefully. 'But it occurs to me that the Seeker might be better employed getting firm intelligence from Wildman's known associates in the city – on his where abouts, and the identities of his co-conspirators. It's possible that some trouble might arise in the city from this. There are Levellers and Fifth Monarchists on almost every corner. With Secretary Thurloe still in his sick bed, it might be politic to keep the Seeker close at hand.'

Without attracting attention, Downing managed to place Elias Ellingworth's file on Meadowe's desk, along with the others of Wildman's associates that had been brought there. He stood back from the activity of the Secretariat, as they drew up lists, issued orders. By the time Seeker arrived, helmet under his arm and Daniel Proctor at his side, everything was ready, and George Downing had not had to make one more intervention. He listened as Meadowe informed Seeker and Proctor of the content of Wildman's latest writing, the urgency that he and his co-conspirators should be found and placed under guard and interrogation. And then came the moment Downing had been waiting for.

Meadowe picked up Elias Ellingworth's file. 'There are

parties out already, raiding suspect printers, but I wish you to accompany me to Clifford's Inn and then to Elias Elling-worth's home at Dove Court. We'll search the place for any hint as to Wildman's whereabouts. If we meet with any resistance from Ellingworth or his sister, I'll have you arrest them.'

Meadowe continued, but Downing didn't wait around to listen. He'd had what he'd been waiting for. He'd been watching Seeker. No one else would have noticed, no one who hadn't been looking for it, very carefully. The merest flicker in the eyes, the slight tensing of the fingers, the unmistakable signs that at last someone had found a way to breach the edifice that was Damian Seeker. As he passed out of Meadowe's room, the Under-Secretary still detailing the soldiers' orders, he glanced at Seeker, bestowed on him a small, powerful smile, a smile of great satisfaction, that could leave the man in no doubt that it was he, George Downing, who had done this.

Still trailing a bemused and yawning Pepys at his heels, Downing strode happily away from the centre of Thurloe's empire. He hadn't gained access to the Royalist files he'd come for, and it seemed Shadrach Jones had returned to haunt him but, all in all, it had been a good night's work.

FIFTEEN

Looking for Wildman

For days now, there had been a great deal of activity in the lanes and alleyways around Drury Lane, so popular with Cromwell's soldiers and officers, who knew the City of London did not want them quartered within its ancient gates. They emerged from doorways and side alleys, like beetles or armoured beasts of some sort, such as Shadrach knew were found in the South Seas. This morning, fewer were headed to St Giles's Fields and so to St Martin's Lane and Westminster than had been on the previous five days. This morning, with grumbled talk of 'printers' and 'pamphlets', most seemed to be headed for the city. Shadrach turned his feet instead towards Tyburn.

He hadn't slept all night. He had risen early, checked that Rhys Evans was securely locked in his chamber, the boys in their dormitory, and gone out to walk the streets, and think. He had questioned William Godmanson into the early hours, pressed him as to what he might know of the man who had befriended and then abducted Edward Yuill and, eventually, just as the boy was weary almost to the point of collapse, he had accepted that William knew no more than he had already told to Seeker, had not seen enough of the man to give any better description than that he had already given.

But it was what Seeker's soldiers had told him as they'd marched him from Cornhill to Holborn after he'd been bundled out of Kent's coffee house yesterday evening that worried him most: they had told him of other children that had gone missing, and where they had gone missing from. Things were being connected that Shadrach would prefer not to have connected, links being made that he would rather were not made. He would have to leave the school again today for a few hours, but he would take better care this time that the Seeker did not discover that fact.

Seeker looked at Meadowe as they alighted from the barge at Temple Stairs and began the march up to Clifford's Inn. Thurloe's deputy was nervous, but was making a good show of commanding an authority Seeker knew he did not properly feel.

'This will be your first raid,' he observed, as he marched alongside Meadowe at the head of his troop.

'Aye, it is.' The Under-Secretary nodded, keeping his eyes firmly to the front. 'It used to be Milton, before his sight grew too poor; he relished it, they tell me, the chance to have his revenge on those who had slighted him. Mr Thurloe has done a good few himself, of course, but I have always managed to remain at my desk. Until now.' He gave a grim sort of smile that told Seeker his desk was precisely where he would prefer to be at that moment.

'Walk into the place as if it's yours to dispose of as you will. Have no regard for person. You are the authority of the state, of the Protector, and I am behind you.'

'Then the state will stand, Captain Seeker,' said Meadowe, brightening a little and quickening his pace.

The gatekeeper in his box was still drowsy from his night's sleep, and startled beyond measure to see the sight advancing on him up Temple Lane. It didn't take a second barked order from Seeker for him to come out of his gatehouse and unbolt the door to Clifford's Inn.

Only the servants were out and about at this hour. No grand Lincoln's Inn this, nor Temple, with their lawns and pleasant bordered walks, but a courtyard of dull honey-eyed stone going green with damp, crumbling walls held together in places, it seemed, by climbing ivy and ancient rambling roses. And yet there was something in it Seeker liked – half-hidden alcoves set with stone benches, pots of terracotta where in the summer herbs must grow, a well where water had been drawn for hundreds of years, birds flitting from the rooftops and gutters, as if the human inhabitants of this place were but transitory intruders into their kingdom. In a grudging moment he admitted to himself that it must be a place where one of such obstinate views as Elias Ellingworth could make himself at home.

The porter chattered nervously as he led the party up a spiral brick stairway in the east wing of Clifford's. 'Mr Ellingworth doesn't live here, though. Not any more. He lodges with his sister, I believe, somewhere off Old Jewry Lane. He has only the one room here now, and not much business. Still . . .'

The sound of many booted feet climbing in unison up the stairs brought some curious young lawyers, still in nightshirts or with their hair as yet unkempt, to their doors. The older, with more of an idea of what such a chorus of feet might mean, bolted their doors firmly and remained behind them.

Ellingworth's room was up a third stairway. 'You'll need your torches, there's not much light gets in these rooms,' said the porter, offering his candle to the soldier beside Meadowe to light his torch by.

The door creaked as he pushed it open, and the porter was about to step inside, when Seeker put a restraining hand on his shoulder. 'You can return to your duties now.'

The sight that greeted Seeker as he followed Meadowe into the room was much as he would have expected – a few thin files ranged on a dusty shelf, and everywhere, on table, chair, window ledge and floor, pamphlets. Pamphlets by Wildman, pamphlets by Ellingworth himself under his long-exposed alias of 'the Sparrow', news-books banned by Milton's Censor Office, declarations and defamations penned by known Levellers, Diggers, Fifth Monarchists even – although over those last Ellingworth had scrawled his contempt.

Meadowe scanned the mound of pamphlets and handwritten papers despondently. 'These will all have to be taken to Whitehall. I will need to question the other lawyers and gentleman of these chambers.' He glanced at the door where the rest of Seeker's troop was waiting. 'Can you give me someone?'

Seeker nodded. 'Sergeant Proctor, take two of the men to attend Mr Meadowe. See also that no one tries to leave.'

As his men began stacking the pamphlets in the crates that had been brought for that purpose, Seeker searched through any handwritten documents he could find, hoping to light on some hint as to where Ellingworth's friend John Wildman might be holed up. There was a small stack of accounts to clients; Seeker leafed through them, noting their names, wondering at those foolish or desperate enough to seek representation from one such as Elias Ellingworth. Letter boxes, caskets, any locked receptacle that had been found had been broken open and its contents gone through, and yet Seeker was not satisfied; there must be something in this small, desolate lawyer's chamber that would afford a hint as to the whereabouts of John Wildman, for it was certain Ellingworth knew them.

He examined the plastered walls, the space between window and shutter, the roof beams. Nothing. Then he looked at the table. A well-enough made thing, good English oak with solid pillar legs, and an armchair of similar manufacture with a worn russet upholstered seat, that must once have been fine. Seeker wondered from what height the Ellingworths had fallen, or had they just slipped, generation by generation, to their current plight? His attention was taken by one of his men, reaching for the old, dusty files that lay on the highest shelf, wobbling and cursing as one of the legs on the joint-stool on which he was standing gave way beneath him. His fellow guard, securing the leather ties on the first crate laughed, but Seeker didn't. The leg shouldn't have given way so easily, nor the stool broken as it had done. He stepped past the cursing man on the floor and picked up the stool.

'Mortice and tenon,' he murmured. He could almost have admired Ellingworth. He would never have suspected him capable of something so ingenious.

'Sir?' asked the soldier by the crate.

'The joints. Legs are secured to the seat by means of a tenon joint drilled through and fixed with willow pegs, but you see here, this tenon is far too short, and the willow pegs are just ends, when they should be a good inch and a half long.'

His two men exchanged dumb looks with one another.

'It's for show,' explained Seeker at last. 'This stool is not for standing on or sitting on at all.' He pulled away the remaining legs with ease, holding up the one part of the stool that was left. 'And this is not a seat, but a box.' Walking over to the small window, gauging the weight of the seat in his hand, Seeker held the piece up to the light and began to examine it carefully. He soon found that the bottom panel slid away, to reveal a cavity inside. And inside the cavity, secured by two wooden runners, was a small book, like a child's commonplace book. Seeker eased the book out and glanced only briefly at its plain hide cover, before opening it to the first page. No title, but a date, in handwriting he had come to know well. This was Elias Ellingworth's journal.

'Should we put that in the crate too, Captain?' asked one of the men.

Seeker flicked through the pages, let his eyes run over some of the words. 'No,' he said slowly. 'This should be kept separate. I'll give it to Mr Meadowe myself.' He put it into his leather bag and secured the clasps as his men secured the second of the two crates. 'We're finished here.'

Downstairs, Meadowe had finished questioning the motley assortment of lawyers, students and younger sons of would-be-gentlemen from out of town who made up the inhabitants of Clifford's. They all carried about them an air of either having seen better days, or having risen from humble beginnings and still intending to rise – making do with Clifford's Inn until they should catch the right eye. None of them had been inclined to risk their position by covering up for Elias Ellingworth to the officers of the Council of State.

Meadowe was already putting on his gloves, turning towards the courtyard that would take them back out onto the street. 'Wildman's been in here to Ellingworth's chamber half a dozen times these last two weeks. If anyone knows where he is, it's our lawyer friend. We'll have to snatch this Sparrow from his perch.' The young Secretary had an uncharacteristic spring in his step as they walked out into the brightening morning. 'Come, Seeker. Dove Court, is it not?'

★

Maria was singing. He could hear her as they turned in opposite the Angel and began to ascend the stairway to the Ellingworths' attic room. It was the song he'd sung to her, his voice low and quiet, breathing it almost into her ear, as they'd lain, her head on his bare shoulder, in the early hours of the night; the song he used to hear his mother sing as they travelled through green woods and over the moors of the north. The words weaved their way down the stairway, almost to the rhythm of his men's feet on the stone beneath them: *Though I am a country lass, A lofty mind I bear, I think myself as good as they, That gay apparel wear.*

On the second verse, though, the words faltered, stopped, and all Seeker could hear was what Maria could hear: a troop of the guard of the Council of State, coming to arrest her brother.

They stopped at the top landing, and at a sign from Meadowe, Seeker struck the door three times. 'Open, in the name of the Lord Protector!'

There was only the smallest of delays, and he had raised an arm to knock a second and last time, when he heard the latch go up and the door opened inwards in front of him. She was in her simple brown woollen gown, one of the only two he had ever seen her in. She had not had the time to dress her hair, and it lay loose about her shoulders, as he had seen it a few times before. Elias was seated at the table, one boot on, the other only half-buttoned, a packed saddlebag at his feet. Facing Seeker, Maria's eyes took in the situation in a moment, and the brief glint of hope he had seen in them vanished almost instantly.

He didn't afford her any preliminaries. 'Step aside, Mistress Ellingworth; our business is with your brother.'

'Then take it to Clifford's Inn, and he will attend you there, when he has had his breakfast.'

It was Philip Meadowe who replied to her, his voice clear and full of authority. 'Oh, we've already been to Clifford's Inn, mistress. Now step aside, before I have the captain arrest you.'

It didn't take long: the attic in Dove Court gave up nothing but Ellingworth's own latest scribbled pages and the lawyer himself, clearly partway through making preparations for a journey – the saddlebag revealing a clean shirt, half a loaf of bread, a lump of hard cheese and a cold leg of boiled fowl, the rest of whose carcass remained on a board on the table, and a purse filled with as much coin as Seeker thought Elias Ellingworth must possess.

Meadowe fingered the goods with distaste. 'Where can you be going to, in such haste and at so early an hour, Mr Ellingworth?'

'I am going to my chambers.'

Seeker snorted. 'With the contents of your larder and every penny you own?' He leaned closer to Elias, ignoring the glare from Maria's eyes. 'You're going to warn Wildman, aren't you?'

The denial was hardly out of Elias's mouth when Daniel Proctor appeared at the top of the stairs. 'Someone beat us to it. Old fellow on the ground floor says there was someone here not twenty minutes since, banging on the door and shouting about the raid at Clifford's.'

'Where's Wildman?' said Seeker.

Elias smiled. 'Out of your reach, Seeker, that's for sure.'

Seeker's patience deserted him. He turned to Proctor. 'Cuff him. Take him to Newgate. Get Colonel Barkstead to send someone from the Tower, if he hasn't told you where Wildman is by the time you get there.'

'No!' shouted Maria, stepping in front of her still seated, benignly smiling brother.

'But yes,' interjected Meadowe. 'And if you continue to impede the Protectorate guard you'll find yourself in the Bridewell.'

By the time Elias was being marched down the stairs, Seeker's guard had finished gathering up his papers and emptying out the chest that contained almost everything the Ellingworths owned that wasn't already out on display and in use. The bells of St Mary-le-Bow rang out for eight o'clock.

'I am to report to Mr Thurloe at eight thirty. I had better get on my way,' said Meadowe, checking his own pocket watch. 'Continue with the raids, and bring me any intelligence you have on Wildman's whereabouts the minute you have it, Seeker.'

Meadowe left, and Seeker sent his remaining men to wait at the bottom of the stairs. In the sudden emptiness of the desolate attic, he could hear Maria's shallow breathing.

'You could have stopped this,' she said, dully.

'No,' he said, stooping to right a chair that had been knocked over by one of his men as they'd dragged Elias away. 'I could not.'

'You could have warned us sooner.'

He spun around, truly angry. 'No, Maria, I couldn't. What do you believe I am? Why do you believe I do this, day in, day out? For entertainment? Because there is nothing else? The world you and your brother think can exist cannot. Man is not capable of the liberty you so loudly demand for him. You think all men to be like your brother? Have you *been* out in the world, Maria? Seen what the world can be? The brute will always rise to the surface without a greater power to curb it.'

'And you would be that power?'

'I would be its arm, I know that I *can* be.'

The anger went from her eyes to leave something more desolate.

'And what about what I know that you can be?'

He surveyed the wreck of the room, the upturned chest, the floor strewn with clothing and bedding, the blue-painted ginger jar of which he had known her to be so fond that had got knocked and broken by the careless swing of a soldier's arm. He felt lead in his stomach. When he spoke, he couldn't look at her.

'I should never have shown you.'

He turned and began to walk down the stairs to where his men waited on the street. He was only halfway down when he heard her begin to sing again, quiet, almost tuneless, the song his troop had interrupted only half an hour before: 'A garland of the fairest flowers shall shield me from the sun.'

'Should we put a watch on the place, Captain?' asked one of his men as he emerged at the bottom.

Seeker looked back up the stairs. 'No. There's nothing more for us here.'

In Kent's Coffee House, Grace was reading through once more the note that had come just as her Uncle Samuel had been closing up the night before. She looked at Gabriel and shook her head. 'You will not do.'

The boy bristled. 'Lady Anne would not have asked for me if she did not think I would do. She says I make the best coffee to be had in London, save for Samuel himself.'

'And so you do, but she would have you serve it too, to her guests in her parlour.'

Gabriel drew in a breath of outrage. 'As I do here, from morning to night, and never a complaint to be had!'

Grace smiled. 'But, Gabriel, our poor coffee room is not the parlour of Lady Anne Winter; even the grandest of our customers has not consorted with the King, as have the guests Lady Anne has invited for tomorrow.'

The boy's chin was up. 'I should think not, not after what that lot did, and to Samuel's leg, too. I'll not bow and scrape to any Royalist. And our Mr Tavener is rarely away from Whitehall, to advise with the Lord Protector himself!'

'That's true. Gabriel, I love you for your loyalty, but if you should go to Lady Anne's today to this coffee party she has planned, bow and scrape is precisely what you will have to do.'

Gabriel looked a little abashed. 'But I will not mean it.'

'I know that. But goodness, child, it is your clothes! We will have to borrow you a suit from one of Mr Tavener's clerks.'

Samuel had made his way over to them from stoking the fire under the first cauldron of the day.

'Boy looks all right to me,' he mumbled. 'Besides, we cannot let him get too close with those people. I like the lady, and I'll tell it to anyone, but a Royalist's a Royalist and such a face to plot on a woman I've rarely seen.'

Grace left on her errand of borrowing the clothes and Samuel was whistling to himself, an old marching tune, when the street door opened. He looked up, ready to tell whoever it was that they would not be ready to serve for an hour yet, but then he stopped. At the top of the stairs stood a woman he hadn't seen in over ten years, but whom he would never mistake.

Samuel stood up as straight as his ruined leg would allow him. 'Dorcas.'

She smiled and started to walk down the steps into the coffee room. 'You remember me then?'

'How could I not? That red hair and those green eyes to break a man's heart. Half of Fairfax's army was in love with you, Dorcas Wells.'

'Hmm. In love with the sound of their own voices, if I remember right,' she said. 'But not you, Samuel.'

'Ah, me, I was too old for love even then, and a soldier for soldiering's sake, though I'd go to war now if General Fairfax were to ask me.'

'I wouldn't say that too loud in these days, Samuel.'

'Where's the harm? The general's taken himself back up to Yorkshire, tends his gardens, reads his books. Not interested in all the power, like Old Nol.'

'That may be, but there's plenty would like Fairfax to come back, plenty in the army are none too pleased with our Lord Protector Cromwell.'

'I didn't think to hear such talk from you, Dorcas.'

'Nor will you. I'm just saying what I hear in my place, the Black Fox, around the streets. You must hear the same.'

Samuel grunted. 'There's that much talk and noise in here I stopped listening long since. But, here, where are my manners? You take yourself a seat there and I'll get the boy to fetch you some chocolate, or will you take a dish of coffee?'

'I've not come for that, Samuel.'

'Aye, but you shall have something anyway. I'll wager whatever's brought you to my door at this hour of the morning will take more than a minute's telling.'

Dorcas relented, and sat down on the chair he'd insisted on pulling out from behind the counter, while he roared at Gabriel to look to his work while he still had it.

'So, tell me,' he said at last, as he settled himself across from her.

Dorcas took a deep breath. 'When you were in the army, Samuel, did you ever know a man named Carter Blyth?'

'Carter Blyth? Can't say I did. Which regiment was he in?'

'Manchester's Infantry, under Crawford.'

'Ah.' He nodded. 'We were with them at Marston, but

there wasn't much time for making acquaintance that day and I never knew any Carter Blyth.'

Samuel saw the disappointment in Dorcas's eyes. 'What's this Carter Blyth to you then, my dear?'

She looked away. 'He did me a wrong once, him and others.' Then, catching the look on Samuel's face she said, 'No, not like that, never laid a finger on me, nothing of that sort, but he did me a wrong all the same, and he knew it. I saw it in his face then and I saw it in his face again the day six weeks ago he walked into the Black Fox. But he wasn't calling himself Carter Blyth then, he was calling himself Gideon Fell.'

Something, a recognition of the name from somewhere, stirred in Samuel and Dorcas Wells saw it.

'You know him?' she said eagerly.

Samuel shook his head. 'No. But I heard that name somewhere before, I'm certain of it. I can ask around, though, discreet like, see if anyone knows where he's to be found.'

Dorcas's voice was bitter. 'Oh, he's been found already, but too late.'

'I don't understand,' said Samuel, very much trying to.

'He's dead.'

'How can you know that?'

'Damian Seeker told me.'

'The Seeker? But . . .' Samuel looked pained. 'This is too deep for me.'

'He knew Carter Blyth had been to the Black Fox, but called him by his other name, Gideon Fell. I told him I didn't know him, Samuel – got my own reasons for that and better not to ask, the way things are in these days – but I did. Carter Blyth thought he could help me, right the wrong of those years past, said he might have discovered something but wasn't yet sure. Now someone has murdered him, and I only have one chance to find out what it is he thought he knew.'

Samuel, seeing her desperation, said, 'And what is that chance, my dear?'

'A boy. A simple boy he had with him. Well, a man, perhaps, by the height and size of him, but he had the face of a boy, and the manner too. Kindly, simple. He wore an apprentice's cap. Someone said they thought they had seen him about Aldgate sometimes, but there aren't many I can ask, Samuel, not many I can trust not to ask me too many questions in return, frighten him off if they know him.'

Samuel nodded, confirming something to himself. 'I think I know such a lad. I think he has been in here.'

She leaned forward, her eyes alight, grabbed his hand. 'Samuel!'

'Ah, but wait, my dear, wait, and I shall see if I can tell you more. Gabriel!' he called to the coffee house boy.

'Yes, Samuel,' said Gabriel, coming quickly over, losing no time in his curiosity to know what this strange early morning visit might be about.

'That lad the Seeker had in here the other night, the one he took to talk to in the private booth there . . .'

'Nathaniel?' ventured Gabriel.

'Aye, that was the boy's name, Nathaniel. What do you know of him?'

'He's a weaver, lives up at Gethsemane with the Fifth Monarchists. But a bit soft – no harm in him and the boys on the street all like him. Mother's a witch.'

'Gabriel!'

'Well, she's one of them preacher-women. Shrivel your heart just listening to her. Funny thing, though, that big dog that used to run after Maria all the time trails everywhere after him now. They're always out and about together, on the streets or out on the earthworks beyond Houndsditch, I hear, and the dog won't let no one near Nathaniel.'

Samuel might have ventured some views he was forming on the ownership of the dog, but Dorcas Wells was already standing up, retying the ribbon on her green velvet cloak, picking up her embroidered suede gloves.

'You're not going up to Gethsemane now, are you, Dorcas? Those Fifth Monarchists are a fierce lot, and your lovely hair alone'll be enough to set them off. Best speak to the Seeker again.'

'No, I don't want the Seeker to know. Don't you worry about me, Samuel. There's nothing they can do to me. I'll find the boy when he's by himself somewhere, just him and his dog.'

When she'd gone, Samuel was lost in his thoughts awhile, and Gabriel tidied up quietly behind him. When Samuel finally leaned on his stick and heaved himself up again, Gabriel asked, 'Who was that, Samuel?'

'That? That was a beautiful woman. Followed her husband to the wars, stayed on after she was widowed.'

'A camp follower, then? I thought they'd be different.'

'Dorcas is different,' Samuel said. 'Mind you,' he added, shuffling off to fetch a roasting pan, 'they're all different, but a woman must eat, and there was little enough to go round in them days.'

But Gabriel wasn't finished. 'It's just – I think I saw her before somewhere.'

'Up Bishopsgate, the Black Fox, that's her place,' said Samuel, without turning around.

'No, it wasn't there.'

The coffee house door opened again, and talk and thoughts of Dorcas were soon forgotten in the measuring against Gabriel of a suit of clothes newly borrowed from one of George Tavener's clerks.

SIXTEEN

The Good Woman of Gethsemane

Elizabeth Crowe felt the fear creep over her like a wave come to shore. It was the worst of times, the very worst of times, for this to have happened. Patience must know she could not leave Gethsemane at a time like this: the moment they had waited upon so long was almost arrived. Messengers had come from the localities – the Midlands, Lincolnshire, Staffordshire; from Nathaniel Rich's regiment in East Anglia and from Vavasor Powell's people in Wales. All was ready and they waited only on the word from Gethsemane that London had risen for the Lord.

But where was Patience? Where in this godless city had she spent the hours of darkness, seen the dawn? Goodwill had no comfort to offer Elizabeth, had rebuked her: the people needed to hear her, to be comforted, fired by the word the Lord had given her. It was not a time to consider the concerns of flesh and blood – when had family been anything to Elizabeth? He had held up to her those words of Christ: 'He that loveth mother or father more than me is not worthy of me: and he that loveth son or daughter more than me is not worthy of me.' Had she not often said it to him? Chastised him for his softness towards his child, that idiot child, a judgement from the Lord? But Patience was different. Patience had a work to do for the Lord, and Patience was *hers*.

She dismissed Goodwill's rebuke and tied on her cloak, to go out into town. No one else would challenge her, and she would be back in time. Her face was set, and few thought to importune Elizabeth Crowe as she went briskly from Aldgate through Cornhill and Cheapside towards St Paul's, and then down Creed Lane. On the streets, one or two faces she knew from her preachings dipped their heads reverently as she passed; she accorded them a brief nod, her mouth a line, discouraging further greeting or attempt at conversation.

Passing the bottom of Old Jewry, she had stepped into a doorway as she had seen Damian Seeker emerge from an alleyway onto the street. Dove Court was there. She remembered a tale Patience had told her, a few days since. She had slapped her daughter there and then, for bringing home a lie, but Patience had sworn it was no lie, no gossip, but the truth: the Seeker, and the lawyer Ellingworth's sister. Patience knew things, she was told things now, that might be of great use to them, and so Elizabeth had believed her at last. Elizabeth had wondered how she might make use of the information, but the look on Seeker's face was one of thunder, not of a man coming from a lovers' tryst.

There were many other soldiers on the streets too, and Elizabeth became careful, looking behind her often to see that she was not watched or followed. By the time she reached Blackfriars Lane, the mass of Bridewell looming closer and closer, Elizabeth became conscious of the thumping of her own heart. Anger at Patience's disappearance had long since turned to fear. Perhaps it had begun as fear. Patience was slipping beyond her control, and Elizabeth didn't know quite when it had started to happen. What had begun with them as a work for the Lord had become something else, and Elizabeth had less and less of a grasp on what that something else was. She should not have trusted her daughter so far, she should have reasserted her control, but she hadn't, and now Patience was missing. The fear of it weighed heavy at the pit of her stomach, and Elizabeth couldn't remember the last time she had felt fear.

The word had not been long in finding its way onto the streets from Kent's coffee house to the gates of Gethsemane: children had been taken from their homes, their place of service, and never seen again. Damian Seeker, they said, was looking for them, but however great her fears, Elizabeth would not ask Seeker to find *her* daughter. As she got deeper into the damp tangle of lanes and the maze of old buildings, her lips began to move in imprecation, her eyes scarcely flickering, her voice low and doom-laden, as if she were threatening God himself.

By the time the bells of Bridewell across the Fleet tolled a mournful nine, Elizabeth Crowe understood that God was no longer listening to her. She had come to the right place, but she had come too late. The rag in her hand, the linen torn from a headdress that she herself had watched her daughter sew, told her all she needed to know. She had warned Patience, but Patience had not heeded her. So be it. Elizabeth dropped the piece of torn linen back onto the dirt in which she had found it and began to make her way back to Gethsemane.

Nathaniel had been out early, running the dog at Hounds-ditch, keeping out of the way. 'Stay out of the way'; 'Get out of my way'; 'Keep out of my way'. He'd heard it all a dozen times before breakfast. Many who had passed through Gethsemane these last few months had returned; the alms-houses were full, and Nathaniel knew these men were here for more than prayer. Major Harrison had addressed them last night, late, and Elizabeth had prayed long over them, until Nathaniel could see one or two of them weary and swaying on their feet. Nathaniel didn't know how anyone could think of sleeping when his mother spoke, such had been the relish with which she detailed the torments prom-ised in the Book of Revelation. Nathaniel had not slept all night for visions of two hundred thousand lion-headed horses issuing from the bottomless pit to breathe fire and smoke and brimstone on those not marked with the seal of God. He had been glad when the hour had come at last to rise from the cold bed of his lonely cell.

As he and the hound came back through the entranceway into the courtyard of Gethsemane, he couldn't see his mother anywhere. Usually, Gethsemane was a happier place for Nathaniel when Elizabeth was gone from it, but not today; her absence from their breakfast table had made his father angry, and Goodwill had been angry already, because of Patience.

No one had seen Patience since before supper last night, no one but Nathaniel. The light had been fading into a final greyness before the dark. Nathaniel had been watching a strange stone, but when Patience had stepped almost silently from the wool store, the stone had fled: a rat.

The movement had caught her eye, and she'd noticed Nathaniel and the dog. She hesitated a moment before turning and walking towards them. She bent down low, to reach him where he was sitting on the ground. The dog snarled, but Patience was not frightened. She brought her face very close to Nathaniel and said, her teeth almost gritted, 'If you tell anyone where I am going, I will poison your dog.'

'But, I don't kn-know where you're going, Patience,' he had said.

'One word that you have even seen me, and I will mete to it a slow death of the greatest agony. You know that is no empty threat.'

Nathaniel nodded. He knew very well. He had seen her once, slowly wringing the neck of a sparrow, for no other reason than that he had taken pleasure in watching it hop about. Another time she had trapped a butterfly, held the terrified creature out towards him, and as he'd reached out to take it, laughed before grinding its beautiful wings to mush between her fingers. But what Patience didn't know was that there had been no need to threaten him: he would never tell where he had seen her go, or who he had seen her on the streets with. Even this morning, with his mother frantic, his father angry, and the old prophetess declaiming on the fate of Jezebel, Nathaniel had not told. He didn't lie, but they hadn't asked him the right questions. The truth was, he didn't know where his sister was, and no, she had not told him where she was going. She hadn't had any bundle with her that might have food or clothes in it, she hadn't looked like someone leaving without any thought to return. They asked him nothing else. Which was as well, for Nathaniel didn't care if Patience was never found at all.

Dorcas Wells had left the instructions for the morning with her cook. She had no worries there; she'd seen Will Tucker feed half a regiment on sheep's innards and a chicken carcass, and a man that could stab a Royalist scout through the eye without giving off the stirring of his pot was not likely to let a kitchen boy slip out of his sight long enough to fall into whatever danger had befallen Isabella, not now that they knew to be watchful.

It would be no small thing for Dorcas to walk into Gethsemane. She knew their sort, those Fifth Monarchists. They'd thought they would have it all their way, once the Royalists had been defeated and the king gone. God's Kingdom here on earth. She knew about the workings of God's Kingdom, the Law of Moses, on earth. Hell, more like, Hell for anyone that wished a life worthy of the name. They hadn't reckoned on Old Nol taking a liking to power, though. Good for him – Dorcas wouldn't have a word against him in the Black Fox. As long as he was there, Lord Protector of whatever he willed, the world would be properly settled; Dorcas's life would be properly settled. She knew the rules and she kept to them, and Damian Seeker and his crew made sure everyone else did too, and the likes of her, and Samuel with his coffee shop, and the young men that ran up and down the road to Gresham and talked of understanding the workings of the world, could just get on with their lives and leave God to others. Dorcas wasn't afraid of much, but the sight of that almshouse gateway filled her with terror. She remembered what her husband used to say to her whenever she'd been frightened. 'What's the worst that can happen?' Dorcas knew now, because the worst that could happen had happened long ago; whatever awaited her through that archway could not come close to it.

Dorcas steeled herself, straightened her shoulders, and went through the gates, but the sight that greeted her was something much different from what she'd expected. No prayer meeting, fervent psalm-singing, not even the thump and rattle of the shuttle across the loom in this place of weavers, but a muster, a muster of armed men, and Thomas Harrison, the most fervent of the Fifth Monarchy men, leading them. Dorcas knew enough to know that no such muster should be taking place in the almshouse courtyard of a group of weavers in the city of London. They were marching on their commander's words, wheeling, fixing bayonets, their backs to her. The certainty, the cold venom in Harrison's voice as he barked out his instructions, sent a chill through her, as did what she could see through the opened door of one of the almshouses: a stockpile of arms, hundreds of them. Dorcas knew her guns from her days following the army. She wasn't close enough to tell exactly what they were – English- or German-made, both probably – but she could see enough to know there were matchlocks, flint-locks, muskets and pistols. The men drilling in the yard were already wearing powder belts, but at Gethsemane was an arsenal for a far greater number of men. Closer to where she stood, beneath the canvas that had been partially lifted from a cart in the corner, she could see things that made her stomach lurch for the memory of what she had seen such do: cavalry swords, quillon daggers, old pikes, crossbows, axes and maces that could rip out a man's innards, pierce his skull or gouge out his brains.

Dorcas was not a fool: today was not the day to do what she'd come for. She stepped quickly backwards into the shadows of the archway, but not before she knew she had caught the eye of the boy, the big, soft boy Carter Blyth had had with him at the Black Fox, and who was standing, with a huge dog by his side, watching not the infantrymen, but her. And he wasn't watching, he was staring. Without knowing why she did it, Dorcas put a finger to her lips and shook her head. The boy inclined his head, as if he under-stood, and Dorcas slipped back out of Gethsemane, unseen by any but Nathaniel.

Out on the street, she thought quickly. What she had just seen was no simple training exercise, but preparation for insurrection, and one that was imminent, by the look of it. But who to tell? The watches of the city wards, the Trained Bands, how could she be certain they wouldn't be among the insurrectionists? Who was to be trusted? Dorcas hurried along Hart Street and up Mark Lane until she came, breathless, to Fenchurch Street. She hailed a passing carter bringing coals from the docks at Wapping to Cheapside, and pulled herself up to sit beside him, careless of the black dust. 'Leave me at the top of Birchin Lane,' she said. It had been the same everywhere, since Dorcas had been thirteen years old: if she asked a man to do something, he would do it, apart from that one time, ten years ago, and Carter Blyth was dead now, anyway. The carter cracked his whip and his pair of horses took up a fine pace through the throng of traffic and people on Cornhill, stopping, in what seemed like no time at all, outside the door of Kent's.

Dorcas was down and through the coffee house door in a moment. The girl behind the counter stepped out and came towards her.

Dorcas looked around her, distracted. 'Where is Samuel?'

'My uncle is at the market on Grasschurch Street. What's wrong?'

'I need to get a message to Damian Seeker, and quickly. I need a swift messenger who can be trusted.'

The skinny boy of about thirteen who'd served Dorcas chocolate the last time she'd been at Kent's emerged from behind the storeroom door. 'I'll find the captain, and you can trust me, Mistress Wells, for he does himself.'

Grace was hesitant. 'You know he said we should not let you out in the streets alone.'

'But I can run like the wind,' pleaded the boy, 'you know it – there's not a single boy in the city runs faster than me, not from Aldgate to Farringdon and all in between, not one. No one will catch me.'

Grace looked to Dorcas Wells. 'Is it really so important?'

Dorcas nodded.

'Fetch pen and ink, Gabriel, and we will write this message down.'

'No,' Dorcas shook her head. 'You must tell him: at Gethsemane, on Aldgate, Thomas Harrison is drilling sixty men and has arms for two hundred more.'

She didn't need to say it twice: Grace knew who and what Harrison was, and so did Gabriel. He had his apron off and Samuel's old buff coat and his cap on in seconds.

'Lose no time,' said Grace, 'and make sure you give your message *only* to Captain Seeker, or one of his men.'

Gabriel nodded, almost bursting with the importance of his mission, and was gone before Grace could tell him to tie up his coat.

Since coming away from Dove Court, they had carried out raids on two printers and another pamphleteer known to consort with the radical Wildman, but neither the brutal efficiency with which their work had been carried out nor the ease which the terrified printers had given up all they knew had been enough to assuage Seeker's mood. He had almost broken his fist smashing through the door of the second printer's shop before his men could ram it, and still it had not helped. After what had passed at Dove Court, he could barely contain his rage. 'Should I ask to be allowed into Ellingworth's prison cell,' he had said to Daniel Proctor, 'don't let me. I would kill him.'

It was when they'd just finished smashing the presses of a known Fifth Monarchist printer off Ave Maria Lane that the ragamuffin coffee boy from Kent's on Birchin Lane had come careering through the crowd of awestruck bystanders to declare that he had an urgent message for the Seeker. One of the guards had tried to stop the boy, but Seeker had ordered him to let him pass. A minute later and a messenger had been sent on horseback, at full speed to Whitehall, to order reinforcements to Gethsemane. The set of Seeker's face as they turned and made for Aldgate told all in his path that there would be no compromises.

They could hear the sounds of Harrison's drill before they even reached the end of Hart Street. Their way was clearer than expected because word had begun to seep onto the streets about what was on hand at Gethsemane, and those with no wish to die that day or end it in one of the Protectorate gaols had left off their lawful business and usual social congress and retreated to their homes. In a very little time, Seeker and his leading men had rounded the head of Woodruffe Lane and were drawn up before the gates of Gethsemane. Seeker raised a hand to bring his men to a halt behind him, and signalling to the other three mounted men of his guard, passed below the archway into the court.

Harrison's men had just begun a musket drill. Seeker remembered how when first he had joined Parliament's army he had practised it and practised it, all twenty movements, until he could have performed it in his sleep. Some of the other men had laughed, for a while. And then there had been the first battle, the carnage at Marston Moor: none of them had ever laughed at Seeker again. And long after he had been assigned to the cavalry, Seeker could have gone through that drill as well as any sergeant on the field. Not like these men before Harrison – those at the back knew what they were doing, but Seeker could see that already the front three rows were out of time. Their timing disintegrated altogether when they noticed the four mounted guards of the Council of State come to a halt beneath the archway of Gethsemane. Harrison was standing at their head, with his back to the entranceway. His tirade of reprimands was brought to an end by a signal to the major-general from one of his men.

Slowly, Harrison turned. His eyes didn't rest on Seeker, or Proctor, or the other two mounted guards, but on the phalanx of men who had come to a halt behind them, beyond the archway and out in the street beyond. Harrison was counting: Seeker could see it in his eyes.

Evidently still weighing the odds, Harrison turned his attention to Seeker.

'You have come to join us at last, Captain?'

'Join you?' responded Seeker levelly, the drawn-out York-shire inflection registering his disgust. 'No, we're not here to join you. We're the four horsemen of the Apocalypse.'

Harrison's accustomed sneer left him and his face hard-ened. 'For the great day of His wrath is come.'

'Aye, it has.' Seeker moved Acheron forward a few paces, as did the other three mounted officers, allowing their men to move around them and begin encircling the Fifth Mon-archist troops in the centre. 'Tell your men to drop their weapons.'

Harrison shook his head. 'Not today. The day of His wrath *is* come.' Then he raised his arm and gave the com-mand to fight.

It was chaos. Seeker's men had only got two thirds of the way round the yard and those of Harrison's men not yet encircled quickly ran through the gap, some managing to get hold of pikes or axes from the weapons cache on the cart, before launching themselves at the Protectorate troops from behind. Those Fifth Monarchists left in the middle attempted to fix bayonets without stabbing their own comrades, or threw down their muskets and rests in favour of swords, daggers or fists. Beside Seeker, Daniel Proctor swung off his horse and plunged into the fray where one of their men was being set upon by three of Harrison's. The other two mounted guards similarly dismounted, but Seeker kept his seat while Acheron, as well accustomed to the din and vio-lence of battle as his master, stood firm beneath him.

Through the clamour, Seeker could hear the increasingly determined barking of the hound, and was glad that Nathaniel had had the sense not to let the beast out. But his focus was on Harrison. His eyes had never left him from the moment the major-general had risen his arm in command to his men to fight, and from his elevated position, Seeker traced the man's movements as he too attempted to reach the weapons cart. There was no sign of armour, other than helmets worn by a few of the men, amongst the Fifth Monarchists, and Harrison's emerald coat and scarlet breeches, his hat embellished with white ostrich feather, marked him out as clearly from his dun and buff-attired troops as if he had been emitting tongues of fire. Even when he looked to have disappeared behind a knot of fighting men, a flash of red or green, a blaze of white feather, would pinpoint him exactly. Seeker held Acheron's rein very light, ready for the moment to dismount. But when Harrison at last reached the weapons cart, Seeker instantly saw it was not to avail himself of pike, axe or halberd, but to raise himself to an elevation almost equal to that of himself. With great agility, Harrison swung himself atop the cart and found his place and balance. His hand was immediately at the leather belt at his waist and the flintlock pistol that hung there. Seeker carried no such weapon out on the streets of London, but in the time it took Harrison to unhook gun, ready the cock and begin to raise his arm, finger on trigger, over the seething clashing crowd to point the weapon directly at him, Seeker's arm had found the horseman's hammer that habitually hung at his saddle. Hefting the weapon in his hand, he swung it up and hurled it with all the precision three decades of hunting in the woods and moors and ten years of killing in the name of Parliament and Republic had taught him. The world around seemed to slow as Harrison continued to raise his pistol, his finger beginning to squeeze on the trigger, while Seeker's hammer, steel pick on one side, four-sided head on the other, spun inexorably through the air to find the firing arm of the major-general. As the spike of the pick ripped through emerald velvet to tear into the muscle of Harrison's upper arm, his hand dropped the pistol and he staggered backwards to topple from the side of the wagon.

Seeker was already on the ground and running, driving his way past knots of writhing arms, legs and steel, pushing aside whatever human obstacle staggered into his path, regardless of whether it was one of the men of Gethsemane or his own lobster-helmeted, steel breastplated soldiers. As he was buffeted by the careering backs, arms and heads of the combatants and his senses assailed by the smells and taste of a rising mix of male sweat, blood and heat, Seeker could feel the exhilaration of his men as they got hand to hand, knife to knife with men who, unlike the printers, lawyers and newsmen they habitually rounded up, fought back.

The clash of steel and clatter of wood as anything that might serve as a weapon was brought to bear on an opponent was drowning out the sound of the dog now, the crying of children, the habitual noise of the world outside

Gethsemane, and had rendered it instead the courtyard of some Royalist stronghold or walled Irish town. As he jettisoned a final barrel standing between himself and the cart Harrison had fallen from, the thought flashed through Seeker's mind that Cromwell would have relished this.

It was simpler to reach Harrison by the underside of the cart than by clambering over it, and so Seeker dropped to his belly and scrambled the last few yards to where the stricken figure in dark-stained emerald and scarlet was struggling to get himself to his feet. Harrison had begun to pull himself up by the uninjured arm, but blood loss was causing his knees to buckle under him. Seeker stretched out his hand and pulled the man's ankle from beneath him, bringing him crashing once more to the dirt. As Seeker dragged himself out from beneath the cart, Harrison turned a dirty and bloodied face towards him. His lip was cut and grit and dirt from the ground had stuck to the blood smeared from mouth to ear. He tried to push himself up once more on his good arm. But Seeker was by this time standing astride him and instead pulled him up by the hair, the long, luscious locks of which this most puritanical of Republicans was so proud. He turned the man round to face him.

'I told you to tell your men to drop their weapons,' said Seeker.

Somehow, with a mouth full of blood and dirt, Harrison managed to engineer a spit.

Still holding his captive by his right hand, Seeker pulled back the fist of his left arm and smashed it into the side of

Harrison's face. The man slumped once more to his knees like a half-filled sack. Seeker dragged him onto the cart, stood up on it himself and picked Harrison up as if the man were a scarecrow he was about to mount on a pole. 'Drop your arms,' he bellowed. 'It's over.'

It was some time before the realisation spread through the seething mass in the courtyard that the Fifth Monarchist leader was beaten, and even then some of his men fought on, but however much they might call God to witness their struggle against the forces of the wicked, their weapons and lack of armour were no match for what the elite of Cromwell's guard had to offer them and eventually Gethsemane was more like a cattle market than a battle scene. With an efficiency pleasing to their captain, Seeker's men soon had the last of the Fifth Monarchists rounded up, tied in irons or put on makeshift stretchers, to be shuffled up to the Tower, or trundled there on carts like so much meat. Broken and bloodied weapons, some helmets of varying manufacture and origin, and scraps of torn clothing littered the dirt and cobbles of the courtyard. For minutes after the last of the struggles stopped, the pigs in their pen had shrieked as if on their way to Smithfield, and there was not a hen left anywhere.

Women and children had been few and far between out in the yard when the Protectorate troops had arrived, and had swiftly barred themselves behind the doors of their almshouse cottages. Slowly, bolts were pulled back, and they began to emerge once more, Elizabeth Crowe at their head. 'What have you done?' she demanded of Seeker, in a voice loaded with hatred.

'God's work,' he said, throwing the words at her over his shoulder as he strode to the caged cart in which Harrison had been placed. Harrison was Seeker's particular responsibility – no Tower for him, yet, but one last interview with the Protector, one last plea from the man he had served so closely and for so long, that he should come back into the fold, or at least pledge to live peaceably and not disturb the Commonwealth. Seeker didn't think the chances of success in that very high, but he was not required to think in this matter, just to do as he was bid, and transport his prisoner, his so highly ranked prisoner, back down the river to Whitehall.

'You think this is all we have, Seeker?' Harrison had managed to drawl as he was bundled into the cart that would take him down to Custom House quay. 'You think we have nothing but our swords and the strength of our arms? That this is all we do to prepare for the coming of the Lord?'

'Tell it to the Lord Protector,' Seeker said, as he slammed shut the cage door and signalled for a guard to padlock it.

'Oh, I will,' said Harrison, 'and more.' He nodded then to Elizabeth Crowe, who was still standing at the front of the community's group of women, guarded on all sides by armed men of Seeker's troop. A smile more chilling than anything Seeker had seen on the battlefield was around her mouth. She started to move her lips in response to Harrison. 'Mene,

Mene, Tekel Upharsin.' The words were taken up in a chant by the rest of the women.

Some of the soldiers started to look a little nervous; Proctor looked to Seeker. 'What are they saying?'

Seeker's voice evinced contempt. They were the words Thurloe had told him were daubed on the walls outside the Banqueting Hall on the night the attempt had been made on Oliver's life after 'Belshazzar's Feast'. 'Nothing Oliver hasn't heard before,' he said to Proctor. ' "God hath numbered thy kingdom and finished it; thou art weighed in the balances and found wanting." And so it goes on. Let him take that to Oliver and see what response he gets.'

'And what about the women?'

Seeker looked up from wiping Harrison's blood from the pick end of his hammer. 'Take them to Bridewell, and put out a search for the daughter, Patience Crowe. Put her in the Fleet prison when you find her.'

'I want my daughter with me,' spat Elizabeth.

'She'll be with you on Tyburn Hill,' said Seeker. He'd clearly given as much time as he planned to Elizabeth Crowe. Turning to Proctor he said, 'Gag her, she's spread enough of her foul pestilence around these streets already. She'll have more than enough occasion to talk when the interrogation committee get to her.'

'What should be done with the crone?' asked Proctor, indicating the open door to the small room from where the prophetess, visibly weakened and in her sickbed, watched them with red-rimmed eyes and loathing on her face. She spotted her moment, and called out in a surprisingly strong, grating voice, 'Remember, Major, tell Cromwell the Lord has spoken: Daniel eleven, thirty-two.'

In as far as he could, Harrison inclined his head towards her, before looking at Seeker and encompassing all Gethsemane with his words: 'Such as do wickedly against the covenant shall be corrupt by flatteries: but the people that do know their God shall be strong and do exploits.'

Seeker looked past Harrison to the old woman watching him malevolently from her bed. He addressed his remarks to Proctor, but never once took his eyes from the woman.

'Exploits. For me, I would throw the old witch in the Thames and be done with it, but the Lord Protector is over-merciful. The streets are polluted enough without we carry her through them. Leave one of the older girls here to tend to her.'

Proctor selected a child of about twelve, with resentful eyes set in what might have been a pretty face. 'You see to her, and if you step one foot out of this door without permission, he will run you through.' He was pointing at a bored-looking guard whose lack of relish at being selected to stand sentry in this place was written on his face.

The last thing Seeker had said to his men before they had entered Gethsemane that day had been to leave the boy Nathaniel Crowe be, and so they had. Goodwill Crowe's son, the dog still at his side, had watched the unfolding of events from the window of the small cell he had shared with the man he had known as Gideon Fell. He had been there, watching his father drill with the other men, when the government troops had arrived, and only now did he slowly emerge from his doorway. His face was ashen, and he did not look at Seeker, hardly seemed to be aware of him, as he slowly walked towards the cart onto which his father had just been loaded. It had been Daniel Proctor who had taken Goodwill down, bested him at last. Seeker's sergeant was as dishevelled as any still standing in the courtyard, the sleeve of his coat ripped and his nose bloodied and swollen, but there was a light in his eye, the light of a good fight, that Seeker had not seen there in some time. When Nathaniel reached the cart he stretched out his hand towards his father, whose wrists were shackled and pinned behind his back. Goodwill inclined his head, gave the boy a brief smile, then turned away, his face filled with sadness. Something in the exchange between father and son – the look on Nathaniel's face, the brief shake of Goodwill's head – gave Seeker hope. There was love there, somewhere.

Nathaniel felt like his stomach was burning. He'd been taught years ago, at the end of a birch switch wielded by Elizabeth, not to cry. But that wasn't what stopped the tears now. He would not shame his father, whatever else might happen.

The Seeker was walking over to him, but Nathaniel didn't want to speak to him. He didn't care about the rest of them, would be glad to see them gone, but he couldn't believe the Seeker was taking his father. He felt the dog tense at his side, but it made no move towards the captain.

Seeker seemed to guess what was in his thoughts. 'I have to take your father with the rest, Nathaniel, but the Lord Protector is a man ready to forgive, and I know your father was a loyal soldier for many years. I will speak for him, but he must spend some time in prison, whatever the outcome.'

Nathaniel nodded and looked up at last. 'He – he is only harsh for my own good, because of Mother.'

It looked as if the Seeker was about to say something in response, but he didn't. Instead, he gestured to the guard on sentry duty. 'I'll have much to do in the coming days, but I'll return here when I can. The man on guard will be told you are free to come and go as you wish, and can have messages sent to me if need be.' He'd half turned away when a thought seemed to strike him. 'And should you need any other help of any sort, and have not the time to get a message to me, the house on Crutched Friars, with the green door—'

'Where Charity used to be?'

Seeker nodded. 'That's the one. Go there. The woman is misguided, but not wicked – I think she has a good heart somewhere – and she will help you if you need it.'

Seeker was about to turn away when Nathaniel haltingly spoke again. 'I – I thought I saw Charity today, only for a moment. But she was taller, and she didn't move like Charity. Perhaps it was her mother.'

'Charity doesn't have a mother,' Seeker said. He looked at Nathaniel strangely. 'Do you mean Lady Anne Winter, the woman in Crutched Friars?'

Nathaniel shook his head. 'No. She looks nothing like Charity.' He had Seeker's full attention now.

'Had you ever seen this woman before?'

'It was the woman Gideon was afraid of, the woman from the Black Fox. She was here this morning, at Gethsemane. I saw her hurrying out of the gate just after Major-General Harrison started the drills.'

Harrison and the few other prisoners remaining in Gethsemane were becoming restive: it was time for the Seeker to be gone. This would have to keep for later. 'Tell no one of this, Nathaniel. All will be well, and I will return as soon as I can.'

Nathaniel nodded, his face solemn, his eyes trying not to betray the confusion raging behind them. Seeker put a firm hand on his shoulder. 'All will be well.'

As he watched the men and women being taken away, Goodwill and Elizabeth among them, Nathaniel wondered if he should have told Seeker about Patience. But Seeker didn't like Patience, Nathaniel remembered, and he probably wouldn't care where she was either.

SEVENTEEN

Lady Anne Winter's Salon

Lady Anne Winter woke to the beginnings of the light. The heavy ochre brocade curtains of her bed were open summer and winter, and despite the sharpness of the January air, she kept her shutters open too, so that the diamond-leaded panes of her bedchamber window were often frosted over by morning. The night had been peaceful at last, after all the commotions down at the old drapers' almshouses they called Gethsemane. Richard had told her the Fifth Monarchists there had been rounded up by the Protectorate guard. When she had ventured her opinion that this was a good sign, he had countered that in this England, the only good sign would be the epitaph carved on Cromwell's tomb.

It might be long enough before that event occurred, but there was much that might be done to hasten it along. Anne Winter sat up against her pillows, and pulled her knees up, resting her chin on her hands. She felt that excitement she had been used to feel on the morning of her birthday, waiting for her brother to tumble through the door to be followed by her scolding nurse, her little dog to jump on her bed, where he was not allowed to be on any other morning.

But today was not her birthday. Today she would play her part in something of greater import than any other she had accomplished in her thirty-two years. She could hear the household stirring below, thought of Charity, the quiet graceful spaces where the girl had been. It had been twelve days now since Seeker had been here, and still nothing from him. Better that Seeker should not take too much interest in her home and household these next few days anyhow.

Downstairs, in the small basement storeroom he had requested as his own, Richard too would be waking, if not already up and making himself ready. He didn't join with the other servants in the kitchen, would not join with her in parlour or hall, but that was his choice and she would not attempt to dissuade him of it. He was not a servant, in the common run of things; neither was he a person of rank, and he resented any who pretended to overlook that fact. His preparations would be simple, she imagined: his knife, the letter, a purse no fuller than it was required to be, nothing as elaborate as those she must make, but her role today was to be a performance, an entertainment to puzzle and divert, whilst on his, with no allowance for error or unforeseen delay, everything might hang. She closed her eyes, preparing to pray, but she didn't pray. She would not pray for Richard, would not concern herself with Richard's mission – all that would be in his own hands. She must give full attention to her own part, and see that she played it well.

The bell of St Katharine Coleman's struck seven – a little time yet until she need rise, and yet curiosity got the better of her. She swung her feet over the side of the bed and found the footstool. Beside it were her favourite red velvet slippers, which she put on for fear of splinters. She would visit Price at the New Exchange to consult on the acquisition of a Turkish carpet. Her mother had disapproved of such ostentation, but Anne Winter reasoned that as no one's feet but her own would touch this carpet, little harm or wear would ever come to it. Besides, she did not need her dead mother's permission, nor that of any other. A favoured woollen shawl around her, she walked to the window, blew her warm breath on the glass, wiped it with the corner of the shawl and looked down onto Crutched Friars.

She smiled as she watched the poor fellow across the road, affecting to be a vendor of gingerbreads and the like, stamping his feet and rubbing his hands to get warm. She would have the cook send him over a warm drink in an hour or so, a well-spiced caudle, to cheer him and help him keep out the cold. He was a new watcher, of course. She had known, when she had sketched them out for Seeker, that that was the last she would see of those particular informers. Well, other than Marvell, but Marvell was different. She wondered, though, what had become of the scarred, bearded one it had taken her a little longer to spot, and who had not appeared for some weeks now, long before Seeker had made the others vanish. She must remember to ask Marvell about him later.

Anne Winter turned away from the window and pulled the silk sash that hung by her bed. It was time to dress, to assume her role for the day.

Andrew Marvell could feel the resentment seething within him. On a day such as today, when secretaries and under-secretaries from everywhere in the department were leading raids on printers and dissidents throughout the city, each with a troop of soldiers buoying him along, or taking part in the interrogation of those already under arrest, Seeker was still insisting that he should attend Anne Winter's salon, in the company of that old Royalist devil William Davenant. Even the useless Bridlington was being permitted to observe and note the interrogations – his uncle, the major-general, no doubt having intervened on his behalf – while he, Marvell, was to take coffee on stiff-backed chairs in some wealthy widow's parlour and pretend amusement at Davenant's supposed wit. What information Seeker expected to be obtained from the episode, Marvell was at a loss to imagine.

'What I expect to obtain from the exercise,' Seeker had rumbled when Marvell had injudiciously complained of his plight to another clerk, not realising Seeker was still in the vicinity, 'is intelligence on the interiors of Anne Winter's house, and of her household. In particular, anything you might glean on the past and present purposes of the Rat would be of use. I wish to know what she and Davenant talk of and do not talk of, whether any others present make any slip or reference whatsoever regarding travel plans or contacts with known suspects at home or abroad. Do I need to teach you your trade, Mr Marvell?'

'N-no,' stuttered an alabaster Marvell. 'It is just that Lady Anne already *knows* I am in the pay of Mr Thurloe.'

'She also knows you practise poetry, and will therefore be more inclined to let you over her door than an unknown face. Yes, she knows what you are about, but there might be something to be gleaned in how she tries to deceive you, and as for the rest, keep your eyes and your ears open. Of course, you might prefer to take Marcus Bridlington's place in the messengers' office.'

At this Marvell drew himself up to the full height of his indignation. 'That will not be necessary, Captain Seeker, I can assure you.'

'Good,' said Seeker, putting on his helmet and calling Proctor after him. 'I will receive your report tonight.'

Almost arrived at Crutched Friars, Marvell examined his feet; the walk through the city had rendered his best boots as grimy as they had been before he had cleaned them that morning in his small lodging at Petty France. Milton had found it for him at a very reasonable rent, not easy to be had in that pleasant part of Westminster, with its proximity to St James's Park and Pall Mall. The proximity to Milton, and Milton's encouraging patronage, had opened the way for him into the many households where men of letters and worldly experience were wont to gather – even Lady

Ranelagh had taken notice of him and complimented him on his verse. Some of the most powerful men in the Commonwealth trusted him to tutor their children and wards, and the Lord Protector himself had begun to call upon his literary gifts. Marvell was gratified, and much engaged, of course, but it was in service at Whitehall, in the offices of state that he wished to excel, and the patronage of artistic friends could only take him so far.

This too, the ageing, blind Latin Secretary, saw very clearly. 'And you will always be near to hand for Whitehall,' Milton had said, 'should you be wanted at short notice by Secretary Thurloe's office.'

And yet today, Marvell thundered to himself all the long way from Pall Mall to Aldgate, when every other agent and officer of the Protectorate seemed to be engaged upon flushing out the last of the Levellers, the Fifth Monarchists, and every other radical suspected of imminent insurrection, here *he* was, making his way to the *salon* of a notorious Royalist widow? Much good would that do him. That the inveterately duplicitous old rogue of a playwright, Davenant, was to be his companion would hardly improve matters. Marvell felt he was going to Anne Winter's house on Crutched Friars to be cleverly made fun of, and he was not sure he saw the point of the exercise, whatever Seeker might think. He was on the edges, again. But Marvell would place himself at the centre, one day – he was determined on that. By the time he reached the green door with the brass crest knocker, his determination had imbued him with a demeanour primed for indignation. Fully prepared to give vent to it, he rapped firmly three times upon the door.

'That'll be him,' said the Rat. 'You know him?'

Gabriel nodded his head wordlessly. Grace had warned him about his manners a hundred times, Samuel about not getting 'inveigled' into wrong ideas by 'whatever company she keeps', and they had both warned him to steer clear of the Rat. It was to be understood, and in a manner that required no explanation, that the Rat was dangerous. Gabriel looked at him as they moved almost silently about one another in the kitchen of Anne Winter's house. This man she called Richard was small, skinny, a bit like Samuel must have been to look at, forty years since. His face was sharp, the nose pointed and the eyes, black as the bottom of the best pot, small and piercing. His sandy hair might have been chewed rather than cut, and he was neither bearded nor clean-shaven, a chin that looked like he might use it to scrape rust off a knife. But there was no rust on Richard's knife. It gleamed in the one shaft of late morning sun that had found its way through the small back window to the kitchen of Anne Winter's house.

The man saw Gabriel's interest. '*Stiletto*,' he said slowly. 'Italian.' He flicked his right wrist and held the knife out, handle on his palm, point towards Gabriel. 'You ever meet an Italian with one of these in his hand and it's already too late. You remember that. Now, get on with brewing that black muck, and I'll go up and let her ladyship's guests in.'

Gabriel was looking at the Rat's boot, into which he had just secreted the stiletto. The Rat smiled, suddenly amused. Gabriel had thought his teeth would be yellow, but they were not: they were white, very white, and sharp. 'Don't worry, boy, I'm not going to kill this Mr Marvell with it.' He leaned a little closer towards him. 'You only kill people who matter, and even then only when something goes wrong. It's only careless people do a lot of killing. I don't plan to kill anyone with this, today. I'll keep it by me though, just in case.'

In spite of himself, it did not take long until Marvell began to find himself at ease in Anne Winter's house. His natural curiosity to see the inside of this house was winning out over his resentment at having been sent there. To his surprise and delight, the composer Henry Lawes was in attendance, as well as the old playwright Davenant.

'My dear fellow,' exclaimed the florid-faced, ruinously-nosed Davenant. 'Such a pleasure to meet you at last! John Milton has told me much of your talents.'

'Mr Milton is too kind.'

At this Davenant roared with laughter, Lawes's eyes widened and Anne Winter smiled. In response to the confusion that must have shown on Marvell's face, she said, 'You must excuse Sir William, Mr Marvell, but it is not often that even his friends hear Milton described as kind. But tell me, how do you enjoy your work for Mr Thurloe?'

Marvell had heard that Lady Anne was not one to abide by convention, but he had not expected her to begin by being quite so direct. His surprise must have shown on his face.

'I am sorry, Mr Marvell, but you must know that I am greatly concerned with the welfare of a young girl who was in my service and a few weeks ago disappeared from my care. I had great hopes Mr Thurloe's agents might have uncovered something in the course of their work, or Captain Seeker even.'

The mention of Seeker snapped Marvell right back to the reality of his situation.

'It is unfortunate, your ladyship, but I have heard nothing. And, I am . . . not quite at liberty to discuss these . . . that is, I am generally employed as a tutor to the sons of gentlemen. I am only in London while my current charge recuperates . . .'

Disappointed hope retreated reluctantly from Lady Anne's eyes, but then she smiled in such a way that Marvell felt he and the others were being gathered up in a circle of light. 'Of course,' she said, 'and it is not long since you were tutor to Lord Fairfax's daughter at Nun Appleton, in your native Yorkshire, is that not so?'

'A-hum, yes, your ladyship,' said Marvell, somewhat perplexed by this sudden change in the direction of questioning.

'Fairfax,' echoed Davenant. 'Now, *he* is a gentleman, and Nun Appleton, they tell me, a perfect delight.'

'Well, yes,' stammered Marvell.

'I have heard,' said Lady Winter, 'that you have written

some poems on the place yourself. It would delight us all to hear them.'

Step by step, although Marvell was made the focus of all their attention, he felt he was being led down an old path against his will. Old poems of his were cited from his Royalist days, cast up to him until he burned with humiliation. As he began to make noises that he would, after all, be unable to tarry any longer, Davenant put out a hand to stay him – they were not finished with him.

'And yet,' said the playwright, 'we have all had to make our accommodations with this new regime, every one of us, and that we must live with as our conscience dictates. But you should know, should you ever come to regret your abandonment of those you formerly allied yourself to, or the King's cause, you will not lack friends here.'

Marvell felt his heart might drop through his stomach, that the room might begin to spin on some unseen axis. People did not say such things to a member of Thurloe's Secretariat, be he ever so lowly. What did it say of him, that here today Davenant had said it to him? To say nothing of what it suggested about the loyalties of Henry Lawes, although Lawes, he could not help but notice, appeared mortified. Lady Anne watched Marvell carefully a moment without saying anything, and then pulled on the heavy embroidered sash by the chimney. 'Enough of such melancholy things. We shall take our coffee now – I have it from the best coffee house in London. Do you enjoy coffee, Mr Marvell?'

★

In the kitchen, Gabriel carefully set out upon a tray the four blue porcelain finians, the most delicate coffee cups he had ever touched, that Lady Winter had shown to him earlier. He had been terrified at first to go near them – in Kent's, only Grace ever handled anything nearly so fine; not even Samuel would trust himself not to break such crockery.

'Your Mr Tavener's wife found them for me, from a Dutch friend whose husband trades to Java, and knows the markets there. Are they not lovely?'

Gabriel had been blunt. 'They are too lovely, your ladyship. I have seen Mr Marvell, and he has clumsy hands – I would not let him near those good cups, and Sir William is an out and out— Well,' he'd corrected himself, 'Samuel says he is sometimes not sober.'

Lady Anne had smiled. 'More cups are easy to be had, Gabriel, but friends perhaps not so. Sir William is a good friend to me, and I hope Mr Marvell might become one. Your thoughtfulness and good sense does you credit, though, and should one of these fine cups get broken, I promise you I will take care to use less fine ones the next time.'

Gabriel had nodded, unconvinced, but had not argued further in defence of the cups. From the store cupboard next to the Rat's room he had then taken some pieces of preserved ginger, some ground cocoa and a cinnamon stick. With a palette knife he had scraped grains from the sugar loaf into a small bowl. As he'd been leaving the storeroom with his small stock of treasures, he'd happened to see through the gap between door and frame where a breeze from the garden had blown it open slightly. He'd glimpsed the Rat's hands, working strangely at the collar of a coat he had never see him wear, and, fearful of drawing further attention on himself, had hurried back to the kitchen.

Lady Anne's good parlour was two floors up, Gabriel knew that much. He'd nothing to do to the coffee now but let it brew. When the Rat left a second time, with a bucket of coals to take up for the fire in the parlour, Gabriel thought of what Seeker had said about keeping his eyes and ears open in this house. He looked around; there wasn't much to see in the kitchen that wouldn't normally be there, for all that Gabriel knew of kitchens in rich women's houses – better-quality dishes, newer implements, a larger scrubbed table perhaps. Nothing worth telling the Seeker of. But when the Rat had come back down the stairway into the kitchen, after letting Marvell and Davenant in and showing them to Lady Anne's parlour, he'd had a rolled-up piece of paper in his hand, and without speaking to Gabriel had gone directly to his room. A moment later he'd come back out of the room, and no sign of the piece of paper.

Hardly thinking what he was doing, Gabriel now went swiftly down the narrow corridor and turned the handle. The click as the door opened sounded to him as if it must have reverberated through the house. Gabriel slipped quickly in and looked around him; there was little to see: two sacks of flour, a jar of preserved fruits the very sight of which made Gabriel's mouth water, a stick and a shovel. In one corner was a musket, in a wooden box on the wall-shelf a pair of pistols. On the floor was a simple straw pallet and a woollen blanket, beside it another roll, of clothing. On a hook on the wall by the bed hung the coat Gabriel had seen the Rat working at earlier. It was of foreign design – such as made Samuel spit on the street if he happened to see any-one pass by wearing one. There was a small empty leather bag, but no chest, no book or journal or papers lying any-where. And yet Gabriel knew he had seen the Rat come in here with a piece of paper in his hand, and come out again without it. If he had not hidden it on his person, it was in here somewhere. Gabriel tried the pockets of the for-eign coat: nothing; but then he noticed the collar, and remembered the Rat's fingers working at it. It did not look quite right. He ran his hand under it and found an opening, as big as his finger. With a little work he brought out the piece of paper folded and hidden inside. He opened it care-fully but could make little sense of what he saw. The paper was of better quality than Gabriel was used to seeing in the myriad pamphlets that seemed to float from all the printers by St Paul's to the door of Kent's coffee house, and there was the design of some sort of bow or knot pressed into it. There were no words on it, just a roughly drawn map – a town, such as a child might hastily draw, then a wavering line out towards a piece of coastline that looked like a fist with a thumb sticking out. It looked like a piece of foolish-ness, but Gabriel knew it could not be foolishness, or the

Rat would never have hidden it away as he had done. As he contemplated the strange sketch, he suddenly heard above him the creak of the door that led to the kitchen stairs. He hastily folded the small map again and replaced it where he had found it. He was standing over his coffee pot again, his heart hammering, when the Rat walked carelessly back into the kitchen.

'They're wanting you up there now. And you've to take that tray of sweetmeats with you too. Well,' mused the Rat, lifting a ball of marzipan that had been coloured and shaped to make an apple, and popping it into his own mouth, 'all but this one.' He laughed and swung jauntily out of the kitchen and down the corridor to his room. By the time Gabriel returned from serving the coffee and sweetmeats to Lady Anne and her guests, the door to the small room at the end of the corridor was wide open, the Rat gone and his bag, pistols and coat with him.

EIGHTEEN

Elias Ellingworth's Journal

It had been the early hours of the morning by the time Seeker had finished processing the prisoners he had taken from Gethsemane. Other known Fifth Monarchists and Leveller agitators had been taken elsewhere in the city and outside it – Christopher Feake, Vavasor Powell, John Spittlehouse and others were under lock and key with Goodwill Crowe. The prisons of London were full – Newgate, Ludgate, the Fleet, and across the river, the Marshalsea and the Clink had been pressed into use. Major-General Thomas Harrison and some others of especial prominence would be in the Tower by now, having resisted Cromwell's heartfelt pleas to make their peace with the Protectorate, to return to the loving fold of their erstwhile brother-in-arms. Men and women of suspect associations had been parcelled up amongst places of security all over London. Elizabeth Crowe had still been declaiming as they'd thrown her into the Bridewell, crying out to God one moment, claiming kinship with Daniel in the lions' den, and demanding that her daughter be brought to her the next. Patience Crowe was yet to be found, Goodwill, not seeming greatly perturbed, had denied any knowledge of where she might be, and Seeker was resolved to leave Bridewell to work its charms on her mother a while before going to interrogate her – he had more pressing matters to attend to.

A few hours' snatched sleep in a corner of the guardroom of Newgate had allowed him no opportunity to examine Elias's journal, but the matter of the lawyer had lurked even at the back of his dreams. Ellingworth would not learn, would never cease in his collusion with the most outspoken, radical enemies of the Protectorate. And with each further step into the half-light of such murky company, the lawyer dragged his sister with him. It could not be long before Seeker found himself having to arrest Maria too. Seeker wondered what madness might have made him think there could be a place for her in this life he had made for himself, of service to the Republic, the Protectorate. Ten years beforehand, he had walked away from the meeting house, high up on Blackmoor, where, before their whole community, his wife had divorced him in favour of another man. With every step away from that meeting house, with every ounce of resilience in him, he had hardened his heart against all that she had been to him, all that he had believed he was to her. And when that was done, as it was done, he had pledged to himself that no other woman would ever reach him. And now, with Maria, that pale, thin, clever, angry, impoverished, defiant woman, too young for him, surely too young and surely too beautiful, he had broken that pledge in pieces. And this was the result, as anyone with any sense might have told him it would be. He could not turn his back on what he had made himself to remake himself again. He would not do it, for there was nothing else he could be.

Nothing had been discovered about John Wildman's whereabouts, and it was becoming more pressing by the minute that one who had so publicly criticised and condemned Cromwell should be brought in and dealt with before he could further stoke the resentments of others. Back in Whitehall, bolting the door of his room, Seeker at last took Elias Ellingworth's journal from his bag and began to read. The entries were not daily, but sporadic, and quite different in nature to the endless reams of political invective Seeker had seen litter the floors of printers from St Paul's to Westminster, or piled upon desks for weary eyes to plough their way through in the Censor Office.

There were many entries about Grace Kent. Ellingworth's love for the coffee man's niece was the worst-kept secret in London. What was less known, although what Seeker had already guessed, was that the lawyer's hesitancy to marry the girl was for fear of dragging her and those she loved into the troubles he knew his writings would bring upon them. He saw, too, the struggle between Ellingworth's desire to create a new England that he could truly be loyal to and believe in, and an impulse to leave, get away, begin anew.

Always anew, thought Seeker. England made anew. Men and women made anew. No one, not the refugee Charles

Stuart in Cologne, claiming to be king of an England that would not have him, to Oliver Cromwell, to the street urchin taken up and given a better life by an old soldier in a London coffee house, not Seeker himself, was living the life they'd been born to. Nor Elias Ellingworth, whose learning should have made him a wealthy man, but whose principles had consigned him to the verge of poverty. None was on the path on which they had first been set. In the pages of the journal, Seeker saw Elias consider at length the possibilities of taking ship, with his sister and with Grace, to the Americas. But Elias knew, as Seeker might have told him, that Samuel Kent would never go to Massachusetts, nor to Maryland nor New Amsterdam either, and that Grace would not go without him.

But if Samuel Kent should die? How long then before Elias married Grace and took her to New England, and his sister Maria with him? Better. Better for her, Seeker told himself.

Maria's name didn't occur often in her brother's journal. She was simply there, in the background, a constant, like the printer's shop or the coffee house. But then, gradually, over the past few weeks, Ellingworth had begun to mention her on her own accord, to show concern for her. The first such entry had been on his recovery after his release from the Tower the previous November, and in it Ellingworth had mentioned with great disgust the journalist Marchamont Nedham, and his insinuations that Maria received night visitors in Dove Court during her brother's convalescence at Kent's.

And so the entries went on, each worse reading for Seeker than the last, as they traced Ellingworth's suspicions that his sister was indeed engaged in an illicit affair, and his eventual disbelief and despair on finally realising whom it was that his sister had involved herself with. Seeker read over the damning entry twice.

I am in despair. I gave my oath to my father that I would protect my sister, and now I have abandoned her to this ruin. I must find a way to detach her from him, or no other will go near her.

Seeker wanted to hurl the journal into the fire, sink the ashes in the Thames. This was what he was to the world. This was what he had made himself. He swallowed down some of the ale he had brought up in a flask from the Swan and forced himself to read on.

As December passed to January, the nature of the entries changed, the change occasioned by the arrival of Shadrach Jones. The first such was written after a visit to Gresham College, where Ellingworth had first encountered the man from Massachusetts, with whom he had been greatly taken.

I made sure to delay him afterwards, and treated him to a jug of good wine that I could not well afford at the Black Fox on Broad Street. I noticed how he paid attention to the young girl serving there, and considered he might be lonely, so far from home, and friendless, being a teacher of boys in a school run by an old Welsh master in his dotage. He had already told me of his desire to hear a talk to be given next week on a new water-pump system, and although I can hardly conceive of a thing more tedious, I suggested that we should go and hear that lecture together, next week, but first that he should take supper with Maria and me in our home. He has accepted my invitation, and I am in hopes that a new and handsome face will shine a light on my sister's jaded world and show her her present folly.

The evening on which Seeker had first found Jones at Dove Court, alone with Maria, was described, as were subsequent visits. Jones seemed to have taken a great interest in every aspect of Maria's life, even her friendship with a Royalist such as Lady Anne Winter. Ellingworth had written,

I was at a loss to explain it, other than that in this England, and in this city especially, we must live cheek by jowl with those whose ideas are much contrary to our own, and that I can conceive of no other way a man might want to live.

Seeker smiled at that, in spite of himself, and as he read on, he found himself unaccountably becoming more interested in what Elias Ellingworth had to say about Shadrach Jones than he was in his speculations about Maria. In particular, an entry from just a few days ago took his attention.

Went with Shadrach to the early evening lecture at Gresham. Heard a very indifferent speaker discourse of some late experiments by Robert Boyle at Oxford. It was with some difficulty that I kept awake throughout, assisted, I think, by the growling

of my own stomach. I had hoped to sup at the Black Fox on our way to Gresham, but Shadrach was averse to the idea, strange, I thought, since he had been so much taken by the place on our previous visit. I was sorry for it, for I had noticed go in up ahead of us George Downing with his clerk Pepys, who is always good company, and some other young and well-dressed fellow, all three of them warmly greeted by Dorcas, who knew them all by name. There were several matters I would have liked to confront Downing with, but Shadrach was very much against it, and so what might have been an entertaining and profitable evening was lost. I begin to fear that Shadrach speaks so little of himself because there is so little to say. He has not much conversation, other than in matters of mechanics, and has a holy terror of the interest Seeker takes in him and his school, from which some boy has gone missing. Absconded, like as not. Perhaps I should not encourage him so much in his interest in Maria, for I suspect she would soon find him dull.

But it was the most recent entry that brought Seeker to his feet.

Came upon Shadrach unexpectedly today on Thames Street. He claimed to be making his way home from observation of the lifting contraptions at the Three Cranes, and to have lost his way, but I am certain this is not true, for I had observed him from a way off, walking with sureness and speed, and coming from the direction of Aldgate, where he tells me he has never been. I do not think I trust him, and begin to wish I had never introduced him to Wildman. I must get a message to Exton to warn him.

Seeker read the entry again and slammed shut the book. In less than a minute he was in Philip Meadowe's room, having scattered three under-secretaries taking instructions from Thurloe's harassed deputy.

'I know where Wildman is hiding out,' he said, pushing the open journal across Meadowe's desk, his finger pointing to the last entry. Meadowe was instantly on his feet, shouting for a messenger. Marcus Bridlington soon appeared, and paled slightly when he saw Seeker, evidently thinking that he was personally the object of Meadowe's summons.

Meadowe was already blowing powder over the scribbled note in his hand. 'Take that to the guardroom at Horse Guard Yard. Give it to Captain Browning.'

Bridlington nodded his understanding and was quickly out of the room and down the corridor without having looked again at Seeker.

Meadowe sank back in his chair with relief. He was beginning to look little healthier than the stricken Chief Secretary for whom he was deputising. 'Exton. We have a garrison near Marlborough – we'll have Wildman by the morning. Good work, Seeker. Where did you find this?'

'Hidden in Ellingworth's chamber at Clifford's Inn.'

'Anything else worthwhile in it?'

Seeker nodded. 'Personal thoughts, mainly. But I think this Shadrach Jones may have some bearing on some business I have been looking into for Mr Thurloe.' He hesitated. 'Shall I leave it with you?'

'What?' said Meadowe, rubbing the heel of a hand into

his eye. 'No, Seeker. If you have read over it, I hardly think I will have to. There is nothing you would miss that I would see, I am certain of it.'

Seeker nodded and left, the journal clasped shut in his hand. Whatever Philip Meadowe might think, he would hand the journal to Thurloe anyway, for Thurloe to read and act upon as he wished. There was enough in the journal, about himself and Maria, that might persuade Cromwell's Secretary of State that Seeker was no longer a man to be trusted. There was enough in the journal to lose Seeker almost everything he had, but if he had not his honesty, then he had nothing. He would give the book to Thurloe.

It was well into the afternoon, and the winter sun low and mellow on the red brick of Whitehall Palace, as Seeker walked up King Street to Wilkinson's cookhouse to take a dish of his favourite fish stew at the small table by the window where he preferred to sit. The gaggle of clerks who had been occupying the table hastily made way for him as he came in. Seeker felt suddenly sick of clerks, of crowded taverns, of duplicity, of men whose eye was ever on their own advancement. He felt sick of London. As he ate, he thought of the fish he had learned to catch as a boy, salmon and trout and eels in the Humber and the Ouse and the Don, of learning to clean them and to cook them over an open fire. He remembered learning to slip into the trees and stay still as a hind when his father told him to, remembered the places his father told him had been common land, watercourses, grazings, woodlands since God had made the earth, remembered running like the wind, faster than the wind, from men on horses who didn't believe the same thing. And now he was the man on the horse from whom others ran. Seeker set his spoon down in the bowl of half-finished stew and left the cookhouse.

He started to walk towards Horse Guard Yard, with a mind to take Acheron out on the gallops in St James's Park, but passing through Holbein Gate he saw Andrew Marvell, evidently got up in his best clothes, coming towards him. His morning's ire with his fellow Yorkshireman was gone, and he was pleased to find someone whose voice, at least, would liberate him from London a half-hour or so. Marvell was preoccupied, his head down, and it took Seeker a moment to get his attention, much to the amusement of others making their way to and from Westminster.

'Oh!' said Marvell startled at last. 'I didn't notice you there, Captain.'

'A novel experience for me,' said Seeker with a smile.

'Yes, yes, I suppose it would be,' responded Marvell, still somewhat preoccupied. Seeker was glad to see that at least he was not in the same truculent frame of mind he had been in when he had been sent out to Aldgate that morning.

'You are just returning from Lady Anne's?' asked Seeker.

Marvell nodded towards the buildings to his right. 'I was about to go and draw up my report.'

'Good,' said Seeker, 'but come and walk with me, you can tell it to me first.'

They passed out through the Tilt Yard and so out into the Park. Marvell looked about him and sighed, unimpressed. 'Were you ever at the Alhambra, Seeker, or at the Archduchess's gardens in Brussels even?'

Seeker shook his head. 'I have rarely been out of England, and even then only to Scotland, and Ireland.'

'Dear God,' said Marvell with some feeling. 'Still, I suppose it must make what London has to offer easier to tolerate.'

'I have little time to appreciate the beauties of London anyway,' said Seeker. 'But tell me of your visit to Crutched Friars. How did her ladyship and that reprobate Davenant receive you?'

'How did they receive me?' grumbled Marvell. 'That is what I am still trying to fathom. They baited me a little, flattered me more, and all in all they tested me.' He looked up at Seeker and screwed up his face as if having suddenly come upon a cherry that was sour. 'I think they may have hopes of turning me.'

At this, Seeker laughed aloud, and it felt good to laugh. 'That woman! Nothing is beyond her, nothing as it might seem. And will she succeed, my friend?'

'I do not *think* so,' answered Marvell, with just the hint of a devilish smile.

They walked on, Marvell occasionally pausing to consider a tree, or study the flight of a particular bird. Seeker questioned him on what he had seen of Lady Anne's house and learned of her household. Little, it transpired, that he had not previously observed himself.

'And what of the man she calls her steward?'

'The Rat?' Marvell grimaced. 'Answered the door to us. Made a show of laughing with Davenant, slapping his back even, as if Sir William was never out of the place. Took up some coals a little later, but I didn't see him again after that. Sir William went down to talk to him about an hour later, just before we left. Then Lady Anne herself showed us out. It was all, as I had feared it would be, a waste of time.'

Seeker shook his head. 'We don't know yet whether your time has been wasted. I have a suspicion Secretary Thurloe might be happy for you to play along in Lady Anne's game a while. Keep me abreast of any further attempts she might make to turn you in the meantime. Now, go and write your report.'

Marvell made to go on and do so, but then stopped. 'She said something about her girl – that servant girl of hers who's gone missing. That you were trying to find her.'

'With little success,' said Seeker.

Marvell nodded without saying anything else, and went on his way.

NINETEEN

At Kent's

It was late afternoon by the time Seeker went through the gateway of Lincoln's Inn. The birds were finishing their labours for the day and returning to trees or rooftops, only a part of the movement, the life, he could sense around him. Ground that had been iron hard only days before began to yield to the late winter sunlight and to anticipate the coming spring. Snowdrops had already thrust through and were beginning to open in clumps around the bases of the huge oaks and elms that lined the walkways of the gardens. Winter was coming to an end and a sense of new beginnings had quietly come into being.

And yet the winter was not over. The city and its liberties might feel cleaner after the raids on Gethsemane, and the Soper Lane church and other likely places, having flushed out so many of the Fifth Monarchist and Leveller conspirators, but he didn't believe Carter Blyth's mission had been completed. Any direct threat to the Protector from Harrison and his followers was probably over, for now, but Seeker was no nearer to knowing why Carter Blyth had met the end that he had, or what had happened to the missing children that Blyth, in his guise as Gideon Fell, had begun trying to track down. Besides, in the bag at his side was Elias Ellingworth's journal, and he could not settle until he had the thing off his hands and into Thurloe's, whatever that might mean for him once the Chief Secretary had read it.

Once arrived in the Chief Secretary's small sitting room at Lincoln's, Seeker was relieved to see the man somewhat further from death than he had seemed when he had last seen him. Thurloe was in good spirits. 'I could hardly be other after yesterday's events, so many of those inimical to Oliver's rule rounded up. I must confess to have taken pleasure in hearing accounts of your dealing with Harrison – the young men of Lincoln's can talk of little else but the fantastical distances your hammer is said to have flown. I see also that if I don't return to Whitehall soon, young Meadowe will be running the country, and I consigned to take notes for Mr Milton!' There was no rancour in Thurloe's words. 'He has done well, has he not, Seeker?'

Seeker nodded in agreement. 'Philip is a good man. He has quietly gone about the business of state and shown himself worthy of your trust in him.'

'Indeed.' And then a rare, momentary sparkle appeared in Thurloe's eyes. 'But he tells me it is you I have to thank for keeping George Downing out of my chair.'

'Which he covets, sir. He is far too often about the corridors of your department. I think he seeks his own advancement by whatever means he can find, and I don't trust him.'

'No more do I, Seeker, but the Lord Protector does, which is why we must keep him close. But you haven't come to me now to talk of George Downing, I think.'

Seeker opened the catch on his leather bag. 'No. I have come to give you this.' He held out towards the Secretary Elias Ellingworth's journal.

Thurloe took it, opened it, and spent some minutes scanning its pages. He looked up at Seeker. 'You have read this?'

Seeker was unmoving. 'I have.'

Thurloe nodded. 'Aye, and still you give it to me.' He closed the journal and returned it to Seeker. 'Keep it in your own chamber, lest we have further need of it. But know this, Damian,' he said, leaning towards Seeker, 'no one will ever know its contents from me.'

Seeker nodded his gratitude and returned the journal to his bag.

Thurloe continued. 'The girl is not under arrest, but still at Dove Court, they tell me.'

So the Chief Secretary knew all anyway. Seeker swallowed. 'Yes.'

'And have you seen her since her brother's arrest?'

Seeker shook his head.

Thurloe looked satisfied. 'Good. Keep it that way. No one will see what I have just read.' He looked up at Seeker. 'There had been rumours, reports already.' Thurloe paused. 'Did anything come of it? Did she show willing to report on her brother?'

'I – no, sir, she didn't.'

'No, I did not think it. But I have put out that should there be any talk of you and the girl Ellingworth, it should be made known that you were operating under my instruction.'

Seeker felt his stomach clench. He did not want this. As if he saw it, Thurloe continued, 'Take care not to risk compromising yourself in this way in future, Damian. You are of too great a value to the Protectorate cause. There are women enough in London, without you associate yourself with such as the girl at Dove Court.'

Seeker said nothing.

'Good,' said Thurloe. 'The episode is past. Let us move on to our proper business.'

Seeker hardly heard anything the Secretary said for the next few moments, for anger at what would be said, in the guardrooms and corridors of Whitehall, the taverns and coffee houses of Westminster and the city, of what had passed between him and Maria, and why. Only on hearing the name of Carter Blyth did he force himself back to what must now occupy his thoughts.

'Harrison or Crowe have nothing to say of him, they tell me.'

'Nothing not already known to us, and I believe they speak the truth – they took him for one of their own and thought little more about him after he had left.'

'Hmm. And Crowe's wife?'

'The woman's like a nettle. I'm letting her stew another night in the Bridewell, see if it will soften her sting a little. But their daughter has gone missing now too.'

'Then find her, Seeker. And find who is behind the disappearances of these children and the death of Carter Blyth – we have enough to contend with without murder and abduction on the streets.'

'I am pushing at a wall,' said Seeker, 'and I think it must soon give.'

'Push hard, Seeker. It says little for our state if even our best officers cannot protect the weakest in it.'

He hadn't been back to Gethsemane since the previous day's raid, but first Seeker had business to attend to at Kent's, business he had not been looking forward to.

There was more than the usual lull when he entered the coffee house. There was wariness in Gabriel's eyes as he held open the door. Instead of smiling, as he had begun to do of late, he looked to the floor and mumbled that the Seeker should come in. Seeker understood instantly what the matter was. 'Come with me over to the counter, and I will explain it to all three of you.'

Grace had, as ever when he appeared at their door at this hour, begun to prepare the warm aromatick she knew he liked. They had come a slow road together, he and Grace, in the last few months since the time of her illness and Elias's false imprisonment, and she had begun, at last, to relax a little in his presence. But not this evening; this evening her movements were stilted, her eyes downcast, although her cheeks were flushed and Seeker could see that civility was an effort for her. Only Samuel, who understood more of the world they lived in than most of the men Seeker ever had dealings with, greeted him in the usual manner, and then waited.

Seeker did not sit, but asked Grace to, and addressed her directly. 'Elias Ellingworth has associated himself with men known to have conspired and fomented dissent against the Protector, to the peril of the state. I know that he has taken care not to meet here with John Wildman or others whose associations might endanger any of you in this coffee house, and I commend him for it. I do not believe he has involved himself in outright treason, and when the rebel Wildman is brought in, if he clears Elias's name of wrongdoing, then he will be returned to his liberty. But you should know that the position Elias is presently in he has put himself into of his own accord.'

Grace nodded. Seeker knew she was not a fool, had seen the pain and worry in her face on occasions when Ellingworth had gone too far. Grace understood.

He continued. 'We had to bring him in, for his own sake as much as anything else. With Wildman on the run, there was a danger that Elias might be tempted to do something unpardonable. I don't mean unforgivable, I mean unpardonable. I have no greater wish than you do to see him swing from a scaffold on Tower Hill, but I can only protect him so far.' There was nothing more to say to them. It was the first time Seeker could remember ever having taken the trouble to explain to a man's friends why he had arrested him, and he didn't know whether he felt diminished or strengthened by it.

Samuel put a hand on his shoulder. 'You sit yourself down there, Captain. Gabriel will bring you your drink.'

Samuel usually left Seeker to himself unless asked otherwise, but this evening, as he warmed his hands on his tankard, it was plain to Seeker that Samuel wanted something of him.

When the old fellow swept the same stretch of floor in front of him a third time, Seeker said, 'What's up, Samuel?'

Samuel leaned on the broom. 'I heard there was a bit of trouble up at Gethsemane yesterday.'

'Aye,' said Seeker, taking a draught of his drink. 'A bit.'

'Just Major-General Harrison and that Goodwill Crowe and his lot taken, was it?'

'Mostly. Left the boy, Nathaniel – he has no part in their schemes, and an old bedridden witch, calls herself a prophetess and a girl to look after her and the young children. I left a guard on the gate, and there's a hound – no harm will come to them.'

'Maria's hound is it, Captain?' said Samuel, a little too casually.

Seeker put down his tankard. 'That's your interest, the dog?'

'No.' Samuel set aside the broom and settled himself awkwardly on a stool opposite Seeker. 'An old friend of mine was here a day or two ago, asking about that boy Nathaniel, the one you had in here with you. I think she had a mind to go up there and look at him. She's no Fifth

Monarchist, Captain, just minds her business, gets on with her life, same as me. She wouldn't be caught up with that sort.'

A chill had crept over Seeker when Samuel had mentioned someone looking for Nathaniel. 'Who is this "friend"?'

'Keeps the Black Fox up Broad Street.'

'Dorcas Wells,' said Seeker slowly.

'She said you'd had dealings with her, Captain.'

'And am like to have more. And what did she want with Nathaniel?'

'Something to do with the fellow he used to go about with, name of Gideon Fell – he'd promised to help her in some way, but she said you'd told her he was dead, and so she went looking for the boy.'

'She told me she knew no Gideon Fell.'

Samuel started to heave himself up from the table. 'Aye, well, Captain, I know nothing of her reasons for that. But Dorcas is not a bad woman, and if she went looking for that lad, she had good cause.'

Seeker needed to get to Gethsemane and, pushing his tankard away, took up his gauntlets and helmet. Gabriel was over beside him before ever he had the helmet on.

'Well, boy?'

The boy swallowed, took a breath. 'Lady Anne's house, Captain Seeker.'

Seeker stopped what he was doing and gave the boy his full attention. 'What about it?'

'I was there, yesterday. She had guests and wished to give them coffee.'

'You were there?'

'I served them.'

Marvell had failed to mention this; Seeker had assumed they had been served by the Rat. 'Who were her guests, boy?'

'That Mr Marvell that's been in here once or twice – talks a lot about poetry and the like, and Mr Lawes, who had his lute with him, and Lady Anne let me stay to hear him play upon it. Mr Lawes is a gentleman. More than that Sir William Davenant.' Gabriel lowered his voice. 'Samuel says he's a terrible Royalist, and not moral, Captain, and Samuel doesn't often talk of morals.'

'No, but with Sir William the subject presents itself. So? What did you hear?'

'Didn't hear much, Captain, but I had a good look about me, like you said I should, and I saw plenty.' And he told Seeker of the *stiletto*, the paper he'd found hidden in the Rat's coat collar, and the Rat's sudden departure from the house.

Seeker called to Grace for paper and pen and handed them to Gabriel. 'Draw me what you saw.'

With great concentration, and with more accuracy than he could have imagined of himself, Gabriel reproduced the simple design of the town, the waving road, and the coastline like a fist with its thumb sticking out.

Seeker frowned. It was nowhere he recognised, but

someone at Whitehall would know it, that was for sure. 'And you were sure there was no writing on it?'

'No, none. But the paper was good and had a strange pattern pressed into it.'

'What kind of pattern?'

'Like that trench Lady Anne is having dug into her garden, for a hedge of roses, she says.'

Thoughts of Nathaniel and Gethsemane were pushed to the back of Seeker's mind. Acheron was back in his stable in Horse Guard Yard, the streets still clogged up with carts and cabs, the tide uncertain. 'How fast can you run, boy?'

A glimmer of excitement came into Gabriel's eye. 'Faster'n any boy in the city.'

'Good. Two miles even?'

'Further, Captain.'

Seeker handed the boy the paper he had just drawn upon. 'Take this and go as fast as you can to Whitehall Palace. Tell the guards I have sent you and you have an urgent message for Secretary Meadowe. Show it only to him and tell him that is where Lady Anne Winter's Rat has gone to. And tell him about the knot.'

'The knot, Captain?'

'The mark embossed on the paper, as Lady Anne would plant her roses, the Sealed Knot.'

TWENTY

A Pattern of Roses

Lady Anne Winter was looking out of the casement window on the half-landing of her house, as the falling darkness enveloped the back garden that stretched as far as the wall of St Katharine Coleman's. She hadn't chosen the house especially for the garden, but already she was coming to love it, the herb garden and vegetable plot, the run for the hens; she was coming too to love the images she saw rising in her mind, the paths she would make, the hedges she would plant around them, the rose arbour. She would have a stonemason make a sundial such as the one they had had at Baxton Hall, that had so fascinated her as a child. Places to play, places to hide – that was what a garden should be. Trees to climb and share secrets in. But there were no children to play in this garden, or to share their secrets. Lady Anne turned from the window and continued down the stairs.

Already, it was a house of absences. Charity's absence, Richard's. Charity's absence was like a whisper, a sudden light breeze on her neck, whereas Richard's filled the house with a tension, an expectation. She had no expectation that

Charity would return, but Richard would, he must. They called him her Rat, she knew that, but he liked the name, took a pride in it, for the cunning, the stealth, the quickness of the rat, and so she didn't mind it for him.

But now there was a hammering on the street door, of a sort that had become familiar to her. At the bottom of the stairs she crossed her tiled floor and opened the door herself.

'Captain Seeker.'

There was no preamble. 'When did he leave?'

'I am sorry, who?'

'Your Rat, the man Richard who paraded himself as your steward, when did he leave?'

She adopted the vague and distracted demeanour that she knew infuriated him. 'This afternoon, I think. I cannot say when, exactly. I was occupied in entertaining my guests – as I am sure you must know. Mr Marvell makes for better company than his face suggests, but then I should have known that already, from the quality of his verse. Do you read much verse, Seeker? Or are you going to tell me that the only verses that interest you are to be found in the Bible? That would be a pity.'

Seeker's face was growing more thunderous with every irrelevant word she uttered, and she could see it was costing him some effort not to be baited. She wondered if he knew they had tried to turn Marvell, planted the idea of turning in his mind, but to ask him now would push him further than she dared.

'When did your Rat leave?' he repeated.

'I told you, I don't know. I was occupied with my guests. Surely,' she said slowly, 'one of your watchers outside was able to tell you when Richard left?' But she knew already that her gamble had paid off, for Richard had checked when he'd opened the door to her guests: as soon as Marvell had entered the house, the poor fellow, the pretended seller of gingerbreads who'd been watching it since dawn, had given up his post and left. None of Thurloe's men had watched her house for the rest of the afternoon, so confident had they been in having one of their own, Marvell, inside it.

She could see the realisation dawn on Seeker too, and his face harden even further. 'Will I ask you a third time, here or in the Tower?'

She knew that he wasn't bluffing. 'Ask Andrew Marvell. He was still sitting here when Sir William went down to give Richard instructions about some matters he had in hand for him, and Sir William, Mr Lawes and Mr Marvell left together very shortly afterwards.'

'Davenant's trip downstairs was but a charade to fool Marvell. Your Rat was long gone by the time he made it.'

Lady Anne only just managed to prevent herself asking Seeker how he could know that. Her mind worked quickly, and alighted almost immediately on Gabriel. Oh, foolish, foolish, to have thought that the boy's evident affection for herself might override his loyalty to Samuel Kent's old, tattered Republican cause. Her thoughts began to travel around the house, the times Gabriel had been here, and she wondered where he might have been and what else he might have seen that he should not have done.

Seeker interrupted her thoughts. 'The paper Davenant brought to your Rat . . .'

She shook her head. 'I saw no such paper.'

This was not enough for Seeker. 'You knew about it though. That was the whole point of your entertainment yesterday – the opportunity for Sir William Davenant to pass information on to this Richard you have harboured in your household on behalf of the Sealed Knot.'

The name on Seeker's lips almost stopped her breath. They had been sure, so sure, so careful and measured in their communications and their planning. How was it Thurloe's men already had the name? Unthinkingly, she reached out a hand to steady herself on the banister of the stair. This time she could not stop the words. 'But how can you know?'

'Your vanity makes you fools. The sign of the Sealed Knot on the paper on which these instructions were drawn? Anyone would think this some play or masque you dabbled in, not matters that have cost good men their lives.'

She repeated, almost for herself, 'I never saw the paper.' Anne Winter could hardly believe the folly of it herself. Seeker was right: a vanity, an unpardonable vanity and it might cost them all very dear. It would have been a sign, of course, to whoever Richard was to present himself to, that he was to be trusted, for she had observed herself that never had any man, save Cromwell himself, had so much the look of a Republican to him. 'I never saw it,' she said again. Fear crept over her whole body, to realise they had employed as their code a symbol Thurloe's men could evidently draw in their sleep.

Seeker's face was as grim as ever she had seen it. She had begun to think that there might be a kind of familiarity grown up between them, but she quickly disabused herself of that idea now.

'Will you give me time to get my cloak, Captain Seeker?' she said.

'Your cloak? What for, woman?'

'You would take me through the streets to the Tower in nothing but this thin gown?' she said, looking down on the lilac satin gown, low cut and with half-length sleeves, she had chosen for entertaining her guests earlier.

He shook his head, almost smiling. 'Oh no. I'm not taking you to the Tower. I'm not taking you anywhere at all. You have something on hand in this house, and until we have your Rat in a trap and squealing – and he will squeal, do not doubt it – you will stay here, and whatever you expect to come to pass in this house will come to pass under full sight of the men who will be stationed here day and night. If your Rat should return, he will find a warmer welcome than he might have looked for, even from you. And don't even consider attempting to get a message to him or anyone else – neither of your remaining servants will be leaving here either.'

Anne Winter sat down on the step she had been standing on, feeling a coldness that had little to do with the thinness of her dress. So much planning had gone into Richard's mission, so much had been prepared to ensure its success, and now everything was imperilled by the observations of a coffee house boy. Only last night, at the risk of great danger of discovery, with so many troops parading through the city, clearing out those suspect of Fifth Monarchism and Leveller sympathies, had the last of the necessary alterations been completed, and now it seemed that all had been in vain. She thought of the excitement there had been in the house when first the architect had arrived to begin his work, how the servants had been caught up in it, knowing something of great import was on hand, but knowing also that they must not ask. Charity had been there then, and so much had she been trusted that Richard had permitted her into the areas of the house that the others were not allowed to see. Anne had searched them a hundred times since, Richard too, but of Charity there was no sign, as confirmed by the architect who had been troubled by the interruptions and eager to get on with his work.

'And what of Charity, Seeker? In all your great concern to know every movement and thought that occurs in my house, have you given a moment to the fate of one innocent girl?'

'I have no idea what you comprehend by the term "innocent", Lady Anne, but I have not forgotten the child. Get up, and come to your study.'

Not understanding what he could have in mind now, Anne Winter followed without arguing. She remembered the one time before that he had been in the house, when she had been its unchallenged mistress, and he an officer of the state whose help she had asked. Even then she had delighted in toying with him, but now, he was master and she had no option but to follow.

He opened the shutters that were still closed from the night, and pulled out the chair behind her desk by the window.

'Sit down,' he said.

'And if I prefer to stand?' she said, summoning some of her old defiance.

'What you prefer to do is hardly my concern. Sit at your desk.'

He was in no humour to spar with her, that was clear, and here in her house, at least, she might yet influence something. From the Tower she would be able to do nothing. Lady Anne sat.

To her surprise, Seeker took a sheet of paper from beneath the lid of the desk, and handed her a pencil from her gilt brass drawing case. 'Draw her likeness.'

'Whose?'

'Charity Penn's. I want to know what she looked like. Head and shoulders will do.'

Her hand shaking a little from the knowledge of his over-bearing proximity, the closeness with which he watched every movement of her pencil, Anne Winter drew. In a very little time, the lines connected with each other, flowed into one another, became the face, the hair of a striking young girl. She had not quite finished when she became aware of a change in Seeker's demeanour. He leaned closer over the desk the better to see; she could almost feel his breath on her skin. And then reached out his hand and picked up the paper. All movement, all sound in the room was suspended a moment, and then he was making for the door, calling for one of the guards from the Aldgate watch whom he had left at the front of the house. Anne Winter heard but didn't understand what she heard. 'Send a messenger to Gethsemane, or wherever he is to be found, and bring Nathaniel Crowe to me here!' She then watched him pace her hallway furiously, all the while raging to himself about the time it was taking the guards he had ordered from Whitehall to get here, and leaving Anne Winter wondering what on earth could connect in his mind the disappearance of Charity with a Fifth Monarchist boy and the mission on which Richard had so clandestinely departed.

Seeker at last sat down in the master's chair in Anne Winter's small parlour, the better to have the light from the fire and the candles burning in the wall sconces. He looked at the paper again, but he knew he didn't really need to see it again. He was seeing, in lines and shadings of pencilled grey, what Carter Blyth had seen in living flesh and bone; he was beginning to realise what Carter Blyth had realised. He'd taken the paper from Anne Winter before she had properly finished, but it didn't matter, because Seeker knew where he had seen Charity Penn before.

It was another twenty minutes before the guards he had sent for from Whitehall arrived, but Nathaniel, the dog in tow, came very quickly. Something lightened in Seeker's heart to see the eagerness in the pair, the desire to please, to earn a word or a kind look. A lighted torch in his hand, he took them down the back stairs from Anne Winter's hall and out into her garden, where he and Nathaniel might speak more freely, where he might be allowed to soften towards them, without being observed.

He set the torch in a bracket on the wall, above a wooden bench halfway down the garden, near to the trench Anne Winter had had dug for the planting of her new hedge. How could Seeker not have connected it before? How was it that these Royalists still believed anything they had on hand could be long hidden from the eyes and ears Thurloe had employed for him about Europe? Seeker wondered if she would have the trench filled in, now that its significance was no secret. The dog sniffed around the animal scents of the deepening night, before coming to settle at his feet.

Seeker unfolded the sketch Anne Winter had made and showed it to Nathaniel. 'Who do you think this is, Nathaniel?'

Nathaniel peered through the gloom as Seeker brought the sketch into the light thrown by the torch. 'Well, it's Charity, who used to live here. But . . .'

Seeker waited, let him think. 'But it's that woman too. The one I thought was her mother.'

'The woman who came to Gethsemane yesterday?'

Nathaniel nodded. 'It is one of them, this picture, most like Charity though, because the other woman was older.'

When the guards he had summoned from Whitehall finally arrived, Seeker gave them their instructions and read with a degree of satisfaction the short note Meadowe had sent to him. It had taken all of five minutes for the location on the south-east coast sketched out by Gabriel from memory of what he had seen of the Rat's secret message to be identified, and their fastest riders had already been sent in pursuit.

The last words of Meadowe's note were, *The other matter of which you spoke is in hand.* The other matter. Seeker had not liked to do it, but it was necessary. He had warned Meadowe that Andrew Marvell should be closely watched, be told nothing of the discovery of the Rat's involvement in some plot of the Sealed Knot. Playing on Seeker's mind was the possibility that Andrew Marvell, as easily as Sir William Davenant, might have handed the embossed paper to the Rat. The fact that Lady Anne Winter had not for a moment questioned his assertion that it had been Davenant troubled him all the more.

All arrangements for the security of Anne Winter's house in place, Seeker said to Nathaniel, 'Come. We are going to Bishopsgate, you and I.'

Dorcas Wells was on her hands and knees in the taproom of the Black Fox, scrubbing the floor. She was conscious of the pot boy circling her, at a distance. He'd started to say, when first he'd come upon her in that attitude a quarter-hour ago, that that was his job, but Dorcas had almost taken the head off him. Don't speak, she thought, Don't say anything. Her heart was as scoured as the floor in front of her; she was at the end of her tether and feared it might snap at any moment, and she did not want her furious despair to unleash itself on this innocent boy.

She took a breath and tried to ignore his presence. She'd covered a third of the floor. She scrubbed on.

The rhythm, like a prayer she repeated to herself over and over, was suddenly interrupted by a loud hammering at the door.

'Tell them we're closed,' she said, without looking up.

The boy repeated the message through the still bolted door.

In response came more hammering and the injunction to open up in the name of the Lord Protector. Dorcas knew the voice and looked to her pot boy, scared now. He turned imploring eyes upon her and she relented. 'Let him in,' she said, getting to her feet and wiping her hands on her apron. She thought of the scenes of men and women being led in manacles from Gethsemane only the day before; she thought of Carter Blyth. 'What's the worst that can happen?'

She'd expected Seeker to be alone, or attended by a troop of soldiers. She hadn't expected him to be here with this boy.

She recovered herself, focused on survival rather than despair. 'What's this?' she said at last. 'Who's this boy?'

Seeker walked down the steps and set his helmet on the counter, told the pot boy to fetch water for the dog. 'No more lies, Dorcas. I have little time to spare, and I am not inclined to waste it on whatever delusions are driving you. You know well enough who he is, and he knows who you are too.'

'He?' She looked from Seeker to Nathaniel. 'How? Did Carter Blyth tell you?'

'Who's Carter Blyth?' asked Nathaniel.

Seeker continued to look at Dorcas as he answered Nathaniel. 'Carter Blyth was the name Gideon used when he was with other people, people who used to know him during the war. Will you tell this woman who you think she is?'

Colour flooded Nathaniel's cheeks. He knew this was important to the woman, and he didn't want to lie. 'I think she must be Charity's mother.'

Dorcas sank into a nearby wooden chair. 'I don't know anyone called Charity.' Then her head rose. She stared at Nathaniel and then Seeker. 'Charity?' she whispered. She leaned towards Nathaniel, beseeching. 'They call her Charity?' Then she was out of her chair. 'Where is she? Take me to where she is!'

Seeker had told the pot boy to bolt the door again against the patrons who could not understand the Black Fox being shut so early, and to build up the fire. He got Dorcas to seat herself on a wooden settle by the hearth, and sat down opposite her. He let Nathaniel stay, though over by the bar. There might be things about Blyth that Nathaniel would need to hear; it wouldn't serve the boy well in the long run to protect him from everything.

'So will you tell it to me now?' he said to the tavern keeper.

Dorcas nodded. Her hands were shaking a little and she began. 'I first met Carter Blyth thirteen years ago, when my husband joined Essex's army, fighting for Parliament. Jude was a man of principle, and he talked of freedoms and rights. They would have called him a Leveller now, I suppose. We hadn't been long married, Jude and I, I'd no other family, so nothing to stay behind for. I didn't mind the marching, the living in camps with all the other followers.' She smiled at Seeker. 'It was a life, same as any other, and better than being apart from him. And then there was Edgehill, and Jude took a Royalist musket ball in the throat. He was dead before they got him off the field. My little girl – Liberty, I called her, because that's what Jude wanted – she was born in a Lincolnshire barn three months later. We managed all right, Liberty and I. The other women were good to us, and I had plenty of work with laundry and mending for the officers. It was after Marston Moor things started to go wrong. Preachers started appearing in the army, men with less learning than you or I, Seeker, but that didn't matter. In a few months they brought in the New Model Army, and the like of me was done for. The Bible, the word of Moses and the prophets, that was all that mattered to them. And a woman with a child and no husband? "Every whore calls herself a widow," that's what they said to me, when they took Liberty from my arms and marched me from the camp. They told me she would have a godly upbringing, and never know she had a mother.'

'But how could a child not have a mother?' asked Nathaniel.

'They told me she'd be raised in one of their hospitals for orphaned children, raised in the fear of God. They took her screaming from my arms and I never saw her again. I asked everywhere, searched everywhere. That was what brought me to London eventually. No one had seen her, no one knew anything of her. But I reasoned that she might find herself here in London, one day, might just walk into the Black Fox, so here I've stayed. All these years, but she never did.'

Dorcas's large green eyes were brimming with tears. Seeker saw a pain, a rawness, that ten years had done nothing to lessen. He knew that rawness, subsumed it every day, as he suspected Dorcas had done hers, until the day Carter Blyth had walked into the Black Fox.

'Tell me about Carter Blyth,' he said.

'Carter Blyth was a sergeant in one of the new regiments. He wasn't one of the fanatics, the Bible thumpers, but he knew his trade in war, and Cromwell liked those men. He was one of the soldiers ordered to take Liberty from me and see me away from the camp. I begged them and I begged them, I was on my knees and offering them anything, but I got only stripes and curses for my pains. He was the one that took her from my arms, but I saw in his eyes that he knew he did wrong. I challenged him with it, but he wouldn't look at me. All the way to the ford on the river nearest our camp that they made me cross and left me at, he wouldn't look at me, but I swore I would remember him. I promised it, and I did remember him.'

'You recognised him when he came into your tavern with Nathaniel here?'

Dorcas nodded. 'It was about the middle of December, a good month before Isabella went missing. I was coming through from the kitchen with a pot of rabbit stew and I happened to look over to that table there by the door just as the man sitting at it looked up. I nearly dropped the pot. I knew straight away that it was Carter Blyth – scarred and bearded he was, but I knew him, all right, and he knew me – I saw that in his eyes. He didn't stay a minute after that. Just got himself and that boy there – Nathaniel, isn't it?'

Nathaniel nodded.

'Got them both out and away before I was halfway across the room. Some stupid drunk tried to tangle with me at the door, and by the time I'd got out on the street, there was no sign of Carter Blyth or the boy. I asked, but nobody could say where they'd gone. I hunted about every day after that. Walking the streets every minute I could spare, but couldn't find anything of them.' She leaned forward, keen that Seeker should understand. 'I didn't know, you see, that he was going by a different name, or that he had got in amongst those fanatics at Gethsemane.'

'And you only found out when I came to you asking about Gideon Fell?'

Dorcas lowered her eyes. 'No. He came back. I lied to you, when I told you I knew nothing of him. I'm sorry for it, but you wear the uniform of the man whose troops took my child from me, and I couldn't risk it.'

Seeker knew that now was the part he had been waiting for. 'You couldn't risk what, Dorcas?' he asked.

'Losing her again,' she said, so quietly the words could hardly be heard.

Seeker sat down at the table. 'Tell me everything, Dorcas. If I can do anything to find your child and return her to you, I will.'

She nodded. 'It was a couple of weeks later, at night, just as I'd got rid of the last drinkers and was closing up. It had been a busy night, with the lectures at Gresham, a lot of young gentlemen from the Inns of Court and clerks and the like, all the way as far as Westminster, had been in. I thought I would never get to my bed. Anyhow, I was at the point of putting up the bolt on the door at last when a man stepped into the light of the street lamp and said my name. Lucky he didn't get this in his throat,' she said, patting the sheath of the knife Seeker had noticed she kept hanging by her waist where other women kept purses. 'It was him, of course, Carter Blyth. He held up his hands to show me he meant no harm, asked if he could come in, said he needed to talk to me. I let him in, but sent my boy there out to get one of the watch to patrol outside, for fear of some trouble. But there was no trouble. He told me first he was sorry about what he'd done, said he didn't ask forgiveness, because he couldn't expect it. Then he asked me if I had ever heard what happened to Liberty after I'd last seen her. Well, that made me angry, and I'd a mind to call in the watch and have him thrown out there and then. "Should he not know better than I?" I asked him. He said again he was sorry, and then he told me all he knew was she was to be sent to a hospital for orphans and foundling children. And then, one day, walking in Aldgate, he'd seen a girl, about eleven or twelve years old, who'd struck him as familiar when she shouldn't have been, and then he'd realised it was because she was the image of me. Of course, I wanted to go there and then, in the night, to Aldgate and find her, but he wouldn't have it. Said he couldn't be certain, and he thought there were some of Thurloe's intelligence people watching her or the place she lived. He said he would come back to me when he understood better of the girl's identity and her circumstances, but that it might take some time, for he would have to take care who he asked, for fear of arousing suspicion amongst those watching her.' She turned again to Seeker. '*That* was the other reason I couldn't tell you of it before, because if your men were already watching her, you might spirit her away a second time, and I might truly never see her again.'

Seeker wondered how it could be that the Protector's regime was so misunderstood that any could think it was in the business of stealing children, but he could hardly argue with Dorcas Wells, whose child had been taken from her once already. 'And did he come back to you? Did he have proofs?'

Dorcas shook her head. 'I never saw Carter Blyth after that night, never heard anything of him until you walked through my door asking about Gideon Fell, and telling me he was dead.'

'But the salt . . .' Seeker said.

'The salt? God in Heaven, Seeker, why do you plague me with questions of that salt?'

'Because it was taken from the house on Aldgate where this girl had been a servant. Before that she had been suffering on the streets, after the poorhouse she'd been raised in was shut down.' Seeker handed her the sketch Anne Winter had made of Charity Penn.

'It's me,' Dorcas said. 'It's me, is it not, more slender, younger . . .?' Then her voice trailed away and she clamped her hand over her mouth. 'Oh, dear Lord, dear God! Liberty. Is it my Liberty?' She stood up, her fingers digging into the table that she clasped. 'Take me to her, Seeker. Take me to her now!'

They were back in Gethsemane, back in Nathaniel's little chamber. It was very late, and the night grown very cold. Seeker lit the fire. Nathaniel had been strangely silent all the way back from Bishopsgate.

'Will she be all right, do you think?' Nathaniel asked.

Seeker pictured the desolate woman they had just left, with instructions to the pot boy to see to it that the mistress was helped to her bed, and watched. The cook, a burly rock of a man who lodged in a room across the street, he'd told to put the bolt back up on the door, and watch it.

'She's had a hard blow, Nathaniel. A second time in her

life and worse, this time, because she had hope. She'll survive, though, Dorcas.'

Nathaniel stroked the dog's head and chewed at his lip. Seeker could see that he was troubled.

'What is it, Nathaniel? What was it at the Black Fox that troubled you?'

'It's something that was there. I have to tell you something that I never told you before, because Gideon told me not to.'

'Gideon was dead before I ever came to know you, Nathaniel, or you me.'

Nathaniel swallowed. 'I know it. But it wasn't just about you, it was about anyone like you, Mr Thurloe's men. He told me I wasn't to tell any of Mr Thurloe's men.'

There it was again. Blyth's distrust of Thurloe's department, of his networks. Seeker felt like he was trying to balance a heavy coin on the finest of threads. He feared almost to speak too loud lest the balance be lost. 'Tell me what it is.'

'That thing, that salt you were talking of, you and Mistress Wells. It was me who left it there, by her sign at the Black Fox.'

Seeker had not expected this. 'You, Nathaniel? But how could you come to have the thing? And why did you leave it at the Black Fox?'

Even in the dim light of the nascent fire, the relief on Nathaniel's face as he began to unburden himself was clear. 'It was the last time I saw Gideon. He'd gone out less than an hour before, off up Crutched Friars, all in dark clothes. When he returned he seemed very agitated and was in a great hurry for something. His hands were all dusty, with soot, and he had something rolled up in a dirty old blanket under his arm. When I asked him what it was, he said it was better that I knew nothing, for what I didn't know could not be forced from me, and,' Nathaniel was downcast, 'I think he knew I was no good at lying.'

'There's no shame in being a poor liar, Nathaniel. Go on.'

'Well, he pushed back his bed then and took out paper and pencil that he kept there. He scribbled a letter.'

'Did you see who it was to, what it said?'

Nathaniel shook his head. 'Gideon had been teaching me my letters, but he'd always taken care that they be written neat and clear – this was like a scrawl, a dozen scribbled lines. I could make out none of it, and he put no mark on the outside when he folded it and sealed it with wax from our candle. He shoved it inside his shirt before the wax can have been properly cooled. Then he turned his back to me and put what he'd been hiding in a sack and told me that if he hadn't come back by dawn, I should take it up to the Black Fox Tavern as soon as I was able, and leave it in some prominent place there, without being noticed if I could. He told me that if anyone on the street questioned me as to what I carried, I should say it was fire irons for Dorcas Wells.'

'And Gideon didn't return before dawn, did he?'

'No,' said Nathaniel, 'nor ever again. I went up to the

Black Fox as soon as I could get away, and waited until the street outside was very busy, and quickly hooked the bag to the sign when one of the trained bands was jostling past on the pavement on their way to the artillery grounds.'

Seeker smiled in admiration. 'I think we might make an agent of you yet, Nathaniel. You know, most people would have tried to go there when the street was very quiet and they thought no one around. And they would surely have been remarked, for the streets of the city are rarely as deserted as they seem, and there is always a pair of eyes at a window, somewhere. Not many would have the sense to hide their deed in a jostling crowd.'

'Truly?' The idea that he had done something well seemed briefly to lift Nathaniel's spirits.

'And Gideon never told you what was in the sack, or where he had got it from?'

Nathaniel shook his head. 'No, and I didn't mean to look, but the sack fell open when I had to jump a ditch at Billiter Lane, and I saw the crest the same as on the green door up Crutched Friars. I still didn't know what it was,' he added. 'Mother keeps our salt in a pot with a lid and when we are permitted to have it it is set on the table in a small bowl, and how much you take watched very carefully.'

Seeker did not doubt it. It would not surprise him to learn Elizabeth Crowe considered the enjoyment of food rather than simply its consumption to be a sin.

'And that was all you knew of this salt, and the last you saw of Gideon Fell?'

'Yes.' Nathaniel's voice was little more than a hoarse whisper. 'I should have followed him. I shouldn't have left him alone.'

'No, lad,' said Seeker, making Nathaniel look into his face. 'You would have endangered yourself and he would never have let you. You did the thing that he needed you to do, and somehow I will get to the bottom of this, but for now I need to get back to Whitehall.' Seeker was about to leave when he thought of something else. 'What happened to the blanket Gideon had the salt hidden in when he came in here?'

Nathaniel was dejected. 'I don't know, he took it with him when he left with his note.'

'Ah, well,' said Seeker. 'It's of little consequence, no doubt. I'll come again as soon as I can. Hold fast, and look after the hound, will you?'

'Of course.'

'And don't fret for your sister. She'll be found.'

Nathaniel didn't look up from the hound whose ears he was stroking. 'Yes,' he said, 'I suppose she will.'

TWENTY-ONE

The Question of Shadrach Jones

Seeker spent the night at Whitehall, in his room near the Cockpit, and woke early. Already, the place was a moving warren of officers, secretaries, couriers, marching along corridors or scurrying; their movements had purpose, but in their purposefulness was an air of satisfaction, an assurance that Seeker was not sure was yet merited. It was too soon for any news of the Rat, but there was plenty of work to be done in cross-checking the files of suspect persons in the area to which the Rat was known to have travelled. Even so, Seeker's thoughts kept returning to the events and revelations of the previous day. Too many things he had heard at the Black Fox and Gethsemane troubled him, and something he had read over casually in Elias Ellingworth's journal was now nagging increasingly at his mind. As the work on the Royalist files drew to a close, Seeker excused himself to Meadowe and returned to his chambers.

The small hide-bound journal that Thurloe had returned to him the previous evening was in a locked drawer in his desk. He took it out and began to go through its entries once more. So taken up had he been with Dorcas's story of her stolen daughter, and Nathaniel's strange tale of Anne Winter's salt, so taken up had he been, in fact, with trying to comprehend the clandestine activities of Carter Blyth, he had almost forgotten the other girl lost to Dorcas Wells: her serving girl, Isabella. Isabella had been at the Black Fox on Blyth's first visit, gone by his second. But Isabella had appeared somewhere else in the tangle of his investigation, if not by name. Seeker turned the pages of the journal carefully, and still he almost missed it, so little attention had he paid it when first he'd read it. He found Ellingworth's entry telling of his first encounter with Shadrach Jones, at an evening lecture at Gresham College on Bishopsgate:

I . . . treated him to a jug of good wine that I could not well afford at the Black Fox on Broad Street. I noticed how he paid attention to the young girl serving there . . .

Entered a few weeks later, after the disappearance of the girl Isabella, Seeker read again,

I had hoped to sup at the Black Fox on our way to Gresham, but Shadrach was averse to the idea, strange, I thought, since he had been so much taken with the place on our previous visit. I was sorry for it, for I had noticed go in up ahead of us George Downing with his clerk Pepys, who is always good company, and some other young and well-dressed fellow, all three of them warmly greeted by Dorcas, who knew them all by name. There

were several matters I would have liked to confront Downing
with, but Shadrach was very much against it . . .

Seeker sat back and read over the two entries again. What
had it been – the missing girl, or Downing? Shadrach Jones
had kept his distance from the Black Fox that night because
of one or the other. A trip to Holborn would be required,
and Seeker would have the truth of it from the New England schoolmaster before the day was out, on that he was
determined. But before Holborn, he had to pay a visit to the
Exchequer.

Westminster was busy, as ever, the shopkeepers and book-
sellers of the Great Hall spilling into the yard, primed to
make the most of whatever shift in political or military
matters the day might bring. The wants of a Protectorate
Secretary were not so different from those of his Royalist
predecessor, the needs of the soldier who might follow him
through a shop door much the same as those that had fought
for the King. Only from the tenor of the books and pamphlets filling the shelves of the bookseller's premises would
a visitor know who was in power.

It seemed fitting that next to this whirlwind of exchanging coin and promissory notes should be the power that
managed the wealth and poverty of the realm. This was not
where the money was made – for that was the city – but
here the decisions were made about how much would be
taken for the state, and how it would be spent. Between
Westminster Hall on the one side, and the Exchequer on

another, the battle for the base-metal soul of the nation was never-endingly played out. Seeker stepped into the Exchequer, a fitting sphere of operation, he thought, for the ambitious, ruthless, puritanical Downing. The doorkeeper did not so much as question him, and the first usher he found in the high-ceilinged, echoing hallway looked like he would rather be swallowed down the neck of his own shirt than deal with Seeker. He was very sorry indeed, but Mr Downing had not been seen that morning. Perhaps Mr Pepys could be of assistance? Seeker was about to draw a forceful analogy involving puppets and their masters when he stopped. Yes, Pepys would do just fine, to begin with.

Downing's clerk walked confidently towards him less than two minutes later. Seeker had heard of him as something of a libertine, too frequent a visitor of taverns and a womaniser of growing reputation, yet the man who presented himself before him was prompt and businesslike. Seeker had seen and heard this Pepys ingratiate himself with others who favoured such an attitude, but was glad that he didn't waste either of their time by attempting to do so with him.

'How can I be of help?'

'Firstly, you can tell me where your master is today, and what business he is about.'

Pepys took a moment. 'Mr Downing is at home in his house in Axe Yard. As to his present business, I don't know, although I imagine the rumoured pursuit of suspect persons will be exercising his mind in some way.'

'I expect it will,' grumbled Seeker. 'You can accompany me to Axe Yard then. I have some questions for you also.'

The clerk didn't look remotely perturbed. 'Should I bring anything in particular with me? Ledgers? Bills? Reports from the Mint?'

'I am not here about the business of the Exchequer.'

'Ah,' said Pepys carefully. 'I see.' The expression on his face suggested that there were indeed many other possible aspects to George Downing's interests, few of which his clerk would find it comfortable to discuss. This suited Seeker very well, and the short walk to Axe Yard took longer than it might have done.

Seeker didn't beat about the bush. 'Tell me what you know of any connection between your employer and a man named Shadrach Jones.'

Pepys registered some surprise but didn't for a minute pretend he had never heard the name. 'The schoolmaster on High Holborn? Yes, he has taken a great deal of interest in him, since first he came across the name in Mr Thurloe's files.'

Seeker had seldom heard such a brazen admission. Of course Downing had rifled Thurloe's files at every opportunity, but he had not expected the man's clerk to volunteer the information so readily. Clearly Pepys felt no great liking or loyalty for his employer. Pepys continued quite cheerfully as they crossed King Street, deftly sidestepping muck on the street and any horseman that crossed their path, happy, it seemed, to be of help, and utterly devoid of any visible awe of Seeker. It was an experience Seeker had rarely had, and he found himself for a moment watching the clerk rather than listening properly to what he said. '. . . at Harvard. Bad feeling between them. Mr Downing was not best pleased to see him turn up in London, I can tell you.'

'Downing and Jones know each other?'

'Well yes,' said Pepys, stopping almost in the way of a carriage transporting two of Cromwell's daughters through the King Street gate out of the palace, and managing somehow to sidestep it just in time while making his bow to the ladies. The carriage driver looked sorry to have been deprived his casualty, and Pepys continued, apparently untroubled by the interlude.

'That is what I've been saying. Shadrach Jones was apparently a student at Harvard when Mr Downing was a teacher there – before he came here to fight for Parliament, of course. I have a suspicion that Jones may have been in some way responsible for Mr Downing having left his position at Harvard so suddenly, and exchanging it for that of a ship's chaplain in the Caribbean.'

'Downing has told you all of this?'

Pepys made a slightly pained face. 'Well – some, the rest I have deduced from comments he has let slip, and from hearsay amongst others come over from Massachusetts. But I do know that he does not like this schoolmaster, and would dearly love to find some reason for his removal.'

Seeker found that he was not in such a hurry to get to Downing as he had first thought, and sensed that there might be more of use to be had from the clever clerk than from the ambitious minister. He told Pepys that he was hungry, and asked him to step into the Axe Tavern with him while he took his dinner.

Seeker made short work of a roasted woodpigeon with a cranberry jelly, while Pepys, looking on with envy, settled for a venison pasty. There was little conversation as Seeker ate, but once he had pushed aside his trencher and wiped his hands, he said, 'Tell me what you know of the Black Fox.'

This was, he could see, unexpected. 'The Black Fox? On Broad Street?'

Seeker, taking a draught of his ale, nodded.

Pepys puffed out his cheeks, in an effort to show due consideration to the matter. 'It is a well kept and congenial place. The tap is clear and the food honest. No, more than honest – it is good. There used to be a very pretty girl worked there, but sadly, I haven't seen her for some time. Isabella, her name was . . .' His voice tailed off wistfully a moment and then he came back to himself. 'I wouldn't wish to tangle with the landlady, mind you. Well, that is . . . I would not wish to *fall out* with her,' he clarified, venturing a lewd smile which he soon realised had been misjudged.

'How often have you been there with Mr Downing.?'

'With Downing?' repeated Pepys, the very familiar environs of the Axe having made him relax more than the occasion warranted. 'Only once. Mr Downing is of a peculiarly puritanical shade, and we seldom socialise together.'

'And why had you gone there that once?'

'Marcus Bridlington – you know, the clerk you, ahem, relocated to the message office – was going up to the lecture at Gresham – he has a great interest in matters scientific, Mr Downing less so. But Downing is very keen to advance himself with those close to the Protector, and desirous of becoming more familiar with Marcus's uncle, Major-General Goffe. I believe there have been hints of an invitation to Marcus's uncle's hunting lodge.'

Seeker's already low opinion of Downing dropped further. For someone of his standing to pander to an inept if well-connected clerk in the hope of currying favour was something that should have been swept away with the head of Charles Stuart.

'Shadrach Jones was not far behind you going up Broad Street that night, in the company of Elias Ellingworth.'

Pepys raised his eyebrows till they were almost hidden by his luxuriant fringe. 'Indeed! Had Mr Downing noticed that, he would have had much to say about it.'

'So none of you did notice them?'

Pepys was emphatic. 'No. Had Mr Downing seen them, a fairly distasteful scene would have ensued, I am certain of it. But we went into the Black Fox and took our supper untroubled.'

'And the lecture?'

'The lecture?'

'That you were all going up to Gresham College to hear?'

'Ah.' Pepys coloured a little. 'Well, I didn't go. You see, there were a couple of musicians came into the Black

Fox — with a lute and a fiddle — and they were uncommonly good. And Mistress Wells has the most beautiful singing voice — do you sing at all, Captain?'

'No,' said Seeker.

'No, no,' conceded Pepys, already looking as if he regretted asking the question, 'perhaps not. Anyhow, I made my excuses, and remained in the tavern, and I'm afraid I abandoned poor Bridlington to the pleasures of Mr Downing's company alone.'

'And of the pretty girl you spoke of, Isabella, there was no sign?'

'No,' said Pepys, nonchalantly wiping the last crumbs of his pasty from his chin. 'None, which is a pity, because she was an uncommonly pretty girl, and clever, too.'

'Clever?'

'Mmm. Took a great interest in what the young men who had been to the science lectures had heard. Engaged in talk about it so much that Dorcas would roundly scold her, although secretly I think she was pleased to have such a bright girl in her place.'

'You're sure it wasn't the young men themselves she was interested in?'

Pepys shook his head. 'I tried her more than once — I am not, you understand, without success in the matter of charming serving girls, but she had no interest in *my* conversation, saying she preferred to talk of mechanics than of music. Ah, well!'

★

Shadrach carefully drew the last line and appraised his work. Those final adjustments would perfect the thing. The boys would still be finishing their dinner, and then, once the parlour was cleared, he'd take them out to the field and let them play football. The early frost had gone and the day was still fine – it would be a release for them, and for him, from the tension they had been living with for the last few days.

He'd been working by the street window, for the light, but was seldom distracted by the sights and sounds of the street in front of him. There had been soldiers everywhere, but he knew what they were for – it was spoken of in every tavern and coffee house, shouted by every bookseller waving pamphlets as he passed: the Fifth Monarchists had been taken, Major-General Harrison was under lock and key and the latest Leveller rising put down before it could begin. Yet something in the sound of a horseman approaching from the direction of St Giles's made him put down his pencil and crane his neck the better to see up the street. The horse was black and powerful, and somehow Shadrach knew before he could fully see him who its rider would be.

Shadrach quickly picked up the drawing he had made; there was no time to put it into the usual hiding place, but his eyes fell on de Caus's *Raison des Forces Mouvantes*, the largest book in his possession, and he hastily placed the drawing between its pages, before returning the heavy tome to the shelf by his bed. Cursing the lack of fire in his own hearth, he snatched up the practice pages he had used and crumpled them in his hand, before hurrying through to

Rhys Evans's chamber, where a fire was always kept for the old man, and throwing them in there. He was still working with a poker at the ashes when the light in the room dimmed and he turned to see the huge form of Damian Seeker fill the doorway.

'You are busy, I see,' said Seeker, advancing into the room.

'I was about to take the boys out for some air and exercise, and I thought I should build up Mr Evans's fire before we left.'

'Most considerate,' said Seeker, moving Jones aside and stooping to lift the corner of a paper which had not quite caught. 'But you would surely have done better to have used those coals.' Without taking his eyes from the paper, he indicated the full basket by the hearth and Shadrach felt his stomach lurch.

Seeker took the poker from him and sifted through the remaining ashes before examining the charred triangle of paper in his hand. 'A locking device of some sort. For a door, I presume?'

'Just some rough sketches,' said Shadrach, his throat dry.

'For what?'

Shadrach scrambled for an answer. 'The door to a pump house.'

Seeker's half smile was almost as terrifying as his frown. 'I hardly think so. There appears to be some sort of pulley mechanism attached to this.'

Shadrach was at a loss for coherent explanation. 'A fancy, out of boredom.'

'Boredom? With a dozen boys to teach and a senile old man to care for? All these lectures at Gresham, your wanderings around the city, visits to taverns and coffee houses, paying court to young women alone in their homes? And still you are bored? Truly,' growled Seeker, 'Massachusetts harbours wonders we have yet to hear of if all the entertainments of London can leave you bored.'

Shadrach was spared the necessity of finding any coherent reply by the intervention of Rhys Evans, who, confined to a high-backed chair in the corner now, had been becoming increasingly agitated since Seeker's arrival. He was muttering to himself, and at first Shadrach couldn't hear what he said, but even when Evans's agitation grew louder, and Shadrach could hear distinct words, he still couldn't understand them. At last, with staring eyes and a voice that was quite terrible, Evans half rose from his chair and stretched a bony hand towards Seeker, pointing a wavering finger and said, 'Morfan!'

He repeated the word twice and then, the effort obviously having exhausted him, sank back into his chair and murmured softly to himself.

For a moment, all else was silence in the room, and then, to Shadrach's astonishment, Seeker let out a hearty laugh and crouched down before the old man, taking the trembling hand and looking into his face. 'Not Morfan, Grandfather, but close enough.'

'I – I don't understand,' managed Shadrach at last.

Relinquishing the old man's hand and standing up again,

Seeker said, 'Morfan was the son of a Welsh goddess. He was a fierce warrior, and ugly as sin.'

'You know Welsh?' said Shadrach.

'Some. My mother was Welsh.'

Shadrach was just considering the information that Seeker had had a mother when Seeker snapped out of his brush with humanity and reverted to the purpose of his visit. He put the salvaged scrap of charred paper into his bag, and told Jones to take him to his own chamber.

Shadrach didn't consider arguing, and they left a still murmuring Rhys Evans in peace, although only after Seeker had made a point of adding coals to the dying fire. Evans was still repeating the name 'Morfan', but it seemed to afford him some comfort now. And then, looking at the two men he said, 'Morfan and Shadrach,' and started to laugh softly to himself. 'Morfan and Shadrach. Shadrach, Meshach and Abednego. Poor Abednego.' He shook his head sadly, and repeated, suddenly melancholy, 'Poor Abednego.' They could hear him carry on doing so even after they had left him and closed the door behind themselves.

Shadrach looked at the door and then glanced apologetically at Seeker. 'He's like that all the time now, only speaks English when he's quoting from the Bible, the rest of the time it's Welsh.'

'He wasn't quoting there,' said Seeker.

'Well,' said Shadrach, puffing out his lips, more confident now, 'perhaps not, but it was certainly a reference to the Book of Daniel, the three children who . . .'

'I *know* what it was,' said Seeker, and Shadrach instantly regretted his folly in correcting a soldier of the New Model Army on a matter of scripture.

'I should see to the boys,' he mumbled, feeling his face redden.

'The boys will see to themselves,' replied Seeker. 'I've told them to go out and exercise in the yard after they've cleared up their dinner things. I set the boy William Godmanson to oversee them – they have no need for you at present, and no one will trouble them – I left my horse tied up at the end of the entranceway.'

Shadrach understood – even the few people in London who did not know that was Damian Seeker's horse would know it was the horse of an army officer, and one to be reckoned with. Nobody would risk drawing the ire, or even the attention of its owner.

It felt to Shadrach that Seeker almost filled the small amount of space in his chamber next to Rhys Evans's. Everything in it – bed, desk, chair, bookshelf, even the trunk he had carried with him from Boston – seemed vulnerable somehow. Shadrach backed up to the window and watched as Seeker put his finger to the wick of the candle on the desk. The wax, still warm and soft, gave under the light pressure. 'Mmm,' said Seeker. He opened the lid of the desk, raised an eyebrow at the very fine pencil box inside, took some time examining ruler, set square, compasses, tested the pencil holder in surprisingly dextrous hands. Then he pushed the pencil box aside, and lifted out

Shadrach's most valuable possession. 'An astrolabe, in gilt brass no less? This must have cost you a pretty penny.'

'My wants are few, and my board here moderate.'

'They must be, though what need a schoolmaster has of an instrument like this, I would be interested to learn.'

'There is no mystery,' said Shadrach, his pride spiked now. 'I told you, I have an interest in mechanics, the possibilities of engineering. I find it useful for measuring, conducting surveys.'

'Mmm.' Seeker appeared to lose interest in the contents of Shadrach's desk.

'So,' he said, turning abruptly, 'George Downing. Enlighten me.'

'What?' said Shadrach.

'Harvard. You and Downing. What happened between you?'

So the other side of the ocean had not been quite far enough. Of all the risks Shadrach had taken, was taking, this was the one to which he'd given least consideration, that somehow his world and that of George Downing would once more collide.

No longer on his guard, no longer alert to Seeker's movements around his room, Shadrach sat down on the narrow bed, his head in his hands.

'Well?' demanded Seeker.

His mouth almost unbearably dry, Shadrach ran the tip of his tongue over his bottom lip. Eventually, he found his voice. 'Whatever he has told you is a lie. With Downing, it is always a lie.'

Seeker's voice was lower, quieter than he had expected. 'Convince me.'

'I was fifteen when I went to Harvard, eleven years ago. The people of our church had raised a scholarship to enable me to go. I still had to take on usher's duties in the college – serving at table, emptying chamber pots, waking the senior students and masters. I didn't mind, so eager was I to learn of mathematics – Copernicus, Brahe, to go beyond the old scholastic certainties of Ptolemy and Aristotle. Perhaps I hoped for too much. In any case, all went well for a time; George Downing was a reader in philosophy to the first-year class with which I had matriculated. He wasn't well liked by any of the boys – always at great pains to remind us of his superior connections, parading his piety, spending more effort looking for opportunities to censure than to teach. He was not greatly popular with his peers either. There were stories that he wasn't to be trusted, that he would sell his friends cheap for any benefit to himself.'

'And?'

'Just before the beginning of my second year, a vacancy arose for a lucrative teaching position in the college. It was known that Downing and another of the junior masters wanted it, but generally noised that despite Downing's superior connections, the other candidate, Walter Coutts, was the preferred choice of the examiners, being better qualified and of a more pleasant disposition. Three days before the trial for the awarding of the place, a young woman presented herself to the College authorities, claiming to have been ravished by this other candidate. The man was brought before them, denying everything, but the woman held to her story, claimed she had proofs – she was able to describe the tutor's chamber in the college and she produced something she claimed to have taken from his room as evidence – a page torn from a prayer book, inscribed by his mother.' Shadrach could feel himself grow increasingly angry as he recalled those events of ten years ago.

'Go on,' said Seeker. 'What happened?'

The tutor was found guilty of assault and lewd conduct, fined and sentenced to lose his place in the college, after having appeared three weeks in sackcloth and ashes in the college chapel.'

'And what has this to do with you and Downing?'

Shadrach looked up. 'As I told you, I cleaned the chambers of the senior scholars and junior masters. I knew Downing had torn that page from Coutts's prayer book, for I'd seen it in his room the day before the girl made her accusations. I went to George Downing, seeking his help for Coutts. He claimed he knew nothing of the prayer book, and I'd do better not to involve myself in such matters. The next day, a young woman who worked in the College kitchens began to shadow me, make knowing suggestions. That was all, but the message was clear enough: what had happened to Walter Coutts might just as easily happen to me. I packed up my belongings and left Boston that day.' The shame of it still filled him. 'I haven't been home since. I wandered Maryland, Virginia. Learned what I could there. But before I left Harvard, I made sure to leave a letter for the Provost, detailing my suspicions that Downing had fabricated the case against Walter Coutts. It was a good few months later that I heard he had left Harvard soon after I had, without public scandal but very suddenly, to join a ship bound for the Caribbean. I hoped never to see his face again.'

'And yet you came to London, where you must have known he was.'

Shadrach shook his head. 'George Downing was not such a figure, not known, in Maryland as he was in Massachusetts. It didn't enter my head that he would have come to England. Even when I arrived here, and began to hear the name, I thought at first it must be some other. I couldn't believe that even one as ambitious as he could have risen so far in life.' His voice became bitter. 'In time, of course, I realised that it was the same man, but it was too late: I was here. I hoped that London was a place big and busy enough that we might never come upon each other, he in his exalted place and I in my low one, but I see that I was wrong.'

There was silence in the room for what seemed to Shadrach to be several moments, save for the low murmur just audible from Rhys Evans's chamber next door, the old man still intoning his mantra of 'Shadrach, Meshach and Abednego,' punctuated by the occasional lament of 'Poor

Abednego'. Shadrach expected some kind of comment, or response, from Seeker to his account of his dealings with George Downing, but none came. Instead, having returned to the perusal of Shadrach's bookshelf, his finger rested on the spine of de Caus's book, the book in which Shadrach had hidden his last drawing. '*Forces Mouvantes*,' mused Seeker, in a passable French. 'Hydraulics. Interesting.'

Shadrach's terror was momentarily replaced by a curiosity as to how Seeker came by this knowledge when the man suddenly turned and said, 'So, tell me about Isabella.'

Shadrach was taken completely by surprise. He stuttered in his attempt at response. 'I kn-know no Isabella.'

'Oh, but you do,' said Seeker, moving away from the shelf. 'You were quite taken with her, it seems, up at the Black Fox. Very pretty, by all accounts. Keen on talk of the new science – there can't have been so many serving girls of that description in there that you don't remember that one.'

Shadrach stared at Seeker a moment, still trying to work out where this latest turn in the interrogation had come from, before at last replying, 'Yes, yes, I do remember now. Straight black hair worn loose, very blue eyes. Quick-witted, as you say.'

'Hmm.' Seeker leafed through a slim book of designs for water closets that Jones had left open on his desk. 'And did you meet with her often?'

'Meet with?' Shadrach swallowed. 'I don't understand. I didn't. She – she is little more than a child. I just spoke to her that one time. Does she say otherwise?'

'She might well do,' said Seeker, 'if she were found.'

Shadrach felt a dread creep through him. He swallowed. 'I don't understand.'

'You don't understand much,' said Seeker, snapping the book shut. 'But what *I* understand is that at least two children with a known connection to you have gone missing. London is too big a place for that to be a coincidence.'

Shadrach began to tremble, felt sweat break out on his brow. 'I swear, Seeker, I didn't . . .'

Seeker turned back from the window, from which he had been watching the boys play at football and leapfrog. He treated Shadrach to a look that chilled the schoolmaster through. 'No doubt. But if you did, it will become known; I will know it, and I will have no mercy.'

TWENTY-TWO

Patience

Elizabeth Crowe had been separated from the other women prisoners – wives and daughters of agitators – who'd been brought to the Bridewell. They'd be let go in a day or two, once the planned uprising had been completely neutralised, its organisers isolated and secured. But Elizabeth Crowe was different, no appendage to her husband, to cook his meals and stitch his clothes, feed his children and do his bidding. She was more than Goodwill Crowe's wife, and where Goodwill and others like him could put arms in the hands of other men, direct their actions, lead them, Elizabeth was the one who would put into their hearts the burning desire for the fight.

The Bridewell warden's room was miserable enough, the poor light serving for little but to cast an occasional glimmer on the old, damp stone of the walls. Little effort had been made, either, to counteract the rank human smell that carried on the air through the endlessly meandering passageways of cells and cellars and yards in which the women were kept, to imbue everything it touched with the same noxious odour. Seeker knew enough of gaols to know that after a while it would be all that the inhabitants, prisoners or guards, knew, and that those who survived to see release would carry the stench with them many weeks, and some, it was said, a lifetime.

The arrival of Elizabeth Crowe, her hands manacled in front of her, did nothing to cheer the room or add to it any suspicion of human warmth. Seeker ordered the manacles removed. The preacher-woman sat down across the small table from him and refused his offer of a beaker of ale from the jug the warden's wife had brought in.

As soon as the door was closed again, Elizabeth Crowe spoke. 'Where is my daughter?'

'That is not the issue of this interview.'

Her eyes, the pupils small and grey, did not seem to move. She hardly blinked. 'I'll discuss nothing else with you.'

'Then your feet will not touch the streets of Aldgate a long time,' said Seeker wearily, writing her name at the top of the sheet of paper in front of him.

'I want to know where my daughter is,' repeated Elizabeth. 'Where are you holding her?'

Seeker looked up from the paper. 'We are not holding her. She was not at Gethsemane when we rounded up you and the others of your sect. You already know that.'

She shook her head, her thin lips pursed more firmly than ever. 'You took her before then.'

Seeker laid the quill pen down on the table. 'Who told you this?'

'I did not need to be told. She left Gethsemane four days ago, after supper. She never returned. One of your people must have taken her under arrest, be holding her in some other prison.'

It was Seeker's turn to be unblinking. 'You can rest assured that that didn't happen. If your daughter's whereabouts are truly unknown to you, she either went of her own accord, or has been taken.' He paused a moment, trying to gauge her reaction – a slight flicker in the otherwise unmoving eyes was all.

'Your daughter is almost a young woman, but you know that children have been going missing of late?'

'Children go missing in the city all the time.'

'These ones haven't simply gone missing, they've been taken – one a few hundred yards from your own door. Are you trying to tell me you haven't heard of this?'

Her eyes shifted away from him. 'I had heard something of it, but they were younger than Patience, who is not a child, and has a family and a home, where these did not.'

'You know a great deal about them, it would seem.'

This time Elizabeth Crowe's mouth achieved what Seeker thought might pass for a smile. 'I do not join in the gossip on the streets, but I hear it. This London you have made is not safe for children on their own.'

'Nor ever was,' replied Seeker. 'But these were not children on their own, no more than was your daughter. Where has she gone, Mistress Crowe?'

'I don't know.'

'And what were you doing searching around Blackfriars two days ago, almost from first light?'

Now he had her. For the first time, Seeker saw something other than contempt in Elizabeth Crowe's eyes: he saw fear.

'Well?'

She examined her hands, her voice as quiet as he had heard it. 'I thought she might have been there.'

'Why?'

Silence.

He took a breath, summoning his patience. 'I'll ask you again.'

Still she would not look at him. 'Because that's where the other one was found – the man who called himself Gideon Fell, who also disappeared from Gethsemane. They found him there, did they not? Bricked up in a wall at Blackfriars?'

'Aye,' said Seeker, 'they did. And you have known from the beginning that your daughter had not been arrested by the Protector's forces.'

Elizabeth Crowe's head whipped up and she almost spat her response at him. 'I have not! Don't tell me your interest in Gideon Fell is what it would have been for any other travelling weaver looking for a roof over his head. You've had your eye on him! Do not ask me to believe Cromwell's men have not been mixed in this somewhere.' She clenched her fists and held her eyes shut as she tried to master her breathing. Calmed at last she looked at him again. There was calculation in her eyes.

'Is Gethsemane cleared out?' she asked him.

'Of most of its vermin. The madwoman Wilkins has been left there to fester, and a girl to see to her and the young children.'

'And my husband's idiot son?'

'Nathaniel is well.'

'Is he still there?'

Seeker nodded.

Elizabeth's lip twisted. 'A stay in Newgate might have put some sense into him.'

Seeker felt disgust. 'He has sense enough, and goodness, which at Gethsemane is in short supply.'

'A fool's a fool, Seeker, and you know nothing of goodness,' she said, and then she would not answer him one thing more. She didn't maintain silence though – silence would have been better. Throughout his questions, even as Seeker spoke, Elizabeth Crowe intoned one chapter of Scripture after another, dwelling on the tribulations of the righteous and the terrors awaiting the ungodly, until the guard on the door thought her mouth must run dry, and long after Seeker had given up and left the room.

But as he descended the steps from the warden's apartments, through the festering corridors of Bridewell, its dank courtyards and back out under its gate and into the light, Seeker was certain of two things: Elizabeth Crowe truly did not know where her daughter was, and Elizabeth Crowe was scared.

★

Patience was cold, but she was used to cold. The wasting of coals was not approved of at Gethsemane, and kindling hard to be got most of the time. Here, in this house, there were hearths aplenty, but he had told her she must not light any, for fear of attracting attention.

Patience had never set foot in such a place, never, in her seventeen years. They had passed by them, of course, at times when they had been travelling, her mother speaking of camels and the eyes of needles, her father enumerating the injustices, the encroachments afflicting the common lands, calling down God's judgement on those who had broken the backs of the poor. Patience had paid lip service to their words, murmured her agreements, but in her heart she had always known that it was in places such as these, not travelling dirt roads or working her fingers to the bone carding cloth, spinning, doing her mother's endless bidding, that she belonged.

She left what he had told her was the 'great parlour' of the house, which for all its grandeur was a cold place, heartless in its way, and began to ascend the great staircase to the floor above. Patience was used to moving quietly. She was careful to make little sound opening the doors of the rooms on the first floor, lest someone else should be there, in spite of his assurances, but all she heard were echoes. The small room he had said she might have for herself, for now, was in the attic, where servants usually slept three to a bed, with neither drapes at the windows nor matting on the floor. It reminded Patience of her cell at Gethsemane, and although she had thanked him for it, she did not like it.

He hadn't come back yesterday, as he had promised he would, and the light of today was growing dim. She reasoned that she would have plenty warning of his coming, every noise in the house echoing through its three floors, amplified so that it sounded louder in her head than did the habitual drone of London that usually enveloped her. There were six doors leading off from the gallery. Patience tried them all in turn. The first was evidently a man's room; empty, it held nevertheless a lingering smell of men, of man, of tobacco smoke, boots, steel, horse. Not him, though; it did not smell of him.

One after another she opened the doors, revealing rooms, some fine, some plain but furnished well. The room which pleased her best was a woman's room – for all that Patience had spent her seventeen years denied womanly things, fripperies, vanities, silks, laces, tapestries, perfumes, ointments and ornament, she knew this to be a woman's room.

Opening the doors of the large oak wardrobe, she brushed her hand through the winter dresses and riding habits hanging there. Her fingers lighted on a heavy green silk bodice shot through with metal threads and lingered a moment. With a little further searching she came upon the skirt that matched. The rough old bloodstone ring she had taken from her mother looked crude and grubby against the silk. She pulled it off her finger and let it fall to the floor. Patience had never worn anything that her father had not woven, nor she or her mother sewn – rough, serviceable woollen dresses in brown or black, bleached linen collars and tuckers, headdresses that heightened rather than masked the plainness of her face. Patience took a fine linen smock, also embroidered with silks and metal threads, from a chest she had opened, and put it on. Then she set to work on the bodice and skirt, agile fingers soon mastering the many hooks, ties and buttons of a rich woman's dress.

Patience appraised herself in the glass. She was not so foolish – she was not foolish at all, in fact – to believe that even now, like this, she might appear beautiful to him, not like the others. But then the others were not here, they would not be here, and not even he could think them lovely now. Besides, no one could have the power over him that she did, for she had the letter. Patience watched herself turn in the long Italian looking glass, ran a finger across her own bare neck and wondered where in this new box of treasures he had put her in she might find a suitable adornment.

Nathaniel and the hound were coming in from their afternoon run out by East Smithfield. The day was fading and it would soon be dusk, later by far than he was usually permitted to be out of Gethsemane, but there was no one there to chastise him for it now. The prophetess would often squawk some intimation of doom his way, but he was learning not to pay too much heed to the sharp tongue of the bedridden crone. If Seeker could remove Elizabeth Crowe, he could certainly remove Mother Wilkins, and he had signalled his desire to do so more than once.

Suddenly, the dog tensed. Nathaniel turned and saw

coming towards them down the Minories a horseman: it was Seeker. Both man and horse looked windswept, exhilarated. Seeker slowed and then brought the animal to a halt before dismounting and allowing himself to be half mauled by the joyous dog.

'I needed to get out of the city, clear my head of its odours,' said Seeker. 'We have been riding out on Hackney Downs; I'd wager he can smell it on us – it's one of his favourite places.'

'He has missed you,' said Nathaniel.

'And I him, but I have my duty to attend to and he his. I hope he guards Gethsemane well.'

'Very well,' said Nathaniel, taking Acheron's bridle as Seeker occupied himself with the hound. 'But I don't think he likes it there. He prowls the courtyard constantly, and old Mother Wilkins keeps her door shut at all times now, for every time anyone opens it, Dog is waiting outside it, watching and growling.'

Seeker looked quizzically at the hound. 'You don't like the tenor of the old witch's preaching, eh? Good boy, neither do I.'

Back at the almshouses, Nathaniel soon had a fire going in the courtyard pit while Seeker fed and watered the horse. The old woman's door was, as was usual now, closed, and the girl who had been left to attend to her careful always to close it again behind her when she went back and forth between the prophetess and the gaggle of small children who had been left in her care, all housed now in the Master's lodging that had been Goodwill and Elizabeth Crowe's quarters.

'Where does your sister usually sleep?' asked Seeker once they had the fire going and the girl had fetched them some ale.

Nathaniel nodded towards the prophetess's cottage. 'In the room next door to Mother Wilkins. Patience pretends to reverence the old woman, but I can see in her eyes that she despises her.'

'Hmm. And you have still had no word from your sister?'

Nathaniel turned his beaker of ale in his hands. 'I've heard nothing. No one has. I asked Margaret there, and she says even Mother Wilkins doesn't know where she is.'

'Are you afraid for her?'

Nathaniel shook his head, and continued to avoid Seeker's eye. 'Patience will be all right. She's a liar and a thief and cruel, and will be a match for whoever might mean her harm.' He looked up at Seeker now. 'I don't wish her harm, I just don't want to see her again. It's better here without her.'

Seeker regarded the boy a minute. There might be something buried deep in there, amid all the cruelties Patience Crowe had heaped upon her brother, that would point to where the girl was. 'Tell me what kind of lies she told, Nathaniel.'

Nathaniel scuffed his boots in the dirt of the courtyard.

'All the usual sort – my parents would ask her to pass some instruction to me, and Patience would claim she had, and watch me be punished for disobedience when the thing was not done, when she had never given me the message at all. At other times she would steal from the larder – an apple, or an egg perhaps, and say she had seen me do it.'

'And your parents always believed her?'

Nathaniel's lip dropped. 'Mother did. I don't think Father always did, but he rarely said anything. Sometimes, if they weren't watching, he'd not whip me as hard as he might have done. Patience usually did watch though; she liked it.'

Seeker swallowed down his anger: this was not the time for that anger – it would keep. But Nathaniel was holding something back from him.

'What other lies did Patience tell, Nathaniel?'

Nathaniel drank down more of his ale.

'She started missing the preachings, saying she felt ill, and Mother would excuse her – it was a thing unheard of. If you could stand up, you went to the preaching, and even Mother Wilkins would be carried there when she felt too weak to walk. There was nothing wrong with Patience.'

'And yet your mother excused her?'

Nathaniel nodded. 'One night I had to leave the meeting room early, to fetch the bread and ale for the people who had come to hear Mother preach. It was usually Patience's task, but Patience had said she was unwell, and so she was given a cordial of ginger and sent to her bed. But when I was going across the courtyard to the kitchen, I noticed the light burning in Patience's window – she was standing by it, and taking down the hood of her cloak. I knew she hadn't been in her bed, but out in the streets somewhere.'

'Did you challenge her about it?'

'Not then,' said Nathaniel glumly, 'for I had the bread and ale to fetch and there would have been a great deal of trouble if I'd come in late with it. I told her the next morning that I knew she had been out.'

'And how did she respond?'

'She threatened to black her own eye and then say that I had hit her if I told anyone of it.'

'So she didn't deny she had been out, then?' said Seeker.

Nathaniel was miserable. 'She laughed about it, mocked me that it was so easy for her to get out of listening to Mother's sermons, to do as she pleased.'

'Did she tell you where she'd gone?'

'No, but I noticed that she did it more and more often.'

Seeker turned his mug of ale in his hand as he considered this.

'Was this before Gideon also stopped attending your mother's meetings or afterwards?'

Nathaniel didn't need to think about it. 'It was before. I . . . I think it was because of Patience that Gideon started to miss services too. I think . . .'

'Nathaniel?'

'I think he might have been following her.'

Seeker had not expected this. 'Did he tell you this?'

'No, she did.'

Seeker moved closer to the boy. 'Why didn't you tell me this before, Nathaniel?'

His face was flushed and tears were brimming on his lashes. 'Because she said horrible things, lewd things about Gideon that I knew were not true. But I think the bit about him following her might have been true.'

'What makes you believe that?'

'I came into our room one day, the room that Gideon and I shared, and I found Patience there, searching through Gideon's things. She was very, very angry, and said that he had stolen something from her. She said it was a book, and she wanted it back. But Patience never had a book, none of us has any book, save Mother's Bible, that is kept in the meeting room, and that Father reads from at all our meals.'

'Did she find the book?'

Nathaniel shook his head.

'And did you ask him about it?'

Nathaniel's reply was almost inaudible. 'There wasn't time.'

'No time? Why not? When was this?'

'That last day, when he came rushing in and wrote the hurried note and gave me the salt to leave at the Black Fox. I wanted to tell him that Patience had been searching through his things, but there was no time. After he left I looked in the secret hiding place he had that Patience had not found. The book was in there.'

Seeker knew what was coming next, and spared Nathaniel the difficulty of telling him. 'It was the book you gave me, the register of the school at the Three Nails, wasn't it?'

'Yes,' said Nathaniel, not looking at him, 'it was.'

Acheron returned safely to his stall in the stables at Horse Guard Yard, Seeker wearily climbed the stairs to his own chamber near the Cockpit. There was a tension of waiting in the air – he knew without having to ask that the Rat had not yet been brought in. Meadowe was walking down the corridor towards him, a sheaf of reports in his hand. The man was a shadow. Seeker could not even tell at first if he had seen him, and had to speak his name twice before Meadowe answered. 'Sorry, Seeker. I hardly know if I'm on my way somewhere, or returning.'

Seeker nodded towards the end of the corridor from which Meadowe had just emerged. 'Have you come from the Cypher Office, by any chance?'

'Yes,' said Meadowe, his face suddenly bright. 'Yes, I have. And I am on my way to Dorislaus at the postal office. I think it possible our Royalist friends have overreached themselves.'

'It is a habit of theirs,' smiled Seeker. Then he lowered his voice. 'And Marvell?'

Meadowe raised his eyebrows and breathed out a heavy sigh. 'Confined to the Censor Office, and not best pleased.'

'I'll talk to him,' said Seeker, 'although for now, I have other business to attend to.'

Closing the door to his room firmly behind him a few minutes later, Seeker unlocked the door of the small wooden cabinet set into the wall and took out the original register of the school at the Three Nails.

He studied it once more, but nothing in it told him why it should have come into Patience Crowe's possession. It seemed clear to Seeker that the girl must have got into the schoolroom at some point, in order to make the switch of the registers. What was not so clear to him was how, or why, she had done it. 'Three,' he said to himself, closing the book. Three young people, between childhood and adulthood – the schoolboy Edward Yuill, Isabella, the serving girl from the Black Fox, and now Patience Crowe – who had some connection to Shadrach Jones, were missing. He would have to return to the Three Nails, to question not Shadrach Jones, but the boys still in his care. It was too late tonight though – they would all be abed, and safe, Seeker hoped.

Wherever Patience Crowe was, Seeker was beginning to think it might be she who held the key to the disappearance of the other missing children, and to the murder of Carter Blyth. He was also convinced that whatever she had done, she could not have not acted alone. Having locked the school register in the wall cabinet once more, Seeker picked up his helmet, put on his cloak, and snuffed out the candle that burned on his desk.

Out in the corridor, he collared the first guard he came across. 'Tell Mr Meadowe if he needs me, I will be found at

Bridewell,' and then he left for the city, leaving the pacifying of Andrew Marvell for another day.

Even in the warming glow of candlelight and the fire that had now been lit in the hearth of the warden's room, Elizabeth Crowe looked no different than she had earlier, or indeed on any of the occasions that he had seen her: bloodless, humourless, as if the misery of the place originated within her rather than in the dirt and despair of her surroundings. Seeker had never seen a human being with eyes so dead, so devoid of life or compassion. He swore to himself that however the events of the next days or weeks might unfold, Nathaniel would not be left at the mercy of this woman.

She looked at him with unconcealed loathing. 'Back again, Seeker. What is it this time?'

'Your daughter.'

There was a brief movement. Elizabeth Crowe's mouth twitched. 'You've found her.'

'No. But I know what she has done.'

The woman didn't even blink. 'What has she done?' Her voice was like one stone grinding against another.

'I believe she has been complicit in the abduction, and perhaps the killing, of four children and in the murder of an agent of the Protectorate.'

Elizabeth smiled her unpleasant smile, a slight relaxation seeming to work its way through her. 'So, Gideon Fell was your spy. Patience tried to tell her father that, but the fool wouldn't believe her. Gideon was a comrade-in-arms, Gideon was one of the chosen. My husband can be blind, and over-soft at times, but I am not, Mr Seeker. Your spy deserved to die: "Then shall ye do unto him, as he had thought to have done unto his brother: so shalt thou put the evil away from among you." He deserved to die, but my daughter did not kill him. A slip of a girl against a man like that?'

It was interesting, thought Seeker, that she had not argued her daughter was too good, too kind a creature for murder, only that she was too slight a thing to do it. 'Who did, then?' he asked, feeling his temper rise in the face of this woman's casual indifference.

She shrugged her shoulders contemptuously. 'How should I know? Tell me where Patience is.'

Seeker got up, unable to trust himself not to strike the complacency from her dead-eyed face. 'How should I know?' he returned. 'With whoever it was helped her take those children, always assuming it wasn't you. Is it a man, Elizabeth? A man that you let her wander the streets like a wanton to see? A man that Gideon Fell saw her with? Is he a good man, do you think? Or do you think perhaps you'll never see your daughter again?'

He had touched a nerve now, he had reached something; behind the death mask of Elizabeth Crowe's face he could see her thoughts racing, but then she rallied herself, her lips clamped shut, and a long, bitter silence filled the room. Seeker had had enough. He called for the guard to come and take her back to her cell. The man appeared and Seeker rose to leave, not even glancing at Elizabeth Crowe, for fear that one more sight of her would cause him to lose his composure. As he reached the door, the same harsh voice like grinding stone stopped him.

'Ashpenaz,' she said. 'That's all I know. She called him Ashpenaz.'

TWENTY-THREE

Marvell's Lists

William Godmanson heard the footsteps cross the school-room floor beneath and the door creak open before being softly closed again. He lay motionless, frightened to move lest he waken any of the other boys. When he heard the outer door close at last, he crept quietly over to the small window of the boys' dormitory, and looked out onto the street. It was still dark, and an icy fog had come up from the river to snake around the houses and streets of Holborn. Yet William could see enough to know the shape of the man who had just left, to recognise the walk. It was not the first time he had been woken by the sound of Shadrach Jones leaving the Three Nails in the night. By the time dawn came, William still had not slept.

The junior clerk from the Censor Office tried to hurry past Seeker, but was jerked to a halt as Seeker placed a heavy hand on his chest. 'Is Mr Marvell in there just now?' he said, indicating the ante-room the clerk had just left.

'Yes, Captain. He's been there all morning.'

'And how is his humour?'

The young man hesitated.

'He's writing a lot, Captain, and muttering. No one wants to stay in there with him.'

'Ah,' said Seeker, 'well, I shall go in full armed, now I know what to expect.'

Marvell was sitting in the corner of the room, by the fire, and was indeed scribbling by the light of three candles, all of which he had placed by himself, regardless of the needs of others in the room.

'Another commission from the Lord Protector?' asked Seeker. 'Do we take aim again at Holland today, or France?'

'Neither. It is a list of my laundry and other linens. Then I begin on one of my books.'

Seeker sat down comfortably in the chair opposite, stretched out his feet before the fire, and wondered how to avoid further antagonising this surly, witty, learned man, whose company gave him so much unexpected pleasure. 'Should we know the reason you find yourself impelled to such urgent tasks?'

'Hmph. I would be astonished if there was anything you didn't know. After all, I am a Royalist, not to be trusted, holed up in here, reading ridiculous pamphlets while insidious milksops like Marcus Bridlington are set loose on the streets of London to protect us all. I am preparing my will, for I expect at any time to be hanged as a Royalist spy, or to be despatched by the Sealed Knot when they override the city – as they surely will, given the quality of some of our agents in the field.'

'No one thinks you're a Royalist spy,' said Seeker, and then corrected himself in response to Marvell's raised eyebrows and pursed lips. 'Well, yes, there are those that do suspect you, but I know that you are not, and I have had you confined here for your own protection, until this present crisis is over, and this latest venture of their Sealed Knot untangled.'

'But why?' pleaded Marvell. 'Why me? How many others started out in the one camp – and I was hardly that – and have ended in the other? Have I not proven myself? The Lord Protector himself trusts me – he asked me to write epigrams for his portrait for the Queen of Sweden, you know!'

'And very fine she thought them, they tell me.'

'Indeed. And the poem he is so delighted with, celebrating the first year of his Protectorate . . .'

'Yes,' agreed Seeker, 'I had heard that that was you, too. And I hear that it is also very fine.'

Marvell's indignation was further inflamed. 'You mean you have not seen it?'

Seeker laughed. 'Andrew, I am a captain of the guard of the Council of State. Last week I heard one of the Lord Protector's advisors comment that I still carry about me the air of a Yorkshire bog, another wager that I wrestle bullocks as a pastime.'

Marvell's eyebrows disappeared further into his hair. 'And what did Cromwell say to that?'

'That he had thrown a bullock or two himself in his time, and that there are worse smells than a Yorkshire bog.'

Marvell laughed. 'That will have silenced them.'

'For a time. But my point is, they think me more ignorant than the hogs Dorcas Wells roasts up at the Black Fox. They don't show me your poems.'

Marvell sighed. 'No. I suppose not. But surely they cannot question my loyalty now? And yet Meadowe confines me to this office like a naughty schoolboy.'

'It was me who advised him to do that, for your own protection. After your visit to Lady Anne's house—'

'It was *you* who sent me there!' blustered Marvell.

'I know. But I didn't expect her and Davenant to try to turn you, and I didn't know her Rat was going to set out on some mission for the Sealed Knot under your very nose.'

Marvell coloured. 'I know. I'm sorry, I should have paid closer attention – they distracted me with flattery.'

'Yes, they did. They think themselves clever – and we do well not to underestimate that woman. Whatever we discover when we finally get this Rat by the tail, I don't want her to be able to seek any kind of leverage by claiming that you were in some way involved.'

'I am not!'

'No. And the closer we keep you to us, the less likely it is that anyone can claim you are. But think, is there anything you might not have told me, might not have put in your report of that gathering that strikes you now as strange or important? Anything spoken of that strikes you as suggestive of some sort of subterfuge, deception, something they might have disguised as—'

Marvell leaned forward, his face aglow. 'Disguise! That's it. That's what she wanted them for, disguises!'

Seeker put up a hand. 'Hold up, Andrew. What disguises? What are you talking about?'

Now it was a different Marvell before him, one in his element, animated rather than sullen, aglow rather than lugubrious, one whose mouth could hardly keep pace with the thoughts chasing each other to his lips.

'It was after I'd recited my poem about Flecknoe . . .'

Seeker went through Marvell's report in his mind, and recalled something about an English priest Marvell had met over ten years ago in Rome. 'Yes?'

'Well, they were greatly entertained, and I, too, found myself quite merry. They asked me for particulars of just how dirty Flecknoe's shirt *was*.' Marvell laughed, and Seeker, bemused, waited. 'Anyhow, that set the company to talk of dress, and then of costume, and Henry Lawes and Sir William began to reminisce on the wonderful costumes worn by the King's Men and players at the Swan and the Fortune and the like, and Lawes mused sadly on whatever might have become of them after the theatres had been shut down, and Lady Anne leaned forward and said, "Why, Henry, some of them are here!" But then Sir William coughed loudly, and she suddenly said, "That is to say, I think I have some sketches in a book somewhere." But that is not what she meant, Seeker, I am certain of it. She has costumes in that house, and unless she means to put on a play – which there was no word of – they must be for something else.'

Seeker followed Marvell's line of thought entirely. Disguises. The Stuarts could not get over their love of masques, of theatre, of playing the other, and in their exile from England it had served them very well. Charles Stuart's own cousin, Rupert of the Rhine, one of his father's best and most ruthless commanders, and one of the best-known faces in Europe, had slipped into the country and away on more than one occasion, unnoticed by the authorities of the Republic, so adept was he at assuming a disguise. Charles himself had only escaped after Worcester by virtue of his disguise as a manservant to a young gentlewoman.

Marvell continued in full flow. 'The plays, Seeker, do you remember, the costumes they had?'

Seeker laughed. 'The players who found their way to the villages and clearings of Yorkshire and Cumbria travelled light. We were to use our imaginations.'

'Indeed, indeed. But did you never go into town, did you never see them in London?'

'I never came near London until General Fairfax had to threaten Parliament in '47, and by then, Andrew, plays were not quite the thing.'

Again Marvell coloured. 'No, I suppose they weren't. But I tell you, Seeker, they had costumes for every part imaginable. Fashions may have changed, but it wouldn't challenge a good seamstress greatly to alter a gown from the 1620s so that it served for now, or a priest's cassock to be an old cloak and breeches for some fellow down on his luck.'

'A good seamstress': the words echoed in Seeker's head,

but it was Anne Winter's voice he heard, not Marvell, and it was when she'd spoken of Charity Penn, 'She was making fair to be a gifted seamstress.' And Anne Winter's own fingers had been pricked by needle points. 'They're sewing disguises in there,' Seeker said at last.

Marvell nodded eagerly. 'A man might walk into Anne Winter's house a prince and walk out of it a washerwoman.'

'Or the other way round,' said Seeker. He stood up. 'Come, Marvell, leave your laundry list; you won't be needing it today.'

TWENTY-FOUR

A Mathematical Problem

Marvell rode alongside Seeker, on a mount of his own choosing from the Whitehall stable. They took four guards with them. As they trotted briskly past Scotland Yard, Seeker noticed George Downing, his clerk Pepys a step behind him, and Bridlington, whom Downing now seemed to have adopted into his own service, emerge onto the street from a coffee house up ahead at Charing Cross. It was Pepys who, deftly retreating to the doorway, called the attention of the other two to the imminent approach of the riding party, and it gave Seeker no little pleasure to see the surprise on Downing and Bridlington's faces as they recognised Marvell as the horseman whose mount they had to jump back to avoid.

The journey eastwards, into and through the city, was achieved at a good pace and without incident. Seeker was not yet ready to mention to Marvell the name of Ashpenaz. Instead, as the demands of cutting through street traffic – human, animal and wheeled – permitted, Marvell and Seeker talked of places, people they had in common in the north. Marvell's childhood had been compassed by light, water, marshland, the great port of Hull, the sea with all the promises it whispered of a world unknown. Seeker's was one that had taken him to high, harsh places, craggy passes and blasted moors, or deep forests, smelling of moss, bark, peat, further into a place peopled by the past and its stories. They were bound, nonetheless, by an understanding that the north was *different*, that they could understand in each other things those from the south, from the city, could not. And they were bound by Fairfax, whom one had served in war and the other in peace, and towards whom both felt complete loyalty.

'Do you think he would have dealt differently with Parliament?' Marvell asked.

Yes, Seeker thought, but didn't say. Instead, he said, 'It doesn't matter what he or anyone else might have done. Fairfax laid down his commission. Cromwell never has, and he is Lord Protector. We are servants of the Protectorate, you and I, Andrew. We don't deal in might-have-beens.'

The rest of the journey was made in a pensive silence, until they turned off Mark Lane onto Hart Street for Crutched Friars. There was a visible stiffening in Seeker's pose, a hardening of his face. 'When we get there, don't be baited – for she will try. I will do the talking.'

Looking at the set of Seeker's face, reflected in that of the four guards riding behind them, Marvell was not disposed to argue.

*

The guard had been placed inside Anne Winter's house, behind the entrance door, not in front of it facing out onto the street as was more usual. It had been agreed with Mead-owe: no one was to know of their pursuit of the Rat, or that her house was suspect. The more confidence in their success they had, the more likely Charles Stuart's plotters were to make a mistake.

The man stood aside as Seeker and Marvell entered the hallway. The four armed guards had been sent in by the back. A startled housemaid dropped the tray she had just carried through from the kitchens. The clatter of pewter on tile would have been enough to summon the inhabitants of the neighbouring house, never mind this one. Anne Winter was at the head of the stair in no time, and descending it in a fury. Her hair was not yet done up, and her dress a simple one. The red shawl around her shoulders somehow seemed to heighten the impression of outrage, but behind the anger, Seeker could see fear.

'What now, Seeker?' she said, throwing her arm out to encompass the party emerging from the back stairway. 'A raid? Or am I to be thrown from my own home, see it turned over to one of Cromwell's favourites? Yourself, per-haps? Do you like my house, Captain Seeker?' She took a moment to steady her breath, until her eye at last lighted on Marvell. 'And Marvell here too? In your so well-*turned coat*.'

Marvell readied himself to reply, but a well-aimed look from Seeker made him think the better of it.

'Coats, Lady Anne, that's what we would have of you,

and gowns and shifts and cloaks and breeches,' said Seeker evenly. 'Where would we find them?'

Anne Winter's brow furrowed and she looked at him as if he had lost his senses. 'Cloaks? Breeches? What in God's name are you talking about man?'

'Not in God's name,' said Seeker, 'but the Protector's. Where are the costumes, Lady Anne?'

The woman could not help but cast a hasty glance at Andrew Marvell. 'I don't know what you're talking about.'

'No?' said Seeker. 'You knew well enough the other day, when Sir William Davenant and Henry Lawes were here to take coffee and be entertained by Marvell here. I think you have mistaken him.'

'It appears I did,' she replied. 'I don't imagine I have been the first, nor will be the last to do so.' She looked directly at Marvell now. 'I thought him a gentleman.'

Seeker could see Marvell's mouth twitch and his face begin to colour, but to the man's credit, he kept his response to himself. Seeker decided she'd had her say.

'That arrogance will see you to the block one day, Lady Anne. Where are the costumes of which you spoke to Davenant and Lawes?'

'I spoke of no costumes.'

This time Marvell was not to be silenced. 'Oh, but you did, my lady. You spoke of the wardrobe of the King's Men, and bragged that you had it here, but Davenant made you shut up.'

'I deny it,' she said coldly.

'Deny it all you like, Lady Anne,' said Seeker. 'Davenant will no doubt join you in your lie, but Henry Lawes will not.' He could see her calculating, she was too confident, too certain. 'I'll ask you again, Lady Anne, where are these costumes?'

'Wherever they are, you won't find them here.'

'Will I not?' he said. The woman seemed to feed off challenging him. He turned to his men. 'Start at the top floor. Take the house apart if you have to.'

She stood there, unmoving, her eyes never leaving his as the four soldiers passed her on the stairs. Seeker wondered if she practised that commanding pose in her looking glass at night, or if the firmness of her hold on the banister was to keep her upright and hide her fear. Once his men had reached the top floor, Seeker said, 'Come, Marvell; we will search the lady's apartments. She has the look of one of these women of the old court, with so many gowns she can hardly know what she has and what she has not.'

'You might have done better to bring Bridlington with you,' responded Marvell. 'If I recall, his reports were full of the cut of so-and-so's jacket and the quality of so-and-so's lace. He would have known what was of today's fashion and manufacture, and what from an earlier time.'

Seeker slapped Marvell on the shoulder, ignoring Anne Winter's look of impotent fury, and said, 'Courage, my friend – you and I can surely tell an old length of cloth from a new one.'

Twenty minutes later, as the piles of gowns, shifts,

bodices, sleeves, collars and cuffs laid out on the bed and floor of Anne Winter's chamber grew ever higher, Seeker was beginning to regret not having brought Bridlington, or even one of the Protector's daughter's lady's maids along with him. Marvell, however, had a better eye for the styles of women's clothing than he, and only one ensemble really gave him pause for thought. There was a short linen waistcoat, a woman's, scalloped at the bottom and embroidered with thick traceries of gold silk thread around flowers and berries of red and green, in an intricate pattern of knots and roses, paired with a red silk skirt with matching tracery. Marvell paused, laid out the garments together as if to picture the woman who might have worn them. He turned to Seeker. 'These are over thirty years old, I would say.'

'Exactly thirty,' said Anne Winter. 'They were my mother's.'

Seeker didn't quibble. They had struck him as familiar the moment Marvell had laid them out together. He remembered where he had seen him before – Anne Winter's mother had been wearing them in the family portrait he had seen in her private parlour on the first occasion he'd been in this house. 'Come,' he said to Marvell, 'there's nothing here.'

Just as they were about to leave the room, the piles of clothing still on the bed and floor, Seeker noticed a button of mother-of-pearl hang loose on its white silk thread from a high-heeled cream velvet slipper.

Seeker picked up the slipper, fingered the button and the loose length of thread from which it hung. 'Where is your sewing box, Lady Anne?'

'What?' She looked truly alarmed for the first time.

'Your sewing box, where you keep your needles and threads and pins and the like for stitching and mending. When I called here two weeks ago, you had pricked your finger on the point of a needle. Where is your sewing box?'

'I . . . I have none. I . . . it went missing at the same time as Charity left.'

'Charity Penn was long gone before I ever set foot in this house. Do better.'

She shook her head, sat down, mindless of the cushion of silk gowns and lace she was crushing beneath her. 'I . . . I have a few things on my dressing table there—'

Seeker walked over, picked up some trinket boxes, opened them. One was made of silver and set with mother-of-pearl, and inside it he found two needles and a dozen pins. He snorted with contempt. 'Am I to believe that a woman so used to luxury relies on these?' He tipped the needles and pins onto the dressing table, where they rolled towards the edge. 'They would hardly serve for mending your handkerchiefs.'

Anne Winter watched the needles and pins roll, drop to the floor, her thoughts chasing them as if somehow they might hold the answer.

'Perhaps the requisite implements are kept below stairs, in the servants' hall?' offered Marvell.

'Oh, perhaps they are,' said Seeker. 'That would be likely enough, in a house such as this. Perhaps Lady Anne has simply forgotten.'

'No, no,' she said, more assured again. 'It is just that I have ordered a new set from the cutlers on Ironmonger Lane, and they are not yet ready.'

'What?' said Seeker. 'The girl has been gone weeks. Feeble, Lady Anne, for one of your reserves of duplicity. We will take this house apart.'

'And you will not find anything,' she said.

Two hours later, Seeker was like an angry bull whose patience was about to desert him. Marvell, having heard of him when in this humour but never before seen it, hadn't ventured a word for nigh on forty minutes. They had searched through the whole house, from cellar to attic. They had lifted rugs, gone through trapdoors, inspected every cupboard for false backs, lifted every picture, every tapestry from the walls, in the search for hidden compartments. Only behind the new wooden wall panelling of Lady Anne's dining parlour did they find some success, exposing cavities of good height but little depth, which she explained away as being for the hiding of valuables, although Seeker thought them ideally suited to the concealment of weaponry. Aside from that, nothing. The Rat's room was as bare as a cell. The gardens and outhouses had been searched, the knot hedge in its middle dug out by two of the guards not quite managing to mask their disgruntlement. 'I told you, did I not? I told you you would find nothing,' said Anne Winter, standing at his side as he overlooked the whole garden from the vantage point of the first-floor landing window.

Her tone was too certain, and she struggled to hide a note of triumph. There was something in this house, and she had begun to relax too much because she had convinced herself now that he wouldn't find it. What had he not seen, or not recognised for what it was when he had seen it? Seeker's forehead tightened in frustration, but he had put off the matter of Ashpenaz long enough – he wouldn't waste any more of his time on Anne Winter today.

Without responding to her, he turned and began to descend the stairs, calling to Marvell, who was examining Anne Winter's dining hall a third time, to go outside and tell the guards there to give off their digging. Seeker had reached the bottom step when Anne Winter, still standing at the window, spoke.

'I think you have overreached yourself this time, Captain. This farrago will be the talk of the taverns and coffee houses before you reach St Paul's.'

He'd stopped where he was when she started to speak, and now he didn't reply. He was hardly listening to her. He was looking instead at his left hand, which was resting on the plain ball finial atop the intricately carved square newel post at the bottom of the banister. It was new, the old, loose newel having been replaced since his last visit here. The Baxton crest had been carved at the top of each of four faces of the post, but the finial itself was a simple, rounded handrest atop a slim wooden disc with a pattern of stars. Seeker had seen such work in other houses, as grand and grander than this – no one went to the trouble of having so fine a balustrade carved only to top it with such a simple head. The head of the newel post on such staircases was reserved for the most intricate and elaborate of carvings. Seeker had seen wood-carved vases overflowing with fruit or foliage, minarets, moulds of a patron's favourite hound, but never, on such a fine stairway, so simple a rounded lump of wood. More strange was that anyone should have gone to the trouble of marking on the wooden disc on which it rested so delicate a pattern of stars. Seeker looked more closely. There were six small, carved wooden stars altogether, and each had a number of small dots, no bigger than a pinhead, leading from the centre to one of its points. The number of dots in each point of the star was different. Seeker looked at the newel post to his right, at the other side of the broad bottom step. Again, beneath the simple rounded hand-rest was a wooden disc decorated with six small carved stars. Again Seeker stooped a little, to examine them more closely. There were no dots on any of the points of these stars. He put his palm over the rounded hand-rest, closed his fingers about it, and started to turn. The newel post, from top to bottom, remained rigid. Seeker crossed back to the post on the left, closed his hand over it and again, started to turn. This time, while the post itself remained rigid, the rounded handhold started to move, and only now did he notice, carved into the bottom of its stem, a small, straight mark, a pointer. He looked at up again at Anne Winter. There was no look of triumph on her face now – it was ashen, and she had run out of lies. Still looking at her, he spoke to the first of the guards who had emerged by the back stairs into the tiled hall. 'Take my horse, ride as fast as you can to White-hall and get Dr Wallis out of the Cryptography Office; bring him back here without delay.'

Wallis carried with him a mildly distracted, benign air that fooled some into believing him absent-minded, other-worldly. Seeker knew differently: Dr John Wallis possessed one of the most astute mathematical minds in England, and from an early stage had served the Republican cause in the matter of deciphering codes. He was not other-worldly, he saw into the heart, the very centre of the way the world worked, understood processes in the minds of men and the things they made that others were not aware of.

'Seeker, they tell me you have a puzzle for me,' he said lightly, pausing to incline his head respectfully to Lady Anne as he tramped across her black and white tiled hallway.

Seeker showed him first the unmoving newel with the unmarked stars, and then, at the other side of the stair, its less rigid, more elaborate partner. A smile spread across Wallis's mouth as he looked from one to the other. 'Hah! Ingenious. So simple, yet so difficult to spot. You have a good eye for these things, Seeker.'

'I've made enough of them in my time,' said Seeker. He saw the look on Anne Winter's face: again, he had managed to surprise her.

'Oh, aye, Lady Anne. I was no more born a soldier than you a traitor.' He'd seen it so often in those of her background – they looked at a person and saw what they expected to see. Such arrogance had cost them dear time and again, and he was certain it was about to do so again, here in her very house.

After testing the unmoving finial once, Wallis lost all interest in it and gave his full, rapt attention to the other. He looked at it, without touching, for almost a minute, then bent a little lower to examine the carvings of the Baxton crest at the top of each side of the newel post. 'Remarkable,' he murmured to himself, before straightening and going back to examine the crests on the other post. 'Careless, of course, but remarkable all the same.'

Seeker had seen Wallis at work before and knew not to interrupt him during this process of observation. Wallis straightened himself again, sniffed, and marched back to the front door, nodding at the guard there to open it for him. He glanced very briefly at the brass crest door knocker, and strode in, pointing to the plainer, unmoving post. 'That's definitely the real one. Real crest, marked on all four sides, but this' – he was back at the other post, beckoning Seeker and pointing to the carved crest on one of its four sides – 'this is the only correct one on this post, for as you can see, the quarters of the escutcheon on the other three sides have been moved around in some way.'

Seeker looked. He knew the Baxton crest well enough: the symbols depicted on the four quarters of the Baxton shield had indeed been transposed on three of the four carved crests.

'Now,' continued Wallis, 'that means that this – the correct crest – is home – the direction in which each of the numbered star points must point. We must just work out the sequence. Pen and paper, if you please,' he said, beginning to turn the disc with his left hand and throwing out his right to no one in particular, awaiting the requested writing materials. Seeker pointed Marvell towards Lady Anne's private study, and a moment later the poet was scribbling numerals and combinations at the cryptographer's dictation. Wallis would turn the finial head, mutter, Marvell would scribble. It went on for almost ten minutes, in which time Seeker's eyes travelled from the odd pairing at the bottom of the stairway to the woman who was now seated on a low footstool by the empty fireplace of her own front hall. Her face was greyer than the remnants of the ashes lying at the bottom of the hearth.

Suddenly, Wallis stood up. 'Write this down,' he commanded Marvell before calling out a sequence of six numbers. Then he beckoned to Seeker. 'Turn the finial head as I tell you.' He repeated the numbers, slowly, and after each, Seeker turned the newel head as instructed. Before calling out the sixth, Wallis turned to Lady Anne, 'Is there anyone here who should move away from where they are currently standing? Any object that you would like to have moved?'

She pointed, her hand shaking a little, towards a large, silver-mounted nautilus shell jug on the hall table set against the wall opposite. 'Perhaps if someone could hold that jug a moment, and if Mr Marvell would like to move away from where he is standing to this side of the hall . . .'

At a flick of Seeker's head, the nearest guard went and took hold of the jug, and Marvell, who was standing almost in the centre of the hallway, looked at his feet, thoroughly alarmed, and stepped briskly across to stand by Lady Anne's footstool.

Seeing that all was ready, Wallis called out the sixth number, Seeker turned the post, and the final pointer clicked into place.

TWENTY-FIVE

The Jew of Malta

It was incredible. Seeker would not have believed it had he not seen it with his own eyes. At the final turn of the post, the final click, a great whirring sound had set up, as if a beast of some sort were waking beneath their feet. A slight trembling began, the hall table against the far wall indeed beginning to shake slightly, and then the section of flooring beneath where Marvell had been standing, about four foot square in all, juddered and dropped six inches before sliding beneath the bottom of the stairway to leave a large, square opening from which a narrow set of steps descended.

Before the exclamations of surprise from the guards in the hallway had died down, or Marvell recovered his composure, Seeker had issued an order for Lady Anne to be manacled.

'The Tower now, I suppose, is it, Seeker?' she said with a resigned smile.

'Not yet awhile,' he said. 'Will you tell us what this is?'

'What it is? I did not know about it. Surely the previous occupant of my house had secrets to hide.'

'I doubt it,' he said. 'But don't trouble yourself. There is nothing hidden that won't be found.'

After that, Anne Winter made no further comment, and ensuring she had guards on either side of her, Seeker, a flaming torch in his hand, descended the stairs, followed by Marvell. Wallis, whose interest had faded by the time the section of floor had slid fully out of sight, pleaded much business back at the Cryptography Office and again making his cursory bow to the lady prisoner of the house, left.

The glow of light from Seeker's torch spread out in a golden and widening circle as he descended. Marvell had also lit a torch, and when he gingerly joined Seeker on the ground floor of the secret chamber he let out a low whistle. 'Astonishing.'

'Yes,' murmured Seeker, but unlike Marvell, he wasn't looking around the long, narrow chamber in which they found themselves, but upwards, at the gap in the ceiling they had just come through. The detached section of floor – whose tiles, he had noticed only while passing down through the space, were of a much more thinly cut marble than those surrounding it – had been carefully and securely balanced on a set of runners, attached to a pulley, which was itself attached to a system of cogs and weights and a chain disappearing up into what he suspected they would find to be the inside of the newel post of the stairs. It was an ingenious piece of work, and he could admire it. He had already admired it, in fact – not made up like this, in three dimensions, a functioning machine, but as part of a scorched drawing rescued from a dying fire. He ran up the narrow stairway and stuck his head through the opening at the top. Looking to his men he said, 'I want two of you to go up to Holborn now. The school at the sign of the Three Nails. Arrest the master, Shadrach Jones, and take him to White-hall. Tell Mr Meadowe he is to be kept under lock and key until I return.' Turning to Lady Anne, he added, 'It was a clever game you played, your ladyship, but the game is up.'

She smiled valiantly. 'Perhaps we have just played but the first hand, Seeker.'

'Perhaps but, if that be so, it will not be you who deals the second.'

Returned to the chamber he began to examine what was down there: a bed, narrow, but made up with the finest of linens topped with an intricately embroidered silk coverlet. A washstand, the bowl and ewer good Bristol gallypot, new and not yet used, by the look of them. Beside the washstand was a fine walnut chair, with sturdy arms and upholstered in black leather, the legs elaborately turned and carved. It was set with an embroidered cushion he thought he might once have seen in her apartments at Whitehall, and was of better quality even than any she had in in her public draw-ing room. Behind the first door, nearest to the chimney shaft, they found a garde robe, the wooden seat and lid looking freshly planed and treated. Seeker lifted the lid and peered down the brick shaft; they could hear running water from a conduit below. Sniffing, he replaced the lid. 'Never used,' he said. Marvell also having satisfied himself of the condition of the water closet, they closed the door, and turned to examination of the small, narrow writing desk with stool, paper, ink, quill pens and pounce pot ready and waiting. If the implements from Anne Winter's own writing set had been fine, these were finer still.

'For whom?' asked Marvell, for this was evidently not intended for her Rat, nor, thought Seeker privately, the prison of a missing child.

'I have an idea,' said Seeker, 'but it seems too fantastic even for that woman.' He held up his torch to lighten the long, dark backdrop to this strange bedchamber. 'Let us examine further back.'

The room seemed to have no end, but to narrow into a long corridor, its ceiling so low that both Seeker and Marvell were constrained to stoop. The floor of the corridor also seemed to slope downwards. At the end of it, they came upon a strong oak door, bolted on the inside.

'That will open easy enough,' said Marvell, slipping the bolt and about to take hold of the iron handle.

'No, wait,' said Seeker, holding up a hand and leaning closer to examine the edge of the door and the jamb. 'It is not hinged.'

Marvell also examined the door more closely. 'Then how?'

Seeker handed him his torch and leaned in towards the iron handle. Grasping it firmly, he pushed sideways, to his left, and the door slowly slid into the wall.

Marvell's mouth was still gaping open when Seeker stepped through the opening to the very narrow space on the other side. He could smell coal dust in the air, and was facing a stack of bulging hempen sacks. He told Marvell to slide the door halfway back, so that he could examine it from the other side. He turned to look at the sacks and again at the door, before letting out a short laugh of grudging admiration.

'What is it?' asked Marvell from the other side.

Seeker laughed again, shook his head. 'Ingenious, yet simple enough. We're down in the coal cellar now, which I'd wager can only otherwise be accessed through a hatch from the back garden. If you came in through that hatch, all you would see would be a bank of sacks of coal. Should you think to shift a good number of those sacks, you would be confronted with what looks like nothing more than an old wood lining to the coal-shed wall. The whole wall this side is covered in it – untreated, dust-blackened pine – and when that door is closed, you wouldn't even notice it's there – there's no handle this side. You need someone on the inside to open it and let you through, one way or the other. Oh, but they've been busy.'

Seeker stepped back through to Marvell's side and slid the door closed again, but without bolting it this time. 'Let's see what else.'

They went back to the bedchamber, their torches before them, and examined the side of the room they had yet to look at. What their torches revealed was a long workbench with two stools set at it, and all the apparatus of a tailor's craft. 'Her sewing box,' said Seeker grimly. Down one side of the darkened backland behind the wooden stairway and against the rear wall, was a series of ancient-looking chests. Seeker opened the first one. 'I think we may have found your Mr Davenant's missing costumes.' The chest, like the others they opened, revealed fine and extravagant sets of clothing from a different age – clothing fit for the stage, and the players, male players all, who would command it. Dresses in the style favoured by the old Queen Elizabeth, or at best James's Anne of Denmark, their cut scandalously low, many of them too big by far for the generality of woman. Veils, headdresses, doublets, short hose, codpieces from another age, but all of the best of quality.

'How is it they are made so fine,' Seeker asked, 'that are just to be trod and paraded across a wooden stage?'

'Ah,' said Marvell, a sort of wonder in his eye and voice, 'but these were not the costumes of just any wandering players: these belonged to the King's Men – much of this would have been gifted from their own wardrobes by men and women at court.' He wandered from chest to chest. Smoothing his hand along fine silks, luxuriant furs, satins almost as bright as when first they had been stitched together. And then he stopped, looked more closely at the chests, at the front of them. 'They're numbered,' he said.

'Probably in accordance with this,' said Seeker, holding out to Marvell a cheaply bound and hastily written looking document.

Marvell took it and examined it by the light of one of the wall torches which they had lit. 'It's an inventory.'

Seeker nodded. 'I daresay you will understand it better than I.'

As Marvell's eyes travelled over the document, Seeker could see a kind of fascinated delight spread over his face. 'Specific costumes identified, play by play – the same to be used for different roles in different plays, of course,' he said.

'Of course,' said Seeker, suppressing a smile. 'But what does this tell us, how does it help us?'

'Well, some are marked as "altered to specifications" – you see here, and here.' He indicated the notes on several pages, relating to costumes from various plays, all made in the same hand.

'Anne Winter's hand,' said Seeker. 'I'd swear to it. But altered to what?'

Marvell had moved over to the long work table. He held up his torch to reveal thin sheets of paper spread out on it, cut patterns for breeches, hose, jackets, shirts. On a sheet beside them was written a list of measurements. Marvell looked at them, his brow furrowed. 'I am no seamstress, Captain – do you make any sense of these?'

Seeker, who had spent his childhood and youth watching his mother cut, stitch and mend every piece of clothing he, his father, his three brothers or his sister wore, knew what he was looking at. 'These are the measurements of a very tall, slim man.'

They searched under the table, where there were more

patterns stored in a long drawer – patterns for a workwoman's dress, a guard's uniform, a hawker, a man of law. All bore the same measurements – even the workwoman's dress.

'It doesn't make sense,' said Marvell. 'These are all for the same person.'

'Yes,' said Seeker, 'it does.' He turned slowly to face Marvell from the darkened corner of the room they had not yet properly examined. 'They are all for a tall young man, with long raven locks and large eyes under dark brows. He is twenty-four years of age. They say he has his mother's sensuous lips.'

Marvell stood back, his chin doubling on itself as he assessed Seeker. 'But how could you know such a thing?'

'Because,' said Seeker, lifting his torch so that it cast its light into the darkened corner he had just been looking at, 'that has been made for the same man.'

Marvell's sudden intake of breath seemed to reverberate around the stone walls of the hidden basement room. What the spreading glow from Seeker's torch revealed was, stretched on wooden hangers suspended from hooks on the ceiling, the separate pieces of a magnificent outfit woven in black silk – the intricately stitched doublet was of the new, short fashion, its sleeves lined with golden brocade slashed to reveal the loose white shirt beneath. The breeches were wide and trimmed with black lace, a garland of golden silk rosettes at its waistband. At the shoulders was pinned a matching black, lace-trimmed cloak. The golden brocade pattern at the edge of the cloak might at first glance have been any current fashionable refrain, but it wasn't. 'His initials,' breathed Marvell.

'Yes,' said Seeker. 'Lady Anne has been very busy, making ready a welcome for her expected guest.' At intervals around the base of the cloak, only an inch apart in a finely entwined golden scroll, were the letters CⅡR.

'Surely she cannot be expecting *him*,' said Marvell.

'You came close to saying it yourself, not four hours ago, more or less,' replied Seeker. 'A man might walk into this house a washerwoman and walk out of it a king.'

Half an hour later, while Seeker accompanied Lady Anne Winter on the short journey from her Aldgate house to the Tower of London, Marvell was still in her basement room, checking the rest of the inventory, on Seeker's orders. 'We need to know exactly what he might be wearing,' Seeker had said.

It had been an ingenious solution, Marvell thought, to the problem of finding disguises at short notice for a tall, slim young man whose appearance and disguises were already a thing of legend. How to disguise a man of such proportions as a woman? In clothes that had been designed to be worn by men in the first place. He went through the inventories and the chests, matching outfits that were there, marking those that were missing, assessing, from the patterns under the table, what they might be altered to. The last list of characters and costumes detailed in the book was for Marlowe's *The Jew of Malta*. Marvell had seen the play performed in the marketplace in Hull when he had been little more than a boy, and it had entranced him. The scheming, cunning Machivel, in particular, had taken hold on his young imagination. He remembered that the murder of one friar, made to look as if it had been done by the other, had frightened him for weeks afterwards, so that his mother had threatened he would go to no more plays. He cast his eye down the list and there they were – Jacomo and Bernardine – with the note *2 sets Blackfriars' robes* set beside it. He checked the relevant box, the last to be opened and bearing signs of having been visited by small vermin, but found only one set of robes, moth-eaten and nibbled about the hems. He checked again. Nothing. He knew that the other boxes had contained no such robes, and adjudged Lady Anne must have used the coarse black woollen garment for something and then forgotten about it. Knowing, however, of Seeker's insistence on nothing out of the ordinary being left out of a report, Marvell noted down the fact of the missing robe nonetheless, shut his book, blew out the torches, and began to make his weary way up the stairs to the better light of the now-absent Anne Winter's hallway.

They put her in the Beauchamp Tower, Meadowe, who had arrived as quickly as he could, having opined that 'it would do the lady no harm to reflect upon the green where other traitresses had lost their heads'. Seeker did not know that he'd ever heard the young Under-Secretary make a joke before. 'Thurloe's on his way, too,' he told Seeker. 'Even you couldn't have pinned him down in that sickroom after he heard this.' The order had gone out that the Rat must be taken alive, and that rather than follow him and whoever he was on his way to meet, they were to be arrested on the spot and brought to London at all possible speed and under the highest security.

'What about Shadrach Jones?'

'Who?' said Meadowe.

'The man who engineered the mechanisms concealing Anne Winter's hidden basement. He is posing as a schoolmaster of Holborn. I sent men to arrest him, and to take him to Whitehall for questioning.'

Meadowe shook his head. 'That's the first I have heard of it. You had better get up there yourself. There are people here aplenty to deal with Lady Anne.'

'You think?' said Seeker dubiously. 'I'd sooner deal with a sack of ferrets.'

He could still hear Meadowe's laughter as he descended the steps from the Beauchamp Tower out onto the green where the scaffold for Henry Tudor's queens had stood. A guard was waiting there, holding the bridle of a newly fed and watered Acheron. Swinging himself up into the saddle, Seeker spurred the horse out of the Postern Gate and urged him on the way to Holborn. He should have felt adrenalin coursing through him, but despite the magnitude of what they had discovered in the long narrow room, cunningly concealed between the other basement cellars of Anne Winter's house, he had a leaden feeling in the pit of his stomach that he could not shake. When first that section of marbled hall floor had begun to slide beneath the rest, he had hoped for a fleeting moment that he was about to discover, alive, those four missing children whose disappearances had so occupied Carter Blyth. His haste to get to Holborn was not only to check that Shadrach Jones had been secured by his men, but also so that he could question the boys again, without Jones being present, before he unleashed himself on the false schoolmaster back down in Whitehall. The school in Holborn connected Edward Yuill with Shadrach Jones; Patience Crowe's possession of the Three Nails' register connected her to Shadrach Jones; Elias Ellingworth's diary connected the girl Isabella from the Black Fox with Shadrach Jones; and now, the mechanical works in Anne Winter's house on Crutched Friars connected Charity Penn with Shadrach Jones. All four children had disappeared. The Three Nails, Gethsemane, the Black Fox, the house on Crutched Friars – movements around all four had been tracked by Carter Blyth, posing as Gideon Fell, and Carter Blyth was dead. And then there was the gardener's boy from Lincoln's Inn – the only one who appeared to have no connection to the Holborn schoolmaster. None that Seeker could yet discern, at any rate. He spurred Acheron faster through the streets of the city, not pausing to warn people to get out of his way, driving himself on towards the Three Nails and the answers he was certain awaited him there.

TWENTY-SIX

Ashpenaz

At the Three Nails, William Godmanson gathered the other boys around him and tried to pretend that he wasn't terrified. They'd heard Seeker's soldiers coming before they'd seen them. They'd been in the middle of an arithmetic lesson, and Mr Jones, whom William had heard come in just as it was time for the younger boys to be wakened, had been in a good humour, though very tired from his night wanderings, which William had taken care not to mention to the others. But then they'd heard voices outside the haberdasher's shop at the entrance to the yard, and two pairs of heavy feet come in unison towards the school door. The boys had stopped listening to Mr Jones, and he'd stopped talking. There had been no knock on the outer door – they heard it crash open without introduction or apology. By the time the door to their classroom itself was being forced open in similar manner, Mr Jones had dropped his pointer and jumped over the nearest bench, clattering one of the younger boys in the eye with an elbow as he did so. He was struggling at the catch of the small back window giving out onto the yard, before smashing it with the same elbow that had caught the schoolboy – it didn't matter; it was too late anyway. One of Seeker's guards had him by the neck of his worn black worsted waistcoat and hauled him backwards. Mr Jones took a flailing swing in response, but he was no fighter, that was plain to see: William could have bested him himself. The guard wasted no further time, but drew back a huge fist and smashed it into the side of Mr Jones's jaw. Blood and teeth splattered out of his mouth as he went down.

'Right, then. This'll be Shadrach Jones?' said the guard to the nearest boy.

The boy nodded vigorously, momentarily struck dumb.

'Well,' said the other guard, 'it'll be a holiday for you lot for the rest of the day. The Seeker wants this one. See you don't make a nuisance of yourselves.' Hooking an arm each under Shadrach Jones's shoulders, they dragged him out of the schoolroom, out of the Three Nails altogether, before slinging the rambling New Englander over the back of one of their horses, and calling behind them that if anyone was asking for Jones, they should enquire of Damian Seeker, at Whitehall.

William had been very firm with the other boys, to stop them from crying, and had set them tasks, as if the events of the morning, the events of the last few weeks, and months even, since the onset of Dr Evans's dotage, were nothing out of the ordinary. But their normality was like a thin thread that had frayed and slipped through so many fingers that now it felt to William he was the only one left holding it.

The glass from the broken window had been swept up and the boy from the cook shop on Holborn had just left after bringing the pot of mutton stew round for their dinner. William had tidied Dr Evans, brought him from his room, and set him in his usual seat at the top of the table. One of the younger boys had just about finished stumbling his way through a Latin grace and William was readying himself to begin ladling out the stew when they heard the horseman come in under the archway of the Three Nails and dismount in the backyard. William ordered the next oldest boy to dish up, and taking a poker from beside the fire, went to stand beside the bolted door as Dr Evans muttered some sort of repeated imprecation in Welsh. Three harsh knocks on the door were followed by three others, and a command that they should open up.

A quarter of an hour later, Seeker had heard everything about Shadrach Jones's night-wanderings that William Godmanson had to tell. It wasn't just by night, but at odd times of the day and evening too, that the under-master had absented himself from the school. He would claim he had a friend to see, some 'business' to put right, a lecture to attend, but always, whenever he went, he took his bag of drawings and measuring instruments with him. William had looked in the bag once when Mr Jones had been at the close-stool in the yard, and seen sketches of some fantastical machine, and a canvas belt holding many compasses, rules and other mathematical instruments William didn't know the use of. Mr Jones had brought back a second bag with him this morning though – William had seen him carry it into his chamber.

A search of Shadrach Jones's chamber soon revealed, hastily and ineffectively concealed beneath his flimsy washstand, a bag of tools – tools whose use Seeker understood very well, for they were those of his own trade before he had abandoned the life of an itinerant carpenter to become a soldier. Jones had not just designed the moveable floor and secret chamber beneath Anne Winter's hall, he must have executed the design, performed some of the necessary carpentry and engineered much of the work himself. It was an astonishing feat. Seeker's mind flitted back to Kent's, the time he had taken Nathaniel there, and Nathaniel had declared Jones to be a carpenter. The boy had obviously noticed what no one else had – Shadrach Jones, his bag of tools to hand, slipping into or out of Anne Winter's house on Crutched Friars. It would have saved a great deal of time, and perhaps some trouble, had Seeker paid as much attention to Nathaniel's casual comment as Nathaniel did to the details of the world around him.

But Jones's activities at Anne Winter's house were not what most interested Seeker at this moment. He told William to take his dinner and then come through to the schoolroom.

'We should bring Dr Evans as well,' said William. 'The

other boys are not so able for him as I, and he might get
past them and out.'

Seeker nodded, and helped the old Welshman take his
dinner before manoeuvring him through to the schoolroom
also. The old schoolmaster thanked him, in Welsh, and
promised to look into the matter of his lost sheep.

When they were at last settled, Seeker said, 'I want to ask
you about a girl who may have been here, and any man that
might have been with her.'

William relaxed a little. 'No girls are permitted here,
Captain, only sometimes Joanna, the girl from the cook
shop across the street, but she is only seven, and only comes
to help her brother fetch the pots back sometimes.'

'The girl I'm talking about is a young woman – about
sixteen or seventeen years of age. She is very plain – sharp
of feature, with small eyes and not at all pretty. She dresses
very plain, too, but clean. Black dress and simple white cuffs
and collar, her hair always covered by a plain white linen
cap, tied under her chin, and perhaps a black-brimmed hat.
Did you ever see such a girl with Shadrach Jones?'

'No, I never saw her with Mr Jones.'

'Oh,' said Seeker, ready to follow up with more questions, but William Godmanson wasn't finished.

'It was before that, before Mr Jones came from Massachusetts. Not long after Dr Evans started his wanderings.
There was one of those Fifth Monarchist women, preaching up in St Giles's Fields. Dr Evans had got that far before
Edward and I realised anything was amiss.'

'Edward Yuill?'

William nodded. 'We . . . we tried to manage things, between us, for the other boys, after Dr Evans started to get a bit . . . wandered in his mind, and before Mr Jones came. Edward left me to see to the younger ones that day, and he went out looking for Dr Evans. Found him at St Giles's, listening to the preacher-woman and shouting at her in Welsh. The woman's daughter helped Edward bring Dr Evans home.'

'And did the daughter stay awhile? Or ever come here again?'

'Not that I knew,' said William. 'But Edward got a bit secret after that.'

'And it was after that that you saw him out with a stranger, practising archery on Conduit Fields?'

William nodded.

'And this man was not with her when she helped William bring Dr Evans back from St Giles's?'

'Not that I saw.' William's brow furrowed. 'You think she knew the man that took Edward?'

Before Seeker could answer, Rhys Evans, who had been becoming increasingly agitated, leaned suddenly forward and grabbed Seeker by the front of his doublet. 'Ashpenaz!' he almost spat in Seeker's face. 'Ashpenaz!'

He held the front of the doublet a moment longer, staring into Seeker's face while William Godmanson sat rooted in his seat, too horrified to intervene. But Seeker gently released the old man's grip, and Evans sat back, spent. The old schoolmaster's eyes lost their focus, and he began murmuring to himself once more.

'Ashpenaz'. The name Elizabeth Crowe had also told him. Neither Cypher Office nor Dorislaus knew of anyone going by the alias of Ashpenaz, but Seeker realised suddenly that it might be a thing more simple than that. 'Bring me a Bible,' he said to William Godmanson.

And there it was, in the Book of Daniel, the favourite text of Goodwill and Elizabeth Crowe and all their like who looked for the imminent reign of Christ on Earth.

And the king spake unto Ashpenaz the master of his eunuchs that he should bring certain of the children of Israel . . . children in whom there was no blemish, but well favoured, and skilful in all wisdom, and cunning in knowledge, and understanding in science, and such as had the ability in them to stand in the king's palace . . .

It was an injunction to find the fairest and most gifted children in the land, and to train them to be attendants and advisors of the king. Daniel had been chosen, and along with him three other children, given the names Shadrach, Meshach and Abednego. Seeker said the names out loud, and Rhys Evans echoed him, nodding, pleased that he had been understood at last. Every one of the missing children whom Carter Blyth had tried to find – the schoolboy Edward Yuill, Anne Winter's housemaid Charity Penn, the girl Isabella from the Black Fox, and Jed, the gardener's boy from Lincoln's Inn – had been talked of as 'fair', 'beautiful', 'of great intelligence', 'gifted'. Something lifted within Seeker: for the first time since he had understood that Carter Blyth had been following the mystery of these disappeared children, he glimpsed the possibility that they might not be dead. Patience Crowe and the man known to her mother, and to Rhys Evans too, as Ashpenaz, had selected and taken children to be trained by the Fifth Monarchists to be the servants of the coming Christ. And Patience Crowe, the shallow, self-serving Patience Crowe, who cared little for the word of God and paid only lip service to her parents' creed, had done this for the game, the fun of it. She had done it with an accomplice to assist her, but Seeker did not believe for a minute that the scheme had been hers.

He left the Three Nails as quickly as was possible after that, having assured William Godmanson that a matron would be sent that day to care for them, a guard placed on their door, and the families of each child written to come and take their sons away. It was the best that could be done. As for Dr Evans, some hospital would be found for him. In the meantime, Seeker had to see Elizabeth Crowe.

'I'll fetch her,' said the warden wearily without waiting to enquire who it was that Seeker wished to see this time. 'She's worse than ever, you know; even the vermin stay away from her.'

Whatever the warden had meant, Goodwill Crowe's wife

certainly looked the worse for her stay in the cells. Her normally pristine linen cap and tucker, like the cuffs on her black sleeves, were becoming stained and grimy. Her pale lips were dry and cracking, and a sty appeared to be forming in her right eye. As soon as she was brought into the room, moreover, Seeker got the unmistakable aroma of the gaol, which hung about her now, claiming her as its own. Seeker had been in many gaols, interviewed many prisoners in worse states than this, but the smell, coming off Elizabeth Crowe as it did, almost caused him to gag.

Her first question was the inevitable one. 'Have you found my daughter?'

'No we have not. Nor have we yet found the others.'

'Others?' she said, attempting to raise her chin in defiance, but much of the fight had gone out of her and her head sank down again. 'I have no interest in any others.'

'What? Not even the special children, those you selected and abducted, to be trained for service?'

There was silence in the room, and then, 'I don't know where they are.'

Seeker felt his fingers clench. 'But you know the children of whom I speak?'

She nodded, still without looking at him. 'The girl from that Royalist woman's house on Crutched Friars, the boy from the school on Holborn, the serving girl from the tavern on Broad Street.'

'What about the gardener's boy from Lincoln's Inn?'

She turned down her lip. 'I know nothing of any such boy.'

Perhaps the boy Jed had, after all, simply run off to sea. 'The other three though? You took them?'

'We were preparing,' she said, her voice dull, 'preparing for the Lord. We were going to train them to be hand servants of Christ, for when he should come to reign. When we had overthrown the usurper Cromwell, removed him from the Palace of Whitehall and from power, and instituted the rule of the godly.'

'What happened?' asked Seeker.

She shook her head. 'I was much busied with my preaching, and too well known about the city. Patience said she would find suitable children who would not be missed, and bring them to me.'

'And she brought those three?'

Elizabeth Crowe's shoulders were hunched. 'I don't know. I never saw them. She said she had them somewhere secure, that another had helped her, someone of influence whose name she wouldn't tell me but whom she said would tell her important things, things about Whitehall, things that could be of use to us.'

'A man?'

She nodded. 'She would not tell me his name, but she called him Ashpenaz. She laughed at the idea he should be named for a eunuch.' Patience's mother raised a face filled with contempt to Seeker. 'I think my daughter was becoming something foul.'

★

Seeker had only just left Bridewell when a messenger from Whitehall came at speed towards him from the direction of the Fleet Bridge. The man was almost as breathless as was his horse. 'You're to lose no time in coming back to Whitehall, Captain. The Rat's been brought in, and Mr Meadowe wants you there when he's questioned.'

Anne Winter's servant was seated on a chair in a small room at the far end of the secretaries' corridor. There were two guards behind him, two to the side of him, and another two on the door. Philip Meadowe sat behind a table a few feet away from the prisoner. Each of the Rat's legs was shackled – one to the chair on which he sat, the other to the ankle of the huge guard to his left. His hands were cuffed behind his back. He made a show of grinning broadly when Seeker entered the room, but Seeker could see the ghost of a grimace of pain, he could see the burst lip, the swollen eye, the torn knees.

'You should see the other fellow,' rasped the Rat, maintaining his grin. Seeker had, or at least he'd seen the two the Rat hadn't killed. The other two soldiers who'd tried to arrest this Royalist agent were lying dead at the foot of a cliff in Kent, the rocks having put to an end what a stiletto through the back of the head in one case, and through an eye in the other, had begun.

Whatever response Seeker might have been tempted to make was forestalled by Meadowe, who got up instantly on seeing him and ushered him out of the interrogation chamber and into his own room.

'We didn't get him,' said Meadowe, having first firmly closed the door to the corridor.

'Didn't get . . .?'

'Charles Stuart,' said Meadowe grimly. 'The agent – the "Rat" as your men call him – spotted the party we had sent to Thanet to bring him in. He had a brazier lit in seconds, and the small boat that had been headed for the shore turned around quick smart and headed back out to sea. We had no decent ships close enough to pick it up – he'll be well on his way back to Flanders by now.' Meadowe's shoulders sank and he rubbed the back of his hand over exhausted eyes. 'We could have had him. He was so close, and we could have had him.'

Seeker cursed softly.

'Mind,' said Meadowe, cheering slightly, 'it could have been worse, all the same. He could have made land without our knowing it. Had you not uncovered their plans, Charles would be on his way to London by now in the guise of a yeoman farmer or some such. The Sealed Knot would be tightening itself around throats all over England. The Protector wouldn't be safe on the . . .' Meadowe had only just managed to stop himself saying 'throne', but the word hung there between them a moment until Seeker broke its spell.

'But he didn't land, and they'll be as rattled by their failure as we have been by how close they came. The discovery of Anne Winter's place will have set them back considerably, and they'll have to start on a new scheme, without Lady Anne and without her Rat.'

'True,' said Meadowe. 'Meanwhile, we must see whether we can make him squeal somewhat. Downing was particularly keen to be allowed a go at the other fellow.'

'The other fellow?' queried Seeker.

'Aye,' said Meadowe. 'Jones, the schoolmaster from Holborn. We'll find out who brought him over here, who their contacts are. The man is an engineer, not a spy; he'll break in there in a few minutes.'

Remembering what Jones himself had told him of the history between the two men, Seeker did not doubt that Jones would break soon, but he wanted the breaking to be before him, and not George Downing; Jones's role in the schemes of the Sealed Knot was becoming clearer by the minute, but Seeker needed to know what he had to say on the matter of Patience Crowe before Downing or the Committee of Examinations rendered him useless. Seeker took a breath. 'I have a request, sir.'

Meadowe flicked a hand. 'Of course. What is it?'

'Get rid of Downing awhile. Tell him Mr Thurloe wants him, that Barkstead at the Tower wants him. Tell him the Lord Protector out at Hampton Court wants him. Just let me have half an hour with Shadrach Jones before George Downing gets to him.'

Curiosity passed through the younger man's eyes, but he didn't ask why. 'All right then,' he said slowly. 'I'll send him across to the Tower, tell him I've had intelligence that the security of the Mint is at threat. That'll keep him away a good while and out of your way – and mine.'

'Thank you.'

Meadowe was already turning. 'But I need you in with the Rat, now. I wouldn't trust a fellow like that not to get out of a locked room with four armed men sitting on top of him. I'll go and get rid of Downing and be with you in a few minutes. I'll send a clerk to take notes until I get there.'

Seeker suppressed a smile. Thurloe would have been proud. A note must be made of everything, no comment, be it ever so casual, left unrecorded. Meadowe could send whom he wished: Seeker wouldn't need any note to remember whatever the Rat might have to tell him. He pushed open the door of the guarded room and found the Royalist agent as he'd left him, bloodied, and smiling, as if he had just played the perfect trick on his opponent. Seeker knew it for a bluff. The man had failed, as had Anne Winter, as had the rest of the Sealed Knot. In his mind's eye, Seeker could see that Knot unravelling, Thurloe, enticed away from his fireside in Lincoln's Inn to the cheerless damp cells of the Tower, gently tugging at its loose end, like a cat, expert at the game and with little fear of the most sleek of rodents.

'About time,' said the Rat. 'I have places to be.'

'You have nowhere to be,' said Seeker, 'this side of Hell.'

'True, perhaps, but on the other side – what work I have to do, to make the place ready for Cromwell and the rest of you. But enough of the pleasantries.' He straightened himself as best he could, adopted the look, ludicrous in his position, of a man of the world. 'We must to business, must we not? Will you trade, Seeker?'

'Your life is hardly worth a trade, *Richard*.' The name seemed altogether too noble for one who lived in the half-light, made his way in the shadows, the gutters, who did the bidding of others, of higher birth, and no doubt their killing for them also. And yet, there was a nobility there, Seeker could see it in the Rat's eyes. This Richard had found a cause and did not scruple to do what had to be done to further it. He did not allow himself the luxury, the compromise, of conscience. He did not pretend loyalty for loyalty's sake, but did his job because it was what he could do well.

The Rat curled a corner of his lip in amusement, a sharp white tooth catching the light from a candle just out of his reach. 'My life? I wouldn't trade my life for a sack of coal, if I were you, Seeker, it's worth less. But I have information.'

'And will you give it?'

The Rat sat back a little, lifted his chin as he made a show of assessing Seeker, assuming the upper hand. 'That depends what you have to offer in return, doesn't it, *Captain*.' He managed to invest the last word with as much derision as Seeker had done his name, but Seeker was in no humour to waste any more time in sparring with the man. He pulled out the chair across the table and leaned towards him, but as he did so, he saw the Rat's eyes lift to the door and a look of recognition come into his eyes, followed by the now familiar crinkle of amusement.

'Well, well, well, I would never have guessed it.'

Seeker had not heard anyone come in, but now turned his

head, following the direction of Richard's gaze: standing in the doorway, writing box in his hands and a sheaf of blank paper under his arm, was Marcus Bridlington.

Seeker's instinct was to tell him to get out, but the Rat's curious reaction, and Bridlington's demeanour – stock-still in the doorway and the colour draining from his face – made him hold his fire. Bridlington became aware of him in the room then, and made an effort to recover himself. 'I . . . the . . . Mr Meadowe sent me, to make notes.'

As well send the cook's boy, thought Seeker, but didn't say it. He pointed to the seat beside him. 'Set up there, and keep your thoughts to yourself.'

'Oh,' said the Rat, affecting to enjoy himself, 'I'm sure he will, although those must be some desperate thoughts, eh, Marcus?'

Seeker bypassed the boy. 'How do you know this clerk?'

Richard snorted. 'Oh, come, Seeker. I know you think us stupid, but really we are not, and even a halfwit would have spotted this fop milksopping his way around Aldgate, trying to look like he wasn't spying for Thurloe.'

'But how do you know his name?'

The response was derisive. 'Because he told it to Lady Anne in front of you, along this very corridor, not three weeks ago, if I recall her telling of it right. Dear God, and I thought some on our side incompetent. Are we done?'

Seeker could have cursed his tongue for allowing him to look so stupid in front of the Rat. In all that had happened since Anne Winter had first come to Whitehall to seek help in the finding of Charity Penn, he had forgotten that exchange outside Thurloe's room between Anne Winter and the boy Bridlington. He shifted, ready to resume the interrogation, but the Rat wasn't finished amusing himself over Bridlington.

'And where is your lady-love today, my fine young Galahad?'

Bridlington reddened, and a glint of anger flashed across his eyes. Seeker noticed his hand shake on the inkpot that he had just set down. 'I—'

'Oh, come, don't be shy. The captain and I are men of the world. We too have known passion.' He glanced at Seeker. 'Well, I have, at least. Though never with such a siren. And one so well set to take after her mother.'

Bridlington, only just seated, began to stand up again, but Seeker put a hand on his shoulder, pushing him back down. 'Sit down.'

Never loosening his grip on the young clerk's shoulder, Seeker leaned towards the Rat, looking straight into his face. 'What girl?' he asked.

Puzzlement showed on the Rat's face. 'You're more interested in *this* than anything else I might have for you?' He looked almost disappointed, as if Seeker had somehow fallen in his estimation.

'What girl?' Seeker repeated.

'Oh, if you're thinking it was Charity Penn—'

'I'm not,' said Seeker, and a third time, 'What girl?'

This time the Rat knew he was in deadly earnest, and all

trace of humour, dissembling, went from his face. 'Some Puritan girl. Her mother's that shrivelled she-troll that preaches her venom out of the weavers' houses at Gethsemane.'

Seeker was just in the process of turning towards Marcus Bridlington when he felt the clerk's teeth sink into the skin of his right hand. Unthinking, he let go Bridlington's shoulder and the clerk was up and making for the door before any of the guards in the room realised what was happening. Seeker was on his feet, the chair beneath him knocked over. As he ran through the door he shouted at the guards not to leave the Rat. Bridlington was remarkably swift on his feet, and had already sent a clerk carrying a three-inch-high pile of papers stumbling into a scullery maid bearing a tray of empty pewterware, scattering papers and mugs in Seeker's path. And then, as suddenly as it had begun, Bridlington's flight smashed to a halt against the broad barrel chest of George Downing, who had just stepped out of Philip Meadowe's room. 'Seeker!' he bellowed. 'What in God's name is going on here?'

Seeker was slower in stopping, and in danger of thumping into the Exchequer Secretary himself. 'Keep hold of him!' he roared to Downing, whose soldier's instinct already had Bridlington's wrists pinned behind his back.

Downing tightened his grip and Bridlington yelped in pain as Seeker reached them.

'So, Captain, what has my young clerk here done to so rouse your ire?'

Seeker looked in disgust at the squirming, expensively

dressed nephew of one of Cromwell's closest supporters. 'He has been instrumental in the abduction, and possible murder, of four children, and in the assassination of a most valued and trusted agent of the Lord Protector. And he has gone by the name of Ashpenaz.'

Bridlington, who all the while was seething and muttering something to himself, suddenly turned to Seeker. 'My uncle—'

Seeker stopped him. 'Your high connections will avail you nothing now. If you cross me further I will have you thrown in a cell so deep within the Tower that neither I nor anyone else will remember where it is. Where did you take those children?'

Bridlington evidently realised the game was up. He gave Seeker one long, last look of contempt before saying, 'Gethsemane – we took them to Gethsemane.'

Seeker was already halfway down the corridor when Bridlington called after him, 'But I didn't kill anyone, Seeker. I swear it and I'd swear it even if Cromwell himself held a knife to my throat. Whoever murdered your agent, it wasn't me.'

TWENTY-SEVEN

Imagined Friends

The light was fading over the city, over Gethsemane, as Seeker and his men arrived. The place was silent, like the silence of Anne Winter's house – locked up, under guard and empty of any human soul. Until dawn broke again, and the officers of the Protectorate resumed their painstaking search of every inch of the place. Thurloe himself had called in at the house on Crutched Friars, Meadowe said, on his way back from questioning Anne Winter at the Tower, to marvel at this new exemplar of Royalist ingenuity. Only a few hours ago, Seeker had stood in that house watching a marble floor open up at his feet, expecting to see the desperate faces of four missing children looking up at him. But the children hadn't been there, in that house at the other end of this street, a few hundred yards and a world away.

Seeker looked around him: fourteen almshouses, and they had searched every one. He listened. The sounds of the street outside continued as ever, but within, the quiet of Gethsemane, so usually a place of industry and community, was unnatural. The shutters to the one window of the prophetess's cell were shut. Through the window of the meeting room, illuminated by a lamp in the window, he could see the girl Margaret they had left to care for the half-dozen young children of the community while their mothers kicked their heels in the Bridewell with Elizabeth Crowe. She was making a show of reading to them from the Bible. Gradually, Seeker became aware of a noise, a rhythm, coming from the loom shed.

Nathaniel was there, cleaning and oiling the loom as the hound lay guard across the door. Daniel Proctor took up his position by it in the doorway. Removing his helmet, Seeker signalled to the hound to remain where it was.

Nathaniel greeted him with a broad smile.

'You're making a good job of that,' Seeker said, nodding to the loom.

'Father showed me. I want to have it perfect for him, when he comes back.' There was a question in those last words that Nathaniel clearly didn't know how to ask. Seeker marvelled at how little love a parent might show to earn the devotion of a child. 'It'll be a few days, perhaps, not much longer. Once all is secure and known to be secure,' he said. 'The Lord Protector doesn't wish to make enemies of those who were his friends. Their ends are the same, after all, your father's and the Protector's: the good of the state, the glory of God.'

Nathaniel nodded. 'Father said that once, something like it. Mother said he was being foolish.'

'Your father's no fool, Nathaniel, and that's why he'll be

free soon enough.' Seeker noticed the boy made no further reference to his mother, nor any enquiry about her.

Seeker told Nathaniel to put down his cloth. 'I need to ask you about the children.'

Nathaniel glanced across the courtyard towards the meeting house. 'I've been helping Margaret with them, since you took all the other women away. She lets me watch over them at their play, show them how to sort the yarns, see that they say their prayers. Dog lets them play with him. They're good children, Captain, they haven't done anything wrong by the Lord Protector.'

'I know that, but I'm talking about the other children, the ones that went missing, the ones Gideon was looking for.'

Nathaniel raised pained eyes towards Seeker. 'Gideon never told me he was looking for any children.'

Seeker pulled up a stool and sat down across from him. 'The things Gideon didn't tell you – they were for your own sake, to keep you from harm.'

'But I could have helped him.'

'Yes, I suspect you could have done.' He held Nathaniel's gaze. 'Have you ever seen any strange children at Gethsemane, any that shouldn't have been here?'

The boy coloured and he looked away from Seeker.

'Nathaniel?'

His voice was very quiet. 'Patience told you.'

Seeker felt suddenly sick.

'I still haven't found Patience. What would she tell me?'

Nathaniel clenched his fists, digging his fingers into his palms so that the knuckles went very white. 'I don't want to go to Bedlam.'

'You won't go to Bedlam, Nathaniel; they'd have to put me there first. Now, what would Patience tell me?'

Still he didn't look at Seeker. 'It was after Gideon came. A boy and then a girl, nearly as old as Patience. I thought I saw them through her window, waving to me. I asked her about them the next morning. She told me there had been no one there, laughed at me for having to imagine friends for myself as I had none. When I told her I *had* seen them, she said that I was lying. But I wasn't lying, I know I wasn't, but she said then that I was mad, and that she would have me sent to Bedlam if I spoke of it again. So I didn't say anything about it to Gideon, in case she heard of it and had me put there.' He took a deep breath. 'She said that was why you were coming, that first time. To take me to Bedlam.'

Seeker cursed Patience Crowe, cursed himself.

'Have you seen those children since?'

A shake of the head.

'Nor another two like them? Charity Penn, perhaps?'

'No, I haven't seen Charity since she went missing.'

Seeker was at a loss. Gethsemane had been searched from top to bottom when Major-General Harrison and his muster had been arrested, taken away, along with Goodwill Crowe and Elizabeth. Bridlington and Patience Crowe must have moved them on somewhere. He was as far from those children as ever.

A door across the courtyard opened, and a young boy bearing a steaming dish began a slow and careful progression from the cookhouse across to the almshouse in which the aged prophetess had her cell. But that too had been searched.

'I see the old crone isn't dead yet,' muttered Proctor.

'It's a wonder her belly doesn't burst,' said Nathaniel.

'Still that prodigious appetite then?' But even as Seeker said the words he let out a roar of frustration at himself.

'What?' said Nathaniel and Proctor in unison.

'You *told* me, only a few days since: Mother Wilkins eats enough for half a dozen. But she's no more meat on her than a sparrow, and hardly shifts from that bed.'

He'd already begun to move at speed across the yard, and was calling for Proctor to come with him. The young boy from the cookhouse took such fright that he leaped in one direction whilst the bowl he'd been carrying flew off in the other.

'But we've already searched in there,' Proctor said as he caught up with Seeker, who was hammering at the door.

'Not everywhere we haven't,' said Seeker, giving up his hammering to shoulder the door open so that the sound of the splintering bar could be heard across the yard.

And there, cowering in her thin grey blankets in a bed made in the recess of the wall, was Anna Wilkins, the prophetess of Holborn. She started to mutter some prayer against them.

'Spare us,' said Seeker, cutting her short. 'Get out of that bed.'

The clawed hands pulled the blankets higher. 'Get out! Lewd, unbridled . . .'

'Dear God, that any man should be so desperate! Get out of that bed, you vile witch, before I throw you out.'

'Is there no decency! In this godless Commonwealth, for a sick, godly woman?'

'Rotten and wicked, more like,' said Seeker. 'Proctor, the other end.' Taking hold of the woman's feet through the blankets he heaved, just as Proctor did at her shoulders, so that the small, scrawny bird frame in its yellowed linen nightdress and cap tumbled, shrieking, to the floor. The dog, beyond itself with agitation, had bounded after them into the cell, and stood growling at the bed.

Ignoring the woman's cries, Seeker pushed aside the straw mattress and remaining blankets from the platform in the wall and revealed what Carter Blyth, so busy following the trails that led from Gethsemane, had not discovered was there: a wooden trapdoor. He wrenched it open by its iron handle, and peered into the darkness beneath.

Darkness, silence, and a strong smell of something animal. 'Bring me a candle,' he said to Proctor, who lit one of the torches their men had brought.

Seeker held it to the opening of the hatch, but could see nothing but the stone floor below, covered in thin rushes. But he heard something, a soft shuffling, not rats – something larger. More than that, there was the overpowering smell, the warm smell, of living human bodies with all their odours, different from the sour decrepitude that permeated the air of the prophetess's own chamber.

There was no stepladder, no rope, nothing by which anyone imprisoned there might find their way up. But there must have been a means for Patience to get down. He looked at the crone who was watching him with a brittle amusement. 'Perhaps you should jump,' she sneered, rubbing at the arm on which she'd landed. She hadn't, however, been able to stop her eyes flitting to the rafters of her chamber and, looking up, Seeker saw an edge of hemp protruding from an exposed wooden beam. Stretching up he brought down a rope ladder with sturdy hooks at the end, which he soon found fitted into two iron rings at the edge of the opening. As he slung the ladder down, he called into the darkness. 'My name is Damian Seeker. I am a captain of the guard of the Council of State. I have come to release you.' The light Proctor was holding above him became dimmer as he descended, but it didn't matter: his eyes were good enough that they discerned in the corner of the room into which he had lowered himself a small and desperate huddle. At first he thought he had got something wrong, missed something, misunderstood something; at first he thought they were all boys, all chained together. As he stepped closer, the tallest of the children got to his knees – his shackles would allow him no further – and shuffled himself in front of the others, spreading his thin arms as wide as he could as if protecting them.

Seeker stood where he was and asked Proctor to come

down with the torch. The sergeant did so, but when he lifted it up that Seeker might better see the huddle in the corner, there was a scrabbling back and frail arms were suddenly lifted to protect eyes from the unaccustomed light. Seeker took a step forward then stopped. He could see now that only two of the children were boys, though the heads of all four had been roughly shorn, the girls like the boys forced to wear thin shirts and tattered breeches. All were barefoot. The place was damp and the air near freezing. Even in the dim light Seeker could see the sores and scabs on their skin.

'Dear God,' said Proctor.

Seeker said nothing for a moment and then, 'God had no part in this.' Slowly, he unclasped his cloak and began to walk towards the children. Proctor did the same. They crouched down and put the cloaks around the thin, shivering, terrified creatures in front of them. 'You're safe now,' said Seeker, 'and we've come to take you home.'

It was several hours later, in the pitch black of the night, that Seeker finally lay down at the doorway of one of the almshouses, the dog stretched out beside him, and lifted the flask John Drake had brought him to his lips.

'What's in it, John?'

'You don't need to know that, but it will help rest your body.'

'I don't want some potion that will send me to sleep. I need to be awake when those children come to.'

'And that will be a good twelve hours yet. Grace and Maria are sitting with them, and two soldiers at each chamber door. You're not needed, Seeker, and they'd be in no state to answer your questions before then anyway.'

Seeker stared at Drake in disbelief. 'Twelve hours?'

The apothecary smiled, attempted conciliation. 'At most, I should think. The effects of the draught will have worn off, and they should be rested enough for you to question them further.'

He knew there was no point in remonstrating further with Drake. The apothecary had only as much interest in the authority of the state as in knowing how to keep himself from its attention. In the treatment of patients, and of these, young and troubled patients, Seeker's business, the pressing need that their accounts should be heard, were of no consequence. 'They need rest, Seeker, and so do you. You'll have your answers when they wake. I imagine you have other things to take your attention? The city has swarmed with soldiers for days. Are the Stuarts at play again?'

'The Stuarts are always at play.'

'And our mysterious Black Friar? You have traced his story by now, I am sure.'

'No, Drake,' said Seeker, almost grinding his teeth. 'I have not. But when these children awake from the potion you have fed them, perhaps I will be a little closer to doing so.'

Drake smiled, his calmness at last washing over Seeker,

who nonetheless poured the draught on the dirt floor. The apothecary shook his head. 'Will you not sleep, my friend? If you can do nothing till morning, why lie awake?'

Seeker's voice was low. 'There are . . . other things that play on my mind. An hour or two's thought will put them in their place.'

Drake glanced towards the doorway of the cell in which the two freed captive girls, Charity Penn and Isabella, washed, fed what they could manage, properly clothed and dosed with medicines, had been put to sleep. He laid a hand on Seeker's shoulder. 'She will come to understand, my friend. Only time, not you taking thought, will bring that about.'

But Seeker knew Maria understood well enough already. He'd known it the minute he'd seen her face, as she'd hurried with Grace, Nathaniel having been sent to fetch them, through the entranceway to Gethsemane. Thurloe's tale had begun to leak out already, and had reached as far as Dove Court: Damian Seeker had used Maria Ellingworth to gather information on her brother and his associates, and that her purpose having been served, he had discarded her. The hurt was like a wall separating them, she on the one side, he on the other. 'Better this way,' Thurloe's voice said in his head. 'Better,' Seeker repeated in his head. Better this one hurt, and then it was over.

He'd gone over to them, a captain of the guard of the Council of State and nothing else. 'There are four children in those houses in a desperate state. An apothecary with physician's skill is on his way, but he will need help. We have started warming water. Will you wash them?' He'd softened his voice then. 'They need kindness, and gentleness. They have known none for many weeks, and I could not think of any others I could ask.'

Maria had avoided his eye, but Grace had put out a hand and lightly touched his. 'We will do whatever is needed,' she said, and then Nathaniel had taken them to where the rescued children were.

The filthy clothes were soon burning in the fire pit in the centre of the yard, new and clean garments having been found in chests in other cells. Food, beef broth and oat bread was brought from the cook shop on Woodruffe Lane.

Seeker would have sent word to Dorcas Wells, but Drake had counselled him to wait. 'The shock for both of them will be very great, however joyful. Let the child wake, and be prepared a little, and let me talk to Mistress Wells.' William Godmanson, though, had been brought from the Three Nails, overjoyed to hear his friend was alive, and allowed to sit with Grace and watch over him. 'I don't understand,' he'd said in a kind of wonder, glancing over to the other bed too, where the gardener's boy from Lincoln's Inn was sleeping, having at last understood that no more harm was to come to his companions.

'Nor do I yet, entirely, but, when they wake,' Seeker pointed to the small table at which he had had paper, pen and ink set, 'I want you to write down every word they say.'

No, Seeker didn't understand. He didn't understand how the pursuit of these four children had brought Carter Blyth to be entombed, in the habit of a Dominican Friar, in a decayed priory a mile from here. And neither did he understand, yet, what had become of Patience Crowe.

She'd retreated at last to the kitchen, where the servants would be, if there were any servants. But there were none here now, had not been in the six days since he'd brought her here. She'd had to do everything for herself, and there was hardly anything left now in the larder. She'd tired, eventually, of wandering upstairs from empty room to empty room. The heavy embroidered silks had become uncomfortable on her skin, she did not like the paintings, and the books in the library were dull – more dull than the Bible, even – and mostly written in tongues and even letters Patience couldn't understand. By yesterday, a fine rash had come out at her wrists and neck, where the lace cuffs and collars she had chosen chafed, and so she had taken them off, and put on her usual plain woollen gown. But still the skin itched, and she could find no ointments anywhere in the house, and she could not make a poultice: he had warned her against going outside, and it would be the wrong time of year to look for garden anemone or thyme anyway.

There had been wood, in a store by the kitchen, and by the fourth day she had got so cold that she had lit the oven. She had spent nearly the whole day down here today. She didn't miss them at Gethsemane, not one of them, but all the same, Patience began to feel resentment creeping over her at how little effort they must have made to find her. She wondered if that was where he was now, at Gethsemane, with those others, those pretty children, when he had promised her so faithfully he would come back here for her. She allowed herself a smile: they weren't so pretty now. Well, that would serve him right.

The night noises were starting again. They were different, so very different from the night noises of Aldgate. They were not human noises, the familiar wicked noises of drunks and bawds rolling through the streets and lanes after curfew, cursing one another, running from the watch; they were not the noises, the slopping and swishing of the night cleansers, the fighting of cats, family arguments or scandalous forbidden songs swaying their way through the air from houses and streets nearby to her opened window at Gethsemane; no, here were the sounds of birds and animals of the night, of the wind through trees, of creaking bushes and snapping twigs, of unknown things whose sounds were only meant for her.

Patience checked again the bolt and bar at the back of the scullery door, another at the top of the kitchen steps where they led to a back stairs and then the great hall of the hunting lodge. The house did not seem still in the night. She knew it for empty and yet it did not feel empty. As darkness fell, she did not dare light a candle even in the kitchen, and the only light was the meagre glow from the oven. There were sounds of doors and shutters rattling softly in draughts, of beams, floorboards creaking above her. She pictured the great hall, hung with deer antlers and a boar's head, and axes and swords long out of use. She wished she had thought to bring one of those axes down with her.

Eventually, she slept. She was not given to dreaming. Not like the prophetess, who spoke through dreams she had pretended to have. She'd been awake though, Mother Wilkins, and keen enough to listen as Patience had *played* with those children. Keen enough to listen, and enjoyed it. Old fraud. Old bitch. There came a smile to Patience's lips as she repeated the words, 'Old bitch,' said them out loud, soothed herself to sleep with them.

But then, deep in the night, as she slept her blank sleep, something began to seep into Patience's mind. A sound, a noise, regular, closer, louder. A horse. She sat bolt upright. His horse. She lit a lamp with a spill from the stove and hastily ran up the kitchen steps, unlocking the door. The combs and pretty jewels she had left on the dressing table upstairs – there would be no time to don again the lace and silk, not tonight, but the combs and jewels she could manage.

Patience had almost reached the foot of the stair in the great hall when the hammering started at the door. She smoothed a hand over her hair – it was not even pinned, but perhaps he would like it better that way. The shadows cast by the antlers and the boar's head across the bare stone floor didn't scare her now. She reached up to light a candle in the sconce near to the door and, smoothing down her hair one last time, she took the large iron key from its hook and carefully turned it in the lock. The hammering stopped, the door knob turned and the door swung open before her into the night. There, standing against the blackness, her lamp revealing a look of supreme satisfaction upon his face, was Andrew Marvell.

TWENTY-EIGHT

The Entrapment of Marcus Bridlington

Thurloe thought the windows might rattle from their frames. Rarely had he seen Seeker so angered.

'In God's name, why would he do such a thing?'

'To prove that he could, I suspect,' said Thurloe, settling comfortably back into his favourite chair, smoothing his hand over the surface of his Whitehall desk, familiarising himself once more with the symbols of his control. Certainly Marvell's actions had proven him right in deciding to set aside Milton's preference for the young Yorkshireman in favour of Philip Meadowe, however fine Milton, or indeed the Protector himself, might think his verse. What Marvell would have done if left in charge during his own recent illness and recuperation at Lincoln's Inn, the Chief Secretary did not like to contemplate.

'And what has Bridlington to say?'

'A great deal, apparently,' said Thurloe. 'The gist of much of it being that he didn't kill anyone, knows nothing of the death of Carter Blyth, and that none of the rest of it is his fault.'

'Oh, is it not,' said Seeker grimly. 'That will remain to be seen.'

'Perhaps,' replied Thurloe. 'His main concern, though, is that he should not have the company of Patience Crowe enforced upon him.'

'He might have considered that before he joined her in her enterprise,' responded Seeker. 'The nature of her charms can hardly have come as a surprise to him.'

'No,' conceded Thurloe, 'but perhaps you should hear his tale for yourself, the better to understand his part in the thing.'

As he watched Seeker turn on his heel, his face brewing a perfect storm, and stride out into the corridor to seek out the manacled Bridlington, Thurloe reflected that the young clerk might have done better to take his chances with Patience Crowe.

Bridlington was chained by the ankle to a bench in the ante-room of an unused office. A pitcher of water and a beaker had been placed on the table in front of him. The look he cast at Seeker as Seeker entered the room was one of outrage and affronted dignity. Recalling the haunted animal looks of the children he had found in a cellar at Gethsemane only the night before, Seeker was not disposed to sympathy. He dismissed the guard, slammed the door behind him, and kicked back the bench opposite Bridlington, slouching down onto it against a wall, his booted feet stretched out before him, in a manner that could leave the clerk in no doubt that there would be no standing on ceremony, no respecting of persons here.

'The truth, or all the uncles in England won't save you.'

Bridlington looked for a moment as if he might be disposed to argue but then persuaded himself otherwise. He poured himself a beaker of the water, his hand shaking a little, and took a moment to summon his courage.

'I knew nothing of Patience Crowe when this all began. I knew nothing of the children, any of them, apart from Edward.'

'Edward Yuill? The boy from Rhys Evans's school?'

Bridlington nodded. 'Since I came to Mr Thurloe's employ, I have often been used as a courier with messages from various personages here to officers quartered around St Giles's and Drury Lane. I had been there one day in late October, delivering instructions to officers at the Red Lion. It was a fine day, mild, still late autumn and little hint yet of winter, and I knew my duties for the day were finished. I had no desire to return here – my fellow clerks have made it plain that they do not seek my society, and I have found nothing of interest in theirs. I was glad to be away from the place. I took a stroll along Holborn, looking into shops and the like, and then decided to walk out to Conduit Fields. As I say, it was a fine day, and there were many others, finished their labours for the day, who had gone out to take the fresh air and to exercise themselves. I saw in the distance a group of boys at sport – from a school nearby, I soon learned. I went a little closer to watch them.' Bridlington allowed himself a smile, and the first honest look Seeker had ever seen him give. 'I never went to school, you see, never had that companionship. I would have given much to join them.'

'But you didn't?' said Seeker.

'I didn't know how, so I just watched.' He played with the beaker in his hands. 'In time, they began to drift away from their game of football to other things, and the oldest eventually called them all and told them they must return to their school for supper. As he picked up their ball, he turned to face me, and he smiled, such a smile as no one has ever given me. I . . . I was . . . transfixed. I had never seen anyone so beautiful.'

Seeker thought of Edward Yuill as he had last seen him, the night before at Gethsemane – bathed at last but his skin grey, his cheeks gaunt, scabs forming on his skin – and yet beneath it all there had been an undeniable beauty and a grace that must have marked the boy out from most of his fellows.

Bridlington continued. 'I started to go up to Holborn whenever I could. I found the location of the school, waited sometimes for the boys to come out again, to go to the fields. The third time I saw them, and Edward saw me, he sent the younger boys to races, and came to ask me if I would like to join them. I pretended at first that I didn't know him, but he was kind, and persisted, and soon we became friends, just we two. Soon, we began to arrange to meet just ourselves. I taught him how to use a bow, he me to climb a tree. It was a time of great happiness for me, for him too, I think.'

'So what happened?'

Bridlington's hands tightened on the beaker in front of him. 'Patience Crowe. I had been detailed with some others to keep an eye on any suspect gatherings at St Giles's, and one day we had information that there was to be some Fifth Monarchist woman preaching there.'

'Elizabeth Crowe,' said Seeker.

Bridlington nodded. 'The woman was dreadful, but a crowd had gathered around her and was growing. She had them almost in a frenzy, but then an old Welsh fellow started to shout at her, too learned for her and in ways she couldn't answer. I recognised him as the master of the Three Nails. I knew from Edward that he had started to wander in his mind. I went over to him, intent on escorting him back to the school, lest there be any trouble, and I thought it would give me the chance to see Edward too, but just as I reached him, Edward himself appeared. We both laughed, which must have seemed strange to the others who had been sent to St Giles's with me, but I don't think any of them noticed. As we both reached out to take hold of the old schoolmaster our hands touched, that is all. A touch, a gentle squeeze, a moment's lingering. And Patience Crowe saw it. She was standing only a yard away, and I saw it in her face, the knowledge and the triumph. She stepped in and said she would help Edward escort the old man home, that there was no need for me to do it. I'd never seen her in my life before, but I knew from that minute, from the look on her face, what she had planned for me, and I let go my hold on Dr Evans, and tried to melt away.'

'And what did she have planned for you?' asked Seeker, although he was fairly sure he knew.

'Blackmail. She helped Edward home with Dr Evans – I later learned she had had her eye on Edward, anyway. I'd hoped to disappear into the crowd, to be gone before she ever came back, never to see her again, but she found me. She said she knew who I was – had seen me at Aldgate, at Crutched Friars, had asked around, knew who my uncle was, in whose employ I was. She threatened to expose me as a sodomite.' Here, he looked up at Seeker, and he was plainly terrified. 'It was only a touch, I swear to it—'

Seeker cut him short. 'Not my concern. Tell me of Patience Crowe.'

Bridlington gathered himself and returned to the bare facts of his narrative. 'She threatened to expose me, unless I did as she bid me. She said it wouldn't matter if what she told people was true or not, that enough had seen me with Edward.'

'What did she demand you do?'

Bridlington's lip curled in derision. 'Her mother had some scheme, out of the Book of Daniel, to find four children to be trained up as servants of Christ in the Second Coming. The woman must be even madder than her daughter.'

'And you were to help Patience abduct these children for her mother?'

Bridlington shook his head. 'Her mother wanted to seek out the children in hospitals, poorhouses, select those she thought most suitable, but Patience said she had a better scheme.' His voice became bitter. 'Patience had a very particular type of child in mind, and I don't think training them for Christ played any part in her plans.'

Seeker thought of everything he had heard of the children from those who knew them. 'She wanted beautiful children.'

'Beautiful, gifted, everything she was not. I had to help her entice them away from their homes, and to the place called Gethsemane.'

Seeker spoke the names. 'Charity Penn, Edward Yuill, Isabella Dray and Jed Cutler.'

'All but the first. I told her, Lady Anne's maid would know me for a watcher of Mr Thurloe's, would never come with me.'

'But the rest?'

Bridlington swallowed. 'With Edward, it was simple: I just asked him to come for a walk with me through the city one night, said it was to meet friends, that I would take him to a coffee house, but that he should tell no one for the fear of the trouble he would be in.' He shut his eyes against the memory. 'He thought it a great game.'

'And the register? How did you effect the switch?'

A half-laugh, with no humour in it. 'Part of the game. I'd got him to tell me the other boys' names, copied them out in a new book, but without his own on it, and told him to swap them, see how long it took the trick to be discovered. It was so simple, so easy to deceive him, because he is good, and I, as you will be aware, am not. But . . .'

'What?'

'The strange thing is, I think the old man, Dr Evans, suspected something, and yet he had wandered so far from his wits we knew no one would listen to him.'

Seeker remembered, the repeated refrain of 'Poor Abednego'; Abednego, one of the fair, gifted children chosen along with the Prophet Daniel to be brought up to serve the king. Yes, Rhys Evans had seen what was happening, but no one had listened to him.

'And Edward trusted me.'

Seeker wasn't about to offer the wretched Bridlington any comfort. 'It was written in your hand? The new register was in your hand?'

'Oh, yes. That day you called for our reports on Anne Winter's house,' the clerk shook his head, 'I thought you were sure to see it, but you asked us to read the reports out ourselves, if you remember . . .'

Seeker cursed himself for carelessness, as Bridlington went on, 'I was sure someone must have the register, spot it soon. I thought once in the night that I had been caught, when Downing had his clerk Pepys wake me and demanded the reports on Lady Anne's house.'

'What?' said Seeker, losing track.

'I thought he had discovered this business, and would recognise my hand, I deliberately took him the wrong file.'

He laughed at the memory. 'I thought he would explode when Pepys discovered it.'

Seeker was struggling to follow this line. 'Downing? In the middle of the night? Which file did you take to him?'

Bridlington shrugged. 'One of little consequence. I think it concerned that lawyer who lives at Dove Court.'

It was said with such indifference. They had done this to him, to him and to Maria: Patience Crowe, George Downing, Marcus Bridlington had done this to them. None of them fit to walk the same streets as her, and yet, step by step, they had colluded in her public humiliation. And he was the cause, and he had let them do it. Seeker wanted to smash Marcus Bridlington into the wall. He took a moment to gain control and forced himself to return to the matter in hand.

'So much for Edward Yuill. The others? The girl from the Black Fox and the gardener's boy from Lincoln's Inn?'

'It was the girl next, Isabella. I knew her from my visits to the tavern coming and going from the lectures at Gresham. She was very pretty, of course, and much importuned by other young men who came into the tavern, although Dorcas would chase them off quick enough. But Isabella didn't mind me – I think she had realised that pretty girls were not of especial interest to me.'

Seeker nodded. 'Go on.'

'She had a very sharp wit and fine mind, and a great interest in science, and in what was to be learned from those who had gone to the lectures, so we would often talk of them.

Patience, who very soon took to following me, discovered our friendship. Once her eye landed on Isabella, she was consumed with venom.'

'She was jealous?' said Seeker.

'Can you imagine? Even if my inclinations had run in that direction. Patience Crowe? Dear God, have you seen her, Seeker?' Distaste was written over his face. 'Anyhow, she declared that Isabella must also be brought to Gethsemane. Edward was in her power by this point, and she hinted at cruelties to be inflicted upon him if I did not bring Isabella to her. So I did. I told Isabella I had a friend from Oxford, who knew Mr Boyle himself, who would show her his experiments. We met near the market at Leadenhall one day, and I took her to Gethsemane. There was some sort of meeting going on in one of the almshouses there, and no one about but Patience and that dreadful old crone who's always pronouncing Cromwell's doom. They took Isabella into the old woman's dwelling and told me to leave.'

'You didn't go inside?'

Bridlington shook his head. 'I don't know what they did with Edward or Isabella once they had them there. I thought that was it, that Patience was finished with me.'

'But she wasn't?'

'No. I was still wondering how I might extricate Edward, and the girl.' He looked up at Seeker. 'Whatever you may think of me, I would not have left them at *her* mercy. But Patience found me a third time. She said we were in trouble.'

He laughed. 'We! As if we had conceived all together, as if she and I were somehow friends.'

Seeker was becoming impatient. 'What trouble?'

'What?' said Bridlington.

'You and Patience Crowe. What trouble were you in?'

'She said a man named Gideon Fell had joined their community, but she had begun to think he was not as he presented himself, rather that he watched her, watched Anne Winter's house, watched me. She said she thought he might be one of Mr Thurloe's agents, but I told her there were none there, at Gethsemane, as far as I knew, and she was allowing her imagination to carry her away. But she would not let it go, and then one day told me she was certain he had been watching us, that he had taken the register of the Three Nails from her chamber, and would show it to Mr Thurloe. So we resolved to follow him. He had arrived at Gethsemane in darkness that night, in a great state of agitation, and gone directly to the chamber he shared with Patience's brother.' He paused to look at Seeker. 'He's a simple boy who has no part in her schemes. Anyway, after about a quarter-hour, this Gideon Fell had left again, in great haste, and a bundle under his arm. We followed him, and although he looked behind him again and again, and must have seen us, I don't think it was us that he feared.'

'He was hiding from another?' said Seeker.

Bridlington nodded. 'I am certain of it. He saw us and didn't seem to care that we saw him. At last we came to the gates of Lincoln's Inn, and I followed him into the gardens while Patience waited outside. Even there, he looked about him, haunted. I hid myself behind a tree and listened as he hailed the gardener's boy who was locking away his tools for the night. I saw him thrust something, a paper, into the boy's hand, and heard him tell him to deliver it to Mr Thurloe, as a matter of urgency. Then he turned and made quickly from the garden by another route. I was certain this paper must contain accusations about me, my association with Patience, lies about myself and Edward. I went by a back path and intercepted the gardener's boy – Jed – whom I knew would know me from the many times I had had to visit the Inn on official business. I told Jed that Mr Thurloe had been called away, but that I would bring the letter to him. He had promised the man, though, that he would deliver it into Mr Thurloe's own hand, and so I was forced to pretend I knew where Mr Thurloe was, and that I would bring him to him.'

'And?' said Seeker, knowing what would come next.

Bridlington's response was barely audible. 'I took him to Gethsemane. Handed him through the door to the crone, told him Mr Thurloe would be on his way.'

'And the letter?'

His voice was full of bitterness. 'Patience has it.'

'She was there?'

'No. When Jed and I left Lincoln's gardens, I could see no sign of her, nor of the man she called Gideon Fell. I never saw him again, and I thought for then all was well, that she had forgotten about me. But she came to me over two weeks ago, telling me his body had been found, that you were on our trail, and that if I didn't get her away she would tell you everything. I should just have killed her. It would have been over sooner.'

'And what of those poor souls she kept like rats in a cellar?'

'They wouldn't have been at her mercy any more.'

'They would have starved to death,' shouted Seeker, his face level with Bridlington's.

'I'm sorry.'

'Oh, you'll have years enough yet to be sorry. Where is she now? Don't even try pretending you don't know.'

'I took her to my uncle's hunting lodge, in Berkshire. She thought I was going to come too, be with her, present her to my family. God!' He laughed. 'As well hang myself.'

'Oh, I doubt you'll hang,' said Seeker, 'though you deserve to. But back to the night at Lincoln's Inn: did you see who it was that Carter Blyth – Gideon Fell – was running from?'

'No.'

'And the letter?'

Bridlington shook his head.

'I never read it before Patience took it.'

TWENTY-NINE

The Last Letter of Carter Blyth

The corridor outside Meadowe's office was a fug of pipe smoke. The Under-Secretary did not look as if he had slept since last Seeker had seen him.

'I haven't,' he said in reply to Seeker's question. 'Mr Thurloe has had me up all night, acquainting him with every piece of business he has missed. He is grilling Morland and Dorislaus as we speak, for fear the postal office has become slack in the weeks of his absence.'

'Get to your bed, then, Philip.'

'Oh, I intend to, but not until I have shown you this,' said Meadowe, grinning broadly through his exhaustion. He signalled to a guard to open the side door to his chamber and there, triumphant, if spattered in mud, sat Andrew Marvell. Beside him, her hands shackled in front of her, was a bedraggled and furious Patience Crowe.

'Well, Captain,' said Meadowe, 'I shall leave you to take Mr Marvell's report, and to question his prisoner.'

Seeker overcame the urge to hang Marvell by his boots out of the window and took a minute to calm himself.

'And where, Andrew, have you been?'

'I have been fetching this,' said Marvell, waving a hand in the direction of his prisoner.

Seeker looked at the woman he had been searching for, without success, for six days. She would keep five minutes longer. He opened the door back through to Meadowe's now empty study. 'A word, Mr Marvell, if you will.'

Marvell, affecting a bravado that took Seeker's breath away, smiled through the grime on his face and followed Seeker through to Meadowe's room. He had hardly closed the door behind him when Seeker rounded on him. 'You have been to Berkshire? Goffe's hunting lodge?'

Marvell nodded, beaming.

Seeker took a moment to calm himself again. 'Would you be good enough to enlighten me as to how you knew where she was and why you chose to go there alone?'

'Well . . .' Marvell sat back, happy at having the chance to tell his story. 'It was when I was left minding Bridlington. When word spread about what the Rat had disclosed about him and Patience Crowe, none of the clerks could believe it – she so plain and of such little account, and he such a fop, with such airs because of his high connections, all the bragging he had done, the seeking to curry favour by making free with his uncle's largesse. And then I remembered.'

'Remembered what?' said Seeker, his impatience building.

'The hunting lodge he bragged of – General Goffe's hunting lodge in Berkshire, some way past Windsor. I knew the general could not be there, and it seemed to me an ideal location, not too far from London, to hide someone, or some people, away.' He cast his eyes down. 'I had in truth hoped to find those children, but unfortunately all I found was that dreadful Crowe girl, who will tell me nothing. But still, it is better than nothing.'

Seeker found his anger subsiding. 'Yes, it is. And we have found the children.'

Marvell's face brightened.

'I will tell you of it later, Andrew, but in God's name – to go off like that, telling no one where you went, on the trail of a matter that has already resulted in the death of one of our best and most experienced agents!' He shook his head. 'It is a wonder I am not talking to a corpse.'

'*Would* you talk to a corpse?' queried Marvell, interested as ever by the idea and not noting the sarcasm.

'To yours, I would. For yours I would make an exception. Never do something so foolish again. Such unregulated behaviour is not our way of operation and can only result in death, discovery or both. You have set back the reputation of good Yorkshire sense a decade at least in these corridors and done yourself no favours.'

Marvell's face had fallen completely now, all triumph and light gone from his eyes. 'But I at least brought you Patience Crowe.'

'Indeed, and it would have been a cold day in Hell before anyone else here had thought of that, but such a rash act must not be repeated. I think Mr Thurloe must soon send you back to your young charge at Eton, where you can write your poems and steer clear of mischief.'

'Oh,' said Marvell, now thoroughly disappointed. 'You will not be interested in the letter, then, nor the Black Friar's robe?'

'Yes, it is certainly his hand.' Astonishment and admiration contended with one another for control of Thurloe's features as he surveyed the letter Seeker had just had Andrew Marvell hand to him. 'You found this in Goffe's lodge?'

'It was amongst the small parcel of belongings Patience Crowe insisted on bringing away with her. I took the liberty of searching through it before we commenced our ride back to London.'

'Did you read it?' enquired Thurloe.

Marvell coloured a little. That he had attempted to read the letter was very clear. He coughed. 'The seal had already been broken, but I am not privy to that particular cypher.'

'Hmm,' said Thurloe. 'Fortunately I am, or at least I recognise it. It looks to have been hastily set down, though. Wallis will be here in a moment, and the contents should become clear.'

The letter was addressed to Chief Secretary Thurloe, at Lincoln's Inn, in a hand Thurloe had confirmed to be that of Carter Blyth, although less tidy than was usual. The cypher in which it was written was that they had agreed upon. 'Blyth was supposed to contact me through the safe house,' commented Thurloe as they waited for the arrival of Wallis. 'He must indeed have been in some very immediate danger, to have tried to contact me so directly at Lincoln's Inn.'

Wallis arrived, Marvell was dismissed to wait in the clerks' room, and warned to say nothing of the business being conducted in the Chief Secretary's room, and Thurloe and Seeker waited in silence while Wallis, a cypher book to hand, to which he only once or twice had to refer, rendered the letter in words they could comprehend. The last words transcribed, he left. Thurloe picked up the pages Wallis had handed him, scanned them once or twice nodding to himself, once raising an eyebrow in surprise, but making no comment as he handed them then to Seeker.

Sir,

I write in haste and fears this may never reach you. My investigations amongst Harrison and the Fifth Monarchists continue, and although I have found no evidence as yet of plans for an attempt on the Protector, I must warn you that I have great fears that someone closely connected to him – Major-General Goffe's own nephew, Marcus Bridlington, who is in your employ – has involved himself with these people at the place called Gethsemane. He is embroiled in some way I have yet to discover with Goodwill Crowes' daughter, Patience, a truly vicious, dissembling girl. I will continue to observe them.

Of more immediate import: I am certain that real danger emanates from the house of Lady Anne Winter. The man who masquerades as her steward is an assassin, and I have tonight discovered a secret chamber in her house which I can only suspect to be envisaged as a safe haven for Royalists of a very high order. The women of the house are busy at a workshop, manufacturing disguises from old costumes, one of which – an old Black Friar's robe – I was able to obtain, as proof, before I was forced to flee the place for fear of discovery.

I can write no longer, for I fear I am followed and watched and will soon be discovered. In the name of his Highness the Lord Protector,

Carter Blyth.

'He was right about that last, at least,' said Thurloe when Seeker at last looked up from the paper.

'Aye, more's the pity,' said Seeker. 'But he near enough had Lady Anne to rights, too. Bridlington was where he got things wrong. I suspect he believed Marcus was involved with the Crowes and Harrison at the behest of Major-General Goffe, and that was why he didn't trust anything to the usual networks.'

'Because he thought them compromised from the bottom to the top,' agreed Thurloe. 'But it was the matter of these disappearing children Bridlington was caught up in?'

'Yes,' said Seeker. 'Blyth obviously hadn't realised that, even when he began looking for the children himself.'

'But his murder, Seeker – we are little further on with that.'

'No,' conceded Seeker, 'but I am in hopes we will learn more when we have spoken to the children. Whatever sleeping draught Drake gave them will have worn off soon. I must get to Gethsemane.'

'I hardly think those children will be of much help in explaining to you the murder of Carter Blyth. It is doubtful they even knew of his existence.'

'I think one at least may be of help in explaining the matter of the Black Friar's gown Blyth removed from Lady Anne's to show you, the one that he was found in.'

Thurloe's eyebrows reached high on his forehead. 'You are going to have to enlighten me, Seeker.'

'I think Mr Marvell might put it better,' said Seeker, opening the door and summoning the weary and bewildered poet back into the Chief Secretary's office.

'Tell Mr Thurloe about the costumes, Andrew.'

And so, revived, Marvell did. 'It was in our search of the underground chamber in Anne Winter's house, when we came across a vast array of costumes. They were left over from the time of the theatre companies favoured by the Stuarts and their court. The costumes were stocked and inventoried according to the plays for which they were most used. A degree of duplication of course occurs, but it is possible to trace each costume if one is thorough.'

'Which you were, I'd wager,' said Thurloe, his interest piqued, liking the unwrapping of the puzzle.

Marvell nodded, pleased. 'There was a note of costumes for use in a play by Christopher Marlowe – *The Jew of Malta*. It said, in what Mr Dorislaus has confirmed to be William Davenant's hand, "All characters provided for", but there was only one set of Black Friar's robes to be found anywhere in that chamber.'

Thurloe leaned towards Seeker, his eyes bright. 'And there are *two* Black Friars in that play, are there not, Damian?'

'I would not know, sir, but Marvell insists it is the case.'

'And Marvell is right. Go on.'

Almost blushing at the unaccustomed praise, Marvell continued. 'The girl who helped Anne Winter prepare those costumes is one of the children currently sleeping sound and under guard at Gethsemane.'

Thurloe sat back and thumped his fist on his desk. 'Then saddle your horse, Seeker, and wake the child!'

THIRTY

Threads

The morning was bright, but the shutters on the windows of the small almshouses were closed.

'Grace says the sunlight would hurt their eyes,' Nathaniel said as he walked quietly with Seeker towards the door.

Grace knew something of waking to a different world, thought Seeker. And Gethsemane this morning felt like a different world; it felt at last as if something good might be nurtured here.

'I didn't know. I didn't know they were here. I would have helped them.'

'I know you would have done, Nathaniel. But you have helped them. I could never have found them without the things you told me.'

'M-my father didn't know either,' added Nathaniel, his eyes filling. 'I am certain of it.'

Seeker stopped and looked into those eyes. 'I think you are right, but we must be certain. You understand he cannot be freed until we are certain about all things?'

'You mean about who killed Gideon too, don't you?'

'Yes, I do.'

'Do you think Patience killed Gideon?'

That question had been troubling Seeker for some days now. 'I don't know, Nathaniel, but I hope we shall soon find out.'

Seeker briefly looked in on the boys who were sitting up in bed, a little bewildered still, but beginning to understand, it seemed, that their ordeal might be over. He could wait until they were stronger.

At the door to the other small bedchamber, he hesitated, before knocking gently. Maria opened the door to him.

There was the smallest moment of hope, recognition on her face, before it closed down to him, to be replaced by a mask of civil indifference.

'Maria,' he said, reaching towards her.

Her body visibly tightened, she took a small step back. 'Captain Seeker. Please do not tire the girls. They are not long wakened. I am going to fetch them some warmed caudle. I will be back presently.'

'Maria,' he said again, but she went past him, as if she had not heard.

The girls were indeed wakened. Pale against the crisp white linen of Gethsemane. Elizabeth Crowe had been a good housewife, for all her other faults. Bunches of herbs, that could not have been there before, hung from the low rafters of the room, giving the place a pleasant, fresh aroma, more redolent of a country parlour than an Aldgate sickroom. Nathaniel, he thought. It would have been Nathaniel.

In the cot to his left was Isabella, the girl from the Black Fox. Though still dulled a little from the effects of Drake's draught, her large blue eyes hinted at something of the intelligence, the quick wit, all had spoken of her as possessing. Her dark hair, short black spikes against the white of the bed sheets, was dulled and dry from the neglect of the past few weeks, but it would grow in time, and its shine return. When she managed to focus and at last recognised him as her liberator of the previous night, she managed to smile. 'Thank you.' The smile and the words warmed him, goodness slowly beginning to wash over the evil that had been this place.

In the other bed, a smaller girl with similarly hacked straw-red hair and her mother's jade eyes watched him warily. Her hands, on the coverlet, were slim and delicate, but the nails broken. The apothecary had applied a healing balm to the chilblains that weeks in the cold cellar had brought to her fingers. Liberty Wells had the fineness of Dorcas's beauty, but not her strength. Even in health, he could see, she would never have her mother's strength. A child such as this would have been broken, shattered and ground to nothing in the streets, had she not been found and taken in by Anne Winter when she had been. Seeker pulled up a stool and sat down by the bed of the young girl who had been denied even her own real name.

'Charity,' he said.

She nodded.

'Do you know who I am?'

Another nod. 'You found us. They say you are the Seeker.'

'That's what people call me. I serve the Lord Protector and you need have no fear of me. I want to talk to you about another man who was also in the Lord Protector's service and who, I think, tried to be your friend.'

A flush of colour crept over the child's cheeks and she looked at her hands, avoiding Seeker's eye. 'Do you mean Gideon?' she said quietly.

'Yes,' said Seeker. 'Tell me about Gideon.'

The child worked at her lip a moment. He could see her thinking. 'It was when I was out on the streets one day, doing an errand for Lady Anne.' Then Charity looked up. 'Does she know where I am?'

'Not yet,' said Seeker. 'We will tell her soon.'

This seemed to satisfy her and she continued. 'Well, I noticed a man looking at me. Not in a bad way, I know that way and it wasn't that kind of look. It was as if he knew me. I hurried on, because Lady Anne had told me I must be careful on the streets.'

'Did you tell her about him?'

She nodded. 'Lady Anne got me to describe him, and it wasn't long before she noticed him too. She said that he was watching the house and that I should be careful of him.'

'But?'

Again she chewed her lip. 'There were some boys one day, calling after me, saying things they should not have done. They started to run after me, and I started to run too, but then the man – Gideon – came and scared them away.

He told me not to be frightened, and asked me for my name. When I told him it was Charity, he asked if I was certain, because he had thought it might be something else. So I told him about the foundling home, and that I didn't know where I had come there from. Then he told me to go home, but not to tell anyone we had spoken.'

'And did you?'

She shook her head. 'He seemed to think there was danger in it, for both of us, and I didn't think it would matter anyway, as I wasn't the person he'd thought. But then a few days later I saw him again, and he asked me about Lady Anne's house. I was careful not to tell him, because I knew many spies watched the house, and by this time Lady Anne was certain he was one of them.' She paused and her brow furrowed.

'What is it?'

'Well, he told me that he was. Is that not strange? Should not a spy pretend to be otherwise?'

Seeker nodded. 'He should. I think perhaps it mattered to Gideon very much that you should trust him.'

'So that he could get into Lady Anne's house?'

'So that he could help you.'

'He said that, that he wanted to help me, that Lady Anne's house was a dangerous place for me to be, but it wasn't, Mr Seeker – it was the safest, kindest place I can ever remember.'

'I think there was another that you don't remember, that Gideon knew about.'

Her voice was almost inaudible. 'He said that too. He said

he thought he might have found my mother. He wanted me to leave Lady Anne's house and go with him to her. I asked him to tell Lady Anne, but he said she had guessed who he was and would never believe him.'

'But you didn't go with him?'

Tears were threatening to brim over the child's lashes. 'I was frightened. I told him if ever I was in danger, I knew a way I could get out of Lady Anne's house, a safe way that the soldiers wouldn't know about.'

'Through the special basement chamber and out by the hidden door to the coal store?'

Wide-eyed with astonishment that he should know, she nodded.

'And did you tell Gideon about this?' he asked gently.

'Yes,' she whispered. 'I did.'

He leaned towards her. 'There is one last thing I must ask about Gideon, Charity. Did you ever see him again?'

She shook her head and now the tears came. 'I think he was in the house. I think he came that night. There was a great commotion in the downstairs chamber, and a thief disturbed who got out by the secret way, and the next morning we saw that a box of costumes had been disturbed, and a friar's robes missing.'

'Was there anything else?'

'Yes, Lady Anne's salt was gone from her dining parlour – the special salt, with her family crest upon it. But why would Gideon have taken that, when there is so much else of value in the house?'

Seeker sighed. 'I think he took it as a message to your mother, should he not be able to get to her himself, a sign telling her where she should find you.'

At that moment, Maria returned with the warmed caudles, and asked him to give the girls a few moments to take them in peace.

'All right,' he said, standing up from the small stool, all at once conscious now of his ungainly size in this small, spare, herb-scented room. 'I would have a word with you first, though, Mistress Ellingworth.'

'I am busy.'

'It will not take a moment.'

She let out an exasperated sigh. 'Once I have helped feed the girls then,' she said.

Only the dog was to be found in the courtyard of Gethsemane, and it came over to Seeker as he slumped down by the girls' almshouse cottage, to sit on the ground, with his back against the wall. The dog seemed to realise that all was not well with its master, and sat quietly by him, allowing his head to be stroked, earnestly looking as if he knew and understood all. 'How do I come back from this, eh, boy? How do I make her see that Thurloe's tale's not true? How do I do it?'

It must have been a quarter-hour before Maria appeared in the doorway. The dog looked up at her with sad eyes, and she allowed herself to stroke it.

'You wanted me?'

Wanted her. The choice of words could hardly have been worse. Every part of him wanted her.

He stood up, brushed some of the dirt from his clothes. 'I need to see you, Maria, to explain.'

'No, you do not. It has been made perfectly clear. I can show you the explanations in print, if you wish, for why you ever dallied with me.'

'Maria, you of all people – you, and your brother, you *know* how this works. You cannot believe there is any truth in the lies Nedham peddled about us in his rag?'

'I know it is what everyone now thinks, now says: you courted me solely in the hopes of gaining intelligence on my brother and his associates. Finding the information through other means, you had no further use for me.'

'But you know, *you know*, that is not true. As God is my witness, I love you and I have loved you every moment since I saw you and you *know* it.'

'I know what is in Nedham's rag and others and it would not be in there if it were not approved by your masters.'

'But not by me.'

'What does it matter, Damian, if it is not approved by you, if still they are your masters?'

He could find no answer for her, and watched, rendered motionless almost, as she turned her back on him and walked away.

The dog, seeming to have comprehended a little more of the situation, slunk down on the dirty cobbles, his head on his paws, his eyes firmly fixed on the ground in front of him.

*

It was almost an hour later that Seeker finally left Gethsemane. The story of Charity's abduction by Patience Crowe had been simple enough: an errand to Petticoat Lane to find a particular silk thread for a special outfit Lady Anne was at work on in the basement workshop; a haberdasher who had no such thread in stock; a kind, plain, Puritan girl, the daughter of a weaver who lived so very close to Charity's own home on Crutched Friars, who was certain her mother had a skein of just such a thread, and would be happy to give it for her ladyship's use. A pleasant walk back into town and to Gethsemane, not five minutes from home, so nearly home, and then the old crone behind the door, the darkened cottage, her hands suddenly bound, the hole in the floor, the fear of falling, the darkness. And then there was the hurting, Patience and the hurting. The mockery, the shearing of her hair. And Marcus Bridlington? She never met him. Edward had spoken of him, asked Patience about him, but Patience had said he wouldn't be seeing Marcus any more.

Charity didn't know how many days it had been; none of them knew. Then Patience had stopped coming, no one had come, and their food had run out, and the water in the barrel been almost finished.

She'd asked Seeker again about Lady Anne, and this time he'd told her. But he'd told her too about another who was being sent for, and that she would know this woman in her heart the moment she saw her.

Just as he had been about to leave, a question came to him

that he had not thought to ask before. 'How did you know it was him?'

Charity was quite exhausted now. 'Who?'

'When Lady Anne's house was broken into, and the salt and robe taken, how did you know it was Gideon Fell?'

She looked at him as if it were a thing so simple. 'Because Richard saw him.'

'Took you long enough.' The Rat's laugh was valiant, but forced. The transfer to the Tower, through busy streets in a wheeled cage, had done little to soothe the broken bones or cuts his captors and interrogators had inflicted on him. No bunches of herbs here either: the place stank.

As Seeker steeled himself to the air of the small and filthy cell, he wondered how it was that the woman who had harboured and protected this man could be accommodated little more than fifty yards away, but in a place of markedly greater comfort. Birth? Or affection for her husband's name? He wondered too if either could save her this time.

'You murdered Carter Blyth.'

The man made an attempt at a shrug. 'I was going to tell you, but you were more interested in General Goffe's little nephew and his blood-curdling amour.' Again the valiant laugh, ending in a croak this time.

'You would never have told me.'

'Well,' conceded the Rat, wrinkling his nose, 'perhaps not, but I would have told you something, to trade.'

'There's no trade for what you've been caught in.'

'Not for me, I'm not that stupid. But the lady. I thought you might go easy on the lady.'

'That's not up to me,' said Seeker. 'What had you planned to trade?'

The Rat considered, shrugged again, the game up. 'Might do you some good. Bridlington and that girl. They followed your man all the way from Gethsemane to Lincoln's Inn. He saw them, mind, but didn't seem to care, too busy looking for me.'

'I know that,' said Seeker. 'Did he find you?'

'Hah!' Again his throat caught in a croak. 'Nah, but I found him. Should have followed your boy, Bridlington – he got the note, I take it? But I made a mistake. Followed Blyth instead, and so did the girl.'

'Patience Crowe?'

'That's right. When he came back out of Lincoln's gardens, she went right up to him, grabbed him by the arm. He tried to throw her off, but she was telling him something that made him stop and listen. I got in a bit closer, so to hear.'

'And?' The Rat was enjoying his moment and Seeker was running out of patience.

'She was telling him she'd found the children, whoever the children were, I don't know. She was asking him to come, saying her mother was behind it all, and she was fearful for them. Don't think he trusted her, but he'd a nice big knife on him, and he went along anyway. I followed them. Down to Blackfriars.'

Blackfriars. 'And what happened there?'

They started to go in amongst the buildings, me following, the girl Patience always saying it was just a little further. Just as Blyth was becoming angry at her, she stood back from a doorway and said, "In here." In he went, and quick as anything, behind him, I saw her hand come up with a brick in it, and the brick smash into the back of his head. Down he went like a sack of coal, and in she went after him, with that brick in her hand. Up it came again, down again and he stopped moving. I was about three feet behind her by this time, pressed in a recess behind a doorway.'

'And you did nothing to stop her?' said Seeker.

'What?' The Rat had screwed up his face in an approximation of contempt. 'When she'd done my job for me, on one of your agents? Why in God's name would I have stopped her? Anyway, she crouched down, checked his breathing, and nodded to herself, quite satisfied it seemed with her work. Then she just stood up, dropped the brick and said, "Give my regards to St Peter." Away she scurried, leaving him there for dead.'

'But he wasn't dead.'

'No,' said the Rat, shaking his head. 'He was not. I slipped in and checked his neck, felt the blood still pulsing. Near enough dead, but not quite, and I wasn't about to leave one of Thurloe's agents, one that had been watching Lady Anne's house, lying there to be found murdered. Your crew would have been at Lady Anne's front door quick as you could saddle that big horse of yours. So I got his own nice big knife and loosened some of those bricks at that old oven. He'd got one of our costumes in a bundle – God knows why – a friar's robe of all things, so I put him in it, for an extra touch, put him in the wall, put back the bricks. Sack of mortar in the yard outside, quick mix with filthy water from the Fleet, fixed them in quick enough. I thought it would be a long day before they ever found him, and then he'd just be taken for one of those old dead friars.' He shook his head again, breathing a humourless laugh. 'I swear to you, though, if I'd known he would wake, I'd just have stuck his knife into him instead. I wouldn't give any man a death like that.'

'And yet you did.'

'I did, and I'll swing for that and all the rest. But you do one thing for me, Seeker, eh?'

It was Seeker's turn to laugh. 'Let's hear it.'

'You catch that wicked bitch. You make her pay.'

'Oh, we have her,' Seeker assured him, 'and she will pay.'

EPILOGUE

London, early March, 1655

The wind was bitter and it would herald more things than the men and women of London knew. Seeker's interview with Thurloe had been a long one, and it would be the last they would have for a good long time too, if Thurloe was to be believed.

'It's coming. Lambert has convinced Cromwell and the rest of the Council will follow. We need to come down hard. The country must be brought under tighter control, the people brought under tighter control. For their own good.'

It was the argument being put again and again around Whitehall, in the Cockpit, in the corridors and arboured walks of Hampton Court, and who could argue against what the generals had decided was for the people's own good, what Thurloe, Cromwell had decided? Only one who thought to spread sedition would even try.

'All the intelligence from abroad tells us the Royalists have another rising planned, and soon. We have some of the names already – it will come to nothing, and the new musters will keep control of the city, but there are plans afoot to put much tighter controls on our Royalist friends – even the ones who've been behaving themselves.'

Seeker knew that. No more Royalists to live quiet in the city, there was talk in the corridors of Whitehall of forcing them to register their movements and seek permission for every journey they made. Anne Winter had been let out of the Tower only long enough to be put into a caged cart and trailed up to Northumbria, where it was thought possible she might do less harm. Cromwell had taken the trouble, though, to ensure that the first part of her journey should be in the company of her steward, the man Richard, that the pair would be paraded out of the city and along Holborn, past St Giles's, to the triple tree at Tyburn, where Lady Anne might 'benefit from the observation of justice served'. There, at Tyburn, a slow and painful death had been meted out to her Rat, and Seeker, also watching, had had to concede that the man had borne it well.

Patience Crowe had also been sent to meet her maker, she at the end of a noose six days before. His days in Newgate, and the revelation of his daughter's wickedness, had done much to make Goodwill Crowe question his own path to salvation, and being forced to watch her daughter hang had finally silenced Elizabeth where all else had failed. Council and Protector, weary of the sects that threatened stability and abandoning something of their zeal for tolerance, had spoken out once and for all against the practices of the Fifth Monarchists and their like. None would be permitted to return to Gethsemane.

Nathaniel wouldn't be returning to Gethsemane either. The health of the boy Jed improved day by day, but it would be a good while until he was strong enough to return to his duties in the gardens of Lincoln's Inn. The masters had hastily agreed to Seeker's forceful suggestion that their old gardener needed at least two young men to help him in his onerous work, and it was there that Seeker had gone to bid Nathaniel and the dog farewell until his return.

Seeker hadn't said goodbye to Maria though. He'd said nothing to her, cut off, shut out from her life since that last day at Gethsemane. Elias had made it clear enough when, all else having failed, Seeker had gone to Dove Court and asked for her openly. Her brother had shaken his head: she would not see him. It was over. She had done with him.

Since that day he'd seen Shadrach Jones not once, but twice, turning off Old Jewry for Dove Court. The second time Seeker had punched the nearest wall so hard he had almost broken his own knuckles. He trained relentlessly in the drill yard, fenced with such venom that it got to the stage no one who could avoid it would practise with him. It didn't help. He hadn't argued long with Thurloe on the matter of Shadrach Jones though, for Thurloe hadn't been disposed to listen. Shadrach Jones had been turned; Shadrach Jones had been freed, his skills too valuable to be lost to the Protectorate, which he was as happy to serve as he had the cause of Charles Stuart. 'It's the puzzle, the test that's the thing for him, you see, Seeker,' Thurloe had said, not seeing there were other things that Shadrach Jones might also care for.

'Forget about him,' Thurloe had said at last. 'I doubt you'll be seeing him in the north.'

The north. In nearly ten years, he had not been back. The army had saved him, liberated him, given him his life anew, and now the army was sending him back. 'The localities, they're the key,' Thurloe had explained. 'The godly are few and of little influence and must be strengthened. The first thing that must be done is for new militias to be raised around the country, and only the best and most trustworthy to command them.'

'Then find another,' Seeker had said.

Thurloe had shaken his head. 'General Lambert wants you there, and Cromwell approves it. Your commission is to York, the orders already sent ahead of you. A new dawn is coming, Seeker.'

It was not dawn, but almost dusk when Seeker stooped his head and crossed the threshold of the Black Fox. The greying chill of the street outside dwindled and died as the pot boy closed the door behind him. The place was full, as ever, but the warmth in it came from more than the fire in the hearth, the many candles burning in their sconces on the wall, the heat from a kitchen that seemed to feed half the footfall of London. The warmth came from the woman who sailed between the tables, laughing, chiding, singing to herself, turning every moment to glance at the young girl who sat behind the counter, happily stitching samplers for the wall, or to place a hand, gift a smile on the serving girl, black hair showing in tufts now beneath her cap and blue eyes shining again.

The place fell silent and Dorcas turned to see who it was had come through the door. She stopped. All motion around her seemed to stop. Puzzlement briefly showed on her face and then something akin to a slow delight came over her. She took a step towards him, reached out a hand. 'Seeker.'

He looked about him, awkward in the silence of the place, began to move towards the small room they had spoken in before. She followed him, and closed the door behind him, before pulling out her own chair and urging him to sit.

He shook his head. 'I can't stay. I leave London in the morning, for Yorkshire. I . . .'

'Yes?'

'I wanted to know that all was well with the girls before I left, to ask if they recover.'

Not sitting herself, Dorcas stood with her back to her accounts table, leaning her hands against its edge. She nodded slowly. 'They recover, day by day. Isabella is almost as strong as ever, as you see, and already asking about books and writings and I know not what that the boy Edward spoke to her of, in their captivity.'

'I'm glad. And your daughter?'

He could see the rush of warmth, of love, go through Dorcas. 'She does well, Seeker. And each day better. She would have us call her Liberty, and although she asks about Lady Anne, she wants all the time to know of her father, and of me, and talks of how long she dreamed that I would find her, long, long before Lady Anne ever saved her from these city's streets. You have mended both our lives.'

Seeker cleared his throat, and tried to find words about his duty, and the good order of the city, but Dorcas shook her head. 'It is all right, you know, that you have a heart. I will not tell anyone.'

He gave a quiet laugh, and looked towards his boots and back to her. 'I doubt if they would believe you anyway.'

Dorcas straightened herself at the table. 'It's nothing to me, what the rest of London believes. But must you really go tomorrow?'

'The Lord Protector wishes it, and so I go.'

'And when do you return?'

He shook his head. 'I don't know.'

The sounds from the tavern parlour only magnified the silence in the small room. Seeker stood a moment, then reached for his hat from where he had set it down.

Dorcas took a breath. 'It's a cold night, Seeker. And a cold bed you go back to, I think.'

'I . . . I can offer nothing,' he said.

'And I ask nothing. I make no demands, have no expectations. And when you return from Yorkshire, you may come back here again, or not, as you will. If you do, you will find me here still, and still I will ask nothing of you. But it's a long road you have ahead of you tomorrow, Seeker, and the night is cold.'

Preachers, Pamphleteers and Prophetesses: the world of Elizabeth Crowe

Readers often ask me about the difficulties of creating strong female characters without making the women in question seem anachronistic in their actions and attitudes. A glimpse into the world against which *The Black Friar* is set should help explain why this is not too much of an issue when dealing with revolutionary England.

Mene, Tekel, Perez. With these words from the book of Daniel, the radical preacher and pamphleteer John Rogers informed Oliver Cromwell that he had been found wanting, and that his time as England's ruler was at an end. Rogers was a Fifth Monarchist, and believed that the English Civil War and the execution of the king had been the necessary preparatives for the rule, in person, of Christ on earth. The Fifth Monarchists had supported Cromwell as Lord General of the godly army who had fought to bring this about, but could not tolerate that he should take upon himself the earthly rule that should be Christ's.

The Fifth Monarchists were only one of a sometimes bewildering number of radical, independent religious sects that sprang up in England in the Revolutionary period – amongst others were Ranters, Baptists, Quakers, Grindletonians, Muggletonians (really!) and Diggers. They were the 'gathered churches' – self-selecting congregations of individuals who had declared their independence of the Church of England. The community of Fifth Monarchists portrayed in *The Black Friar* is fictional, but the city of London was at this period seething with radical sects, and a common factor to them was a heightened belief in the rights and capacities of women in society. The patriarchy that underpinned English society from top to bottom was challenged at all levels by the attack on king and hierarchical church. Just as the monarchy and the Church of England stood and fell together, so too was it impossible to untangle the clamour for political and economic freedoms from that for religious freedom. People of little or no education preached as the inspiration led them. And amongst those who preached were women.

Rogers, the Fifth Monarchist, advised men not to 'wrong them [women] of their liberty of voting and speaking in common affairs. To women, I say, I wish you be not too forward [John Rees, quoting Rogers in his 2016 work, *The Levellers*, suggests that Rogers' own wife *was* perhaps a little too forward] and yet, not too backward, but hold fast your liberty … ye ought not by your silence to betray your liberty.'

The Fifth Monarchists, like the other, shifting, groups of people who attended the 'gathered' churches also met with one another in inns and taverns, where they also discussed their ideas for religious and political freedoms. Amongst those same, shifting groups again are to be found the many pamphleteers and printers who disseminated their ideas to the wider population. The churches of Coleman Street, the inns and taverns and printers of Bishopsgate and Lothbury, seethed with radicals who petitioned, printed, protested and preached, and amongst their most prominent figures were women.

It is against this historical background that I have set the character of Elizabeth Crowe. Elizabeth and her daughter Patience, are, according to the demands of the story, deeply unpleasant individuals, but there were many brave and remarkable radical women active in London in the Civil War period. Katherine Chidley, for instance, wife of a Shrewsbury haberdasher and a mother of seven, led an independent church on Coleman Street alongside her son, wrote and printed pamphlets attacking learned and power-ful men, presented petitions, in person, to Parliament, and was prominent in the Leveller movement. Such able and outspoken women, of course, drew a special kind of oppro-brium from their political opponents: when Anna Hemstel spoke for two hours to an assembled crowd of women who had come from far and wide to hear her, it was claimed her audience had only come because of the pig that was being roasted for the occasion. One adversary derided radical female gatherings in the following manner: 'Where their university is, I cannot tell, but I suppose that Bedlam or Bridewell would be two convenient places for them.' Bedlam, of course, was a lunatic asylum; Bridewell a women's prison and house of correction.

Damian Seeker had been brought up in a Seeker sect in the north of England. The Seekers, who believed the individual should look for the light of God within themselves, were a group who had been active in the Elizabethan period, before going underground only to re-emerge in the revolutionary period. Just as Seeker's wife had divorced him by the simple expedient of announcing it before their congregation, the radical sects' attitudes to monogamy and to divorce were unconventional, and as such were seized upon by their opponents to denigrate women preachers. Mary Gadbury, a woman preacher from the Coleman Street area of the city, was deserted by her husband, but it was nevertheless she who was criticised and blamed for it. She was later whipped and sent to Bridewell following an association with a fellow, male, preacher whom she believed to be the Messiah. Naturally, Mary was more severely punished than the man involved. Another woman preacher out of Coleman Street was the Baptist Mrs Attaway, a lace-seller to trade. In the mid-1640s, she claimed to speak regularly to an audience of a thousand women. But women such as Mrs Attaway threatened the patriarchy, particularly as she argued that a Christian should not have to tolerate marriage to an anti-Christian; she saw no sin in her relationship with the also-married William Jenny, although traditionalists regarded them as living in plain adultery.

That the Presbyterian polemicist Thomas Edwards, in the pages of *Gangraena*, his assault on the radicals of the period, should devote some of his horror towards women preachers suggests that, despite bawdy vitriol, they were taken seriously by their opponents. St Paul's injunction, repeated by Seeker in *The Black Friar*, that a woman should keep silent and not be suffered to teach, was powerless in the face of the phenomenon of women prophets, for prophets were chosen by God as his mouthpieces. In a period in which no one was more prone than Oliver Cromwell himself to justifying political acts and events of national importance as manifestations of the divine will, some prophetesses were, for a time, taken very seriously indeed.

For instance, in the winter of 1648–9, the critical period leading up to the trial and execution of the king, the prophetess Elizabeth Pool had presented to the army's Council of Officers her vision of the army as the cure for the ills of the nation. Liking what they heard, the officers called her back a week later, when she told them that while they had the right to imprison the king, it was not the Divine will that they should execute him. Another prophetess, the Fifth Monarchist Mary Cary, who described herself as a 'minister', would later defend the killing of the king.

Best known, perhaps, of all the prophetesses at the time was Anna Trapnel. From early adolescence in radical Stepney, Anna had desperately yearned for a meaningful religious conversion. This finally came in 1642, when listening to the preaching of John Simpson, who went on, as did she, to become a Fifth Monarchist. Anna's first, ecstatic vision of a New Jerusalem came as she watched the approach to London of the New Model Army in 1647. By 1653 she had become a very public figure. Her prophesying, induced by extreme fasting, was observed by crowds who flocked to the house in Whitehall in which she lay bedridden. Initially viewing Cromwell as Gideon, chosen by the Lord to do great things, she came to see him, in the manner of the Fifth Monarchists, as a horn of the Beast. Eventually, Cromwell sent her to Bridewell, to be flogged.

Anna Trapnel may have been a very troubled young woman, who in a different age would have been treated very differently, but some key figures in the radical movement of the period such as church leader and pamphleteer Katherine Chidley, the Leveller printer Mary Overton, and Elizabeth Lilburne, wife of leading Leveller 'Freeborn' John Lilburne, showed tremendous ability, pragmatism and courage in the face of abuse and great personal hardship and tribulation.

The biggest difficulty facing historical novelists in creating strong female characters is not the material they have to work with, but our perception of the role and achievements of women in past times. Given the circumstances and role models offered by revolutionary England, it is not at all difficult to conceive of such characters living and operating in Oliver Cromwell's London.